INHUMAN CRIMES

They're killers from our worst nightmares whose crimes defy description and understanding.

They're real life vampires, cannibals, human butchers—the merchants of grisly, unnatural death. And, they live among us.

Until they get caught.

Now, from the authentic files of TRUE DETECTIVE MAGAZINE, read the chilling stories of the most BIZARRE MURDERERS in the annals of crime.

That is, if you can take it.

THEY'RE NOT FOR THE FAINT-HEARTED — TRUE CRIME FROM PINNACLE BOOKS!

APPOINTMENT FOR MURDER (238, $3.95)
by Susan Crain Bakos

Who would have thought that a well-respected, prestigious dentist could, over the course of twenty-two years, murder five men and two women? And that the generous and well-loved Dr. Glennon Engleman was capable of premeditative murder, of shooting and blowing up his victims, all in the name of greed?

Renowned journalist Susan Crain Bakos paints a gripping psychological portrait of the charismatic man who sexually tortured young women and primed them to marry his future victims. But Engleman made one fatal mistake in his sex scam for money, and what followed was the unravelling of his horrific crimes.

EDWARD GEIN: AMERICA'S MOST BIZARRE MURDERER (187, $3.95)
by Judge Robert H. Gollman

— *There were skulls on his bedposts.*
— *A heart was found in a saucepan on the stove.*
— *Gein danced in the moonlight wearing the face, breasts and hair of one of his victims.*

Edward Gein. He inspired two of the most terrifying films ever made: Alfred Hitchcock's "Psycho" and Tobe Hooper's "The Texas Chain Saw Massacre."

Here are the horrible facts of "the case of the century", as told by Judge Robert H. Gollman, before whom Gein stood trial. What drove this reclusive bachelor to murder, mutilation, fraticide, grave-robbing and cannibalism—a catalogue of atrocities still unparalleled in the annals of crime?

Judge Gollman's account, which includes transcripts from the trial, is a straight-forward, riveting, and chilling descent into one man's madness.

Includes 8 pages of graphic police photographs.

BIZARRE MURDERERS

EDITED BY
ROSE G. MANDELSBERG

PINNACLE BOOKS
WINDSOR PUBLISHING CORP.

A special thanks to Sergeant Leonard Muuss of the Bureau of Criminal Identification, Middlesex County Sheriff's Department, Sergeant Don Bond of the Springfield, Oregon Police Department and Detective Robert Leonard, Las Vegas Metropolitan Police Department without whose efforts this book could not have been possible.

PINNACLE BOOKS

are published by

Windsor Publishing Corp.
475 Park Avenue South
New York, NY 10016

First Printing: March, 1991.

Printed in the United States of America

TABLE OF CONTENTS

"THE CANNIBAL & THE FLOATING BODY PARTS"

by Gary Ebbels

It was May 15, 1985, and the Nevada desert was beginning to heat up, surpassing the 100-degree mark every day. It would be that way in the Las Vegas Valley until the end of September. Las Vegans are used to such heat, and they are rarely bothered by it.

But workers at the Las Vegas Waste Water Treatment Plant found something this day that they could not take in stride.

In the sewage streaming into the plant this particular afternoon, a worker spotted what appeared to be a human finger. He called a fellow worker over for a look. The fellow worker agreed that there was indeed a human finger floating in the sewage.

Obviously, someone in Las Vegas had flushed it down a toilet. That was how it ended up at the sewage treatment plant. But there was more . . .

One of the workers also spotted a toe and then another toe, floating near the finger.

Another pointed out an ear—a human ear—floating near the digits. A supervisor was hurriedly called by one of the workers. By the time he got to the workers, still another body part had been found in the sewage. The body part this time was a man's sex organ.

The body parts were fished out of the sewage, and the Las Vegas Metropolitan Police Department was notified.

Although a complete corpse had not floated in on the sewage, it was apparent someone was dead and that these were just a few of his body parts. These were the ones someone was able to flush down a toilet.

Homicide Detectives Bob Leonard and Norm Ziola responded to the call from the treatment plant. They interviewed the workers who had found the body parts. The workers said the parts probably had been flushed down a toilet that very day, because it does not take long for sewage to get into the treatment plant.

The detectives placed the body parts into individual plastic bags. They would be taken back to the police lab for analysis. The finger would be rolled for a print.

At the time, it appeared that the fingerprint might be the only thing that would reveal the identity of the hacking victim. The blood would also be analyzed and typed, and the skin would be carefully examined. There was little doubt in the minds of the detectives that the parts belonged to the same person, but the lab would have to verify it with scientific proof.

When Leonard and Ziola returned to headquarters, they turned the body parts over to Kim Groover and Hank Truszkowski, identification experts who would perform the analysis.

There was little more the sleuths could do with the case at this point. They knew someone had been a victim of foul play, but they didn't know who it was. They didn't even have a complete corpse on which they could at least hang a John Doe tag.

It was the morning of May 16th, and a blood donor center in Las Vegas was doing a brisk business. But business came to a hasty halt when a passerby rushed in and said he had just seen some body parts in a dumpster out back. He said he had seen an arm and a leg sticking out of the dumpster.

An official at the blood donor center immediately telephoned the police department. Both Ziola and Leonard were at their desks working on their files when the call came in. Since they had worked on the case of the body parts found at the sewage treatment plant a day earlier, they were dispatched to the blood donor center. There was a good chance that these body parts belonged to the same man whose smaller parts were flushed down a toilet the previous day.

9

The police operator asked that no one at the blood donor center touch the arm and the leg in the dumpster. He said it was necessary for the detectives to view the scene just the way the passerby who made the grisly discovery had viewed it. He also asked that the passerby remain at the blood donor center, so he could give the detectives a statement.

As they had when they arrived at the sewage treatment plant, the sleuths brought with them plastic bags. These bags were bigger than the ones used the day before, because the two body parts on this occasion were bigger.

These parts, assuming they belonged to the same victim whose parts were found the previous day, had been too big for the slayer to flush down a toilet.

Ziola and Leonard returned to headquarters with the arm, which was handless, and the leg, and turned them over to the lab. Joining Groover and Truszkowski in the analysis at this point were two more identification experts, Nancy Kingsbury and Dave Welch.

The blood in the parts found a day earlier was Type O, according to the analysis performed by Groover and Truszkowski. The blood on the latest body parts to be found would now be analyzed. The skin would also be compared with the skin on the parts found floating in the sewage.

The detectives, meanwhile, were working on the theory that all the parts found so far belonged to the same man. There had been no duplication of parts thus far. Furthermore the flesh on both sets of parts was fresh. Even in the May heat, the parts had not yet begun to rot, indicating the victim had been dead only a day or two.

This dovetailed nicely with the information from the worker at the treatment plant that sewage flows rapidly once a toilet in town is flushed.

If the identification experts should be unsuccessful in matching the two sets of parts, it would mean a hacker in Las Vegas had already claimed two victims, and was probably lurking somewhere looking for another.

The sleuths still had no idea who the victim was, assuming there was only one victim. The finger had been rolled for a print, but that print would only be useful in verifying identification once a tentative identification was made.

They didn't even know what the cause of death was, because there was no corpse on which an autopsy could be performed.

Had the victim been stabbed? Had he been shot? Had he been strangled? Had he been bludgeoned?

How do you solve a murder when you don't have a corpse, and you don't have the identify of the victim, and you don't have any witnesses coming forward?

These were the questions that haunted the two detectives who had been charged with the task of solving this slaying.

On May 17th, the identification experts reported to Ziola and Leonard. They said they had all come to the same conclusion—that all the parts gathered so far belonged to the same man. The blood type was the same and the consistency of the skin was identical.

While the idea of someone being hacked up and his body parts scattered around town was a revolting one, the detectives were relieved by the findings of the identification experts. It meant there was only one victim, and a madman was not stalking his way through Las Vegas, hacking victims at will.

Now all the sleuths had to do was find the killer.

It was late in the afternoon on May 17th when a call came into headquarters. The call was from someone in a downtown hotel. The caller said someone had just come into the hotel and announced he had found some human body parts in a dumpster in a nearby alley.

Again armed with plastic bags, Ziola and Leonard immediately headed for the hotel.

Once there, they were led to a dumpster. In it, and beside it, were some body parts. There was part of a leg, and a hand with no fingers. There was also an ankle and part of a shoulder.

Again, the detectives theorized these parts must belong to the same man whose parts had been found the previous two days, since there was still no duplication.

But body parts weren't all the detectives found this time. Also lying by the dumpster were some large pieces of plasterboard. These pieces of building material gave the sleuths their first possible clue in this incredibly grisly case.

There is an area not far from downtown Las Vegas where there are several shanties, most of which are built of the same material as that found beside the dumpster. If the material was dumped there with the body parts, the secret to the murder and mutilation could lie somewhere in the shanties.

The detectives turned the body parts over to a uniformed officer to take to the lab. The sleuths left the alley and headed for the shanties. They knocked on doors and asked questions.

But they found themselves getting nowhere in a hurry. No one had any information to offer. No one in the area had seen anything suspicious, and no one was saying anything suspicious in answering the detectives' questions. They hadn't knocked on all the doors yet, but they were getting disappointed as they worked their way through the area.

The disappointment didn't last long, though.

They came upon a shanty with blood on the exterior near the front door. It wasn't a lot of blood, and there was no telling how long it had been there. But it was blood just the same, and it could be the blood of the mutilation victim, the probers reasoned.

The detectives knocked on the door and were greeted by two men. As they started to ask questions about the blood, one of the men grew evasive. He explained that there had been a fight at the dwelling in recent days, and that the blood on the building was a result of the fight. He added that no one had been seriously injured.

The other man said that if there had been a fight, he knew nothing about it, because he hadn't been home much in recent days. He said he had been out job hunting. He said he hadn't even seen his other roommate in recent days.

The detectives asked about the "other roommate," and again the man who had been evasive about the fight and the blood answered the question. He explained that the man no longer lived there. He said he had moved out just a few days earlier.

The other man said he had been unaware of that development, but reminded the detectives he had not been home much.

The sleuths agreed there were some explanations missing, and that they weren't going to get them at the shanty. They decided to take both men to headquarters for extensive questioning.

The landlord was also contacted after they arrived at headquarters. He said the third roommate was Patrick Fogarty, 36, who hailed from an eastern state.

The print, rolled from the finger that had been found floating in the sewage, was immediately dispatched to Fogarty's hometown police department. It was possible his fingerprints might be on file. If they were on file and they did match, the detectives would finally have the identity of the hacking victim.

The interrogation of the two men lasted into the night. Some five hours later, the man who said he had not been home much was released. The detectives had been successful in contacting some of his prospective employers, and they confirmed he had been with them, seeking work, in recent days.

But the other man, Michael Yarbrough, 33, was kept in the Clark County Jail on suspicion of murder. The detectives knew they had very little with which to hold Yarbrough for long.

Meanwhile, the fingerprint was sent to the east through an overnight carrier, so they could get telephone confirmation from Fogarty's hometown police department one way or the other the next day. If his fingerprints were on file with the department, so too would be his blood type.

The morning of May 18th saw detectives checking with the identification experts who performed the analysis of the body parts found in the downtown alley. Again, the blood was Type O, and again the skin consistency matched that on the other body parts. Their conclusion was that all pieces were parts of the same man.

There had still been no duplication of parts.

While the detectives checked with the identification experts at headquarters, a lab crew was going over the shanty once occupied by Fogarty, Yarbrough and the third man. A sample of the dried blood was scraped from the outside of the dwelling. A hatchet found inside the building was confiscated.

When the lab crew returned to headquarters, the blood sample was turned over to the identification experts for typing. The hatchet was booked into the police evidence vault.

The detectives, though, found themselves in a situation much like a quarterback running a two-minute drill. With the evidence they had so far, they would not be able to hold Yarbrough much longer.

On the afternoon of May 19th, they made contact with Fogarty's hometown police department. They were told his fingerprints were on file and so was his blood type. And, yes, they had compared Fogarty's fingerprints with the single print sent to them by the detectives.

They matched, too.

The print sent from Vegas belonged to Patrick Fogarty. Fogarty's blood was Type O, according to the desk sergeant from the east.

Before being booked into the evidence vault, the hatchet seized at Yarbrough's residence had been dusted for fingerprints. Yarbrough's fingerprints were found on it.

This didn't strengthen the case much, but the revelation that the dead man was Yarbrough's roommate did. This, and the fact that blood was found on the outside of the shanty, and the same type of plasterboard used in the construction of the shanty was found by the last group of body parts, built enough of a case to formally charge Michael Yarbrough with the murder of his roommate.

A sample of Yarbrough's blood was taken and typed when he was booked into the jail. It was found that he had Type A blood.

Yarbrough was still maintaining his right to remain silent, even though the detectives were starting to build a case. The blood taken from the outside of the shanty was typed by the identification experts who had been working the case from the scientific angle. They reported to the sleuths that it was Type O blood, the same type that once pumped through Patrick Fogarty's veins.

That meant Yarbrough, when and if he decided to talk, would not be able to say that it was his blood on the building.

Meanwhile, news of the day-to-day discovery of human body parts around town had Las Vegas buzzing. It was front page news every day. Television stations led off their newscasts with reports on the grisly findings.

It also remained front page news and top-of-the-newscast material when Yarbrough was jailed on the murder charge.

One Las Vegas television reporter, trying to keep ahead of the others with his coverage, managed to get Yarbrough to grant him an interview in the county jail, just three days after the arrest. And while he had nothing to say to the detectives, he had plenty to say to the television newsman, who made a videotape of the interview.

He told the newsman he had, indeed, murdered Patrick Fogarty. He said he did it in self-defense, though. He told the newsman, and all who viewed the videotape on the six o'clock news, the following shocking story:

He and Fogarty had been arguing, and Fogarty came at him with the hatchet. Yarbrough grabbed a cord and made a lasso out of it. He lassoed Fogarty and pulled as hard as he could on the cord. He pulled so hard he strangled Fogarty to death.

When he saw what he had done, Yarbrough said, he placed the corpse in the bathtub and then went into the kitchen for a knife. He returned to the bathtub with that knife.

That's when he started cutting up his dead roommate.

The first thing he did was cut out Fogarty's eyes and throw them in the toilet. He flushed them away, and then he started cutting again. He sliced off a finger and flushed it. Then an ear, and so on.

When Yarbrough started cutting off the larger parts of Fogarty's body, he realized he could not simply flush them away. The arms, legs, head and the torso would have to be disposed of differently. He said he set about Las Vegas after the sun went down on May 15th and started dropping off parts in different garbage dumpsters.

Yarbrough said he didn't remember all the places he left off chunks of Fogarty's body.

All the while he was cutting up the body, and all the while he was scattering it about town, he had the desire—the urge—to eat human flesh.

The interview tape was played at the beginning of the six o'clock news, and the detectives working the case were among the horrified viewers. While the sleuths had had only a circumstantial case before the interview was aired, they now had an air-tight case against Yarbrough.

With the admission of guilt documented on videotape, the bail setting on Yarbrough was removed. He was ordered held in the county jail without bail.

The prosecution of the case was placed in the hands of Deputy District Attorney David P. Schwartz. The case was bound over for trial by a justice of the peace, following a Justice Court preliminary hearing. Such hearings are conducted as mini-trials.

It is the duty of the prosecutor to show the presiding justice of the peace that the state has enough evidence against the defendant to warrant a District Court trial by jury.

Schwartz had little difficulty showing the presiding justice of the peace he had a good case against Yarbrough. But even though the case against Yarbrough was extremely strong, Schwartz was a little worried about taking it before a jury, because of Yarbrough's insistence that he killed in self-defense. Yarbrough was the only living witness to the killing. No independent observer could tell a jury what happened.

D.A. Schwartz was not worried about getting a conviction of some sort. It was just that he wanted a first-degree murder conviction and a sentence of death by lethal injection. In order to exercise all his options, Schwartz alleged the use of a deadly weapon in the commission of a crime. This would bring about an automatic double penalty under Nevada statutes, in case he came up short of the death penalty.

Trial was scheduled for October in the courtroom of District Judge Stephen Huffaker. Defense attempts to get the case dismissed, on a technicality of some kind, failed throughout the summer months.

Now Yarbrough would have to face a jury of his peers.

The prosecutor's key witness was the television reporter who videotaped the jailhouse interview with Yarbrough—the one that was shown on the six o'clock news three days after Yarbrough's arrest. The reporter testified that he, indeed, conducted the interview and got the admissions out of Yarbrough. When he was through testifying, the videotape was shown to the jury.

Later, when it was Yarbrough's turn to take the

witness stand, he repeated what he had said on tape, maintaining that he had murdered in self defense.

Someone on the jury must have bought the self-defense story, because it took the panel seven and a half hours to come back to Judge Huffaker's courtroom with the required unanimous verdict. Just the same, it was the verdict Schwartz wanted. The jurors found Yarbrough guilty of first-degree murder.

It would now be their job to set a punishment. They would sit through a penalty hearing, and then retire to deliberate the punishment.

As was the case in the guilt phase of the trial, it would be necessary for the jury to reach a unanimous verdict regarding punishment. The jurors would have the option of sentencing Yarbrough to prison for life, with or without the possibility of parole, or to death by lethal injection.

After hearing D.A. Schwartz argue for the death penalty, and after hearing Yarbrough's public defender attorney put on a case for mercy, which included testimony by one of Yarbrough's relatives, the jurors again returned to the deliberating room.

When they came back with their verdict this time, they brought good news for Yarbrough.

His life would be spared.

On top of that, he might once again be a free man. The jurors tacked a parole possibility onto his mandatory life prison sentence.

Normally, this would mean he could be paroled after serving only 10 years behind bars. Since Schwartz had been clever enough to allege the use of a deadly weapon in the commission of a crime, though, Yarbrough would be caged for at least 20 years before becoming eligible for parole.

When the trial was over, Schwartz said he thought Yarbrough's family was the reason the jurors gave him life with the parole possibility.

"They were in court every day, showing the remorse that Yarbrough never did," said the veteran prosecutor. "I think they may have had an impact on the jury."

Patrick Fogarty's head and torso were never recovered.

"WHO LACED THE ICE CREAM WITH ARSENIC?"

by Gary Miller

January and February, 1977 were bitter cold months in Louisville, Kentucky, but Morris Lee Amos had worked just about every day for the past 30 years, and he wasn't about to let a little cold weather stop him from getting his job done. For the past several weeks, after coming home from work, he had begun renovating the garage to his four-bedroom home. He was almost finished with the job by February when the problems started.

First, there was the diarrhea. Almost every day, he experienced painful cramps which doubled him over. He figured it was a virus bothering him, but there were other complications: the aches and pains along his arms and the listlessness: By the time he got home from work during the day, he could barely lift his arms, and he was so thoroughly fatigued that any thought of working on his garage was quickly put on the back-burner. He decided he'd have to wait until the end of the winter season to continue renovating.

Reducing his workload, however, did not have much of an effect on Amos's health. He began to deteriorate quickly, losing thirty pounds within a few short weeks. He stayed home from work for the first time in years in an attempt to renew his health. His wife tried all sorts of remedies on him. She spent hours over the stove cooking up steaming pots of hot chicken broth and spoon-fed it to him. She had also brought him gallons of ice-cream to cool the hot burning sensation in his stomach. But nothing she tried seemed to work on him.

Instead, Amos's condition worsened. He complained about numbness in his fingertips and arms, and of increasing pain in his chest. He went to his private physician and was given blood tests, but when the lab report came back, there was little the doctor could make out. Amos's white blood count had decreased to a danger-ously low level, but there was no apparent reason for this reduction. The doctor advised him to take vitamins, and put him on a high protein diet.

But as the days passed, the dietary routine seemed to have little effect. Amos's wife fed him double portions of breakfast, lunch and dinner, but Amos continued to lose weight; and, in addi-tion to his painful cramps, he became increasingly thirsty. He drank gallons of water, but couldn't quench his burning thirst.

The next time Amos went to see the doctor, he had to be helped along by his wife. She stayed by his side to make sure he didn't fall. His balance seemed precarious, and he complained that he could hardly move a muscle. The physician noticed that Amos's fingertips were blue, and his face ashen and pasty. He checked Amos's heart, and, for the first time, the doctor recognized an irregular beat.

Overwork wasn't the best explanation for Amos's deteriorating condition, but after discussing the situation with other members of the staff, it was the only cause he could come up with that would explain the irregular heartbeat and other symptoms. He could do little else but caution Amos to reduce his physical activity.

"Take a few more weeks off work," he advised.

The following week, on February 15th, Amos's family called the physician. Amos was in such bad condition that he couldn't even get out of bed. The doctor sent him to nearby Suburban Hospital, where Amos was given numerous tests to determine the cause of his illness.

Lying in his hospital bed, Amos was a pathetic figure of his former robust self. His skin stretched tightly across his face, revealing the contours of his skull; and his once thick, muscular arms were now but thin, gangly appendages that lay lifeless by his side.

An examination of his blood revealed an almost complete absence of any white blood cells.

"If this patient catches a cold, he's a goner," one of the attending physicians pointed out. "He's got nothing to fight off a disease."

All attempts at diagnosing the cause of Amos's white blood count reduction met with a total blank. Physicians discussed possible causes. Some argued that Amos was suffering from a rare, as yet unidentified virus, while other doctors believed it was Muscular Dystrophy.

Muscular Dystrophy would have explained the almost total loss of physical mobility, but there were too many problems with this diagnosis. First of all, Amos's condition had deteriorated much too rapidly in comparison with other Muscular Dystrophy cases. Secondly, the loss of weight, white blood count reduction, dizziness and chest pains were symptoms usually not associated with that disease.

The doctors questioned Amos's wife to ascertain if he had been in contact with anyone in the past few months who displayed similar symptoms, but the woman could recall no one.

The doctors realized further testing was in order. They planned on monitoring his vital signs for the next several days while continuing to run tests. But only two days after being admitted into the hospital, on February 17, 1977, Amos jerked upright in his bed as if he had been kicked in the back, and then he slumped down on his mattress, dead.

One of the physicians had the thankless task of informing Amos's family of his death. They phoned his wife at her home and asked her to come to the hospital, explaining only that her husband was in serious condition. When she arrived with other family members, a doctor went out to meet them and broke the news.

After giving the family time to vent their emotions, the physician ushered them into an office and asked a crucial question.

"As far as we know," he said, "Mr. Amos died of a heart attack. It happened suddenly and there was nothing that could be done to help. We would like to perform a postmortem," he added. At that suggestion, the doctor was cut short by Amos's wife who said her husband wouldn't have wanted it.

The doctor explained that the autopsy would allow them to determine what exactly caused his complete deterioration and death. Nevertheless, he was given a flat, irrevocable veto.

Without the autopsy, the determination of death could only be an educated guess. Amos's death certificate read cause of death as a minor coronary infarction or heart attack, and things were left at that.

Amos's funeral took place later that day. Friends and relatives of the deceased who attended the proceeding were in shock at the loss.

"I wouldn't have believed it if I hadn't seen it,"

said a neighbor. "He was such a big man, strong, healthy. And just like that, he wasted away. Never saw anything like it in my life."

"So young," a woman said. "Forty-six years old and so young looking."

"It was his ticker that got him," said another neighbor. "You never know when it's gonna go on you."

"It's God's will," said a close friend of Amos's. "He takes those he loves most."

With the funeral proceedings concluded and the corpse interred, the torturous last days of Morris Amos had come to an end.

Life for his family, though, went on. His wife received social security checks and was able to continue paying off the mortgage on their home. Over the following years, the sudden demise of Morris Amos became just a sad memory to his family and the community—until four years later in April of '82 when another man began visiting the local hospital complaining of symptoms similar to those which Morris Amos had suffered.

There was the violent, burning stomach cramps and diarrhea; the unquenchable thirst and the numbness in the arms and legs. The man also complained that his breath smelled of garlic, and that he constantly had a metallic taste in his mouth.

The first few times he went to the hospital, doctors thought he was suffering from iron deficiency. He was given a change of diet but it was of no help. Like Amos, the man began losing weight rapidly, and his mobility became so markedly deficient that he could barely even tie his shoelaces.

His condition stumped doctors at the hospital. Every diagnosis they came up with was shot full of holes by other symptoms the man displayed, and as the days continued to close in, the man's health deteriorated rapidly. His relative brought him to the hospital on several occasions, barely hiding her grief at the suddenness of his change.

But the hospital physicians were at a loss to determine its cause.

Eventually, a blood specialist was called in, and a battery of tests was scheduled. The patient was kept at the hospital during this time; and almost as suddenly as he had become ill, he showed a marked improvement. The physicians were mildly surprised at the man's fortuitous turnabout. The longer the man stayed at the hospital, the more his health improved, and, finally, he was able to return home and continue his normal activities. As for the cause of his apparent illness, physicians attributed it to a blocked intestinal passage.

The matter was left at that until a few months later when the man's relative phoned the hospital again, informing doctors that his condition had drastically worsened.

An ambulance was immediately dispatched to his home and rushed him to the hospital. The man could hardly speak, and he was almost totally paralyzed, barely able to lift even a finger.

Doctors called a rush meeting to discuss their patient's situation.

"All tests show a marked decrease of white blood cells," said the blood specialist.

"Did the tests show any causes?" asked one physician.

"You know as well as I do there could be a number of causes," the specialist answered, "but not one of them fits perfectly with the symptoms. I'm at a loss here. If somebody could provide some input, I'd appreciate it."

"Did you eliminate the possibility of a virus?" one doctor asked.

"There's no evidence, other than a normal amount of antibodies in the blood. I'd be surprised if what we have here is a virus."

"Have you tested for poison?"

"No," the specialist answered with a questioning look. "There was no need to. We have no suspicion of a poisoning."

"It wouldn't hurt if we gave it a shot," the other physician suggested. He was a small pudgy man with a huge forehead and puffy cheeks, but his eyes were sharp and penetrating, and the other doctors respected his opinions. They all agreed that it was worth conducting a number of tests concentrating on the possibility of poison.

The patient, meanwhile, was put on intravenous and his intake and output fluids were monitored for any possible changes. The patient's urine as well as hair samples was sent to the lab for analysis, concentrating this time on examining it for the presence of poison.

The next day, before test results came back from the medical laboratory, the patient's female relative came by to visit him. As always, she was affectionate with him. He looked so pale and wan, and he could barely move, so she fed him herself. Only the best for him. She took the container of ice cream from her bag and showed it to him. It was his favorite. She lovingly spoonfed him the creamy confection until he had consumed the entire contents. She then dropped the container in the wastebasket, walked over to the nurse's quarters, asking them to take good care of the patient and then left.

Only shortly afterwards, the lab tests run on the patient's hair and urine came back, and a hurried conference was called.

Normally, an average person has approximately 200 milligrams of arsenic in his urine. The tests just completed on the patient's urine showed approximately 20,000 milligrams of the poison, enough to completely incapacitate a person or kill him!

The decision was immediately made to contact the Jefferson County Police with their discovery. Homicide Detective Danny Crady arrived with several other investigators and was given a summary of the doctors' findings.

"There's too much of the poison to have been inhaled," a doctor explained. "The only way such a great amount of arsenic could have gotten into his body is by oral ingestion."

"You mean somebody fed him the stuff," an investigator quipped.

"Yes. That's it exactly," the physician answered.

"Do you know who normally prepares (the patient's) meals?" a prober asked.

The doctors advised the investigators to ask the nurses who had the responsibility of monitoring all the patient's meals in the hospital. As for what he ate and who prepared his food outside the hospital, the investigators would have to find that out on their own.

Two Jefferson County lawmen got the patient's room number and immediately rushed down there. Upon questioning the nurse in charge of this patient's oral intake, the probers were told that the patient was restricted to a hospital diet, but if a family member brought a little snack, the nurse usually allowed it. It couldn't really hurt. As a matter of fact, the nurse said, the patient's relative, Pauline Rogers, was there just a few minutes before, feeding the patient some ice cream.

The lawmen checked by the patient's bed and found the empty container of ice cream. This item was brought to the crime laboratory where the remainder of its contents were tested. Results showed an abnormally high amount of arsenic in the container.

This was enough for Detectives Danny Crady and Bobby Jones to get a warrant to search Pauline Roger's home.

Only shortly thereafter, investigators went through her house with a fine-tooth comb, but after hours of fruitless searching without any discovery, the probers gave up in frustration.

When probers checked into Pauline Rogers background, they learned that back in 1977 her husband, Morris Amos, had succumbed to a puzzling heart ailment.

Jefferson County Homicide Detective John Spellman was assigned to uncover any details about Amos's sudden death. He started his probe by contacting County Coroner Richard Greathouse about the possibility that Amos was poisoned by his wife, now known as Pauline Rogers.

Greathouse began his own investigation into Amos's death while Detective Spellman made contact with potential witnesses.

One relative of Amos told Spellman that Rogers and Amos had been married for 11 years before Amos became sick. "He never missed a day of work till he became sick," the relative said. "Then all of a sudden he was losing weight, and got pale and cranky."

About Pauline Rogers, witnesses told Detective Spellman that she was a real friendly woman. "You'd just like to spend the day with her," said one neighbor. "She had a hell of a personality . . . always joking."

Others described the suspected poisoner as a person obsessed with neatness. "Her house was spotless. You could eat off it," recalled a neighbor who had often visited.

And the garden; there was always that beautiful garden of hers. "She'd put out all these kinds of fruits and vegetables. Why, she had these big cucumbers growing out there; potatoes too, and flowers," the neighbor remembered.

Spellman realized that anyone interested in gardening would usually have some knowledge of arsenic and its uses. She would have no problem, Spellman knew, of getting hold of the poison.

But as for using it, so far there was no witness pointing to that—until he spoke to a close relative of Amos, who told him about the doctors' request to conduct a postmortem and of Pauline's rejection of such an idea. According to the relative, she "didn't want anybody cutting on him."

Here was the first substantial clue that Pauline Rogers had something to hide, which an autopsy might unearth—that Amos had, indeed, succumbed to poisoning.

The results of Spellman's canvass was further verified by County Coroner Richard Greathouse, who had already conferred with the physicians at the Suburban Hospital where Amos had died.

According to Greathouse, Amos's physician believed the cause of death was "some sort of cardiovascular collapse," but the physician also had added that there had been some suspicion about the rapidity of Amos's demise and the bizarre symptoms of his illness.

Coroner Greathouse was annoyed that he hadn't been notified of these suspicions at the time: "We would have ordered an autopsy over her (Pauline Rogers) objections if we had been notified," he said.

But the autopsy could still be performed, Greathouse told Det. Spellman. Even though Amos had been buried five years before, the body would be "preserved well enough to perform a decent autopsy. If we are looking for arsenic," he explained, "it wouldn't matter if he'd been down there 50 years; arsenic stays in the hair and nails."

After conferring with homicide detectives, Greathouse signed an exhumation order. Then, in order to quell any objections from the public, who might perceive the disinterment as a ghoulish act, he made a formal announcement explaining his reason:

"A coroner can order disinterment if he has reasonable and just cause to believe the death was not a natural one. I certainly do in this case."

Early in the morning on June 4, 1982, men in overalls began shoveling away clumps of dirt on a burial mound at the Middletown Cemetery. Lacking backhoes to break the hard crusted ground, the workers had a hard time making headway. Their shovels arced in the air and came crashing down on the stiff unmoving earth. After several hours, they had only gotten down about a foot, and yet their sweat was pouring off their faces. They wiped their foreheads and continued on.

By late afternoon, the cracking sound of metal on wood indicated the diggers had finally achieved their goal.

Two long, thickly braided ropes were shoved under the casket. Two ends stuck out from one side and two from the other. The workmen then lifted themselves out of the burial ground and, holding onto the four lengths of rope, they slowly began walking backwards, and the pine casket suddenly rose upwards as though being lifted by some extraterrestrial force. It was soon laid beside the gravesite and, in a short while, brought to a morgue wagon to be transported to University Hospital, where an autopsy would be performed on the remains.

The following day, on June 5th, Coroner Greathouse announced that cause of death of Morris Amos was not a heart attack as had been listed.

The victim's remains "showed no obvious cause of death," he explained. "Under normal circumstances we would have found scars on the walls of the heart if it had been a heart attack."

Tissue samples from Amos's body had already been sent to the state toxicology laboratory in

Frankfort for testing.

In the meantime, Investigators Danny Crady and Bobby Jones had placed Pauline Rogers under arrest and charged her with murder.

She was able to post a $2,500 bond, and was soon out of jail. But the next day, June 7th, she was hospitalized for extreme stomach cramps, and, shockingly, it was learned that she herself had ingested arsenic.

While Pauline Rogers was recuperating, the case against her began to firm up with the results of the toxicology analysis of Amos's tissue sample. Examination of the tissues showed an abnormally high amount of arsenic in several organs. 18,000 micrograms were discovered in the liver, 470 in the stomach and 460 in the hair.

The arsenic presence in the hair indicated that Morris Amos had not only died from a lethal dosage of the poison, but also that it had been administered over a long period of time, a year or more.

With the overwhelming evidence of murder and attempted murder pointing to Pauline Rogers, Assistant Commonwealth Attorney Bill Duncan decided to prosecute her. He planned on handling both cases—the attempted murder of her relative and the murder of Morris Amos—separately.

In early August 1982, Pauline Rogers was indicted for both charges by a Jefferson County grand jury.

Her trial for the attempted murder charges did

not begin until the following year in June of 1983. During that time, Detective Danny Crady firmed up the case against her with incriminating eyewitness testimony.

At the attempted murder trial, these witnesses revealed that Rogers had brought candy and other "goodies" to the hospital.

When Crady took the stand, he revealed that during an interrogation session with the defendant, she had admitted sprinkling these "candy gifts" with ant medicine, her term for the arsenic.

Another crucial prosecution witness was the nurse at the hospital who remembered seeing Pauline bringing the arsenic-laced ice cream to her relative.

With this kind of damning testimony to back up his case, Prosecutor Bill Duncan was able to convince the jury of Pauline Rogers' guilt. On June 24th, she was convicted of attempted murder; and the next month, July 15th, Circuit Court Judge Laurence Higgins sentenced her to 20 years in prison, the maximum sentence under law for attempted murder.

Pauline Rogers' trial for the murder of Morris Amos took place within the next few weeks. Prosecutor Duncan was able to use much of the evidence presented in the first trial since it was directly related to, and offered proof of, the Morris Amos homicide.

The most crucial evidence against Rogers in the second trial was, of course, the lethal amount of arsenic discovered in Amos's body.

In early September of 1983, Pauline Rogers was again found guilty, this time of second-degree murder of Morris Amos. On September 23rd, Judge Higgins sentenced her to an additional 20 years in prison, to run consecutively with her 20-year term for attempted murder. So, in effect, Pauline Rogers has a 40-year stretch ahead of her as a result of her crimes.

"WHO BEHEADED THE BISEXUAL NYMPHO?"

by Andrew Lowen

James Dunne had to stop. He'd had a few beers at lunchtime, and his bladder felt as if it was about to burst. He couldn't hold out a minute more.

The country road between the cities of Exeter and Torquay in Devon County, near the southwest coast, was unusually quiet that September afternoon. Dunne, a travelling salesman, steered his two-door metallic bronze Ford Capri on to the brownish grass verge. The late-summer sun had scorched the earth and painted premature autumn brands on the greenery.

The woodland seemed to close in on the traveller as he stepped from his vehicle. Everywhere there were trees, shrubland, heather and bracken. Poisonous snakes—adders—slithered away from the sound of crunching feet as Dunne hurried for the privacy offered by the dark interior of the forest, already lowering his fly.

As he stood there urinating, finding relief, his eyes began to become accustomed to the overpowering gloom. Just to his right something bright and pink caught his eye. The color was all wrong, far too vivid and harsh to belong to nature.

Now he could see better, more clearly. Everything was beginning to take shape. Outlines were falling into place. The salmon-pink represented a pair of shorts, women's hotpants. As he lowered his head to get a closer look, the stench almost knocked him out. Before staggering backwards and dashing from the forest, he spotted a most unusual T-shirt, bearing the marking: "Souvenir du Maroc." Both hot pants and T-shirt were on a body—a horribly decomposed body.

When Detective Chief Inspector Jeff Henthorne arrived on the scene roughly an hour later from his headquarters in Exeter, he was immediately struck more by what was missing than by what had been found. The woman's body was headless.

The worms and other wildlife had really gotten to work on the body and it was a sight that brought on nausea even to the most strong-stomached officers who were drafted into the area to conduct an inch-by-inch search of the forest.

"Basically, we're looking for any clue, however small," Henthorne stressed at the briefing. "But what we need to find most urgently is the missing head. That's what we want most of all."

Troops from nearby army camps joined the ever-expanding special task force, while the rotting remains of the unknown homicide victim were placed into a plastic morgue bag and transported in a coroner's vehicle to the Exeter Royal Infirmary, where an autopsy was started that same evening, September 23, 1983.

Henthorne remained at the forest until nightfall, but no clues had been found since the cops had been alerted. No shoes. No handbag. No handkerchief. No bra. No head.

The police doctor who had been dispatched to the forest had refused to conduct a preliminary medical examination.

"Pointless," he told the inspector. "The body is far too gone to be examined in these conditions. I could only hinder, not help. All I can tell you, without even looking any further, is that she's been dead a helluva long time."

Henthorne could have told the doctor that!

Late September, it's dark by 8:30 p.m. in the south of Britain. Henthorne and his top brass entourage were back in his office by nine p.m. Dunne was still in custody and now it was time for the inspector and a detective sergeant, Rod Saltmarsh, to interrogate the witness more closely.

This second interview was conducted in a special room set aside for this kind of inquisition, in the basement and next to the cell-block. Dunne had been plied with coffee and sandwiches, and there was nothing aggressive about the police attitude. He was there to help the cops with their inquiries, and nothing more. Henthorne was the first to state categorically to the press that Dunne was not a suspect and that he would be free to go home as soon as the cops were sure that the witness had recalled everything.

Dunne explained why he had pulled up at that precise spot in the forest. Grass stained with his urine was taken to the laboratory. Scientific tests on that urine established that it had come from the witness's bladder. Henthorne was satisfied. Almost.

"Have you used that stretch of forest road before?" the inspector inquired.

"Sure," was the reply, "two or three times a week. I'm a travelling salesman. I've told you that. I'm always on the road. That road in particular."

"Do you often stop for any reason when you're on that road?" Henthorne asked.

"Never done it before," Dunne answered spontaneously.

"You didn't know the body was there?" Henthorne pressed.

"Of course I didn't."

"Funny you should stop at that exact spot," the inspector commented, testing.

"Someone had to find the body sooner or later.

You could say the same thing about anyone who finds any body."

The inspector was satisfied. Smiles were turned on. Hands were shaken. An official statement was dictated and signed. Then the witness was allowed to go home, everyone on friendly terms.

The autopsy was not concluded until six a.m. on September 24th, the day after the decomposed body was found.

Dr. Hugh Dykes, a pathologist attached to the Home Office, presented the official report to the inspector. The victim had died from gunshot wounds to the throat and chest. Two bullets had passed through the heart, fracturing a rib and finally coming to rest in the left lung.

"Death would have been instantaneous," the doctor stated.

When it came to the date and time of death, the pathologist was far less dogmatic. "We're talking about months rather than days or even weeks," he said. "I cannot be more precise. "I'm sorry. But weather and environmental conditions have such an influence on these things that I would be doing you a disservice to try to be more definite.

"However, I can tell you a few things which may be of help. Firstly, the head was severed from the rest of the body sometime after death, in my opinion.

"Secondly, the body has been kept in several different places since the murder, I believe. We took quite an amount of dirt, as you would expect, from the body. Under the microscope, we discovered vast differences. Much of the dirt was household dust. Several splinters were extracted from the skin. Not the sort of wood you find in a forest, though. More the kind of material you'd expect to find in a log cabin."

"Such as in a woodcutter's or gamekeepr's cottage?" the inspector demanded.

"Exactly. Or something like a sauna; a Swedish log sauna. It was that sort of timber."

"Interesting," Inspector Henthorne remarked, writing "sauna, gamekeeper and woodcutter" in his notebook.

"Thirdly," said the pathologist, "there's no evidence of rape. No damage to the vaginal cavity, except that which has been caused by forest bugs, rats and foxes. It's my opinion, however, that she hadn't been sexually assaulted. Could be wrong, but I don't think so. Neither was she pregnant, or anything like that."

The bullets which had proven so lethal were immediately handed over to ballistics. Later, Henthorne was told they were "from a Marlin .303 rifle. Fired from close range. She'd have had no chance. Not with a weapon like that from such a short distance."

Henthorne hurriedly called a conference with his team. He shared with them everything he knew. He stressed the fact that public cooperation was vital. "Hence, we have to bring in the press on our side right at the outset," he informed them. "This is one of those occasions when we can't get along without them."

Inspector Henthorne announced that he intended to ensure that every newspaper, TV channel and radio station carried a bulletin of the homicide, giving a description of the clothes from on the body.

Checks would be made on everyone in the nation who had been issued a gun license for a Marlin .303 rifle. The missing persons file at Scotland Yard would be scrutinized: an easy job. An instant read-out could be obtained on the computer at the Devonshire police headquarters: All the county HQ computers are plugged into the central computer files at Scotland Yard, London.

In his autopsy report, the doctor had estimated from skin tissues, that the victim's age was "not younger than 22 and no older than 35." Not very illuminating, but better than nothing. It certainly ruled out kids and pensioners.

Priority was placed on finding the missing head. The search of the forest would continue "day after day, week after week, month after month until it is found," the inspector ordered. More troops were to be drafted into the hunt. Men and women from a nearby air force base were also to join the team.

"I am convinced that the head is somewhere in that forest," Henthorne said. "It has to be.

Maybe it's been buried. So we must be on the look out for shifted soil, uprooted undergrowth. It's going to be a devil of a job, but it has to be done."

Fingerprints taken from the dead woman were fed into Scotland Yard's central fingerprint computer, but to no avail. There was no match. So the victim didn't appear to have a police record of any consequence. An examination for surgical scars on the body had been fruitless. No appendix scar. No indication that she'd ever had an abortion or miscarriage. Certainly she'd never given birth.

During the next couple of days, the murder hunt received saturation coverage on television, radio, and in the newspapers. Henthorne made several TV appearances. A woman cop modeled identical hotpants and T-shirt to the ones the victim had been wearing. Det. Sgt. Walt Mitchener posed with a Marlin .303 rifle in front of TV cameras.

"Someone must know the identity of a young woman who used to wear pink hot pants and a T-shirt bearing the inscription 'Souvenir du Maroc.'" Henthorne appealed to the public. "A woman who hasn't been around lately. Someone who disappeared suddenly. Perhaps she had a hairdressing appointment and didn't show. Perhaps she hasn't been seen for a while in her local shops. Perhaps her friends have been wondering why she hasn't called.

"Someone in this world must be missing this young woman. She has been brutally, wickedly destroyed. Beheaded. Please think. Please help. After all, you could be next, or your daughter, or your wife."

Sgt. Mitchener talked about the rifle, appealing to all gunsmiths. "We want to hear from anyone who has sold a similar rifle lately," he explained. "All information will be treated in strict confidence. We're not interested in prosecuting anyone for a breach of the gun laws. All we're concerned about is catching a killer."

The missing persons computer threw up more than 200 "possibles." More detectives, mainly youngsters only a few months out of uniform, were recruited to the team to cope with this end of the operation. "Follow every lead," they were ordered. "Check it out. Identifying the victim is now the No. One priority."

During the following week, the relatives and friends of 200-plus missing women in the appropriate age range were interviewed. Statements were taken, photographs were examined, the pathologist was consulted, but every lead turned into a dead-end. A short list of 200-plus became a smudged dossier of cross-off names. Neither had anyone come forward with any positive information relating to the rifle. The search in the forest had been remarkable only for its futility. Not an additional clue had been uncovered.

Henthorne could not believe that this was happening to him. It was all so unreal. At the outset, he would have bet his life on the missing head showing up quickly. During the search, he had hardly slept. Neither had the rest of his team. Tempers were becoming frayed. Spirits were low. Frustration ruled.

Henthorne decided that it was time for another TV blitz. Arrangements were made for him to make yet another personal appeal on the nationwide BBC News program at nine p.m. that day, October 3rd. He repeated much of his earlier broadcasts, concentrating on the hot pants and the T-shirt. He'd decided to forget the age, just in case the medical scientists were off the mark on that score.

The inspector had hardly returned to his office from the local BBC TV studio, when an excited detective constable shouted across the special operations room:

"Chief! Chief! I've got a woman on the line who says she can identify the victim. She doesn't sound like a nut. Sounds very respectable."

Henthorne had encountered many well-spoken, articulate nuts in his career, so there was no sign of elation in his voice when he took over the call, pushing the young greenhorn from his desk in a room crammed full of detectives working on just one case.

Inspector Henthorne introduced himself, and the caller replied: "Oh, yes, I've just seen you on TV, that's why I'm calling. I can identify the headless woman for you, I think. What's more, if I'm right about her identity, I can also name the killer for you."

Now the excitement was beginning to show as Henthorne asked: "Why have you waited so long before calling me?"

"So long!" the woman exclaimed. "It's only a few minutes since you were on TV."

"But I've made many appeals during the past week or so," Henthorne countered.

"Ah! But we've only just returned from a foreign holiday," the woman explained. "We'd only been indoors an hour when he switched on the TV and there you were."

Satisfied, Henthorne said: "Okay, who is she?"

Monika Telling," came the reply. "She lived with her husband at Lambourn House in the village of Bledlow, near High Wycombe." That's in Buckinghamshire County, some 250 miles northeast of where the body was found in the forest.

Henthorne's heart sank. Could this really be the woman? Would the killer really have chanced driving the body so far before dumping it? He was preparing himself for yet another disappointment, when the caller went on: "She often wore salmon-pink hot pants, but it was the description of the T-shirt that struck me. What's more, her husband, Michael Telling, has just confessed to me and my husband that he did it. He's just left. He's been on holiday with us."

The caller's name and address were taken, and

the woman was told that a car would be sent from her local police station and that she and her husband would be driven to the murder HQ in Devon County that same night.

The car carrying Mrs. Daisy Walters and husband Frederick arrived at the Exeter police headquarters around two a.m. They were shown straight up to Henthorne's office, where he and Sgt. Mitchener were waiting anxiously, both of them pacing up and down like expectant fathers.

After the handshakes, Henthorne got straight down to business. "Tell me everything," he demanded. "Starting with the woman and then the husband who, you say, killed her."

The following statement was taken from Mrs. Walters during the following three hours: "I've often seen Mrs. Telling in garish pink hot pants and the T-shirt you described and showed on TV. I don't like speaking ill of the dead, but she loved to show off her body to other men. She led Michael a hell of a life.

"Ever since I knew them, she was on drugs, and she was having regular lesbian affairs, in addition to sleeping around with other men. She was always taunting her husband about these affairs, even in public at dinner parties and occasions like that. Any other man would have killed her long ago.

"Then, about six months ago, Michael came round for a drink and announced that his wife had packed her bags and left him. He seemed so relieved and we felt delighted for him. Secretly, we believed it was the best thing that could have happened to him. 'Now you can start living again, really living,' I told him.

"We'd been friends for a long time. So much so that we invited him to come along with us on our holiday in Spain for two weeks. When we got back, I made coffee and we were relaxing in the lounge when we saw the police appeal for witnesses.

"Michael ran from the room and I could hear him vomiting in the bathroom. I didn't pay too much attention because he's a diabetic and if he does not eat, he gets sick. When he came back into the room, he broke down sobbing and confessed. We didn't believe him at first, but then it all began to add up. You know, his wife suddenly leaving all those months ago and then a body being found wearing those striking, unforgettable clothes. In the end, I just had to believe him.

"A few minutes later, he said he wanted to return home and be alone. I talked things over with my husband, and we both decided, although we feel dreadful about it, that it was our duty to inform the police."

The statement was duly signed and sworn by the witness. A similar statement was also signed by Mr. Walters.

"What does Telling do for a living?" Henthorne then asked.

"Don't you know who we're talking about?"

Mrs. Walters asked incredulously, looking in disbelief at her husband.

"No," replied Henthorne, shaking his head. "Should the name mean something to me?"

"Hell it should!" she exclaimed. "Michael is the second cousin of a lord. Although he is only 34, he's one of the five richest men in the United Kingdom." The cops were to discover that his world-wide empire was worth over a billion dollars. His dynasty ran from a cattle ranch in the United States to a chain of butcher shops, from Argentina to Zimbabwe. He had married his wealthy socialite California wife just 17 months previously. This was his second marriage.

The hot pants and T-shirt were shown to the Walters. "I'd swear they are the clothes I've seen Mrs. Telling wearing," said Mrs. Walters.

Without any further delay, Henthorne and Mitchener drove north, taking Mr. and Mrs. Walters with them. After dropping the couple off at their home, Henthorne drove two miles further to the vast estate of Michael Telling, who was walking his dogs at the time in the sprawling grounds.

Telling was immediately arrested and taken to the local police station where he was questioned for several hours. He was told of the statement which had been made by the Walters. "Did you tell them that you killed your wife?" he was asked by Henthorne.

"Yes, I did," he answered.

"And is that the truth?" the inspector then

inquired.

"Yes, it is," came the reply.

Henthorne then said, "Did you hide the body of your wife in a forest between Exeter and Torquay?"

"I didn't hide her," Telling maintained, "I just threw her away. She was there for anybody to find who walked that way."

"What about her head?"

"Oh, I couldn't part with that," Telling explained. "She was so beautiful. Her head was far too lovely to be thrown away with the rest of her."

"When did you cut off the head?" Henthorne probed.

"In the forest," Telling replied. "I hired a van and drove to Exeter. I'd wrapped her body in motorcycle covers. I had an axe with me and, after unloading Monika into the forest, I knelt beside her and chopped off her head. It came off very easily."

"And where did you put your wife's head?" Henthorne demanded.

"I wrapped it up and took it home with me," he said matter-of-factly.

Concealing his revulsion, the inspector pressed on with the inquisition. "Where is your wife's head now?"

The suspect hesitated a moment, then shook his head, finally answering: "I'm sorry, I can't tell you that."

"Why not?" Henthorne snapped, not liking the answer he'd just received.

"Because I can't part with that. I won't allow anyone to take that away from me."

Henthorne decided on a different approach. "Why did you do it, Mr. Telling?"

"Because I couldn't take anymore."

"Anymore of what?"

"She was always ridiculing me."

"What about?"

"Being no good as a lover. She said I'd never satisfied her once in all our nights together. She even preferred other women to me. She would make love with other women in front of me on the carpet while I was watching television. Sometimes she'd take women to bed with her and I'd have to sleep downstairs or in one of the spare bedrooms.

"At other times, she'd bring home other men and *do it* while I was in the house. It was revolting. I pleaded with her, but that seemed only to make matters worse. 'You weakling!' she'd roar at me. 'You're not a man. You're not even a mouse. At least mice can screw!'

"On top of that, she was also an alcoholic and was hooked on drugs. She'd been attending Alcoholics Anonymous for some time. But I still loved her. I still love her now. That's why her head will stay with me forever."

Henthorne continued with his soft approach. "Tell me how it happened, please? How you shot her?"

"She was screaming at me," Telling explained. "Going wild. Telling me that she was going out to find another lover and that she'd be bringing him or her back to our home for the night. Then she yelled: 'You're mental! You're nuts! Why don't you go back to the asylum where you belong.' That was the end of everything."

"What did she mean by that?"

Telling lowered his head and went into deep thought before answering: "When I was younger, I needed psychiatric treatment. I had a problem."

The cops were later to discover that the suspect had spent a period in a mental institution as a voluntary patient. As a child, he'd been educated at special schools because of his anti-social behavior. Several times he'd threatened to kill his own mother; he'd smashed up rooms and had cracked a milk bottle over the head of a clergyman's daughter. Twice he'd attempted suicide.

"Tell me more about the shooting?" Henthorne probed.

"I just grabbed my rifle and let her have it," Telling replied. "It was as simple as that. She was running at me, charging. I thought she was attacking me. There were a hundred and one reasons why I did it.

"I kissed her and told her how sorry I was for what I'd done. I put her in a spare bedroom, and I kissed her every day. Then I stored it in a sauna cabin in one of our outhouses in the grounds. I kept her there until one day—I can't remember the exact date—I hired a van and took her away, to the forest, to her place of rest."

The cops were later to discover that he had made love to two women, on separate nights, while his wife's body lay on the floor of the spare bedroom, which could be reached via an adjoining door.

During that initial interrogation, Henthorne finally returned to the one remaining mystery. "Where is your wife's head, Mr. Telling? It's no use trying to hold out any longer. You've told us everything else. You might just as well come clean on everything."

By this time, a search warrant had been obtained from a magistrate. While the suspect was driven south to the headquarters of the murder hunt in Exeter, the cops began searching his home and grounds. A search that lasted barely an hour.

In the trunk of a white mini car and wrapped in a plastic bag, the cops found the missing head of Telling's wife, who had died at the tender age of 27. The murder weapon was discovered hidden under the floorboards of the sauna cubicle. Later, Telling was to admit that he'd bought the rifle in Australia, explaining why all the cops' efforts to trace the weapon had failed so miserably.

Michael Telling was duly charged with the murder of his wife and his trial was held at Exeter Crown Court in June, 1984, where he pleaded not guilty. However, he pleaded guilty to manslaughter on the grounds of diminished responsibility, which the Crown refused to accept.

Telling maintained that he'd cut off his wife's head because he couldn't bear to be completely parted from her. The prosecution, however, alleged that the head was chopped off because the accused knew his wife could easily be identified from the dental surgery which she'd undergone shortly before her brutal death.

"The severing of the head was a calculated gamble to prevent the police from identifying the body in the forest," Alan Rawley, QC, prosecuting attorney, insisted.

The defense case relied heavily on the victim's alleged deviant sexual behavior and alcoholism. But the judge warned the jury not to be unduly influenced by sordid scandal stories about a young woman who was in no position to stand in court and defend her good name and honor.

The court heard about wild, naked parties at Telling's home and midnight nude bathing in his swimming pool, followed by lovemaking sessions between guests on the patio and lawns and in the stables. But the accused was never a participator. Always he was on the sidelines, forlornly watching from the outside, a man who did not fit anywhere, not even in his own home.

Defense counsel, the legendary Mr. George Carman, QC, who seems to land a starring role in all the contemporary epic British trials, pleaded with the jury not to reject his client. "He has suffered throughout his life rejection after rejection after rejection — and has been the victim of rejection. Are you going to deliver a final and ultimate rejection? I suspect not."

The jury, after many hours of soul-searching, cleared Telling of homicide, but convicted him of manslaughter. The judge, Mr. Justice Sheldon, had no hesitation sending one of Britain's wealthiest young men to jail for life.

And the change in Telling's life was brought home to him as he waited in the cells beneath the court to be taken to Exeter prison. When his lunch was taken to him by a guard, he asked for a bottle of his favorite claret wine to help down the meal. "I can't eat any meals without a bottle of wine," he told the guard.

"You've got plenty of time to learn how to do without!" retorted the guard. "The rest of your life, to be exact! You're a prisoner now, no longer on remand. Such privileges are no longer available to you."

EDITOR'S NOTE:
James Dunne, Daisy and Frederick Walters are not the real names of the persons so named in the foregoing story. Fictitious names have been used because there is no reason for public interest in the identities of these persons.

"CHEF CHOKED ON A BOTTLE OF TABASCO SAUCE!"

by Bob Carlsen

Henry D. Johnson, 57, of Seattle, Washington could put together a pretty good plate of food. That's why the experienced chef had a job at a well-known restaurant near his home on 20th Avenue South in Seattle. Over the years he'd built a reputation for himself, and several persons from his own neighborhood frequented the restaurant because of his abilities in the kitchen.

It was Monday, October 24, 1983 when Henry Johnson's next door neighbor left his home early in the morning. The neighbor was headed for work and intended to stop off at the restaurant for a cup of coffee and donut. As he backed his car out of his driveway, he noticed that Henry Johnson's house lights were on. That seemed odd, since Henry usually left his house dark when he went to work early in the morning.

The neighbor thought nothing more of it and

drove to the restaurant. However, when he arrived there, he found things in turmoil.

"What's the matter?" the neighbor asked the morning manager, who was not in a pleasant mood.

"Johnson didn't show up for work yet," the manager growled while hustling behind the counter. "We're shorthanded and look at the crowd."

"Geez, he must be awake," the neighbor said. "When I left the house I saw all his lights on. I wonder if he's sick."

"He could have at least called in," the manager muttered.

Henry's neighbor went to the pay phone, dropped a quarter and dialed his friend's home. There was no answer. He hung up, retrieved his coin from the return box, dropped it into the slot again and dialed his home.

"Honey," he said to his wife when she answered. "Look out the window and see if Henry's lights are still on, will you?"

"They're on," she said upon her return to the telephone. "Why do you ask?"

"Henry hasn't shown up for work yet, and he's not answering his telephone. I don't have time to go back to the house and check on him. It'll make me late for work. Could you go over and see if he's okay?"

"Sure," his wife responded. She hung up the phone and got dressed. Her husband was on his way to work when she walked to Henry's house, knocked on the door but got no response.

The door was unlocked, so she entered the small, wood frame house. She was stopped cold in her tracks when she entered the living room. Her husky friend, Henry D. Johnson, was trussed up and apparently quite dead on the living room floor. His nearly naked body was bound and gagged.

The woman ran back to her own home and telephoned for help. Police and paramedics were soon on the way.

It took but a few seconds for the paramedics to determine that they could no nothing for Henry Johnson. They did not disturb the body, and officers called for homicide detectives and the medical examiner.

Officers Lawrence Dimmitt and William Tighe, Sr. secured the crime scene until others arrived. Detective-Sergeant Harlan Bollinger was the chief investigating officer on the case, and Detectives Dwight Chamberlain and Richard Krogh assisted him.

It was apparent to the detectives that Henry Johnson had been the victim of some type of torture slaying. He had suffered numerous facial bruises and there was a deep cut over his left eye.

Blood was spattered throughout various portions of the living room and other parts of the house, which indicated that Henry may have put up a struggle before being subdued by his killer or killers. There also were bruises on his hands which could have been either defensive or offensive wounds.

Detectives didn't disturb the body. The actual examination of the corpse was left up to Dr. John Eisele, a medical examiner from King County. Dr. Eisele found that the victim's pants had been knotted around his head and tied in front. The victim's undershirt was pulled up to his shoulders. He had on boxer shorts and socks. He'd been gagged with a towel, and a bottle of Tabasco sauce had been stuck into his mouth in such a manner that the gag prevented him from pushing the bottle of hot sauce out of his mouth with his tongue.

The killer had tied Henry up with the telephone and vacuum cleaner cords and towels in a very complex fashion. Preliminary examination indicated that Henry had died a slow death. The hot sauce caused him to slowly asphyxiate, was their preliminary conclusion. A subsequent autopsy would determine that the hot sauce was a contributing factor but not the primary cause of death.

Detectives questioned the neighbor woman and learned the circumstances leading up to the discovery of the body. She could add nothing more to the mystery other than to say Henry was normally a tidy housekeeper and worked as a chef at the nearby restaurant.

A detective went to the restaurant while others

continued the crime scene investigation.

Blood samples were gathered from various portions of the house. Blood was lifted from the coffee table, two end tables, from drawers in the kitchen, cabinet doors under the sink, the bedroom closet door and the wall leading to the bathroom. Bloody footprints were discovered on the floor in front of the kitchen sink. The extensive gathering of blood samples by crime scene technicians would later prove to be an important factor in the case, as more than one blood type would be found.

Detectives learned from the restaurant manager that Henry had been paid the previous Friday and would have had about $500 in cash if he hadn't deposited the money in the bank. A check with banking records revealed that Henry hadn't made a deposit recently. No money was found at the murder scene, so detectives concluded that robbery was at least part of the motive.

Considering how the victim had been found nearly naked, tied up and slowly strangled, detectives also considered the possibility that sexual torture might have been involved.

"There could be a combination of motives here," Sergeant Bollinger told the other police investigators.

Bloodstains were found beneath a pile of clothes near the victim. This indicated to detectives that part of the victim's clothes must have been removed after the assault occurred and the man was subdued. Otherwise, why would the bloodstains be found on the floor under the clothes? If the clothes had been removed first, then blood would have gotten on them and not on the floor under them. This would prove to be an important clue later in the case when detectives had to consider the suspect's excuse for the horrible assault.

The victim's false teeth were found in the bathroom, a pair of glasses were in the bedroom and a second pair on the living room floor. A search of the victim's pickup truck turned up a pornographic magazine depicting a woman performing various sex acts with a male. This magazine, depicting heterosexual activity, also would prove to be an important clue once the suspect in the murder was found.

Detectives talked to relatives who lived elsewhere in the city, and they said that in addition to the $500 that was missing, a distinctive silver ring with diamond stone which Henry always wore was missing from his hand, along with an expensive gold watch and a second, less distinctive ring.

After completing their crime scene investigation and questioning those closest to Henry, detectives fanned out through the neighborhood to determine if anybody had seen the victim on Saturday and Sunday. They knew he'd been alive the previous Friday when he had gone to work and gotten his paycheck.

Detectives found a woman who lived on the same street who claimed to have seen Henry Johnson on Saturday at 6:20 p.m. "He was getting into a cab with another person," the witness told detectives "He appeared to be normal at the time, like nothing was wrong."

So Henry had been spotted alive at 6:30 on Saturday. That meant the murder occurred sometime Saturday evening or Sunday, perhaps as late as Monday morning.

The woman couldn't remember the license number of the cab company. Detectives knew it wouldn't be too difficult to nail that information down, however.

Detective Bollinger learned that Henry Johnson was not a homeowner. He rented the house. A check with relatives and the county assessor's office determined the name of the property owner. Detectives contacted the landlord who told them that he'd been to the house on Saturday to pick up some rent due him.

"Henry kept the house in good condition," the landlord told detectives. "I visited him around four o'clock on Saturday. Johnson jokingly introduced another young guy as his nephew, but I know it wasn't his nephew. At the time the house looked neat, except for the kitchen cabinet, which was cluttered. Johnson was drinking whiskey. The other guy was drinking beer."

"Could you describe the other person?" the landlord was asked.

"He was sitting down most of the time I saw him. But I'd estimate he was over six feet tall, 180 to 200 pounds. He had brown hair."

The landlord said he'd never seen the young man before, and he guessed that the guy might have been a stranger who Johnson was letting spend a couple days. Henry was known for being a kind-hearted person, and it didn't surprise the landlord in the least that perhaps he'd felt sorry for a street person when the October nights turned bitterly cold.

Detectives contacted the local taxicab companies and determined the one which Johnson and his killer had used that Saturday. Sleuths learned that the two men had used cabs to get both to and from a popular nightspot.

The cab driver who picked the two up at Johnson's home at 6:30 told detectives that upon entering the cab, Johnson told the driver, "I want to show my son a good time. Can you recommend any place?"

The cab driver took them to a very popular Seattle lounge. Detectives next interviewed patrons at the lounge; several admitted being there the previous Saturday. Some of the patrons remembered Johnson, but nobody knew who the strange young man was who accompanied him. Johnson had, at times, introduced the young man as his son, at other times, as his nephew. Through witnesses, detectives determined that the young man was neither. It was a mystery as to why Johnson had been introducing the young man this way.

The cab driver, who returned Johnson and his friend home, recalled he picked the two up from the lounge around 11:30 p.m.

"The older guy paid me with a twenty dollar bill," he told the detectives. "It looked like he had quite a roll of twenties." That corresponded with what some of the lounge patrons had told detectives—Johnson appeared to have been packing quite a bit of money with him on Saturday evening.

As detectives spent several days gathering all of this information, the medical examiner's report came in from Dr. Eisele. Eisele determined that Johnson had suffered internal neck injuries indicative of being strangled with somebody's hands. The facial injuries and the Tabasco hot sauce stuck in his mouth were contributing factors to the primary cause of death—strangulation.

Detective Bollinger did get some good news from crime laboratory Criminologist Carol Murren. Most of the blood that had been found in Johnson's home had been his, Type A.

However, one blood sample had been lifted from one of the end tables. This sample tested out to be Type O, most likely the killer's type. This, along with other evidence gathered over the two-week investigation, would enable Detective Bollinger to eventually nail a killer.

The investigation continued but probers could

get no useful leads from persons in the neighborhood. The search expanded and sleuths turned up a crucial lead at a convenience store several blocks from the victim's home.

Detectives learned that on Sunday morning a young man who stood more than six feet tall had been hanging around the convenience store and was questioning customers about the possibility of getting a ride north. The clerk who'd been working the shift told detectives the name of the customer who agreed to give the young man a ride.

"The customer is a regular of ours," the clerk told detectives. "I'm sure he didn't know the guy who was looking for the ride. But the guy was packing such a wad of dough, it was hard to pass up the offer."

Detectives contacted the man who had chauffeured the suspected killer out of town. The man readily admitted giving the suspect a ride.

"It was between 1:30 and 2:00 a.m. when I gave the guy a ride. He had been drinking, that was obvious. He wanted to go north to LaConner," the witness told Detective Bollinger.

Initially, the suspect offered the man $50 to drive him up to LaConner. But that fee was increased to $100. That fact caught the detective's attention, and he queried more about it.

"At first he gave me a fifty dollar bill," the driver recalled. "But then he paid me $100 total, using twenties. That was after we got stopped."

Detective Bollinger saw a ray of hope. "You got stopped?"

"Yes," the man sheepishly admitted. "Because the tabs on my license plate were expired. I got stopped on the freeway by a state policeman."

"During this stop, did anything unusual happen?"

"It's funny that you mention that," the witness said. "Because this guy started acting really weird. The policeman took all of our identifications (there were three) to his car and this guy pulls out a knife and put it to his own throat and said, 'If this doesn't end pretty soon, I'll end it for them.' I told the guy, 'Nothing is that bad. The cop is only going to give me a ticket.' And that's all he did. I knew it would come to $37, so that's when I told this guy I was giving the ride to that it wouldn't even pay me to drive all the way up to LaConner. That's when he paid me the hundred."

"Did this guy say anything about being in a fight or killing someone?"

"He said he beat a guy up pretty bad and didn't know if he was alive. He said he needed the ride because some other dudes were after him."

The driver went on to say how they got stopped a second time farther north because the car had defective lights. He was just given a warning for that offense, however. But after being stopped the second time, the murder suspect then took off on foot. He apparently wanted no more dealings with the police at all.

Detectives contacted Washington State Patrol headquarters and determined the name of the trooper who had issued the $37 ticket on Sunday morning. Through him, they learned the identities of all three persons who had been in the car that morning. Two of the names the sleuths already knew because the driver had told them his friend's name. But the driver hadn't known the name of the third person, the suspect.

From notes in the trooper's log, detectives determined his identity as being Kevin Mark Christianson, born March 15, 1960. He was a California native.

The trail led detectives to LaConner, Washington where they learned that Christianson apparently had gotten stranded in the small community. He had left his backpack and other gear at a store and had returned to get it several days later. The period of time he was absent corresponded to the three-day period detectives had placed him in Seattle—Friday, Saturday and Sunday.

A background check on the suspect determined that he'd had trouble in the military, and in October of 1983 he had been touring Alaska, Canada and Washington State. He'd spent about a week's time in LaConner and Seattle, detectives determined.

From LaConner, sleuths traced Christianson's

movements to a motel in Everett, Washington where he had registered under an alias of Mark Mosely. After he checked out of the motel the next morning, the maid found a silver ring. No stone was in the ring, she told detectives. Christianson apparently had pried the diamond out of the ring so he could sell it. Probers reasoned he knew that selling the ring would make it easier to trace, so he just pawned the diamond.

Detectives were unable to find out where Christianson had gone after leaving the Everett motel. But since Everett was south of LaConner, sleuths figured that the suspect was probably headed back to his old stomping grounds of San Rafael, California. Lawmen in that city were contacted.

Detective Bollinger's theory that the suspect was headed back to California eventually proved to be correct. First, the suspect went to Pomona in Southern California. After a stay there with friends, he went to his home town of San Rafael on the San Francisco Bay. Upon his arrival there, he was arrested without incident and Sergeant David Johnson of the San Rafael Police Department contacted Detective Bollinger in Seattle with the news.

On November 9, 1983 Detective Bollinger came face to face with his adversary for the first time. The sleuth studied the man's face, noting every detail, and his eyes trailed down to the suspect's hands where there was evidence of an old bruise on the suspect's right knuckles.

Sergeant Johnson was present when Sergeant Bollinger administered Kevin Christianson his rights. The suspect acknowledged that he understood his rights and he agreed to talk to the detective.

Bollinger questioned him about his bruised right hand.

"I got ripped off," Christianson told the detective. He said his jacket and travel bag had been stolen, and in the ensuing scuffle, his hand got bruised.

Sergeant Bollinger explained that he was there to question Christianson about any connection he may have had with Henry D. Johnson.

"How is Henry?" Christianson asked Bollinger. The detective wasn't sure if Christianson was asking a legitimate question or just being coy. The latter possibility seemed more likely. Johnson had taken such a beating that Christianson must have known that he was dead. Detective Bollinger told the suspect that Johnson was murdered.

Christianson appeared to be anxious to tell his side of the story and began with his arrival in LaConner, Washington. He had left his backpack at an Indian reservation store so he could explore some of the beautiful countryside. But upon his return, he found the store closed. He went to Seattle in search of a mission.

That struck Detective Bollinger as being odd. Seattle was quite a long distance away. LaConner was in Skagit County, Seattle in King County, and Snohomish County lay between the two.

On Friday evening, Henry Johnson picked him up in Seattle. He'd been driving a blue Pinto and had asked, "Can I help you?"

Christianson slept on a hide-a-bed sofa in Johnson's living room Friday evening. They spent Saturday together and went out drinking Saturday night.

Up to that point in the story, Christianson told Detective Bollinger nothing new. The sleuths had determined all these things through their investigation.

It was late Saturday night or early Sunday morning when Christianson and Johnson argued, the suspect told Bollinger. Christianson claimed the victim started making homosexual advances. He was dressed in his underclothes. His other clothes were piled on the living room floor when he approached Christianson, according to the suspect's confession, which later was admitted into court proceedings.

Detectives had serious doubts as to the veracity of this part of the suspect's confession, however. If the victim had partially stripped and made sexual advances, why was it that the victim's clothes had been found covering a section of the floor that was bloodstained?

If he'd stripped and left his clothes on the floor, and then the fight ensued, how did the blood get under the pile of clothes?

And the second thing that indicated the victim

was not a homosexual was the pornographic magazine that had been found in his pickup. If he was a homosexual, why was it he had only one porno magazine, and that one depicted a man and a woman in the throes of wild sexual gratification? Detectives suspected that Christianson, through his accusation of being homosexually accosted, was laying the groundwork for a neat defense.

Christianson said he declined the older man's advances. Harsh words were exchanged. "You wanna get tough? I'll show you tough!" Johnson cried, according to Christianson's version of what transpired. Johnson approached angrily, and Christianson hit him and he fell. When Johnson tried to get up, Christianson hit him again. He tied the victim up, gagged him and put the Tabasco sauce bottle in his mouth. He said he didn't want Johnson to choke, and that's why he put the bottle in his mouth. He figured the bottle would keep a small portion of the gag open, and afford a breathing hole.

If it wasn't murder the detectives were investigating, they might have laughed out loud at that excuse. You don't let a bottle of hot sauce slowly drip into a gagged person's throat to help him breathe. It's a form of torture. But Christianson steadfastly denied wanting to kill Johnson.

"Okay," Sergeant Bollinger said, concluding the interview. "So you hit him a few times and then you had to tie him up? You tied him up with the telephone cord and the v.c. cord? Are you saying that you don't remember everything you did to him, then? Is that what you're saying?"

"Yes," Christianson replied.

Sergeant Bollinger knew that the confession was important because in it Christianson admitted beating and trussing up his victim. Bollinger figured evidence that officers had gathered would disprove the suspect's contention of self defense.

Christianson was extradited back to Seattle. He went on trial before King County Superior Court Judge H. Joseph Coleman in March of 1984.

The prosecutor charged the defendant with first-degree murder. He contended that Christianson temporarily moved in with Johnson so he could prey upon his victim, and rob him when the occasion arose.

The defense claimed that Christianson was somewhat psychotic and he had a terrible fear of homosexual rape. When the older man approached, Christianson exploded in a rage triggered by his psychotic fear of being raped. The defense contended that Christianson committed, at worst, manslaughter.

The defense also contended that Christianson was suffering from diminished capacity at the time of the killing. A well-respected clinical psychologist testified that there is evidence for and against the conclusion that Christianson was psychotic when he killed Johnson.

The psychologist confirmed that Christianson

is a deeply disturbed person, capable of becoming psychotic under extreme duress or when he is drinking or taking drugs.

Christianson told Judge Coleman that on the evening he went out with Johnson, he drank heavily and also ate psychedelic mushrooms that he'd picked earlier in the woods.

According to the psychologist, Christianson had an exaggerated fear of homosexual rape.

Judge Coleman felt that the nature of the crime warranted a conviction harsher than just manslaughter, which the defense was pushing. On the other side of the token, the judge wasn't fully convinced that Christianson had formed the necessary premeditation to warrant a first-degree murder conviction.

On March 22, 1984 Judge Coleman convicted Christianson of second-degree murder. On May 10, 1984 he sentenced Christianson to 20 years in prison for the murder of Johnson. Christianson is presently serving his sentence.

"THE LITTLE BOY WAS BOILED IN LYE!"

by Joseph Koenig

In the afternoon, five-year-old Jason Foreman went out to play with his brother. The boys went quickly behind their Schaeffer Street home to the spacious yard which led to a thin stretch of woods. There they met three other youngsters and pretty soon all five of them were making their way through the trees to the edge of a large housing project. When they got there, one of the boys said something that wasn't appreciated by the others. There were more words and one thing led to another and then the boys were throwing rocks at each other. Jason didn't care for that. About half an hour after coming outside on that fine spring day, he told his brother he was going home.

It was a short walk back to the house on Schaeffer Street where Jason had settled with his family five years earlier. The Foremans had moved to the tiny settlement of Peace Dale, Rhode Island, from Virginia in the months after Jason's birth to be close to the boy's grandparents and great-grandmother. They came to love the quaint colonial villages and excellent bathing beaches on the western shore of Narragansett Bay. In their short time in the area, Jason's father had become president of the Peace Dale fire department.

Jason Douglas Foreman did not make it back home on the warm Sunday afternoon of May 18, 1975. At 4:30, when he had been gone about an hour, his father got into the car and went out looking for the youngest of his three children. By six o'clock, when there was still no sign of the boy, the family phoned police. Sixty minutes later, the Peace Dale fire alarm was sounded, signalling an urgent need for volunteers.

In no time, a large body of searchers had gathered at the firehouse. They were told that the object of their effort was a slender, blue-eyed, blond-haired boy who carried barely 45 pounds on his four-foot frame. There were freckles on Jason's nose and a small scar on his upper lip. Because he still sucked his thumb, his front teeth protruded a bit and, as a result, he slurred his words. When he went out at 3:30 that afternoon, he was wearing maroon pants with a lion patch on the right knee and a short-sleeve polo shirt.

Not a trace of the missing child was found that night, nor the next day—despite an expanded

80

hunt. On Tuesday, May 20th, the searchers gathered again. They were split into two groups—one under the command of South Kingstown Police Detective Sergeant Richard Brown at a field behind a gas station on Kingstown Road south of Kingstown; the other, under the command of South Kingstown Police Captain H. Ronald Hawksley, the veteran officer in overall charge of the probe, assembled a short walk from the Foreman home.

The first group spread out from the gas station to pore through an area several square miles in size. It was swampy, densely vegetated terrain extending all the way south to St. Francis Cemetery. About 2:30, as they hacked through the brambles, some 40 members of citizens band radio clubs from all over the state showed up in South Kingstown. They were joined, later, by some 25 troopers and bloodhounds.

Also joining the more than 150 searchers was a professional psychic, a Providence woman who told that the missing boy would be found along the eastern shore of California Jim Pond. About 1:30 that afternoon, the woman joined the searchers combing the edge of the tiny body of water a few blocks west of Schaeffer Street. She told officers that she had "experienced" Jason's presence in the area. But two canoe searchers—one just before dusk—turned up no indication that the boy had ever been there.

At the end of a long day, the searchers had

nothing to show for their time but a pair of red children's sneakers, which had been found in some woods off Curtis Corner Road, and a plastic squirt gun. But when these were shown to Jason's family, it was quickly determined that they were not the property of the missing child.

Interviewed by reporters, Captain Hawksley was asked why police had brought the psychic into the search.

"We have nothing else to go on," he confessed. "The woman was sincere and we are checking out every angle." He went on to say that his department was eager to speak with anyone who thought they had some information pertinent to the probe.

On Wednesday, police and civilian volunteers beat the bushes across a wide area from Peace Dale South into the business district of neighboring Wakefield and then east to the Pettaquamscutt River. A few officers kept up the hunt on a round-the-clock basis as they had since the boy disappeared.

Increasingly, police were coming to accept the likelihood that little Jason Foreman had been the victim of foul play and troopers began administering lie detector tests to a number of Peace Dale teenagers in an attempt at confirming their insistence that they knew nothing of the boy's disappearance. At the same time, South Kingstown police began routine background checks on all persons with criminal records showing child molestation and sexual offenses. The Federal Bureau of Investigation was advised of their progress.

"The likelihood of foul play increases each day we don't find the child," Captain Hawksley told inquiring reporters.

From other investigators newsmen learned that a number of area residents had been brought to South Kingstown police headquarters for interrogation. Among them was a 29-year-old Narragansett woman who had been arrested at her home about noon and charged with making harassing phone calls to the Foreman house. The woman, who allegedly told the child's parents that she was holding the boy, was released under $500 personal recognizance pending arraignment.

Detective Sergeant Brown told newsmen that the search for Jason Foreman would continue through the Memorial Day weekend, "until we find the boy, or learn something else." He added that the search would be expanded into the countryside.

The following morning, when searchers gathered at the Kingstown Road service station, they were two men light. Both of them had been treated at South County Hospital for injuries suffered during Wednesday's search—one for an eye problem, the other for heat exhaustion. Both were expected to be all right.

Next day, some 200 police and volunteers joined forces to scour a seven square-mile swath of Peace Dale.

"They hit all the areas," Detective Sergeant Brown told newsmen that night.

Chief among those areas was California Jim Pond. Half a dozen volunteer divers from the Newport Naval Base opened the dam gates on the pond about a mile from the Foreman home to search for the boy's body.

South Kingstown Police Chief Clinton Salisbury told reporters that he had decided to have the pond lowered by about six feet so that searchers in helicopters could see the bottom.

"All the kids in town go fishing there," another investigator said, "so it seems like a good place to try. The water level is going down about three inches an hour and we should have the copters up pretty soon."

Joining the Navy searchers, Thursday, were CB units from all over Rhode Island, as well as off-duty policemen from area towns, Civil Air Patrol groups from Quonset Point, Kent County and Smithfield, plus hospital workers and about 15 high school students on trail bikes.

"They're discouraged and disappointed, but they just won't quit," Captain Hawksley said. He added that a massive search was planned for Saturday. "I don't want to put something like this off until next week," he said. "Our goal is to find that boy."

Saturday's effort, he continued, "will not be the grand finale by any means. When we call this thing off, it will be for one reason—that we don't have anywhere to go."

For the big hunt civilian volunteers were advised to wear protective clothing and report in groups by 9 a.m., to the Keaney Gymnasium parking lot at the University of Rhode Island campus in Kingstown. Joining them would be officials from local rescue units—who would work out of the South Road Elementary School and Curtis Corner Road junior high in Kingston—and National Guard units and Navy and Marine units from all over Rhode Island and eastern Massachusetts.

Also contributing to the hunt was the Textron Corporation, which loaned its company helicopter, and the New York state police, which dispatched Trooper Ralph D. Suffolk, Jr., who brought two specially trained dogs. The Wakefield Rotary Club and the National Finance Corporation announced that they had started a reward fund for information leading to Jason Foreman's return.

Some 650 police and civilian volunteers turned out on Saturday to hunt for the boy, backed up by another 150 communications, first aid and food workers. Countless others helped without identifying themselves to the authorities.

"I'm amazed at the ground they covered," Captain Hawksley said. "The word 'humble' came alive this week. I can't believe it."

The searchers were instructed to link arms and

march through an eight square mile area surrounding the Foreman place.

"Search arm in arm in a straight line," they were ordered, "with the slowest person setting the pace."

"Check every bush. Leave nothing out. Don't just look at the ground. There are trees which he could have climbed."

The volunteers were divided into groups of 40, armed with at least one walkie talkie and a radio monitor.

From the junior high school, fire and rescue units fanned out to check waterways from Point Juditch Pond to the North Kingstown end of the Pettaquamscutt River, to the Queen's River in Richmond and to the salt ponds in Green Hill. Other searchers were assigned to check out rivers in the Great Swamp.

But despite the massive turnout, the result was the same as it had been all week. Not a trace of the missing child was found. Before going home for the night, the searchers were asked to report to command headquarters at the Keaney Gym at 9:00 on Sunday morning for another look for the child.

Early on Sunday morning, as the searchers heard their instructions for the day, worshippers at the Peace Dale Congregational Church listened to what was going on in the community.

"This has been a very trying and emotion-filled week for the people of South County," said the

Reverend Lawrence A. Washburn.

"What man, having a hundred sheep, if he has lost one of them, does not leave the 99 in the wilderness and go after the one he has lost until he has found it?"

Speaking with newsmen as some 400 searchers beat the bushes for the boy, Captain Hawksley said that it was becoming apparent that Jason was not anywhere inside the 30-square-mile search area.

"I feel the search has been conducted to such a degree that the boy isn't in there," Hawkley said.

Although he hadn't any evidence, he had a "feeling" that the child had been "adopted" by an abductor.

"I don't think it happens every day," he said, "but I think it happens more than we realize."

Hawksley added that the search would continue until the entire area had been covered.

"Finding that boy alive will be the biggest thrill of my life," he said.

But Sunday's effort was also a failure, despite the help of two men who flew a small fixed wing airplane out of Weatherly Airport to scan the area from the skies.

There was another search for Jason on Monday, but to no one's surprise it, too, was a failure. Late on Monday night, Captain Hawksley announced that the formal effort was being called off, although searchers willing to hunt on their own would be advised to do so in groups.

"We haven't developed one single clue," Hawksley conceded sadly.

About all that the searchers had found during the eight-day hunt was a bomb which had turned up on the shores of California Jim Pond. The Navy had been called and a bomb squad from Newport determined that the explosive device was a dud used for practice during World War II.

Despite the end of the massive effort, the hunt for Jason Foreman was, in many ways, only beginning. South Kingstown police printed and distributed some 10,000 posters on the boy, which were paid for by Jason's family. The nationwide response produced leads which brought investigators as far afield as California, Montana, western Pennsylvania and New Jersey. In Rhode Island more than 100 persons were given lie detector tests, including 20 area sex offenders. Roadblocks were set up near the Foreman home so that motorists could be asked who they were and what they were doing in the neighborhood.

And at least once each week Captain Hawksley met with Jason's mother to apprise her of the latest developments in the case and to discuss further avenues of search. Nearly 18 months would pass by, however, before he had something positive to report.

It was September 5, 1976, when a state police officer making routine traffic checks in Waterloo, New York, in the Finger Lakes district, pulled over a car in which he found a starter's pistol, nude photos of young boys and flyers offering a large reward for the safe return of a five-year-old Brockton, Massachusetts, boy missing since June of 1974. The driver, 29-year-old Henry Pauli, of Providence, who had been implicated in sexual assaults on young boys in at least seven states, was taken into custody on charges of carrying a blank pistol. Turned over to Rhode Island authorities, he was charged with one count of indecent assault and two of sodomy involving boys between the ages of six and eight. Then it was the turn of Massachusetts lawmen to have a go with Pauli. On September 16th, he was charged in Brockton District Court with the first-degree murder of the Brockton boy, whom he alleged to have lured into a wooded area on the pretext of looking for a lost puppy.

"From what we've been able to find out," a Bay State homicide prober said, "Pauli spotted the boy at the Hancock playground, about a mile and a quarter from the boy's home, and then the two of them walked together about half a mile to a spot behind the Melrose Cemetery where the boy was sexually assaulted. After that, we think Pauli panicked and fled the area and the poor kid died of a combination of internal injuries and exposure."

In Brockton, local and state police hurried to a wooded area in the west side of the city to begin a search for the boy on the basis of information allegedly obtained from Pauli. The site was just off North Pearl Street, behind the cemetery.

"We're bringing metal detectors," one investigator said. "If we have some luck, maybe it'll pick up the presence of a zipper on the boy's clothing, or the metal eyelets in his sneakers."

Captain Hawksley told reporters that he would travel to Brockton to review evidence obtained by local police. The day before, he noted, Pauli had come to South Kingstown to drive around with homicide probers.

"We cruised the Peace Dale and Wakefield areas with him," Hawksley said, "but were unable to establish anything."

Hawksley added that he had no plans to charge Pauli in connection with the Foreman case and didn't expect to have any, "unless we find a body."

An investigation in Pauli's activities revealed that in 1973 and 1974 he had worked in the South Kingstown area as a delivery man for a vending company. But at the time of Jason's disappearance he was employed in Providence as a hospital janitor.

Despite the high hopes of Bay State investigators, the Brockton boy's body was never found and a Plymouth County grand jury refused to indict Pauli on the murder charge. And in Rhode Island, detectives were also forced to concede that Pauli had not panned out as a suspect.

Captain Hawksley returned to the routine that had marked the earlier stages of his investigation.

Once a week there was a progress report for Mrs. Foreman and frequent meetings with his probers. But the main burden of the case fell on his own shoulders. In the years to come he would run down countless cases of other missing children and once would follow a Peace Dale family all the way to Canada on the chance that one of its members knew something about what had happened to Jason. At one point, he had packed his bags and was about to take a plane to New Jersey, where he would meet a child who matched Jason's description, when word reached him that the boy could not be Jason.

In the third week of April, 1982, nearly seven years after Jason had vanished, Captain Hawksley again packed his bags, this time for a visit to West Virginia, where he hoped to speak with a relative of the boy, who would now be 12 years old. But once again the flight was called off. Only this time, for the most dramatic reasons of all.

When 14-year-old Kelly Spanier's father came home from work on Thursday evening, April 15th, and saw a pile of his son's newspapers lying undelivered on the front porch, he knew at once that something was the matter. Kelly, an eighth grader at South Kingstown High, was an unusually reliable, conscientious boy with an extremely business-like attitude about his paper route. The elder Spanier went out into his Peace Dale neighborhood to hunt for his son.

When Spanier had no luck in finding the boy, he was joined by one of his neighbors—Jason Foreman's father. But the two of them would accomplish no more than Spanier had alone; for at that very moment Kelly was lying unconscious in a house on nearby Schaeffer Street.

The afternoon had begun quite normally for Kelly. After school he had come home and picked up his papers and begun delivering them throughout his Peace Dale neighborhood. As he passed the home of Michael Everett Woodmansee on Schaeffer Street, the heavyset 23-year-old invited him inside. This was not the first time Michael had asked him in, Kelly would report, but this time he accepted. Michael reportedly offered him some liquor, which he also accepted, and after a few drinks Kelly passed out.

When he came to, Kelly would report, it was to find a red bandana wrapped around his neck and Michael twisting it for all he was worth. Kelly managed to get his fingers underneath the cloth and suck in enough air to revive himself. Then, with one final burst of strength, he broke free from the older youth and fled the house.

At about 7:00 that evening, Kelly's father phoned South Kingstown police to report the incident. Investigators quickly contacted the Woodmansee home, where young Michael reportedly told them he would gladly appear at police headquarters to talk about it. Meanwhile, Kelly was brought to South County Hospital for treatment of cuts on the neck.

Although the details of their conversation have not been made public, there was something in the story that Michael Woodmansee told South Kingstown police which convinced them that they had better hurry out to Schaeffer Street and have a look around. It was 11:00 on Friday morning when they showed up at the Woodmansee home, moments later when they looked inside a cardboard box on top of a cabinet in Michael's second-floor bedroom and felt their hearts catch in their throats. For inside the box were about two dozen bones and the skull of what in life had been a child. Nearby, in the cabinet, the officers reportedly found a recently authored journal describing the abduction of Jason Foreman.

After a medical examiner got a look at the remains and identified them as those of a boy between the ages of four and a half and five and a half, Michael Woodmansee was charged with the first-degree murder of Jason Foreman and assault with intent to murder Kelly Spanier. Though Woodmansee was just 16 years old at the time of Jason's death, South Kingstown police said that they would seek to have him treated as an adult in the courts. Woodmansee spent the weekend at the Institute of Mental Health in Cranston, undergoing psychiatric evaluation to determine if he were mentally competent to stand trial.

"My feeling is that Family Court doesn't have jurisdiction over a 23-year old," Attorney General

Dennis J. Roberts II would tell reporters. "It is the intent of the attorney general and the South Kingstown police to ask that he be treated in every respect as an adult."

On Monday, Rhode Island's Deputy chief medical examiner, Dr. Arthur C. Burns, and Dr. Michael Scala, an orthopedic surgeon, examined the bones found in the Woodmansee home in an attempt at formally identifying the remains. Burns later would tell newsmen that it appeared as if the flesh had been stripped from the bones, not with a knife or other flensing tool, but with some sort of chemical process.

"They have been somewhere for quite a while, protected," Burns said in noting that the bones showed no signs of weathering. He added that his office had not yet formally identified the remains or determined a cause of death.

Identification would not come easily, veteran probers noted. The most common means of identification in such cases, the use of dental charts, would be impossible because at the age of five Jason Foreman apparently had no dental history. Anthropologists were being requested to lend their skills.

As news of the shocking arrest spread across Peace Dale, newsmen swarmed to the tiny community eager for any bit of information they could glean about Michael Woodmansee. They were told of a shy, bookish youngster who seemed to spend most of his time sprawled on the front porch of his home puffing on cigarettes as he worked his way through a pile of books. Often the youngster was seen chatting with neighborhood children and from time to time played football in a vacant lot across the street.

"He was a loner," one of the neighbors said. "You hardly ever saw him with anyone but the kids from around the block."

Something of an amateur actor, Woodmansee reportedly had won a bit part in a South County Players' production of "Mousetrap," slated to be staged in June. His role was to have been that of Christopher Wren, a murder suspect.

On Tuesday, April 20, 1982 Michael Woodmansee entered no plea during a six-minute arraignment at District Court in West Kingstown. Judge Paul J. Del Nero ordered him held without bail at the Institute of Mental Health, where he would undergo additional mental testing and neurological assessment.

Although Judge Del Nero ordered Woodmansee's preliminary psychiatric evaluation sealed, newsmen learned that the young man had been determined to be competent to stand trial. However, it had been suggested that he be returned to the Institute of Mental Health for neurological assessment.

Also on Tuesday, Dr. Burns told newsmen that, along with Dr. Scala, he had reached a "very, very rough estimate" of the height and weight of the victim.

"There's nothing," he added, "to indicate at this point that we are not dealing with Jason's remains."

When he was asked how the child's bones could have been cleaned of flesh in a chemical process, he answered, "To be crude, it's a matter of boiling them with lye, a weak lye-type solution and soap."

On Thursday, July 22nd, the Washington County grand jury indicted Michael Woodmansee for the murder of Jason Foreman.

EDITOR'S NOTE:

The names Henry Pauli and Kelly Spanier are fictitious and have been used because there is no reason for public interest in their true identities.

"A PILE OF HUMAN BONES FILLED THE CHAMBER OF HORRORS!"

by Andrew Lowen

A young couple living in a ground floor apartment at 23, Cranley Gardens, Muswell Hill, London became anxious when a communal lavatory on the first floor was blocked.

Someone else in that same house had already written an indignant letter to the landlord's agents, complaining about an "unpleasant smell" and demanding action, "without further delay."

The letter carried more muscle than the complaint from the couple. Its author was Dennis Nilsen, a former cop, and at the time a civil servant, heading a job center which helps the unemployed find work.

Consequently, a Dyno-Rod engineer was sent to investigate, and as he lifted the manhole in the back garden, he was overcome by the choking stench of rotting flesh buried within.

Underneath the cover, he found that to a depth

of eight inches there were between 30 and 40 pieces of flesh of different sizes, some mere strips, others as large as a fist.

The engineer phoned his company and asked whether he should call the cops, but was told to wait until the following morning when the manager would take a look. It was then 5:00 p.m. The date was February 8, 1983.

No one in that sleepy suburb of north London that night could possibly have imagined that the following day evidence would be uncovered of the most horrendous mass murder crime committed this century in Britain.

On the night of Feb. 8th, the young couple on the ground floor heard footsteps going to and from the top floor where bachelor Nilsen lived alone in a small, self-contained, two-room apartment.

The plodding footsteps up and down the creaky, bare timber stairs continued for more than an hour, so the couple, dressed in their bedclothes, left their apartment to investigate. As they did so, they heard the sound of a manhole cover being replaced just outside the front door.

When they opened the front door, Nilsen was standing on the doorstep and he looked startled, explaining: "You gave me a fright. I thought everyone in the house was in bed . . . asleep."

It was then a few minutes after midnight. The day of November 9th had just begun. A day that will live forever in the minds of the residents of sedate Cranley Gardens, a middleclass refuge, just a few miles north of downtown London. It's an area of white lace curtains, fading Victorian property, not fashionable but boasting a sort of frayed, shabby elegance. Not a wealthy area, but respectable; a small patch of London where most of the people still find the time and the inclination to get on their knees during Sunday.

At 8:45 a.m., Nilsen left for his office in Kentish Town, a brief ride. Kentish Town, another northern suburb, is closer to downtown and it's more grimy and depressing than Muswell Hill. He was in his office by nine, ready to deal with the early rush of the despairing jobless.

By 9:15, the engineer, accompanied by his boss, had returned to 23 Cranley Gardens. This time, the engineer found only a few pieces of flesh underneath the manhole cover, together with four small bones.

"Someone's been here during the night," he declared. His boss, holding his nose, hurried to the nearest public pay phone and called the cops.

It did not take Detective Chief Inspector Peter Jay and his men long to make the six-mile journey north from Scotland Yard.

After a cursory inspection, Inspector Jay radioed for an "army" of men. All day the detectives dug up the garden at the rear of the house, cleared and searched drains and toured the labyrinthine network of sewers under the roads and properties.

99

When Nilsen returned home from work at 6:00 p.m., the cops were waiting for him. Nilsen invited Jay and two of his senior colleagues into his apartment, after learning that the cops were already in possession of a search warrant.

Without any preamble, Jay questioned the ex-cop about the blocked drain, telling the suspect what had been found. "We know they are human flesh and bones," said Jay.

To which Nilsen replied earnestly: "Oh, good grief. Oh, how awful!"

Jay looked Nilsen long and hard in the eye before pressing: "Where is the rest of the body? I'm sure you can tell me everything I want to know."

Nilsen met the chief cop's stare and answered unemotionally, voice steady and controlled: "In two plastic bags in the wardrobe next door. Yes, I can tell you everything. I do want to make a statement. Can we get this over with now?"

Before cuffing him and taking him to Scotland Yard, Inspector Jay asked Nilsen: "Are we talking about one body or two?"

Without blinking or a pause, Nilsen replied in his articulate, well-spoken manner: "Sixteen to be precise!"

The answer hit the inspector like a poleaxe between the eyes. At first, he didn't know whether to believe the suspect. The enormity of the confession was even too big for a man of Inspector Jay's experience to absorb and find credible in one unbelievable hearing.

100

After the customary search of the suspect, Nilsen was led to Jay's car and driven through the evening rush hour traffic to Scotland Yard, the ride taking almost an hour longer than it would have done in any off-peak period.

After getting Nilsen settled into one of the Yard's interview-rooms, he was officially cautioned by Jay in front of witnesses and then invited to make a formal written statement, which he readily agreed to do, with the words: "Let's get started, shall we?"

As an ex-cop, he was almost as familiar with the routine as was Inspector Jay and his men.

And then, for two days, almost nonstop, Dennis Nilsen poured out a story of horror, blood, gore, massacre and mutilation that was to sicken and horrify even the most hardened cops on the case.

Nilsen said that he had first murdered in December, 1978, though he couldn't remember the exact date. He had then been living in a ground floor apartment in Melrose Avenue, Cricklewood, another suburb of north London, though less salubrious than Muswell Hill.

"Did you kill again at that address?" he was asked.

"Oh, yes," he replied evenly and without hesitation. "I can give you the precise number. I killed 12 people at my home in Melrose Avenue."

"All men?" Jay asked.

"Oh, yes," Nilsen retorted, almost indignantly.

"I wouldn't harm a lady. Gentlemen don't do things like that. I was brought up to respect ladies. I just killed men. Young men. Worthless types. The sort of men that pollute society. I hope I'm making myself clear."

Inspector Jay was beginning to get the picture.

Nilsen went on to describe in his statement how he would befriend drifters—many of them out of work homosexuals who were living rough in London—invite them back to his home, where he would slay them.

One of his victims was 25-year-old William Sutherland, a heavy drinking Scotsman who survived by panhandling in London.

They met in a pub near Piccadilly Circus, the very heart of downtown London, amid the flashing neon lights, strip clubs, gay bars, massage parlors and call-girl haunts. It's all tinsel at night, but as tawdry as hell beneath the superficial veneer.

In his statement, Nilsen admitted: "We had a great binge and I killed Billy Sutherland. I remember having a tie round his neck and pulling. I don't recall him struggling, but I think he must have done.

"When he was dead, I stood back and looked at him, as casually as that. Then I put his body under the floorboards, possibly two days later.

"Later, I dissected the body and put the pieces in a suitcase, which I hid in a garden shed. A week or so after that, I burned the suitcase. I stood watching the fire and I could smell the burning meat. It was just like cooking a steak. The meat sizzled and splashed. I felt nothing."

Nilsen didn't know the identity of most of the young men he murdered. He told cops: "I didn't want to know their names. They were just trash. I just wanted them dead. I was helping people like you. I'm still a policeman at heart. I was getting them off the streets—forever. Making your job easier."

He then went on to describe how he killed a skinhead, aged between 17 and 21, who had a London accent and boasted about his toughness and drinking ability.

Nilsen had described himself to the skinhead as "an under-exercised clerical pen-pusher."

After a drinking session the skinhead passed out in Nilsen's apartment. "I didn't think he was very tough," Nilsen told the cops.

"I removed my tie and put it round his neck and strangled him. End of the day; end of the drinking; end of a person.

"I didn't always succeed in killing my intended victims. I had a failure rate. Not a high one, but a number did escape. That would make me very angry and I would try extra hard next time.

"After a failure, I always made an excellent job of my next victim. I strangled most of them with a tie before cutting them up and disposing of the meat in whatever way happened to appeal on the day. I didn't believe in too much forward-planning because that would have taken away the spontaneity of it all, spoiling the fun.

"I started off with about 15 ties. Now I have only one left, a clip-on. I never used the same tie for killing twice. I liked to use a fresh tie on each victim."

At one point during the questioning, Nilsen was asked about his sex life.

After a full minute of heavy thought and silence, he replied: "Physically, I'm bisexual. Emotionally, I'm homosexual. Many of the people I killed were male prostitutes or rent boys."

He became angry with the cops when they suggested that the victims were slain because they rejected Nilsen's homosexual advances.

"Not true!" he stormed. "There was no sexual horseplay before they died. There was no sexual motive. They died because I enjoy killing. Okay? I didn't want to screw any of them. All I ever wanted from them was the thrill of seeing them dead. I was easily pleased."

During the next few days, Inspector Jay and his men tried to find out what exactly went on in the mind of Dennis Nilsen, a neat, almost timid clerk-like figure who seemed to be hiding behind his thick spectacles.

One moment he would quote poetry to the cops and the next he would break down sobbing. Coldly he told the detectives: "I have no tears for my victims. I have no tears for myself."

During the days and nights of almost non-stop

interrogation, he once bragged: "I will be remembered as a major killer. They'll read about me all over the world. My name will not be forgotten in a hurry."

Psychiatrists joined the police team and slowly they began to build a picture of a lonely man, who throughout his life longed for friendship and to feel that he was wanted. He had tried desperately to build a stable relationship but always failed, sinking deeper and deeper into his own dark fantasies.

The "shrinks" believed that Nilsen's unhappy childhood in the Grampian village of Strichen left a mark on him that he is to carry for the rest of his days. He is solitary, introspective and studious.

To doctors, Nilsen described himself in childhood as a person who always felt quite alone, often lost in his own dark fantasies.

They concluded that he'd become totally withdrawn within himself and probably hadn't had an emotional relationship since the tender age of six.

Nilsen's escape from his unhappy childhood was to the British Army, enlisting on August 28, 1961, three months before his 16th birthday. He served Queen and country well and faithfully for 12 years.

After the Army, Nilsen joined the police as a trainee constable in Willesden, yet another north London suburb. But he did not make the police force his career, leaving to get a job as a security guard. While a security officer, he rented a one-room apartment in Teignmouth Road, a short walk from Melrose Avenue.

And, of course, it was at his homes on Melrose Avenue and Cranley Gardens that he killed and cut up his victims.

One police psychiatrist told Jay: "To Nilsen, the victims were a chance of friendship. Even after he slaughtered them, their bodies were his friends because they were a presence. They were better than being empty, completely alone."

Sleuths learned Nilsen met all his victims in the down-and-out haunts of London, which attracted either lonely homosexuals or friendless drifters.

Over his favorite drink, Bacardi and whisky mixed, he would sit alone in the bars eyeing those he could befriend.

The build-up was always the same: a few pints of beer, then Bacardi and whisky, with Nilsen insisting that he pay for the drinks for his new-found *friend*.

Back in Nilsen's apartment, he would drink massive quantities of his favorite drink, and listen to his kind of music—chart-toppers like Superman by Laurie Anderson and Criminal Record by Rick Wakeman.

The combination of music and drink brought on a hypnotic trance during which Nilsen believed he was a kind of god who could do exactly what he liked.

He told police about the moment of each

crime, saying: "I was amazingly strong. I stored the body of Sutherland alongside two other corpses in plastic bags under the floor. Every day I would spray the room with air freshener."

Another victim was 16-year-old Martyn Duffey, a student caterer from the city of Birkenhead, near Liverpool, in the northwest. After strangling Duffey, Nilsen used Duffey's own set of kitchen knives to dismember him.

Malcolm Barlow, aged 17, from another northern industrial city, Rotherham, believed he had found a true friend in Nilsen.

Barlow, something of a pathetic figure, was an epileptic. His parents had died while he was still at school. Barlow was strangled, chopped up into 60 pieces and fried in a specially-made bonfire in the garden because he had cried in front of Nilsen when talking about how much he missed his mother and father.

"Weak men make me sick," Nilsen explained to Jay, making it clear why Barlow was killed.

The most unusual of the murders was that of English-born Canadian Kenneth Ockenden, who was on a three-month holiday in Surrey county. He was highly intelligent and was not a penniless drifter.

He and Nilsen appeared to have struck up a good friendship over a few drinks in the Golden Lion pub, Soho—the red light district of London's swinging West End. They even went together on a sight-seeing tour of the capital.

But when they arrived back at Nilsen's apartment in Melrose Avenue, Ockenden made the mistake of asking to listen to some stereo music. And as he sat in an armchair with the headphones on, Nilsen looped the flex round the Canadian's neck and strangled him.

Archibald Allen, 28, from Glasgow, a tough Scottish city, was strangled as he ate an omelette which Nilsen had cooked for him.

Allen had arrived in London following a love affair that had run out of steam. The carved up parts of his body were the chunks of human meat that the cops discovered under the manhole in the garden of 23, Cranley Gardens, after being called to the scene by the Dyno-Rod engineer on February 8th.

Nilsen's final victim was another Scotsman—Stephen Sinclair, aged 20, a heavy drinker who was also a drug addict. They met in The George pub in London's Charing Cross Road and, after a meal, went to Nilsen's apartment in Cranley Gardens.

When the cops raided the apartment on February 9th, the lower half of Sinclair's body was in a bathroom cupboard. Other sections were in the two plastic bags and more human flesh had been flushed down the sewer.

In another part of his statement, Nilsen wrote: "I have been collecting bodies. Dead bodies. Some people collect stamps or stuffed birds. I like to have dead bodies around me. It makes me feel good and secure. Living people scare me. The dead are so much more predictable. They don't cause pain. They don't double-cross you. Dead people make the best friends."

Because the victims were homeless men, either without any known relatives or with parents who were pleased to see the back of them, the task of identifying the bodies was a thankless job, almost an impossible one. In the end, the cops were able to positively identify only seven of the total number of victims, even though more than 1,000 separate pieces of human remains were found on the premises of the two properties—in the houses, gardens, sewers and pipes.

It was on February 12th that Nilsen was charged with the murder of Stephen Sinclair, who was quickly identified. He'd been the last victim. This served as a holding charge. Two months later, he was charged with six indictments.

Still the cops pursued their inquiries, trying desperately to put names to more victims, imploring mothers, fathers, wives, aunts and uncles to contact their nearest police station if any young man in their family had been missing.

Meanwhile, Nilsen was writing letters from prison to the detective who had arrested him!

In the first letter to Jay, 37-year-old Nilsen wrote: "There is no disputing I'm a violent killer under certain circumstances.

"It amazes me that I have no tears for these victims. I have no tears for myself or those bereaved by my action. I am a weak person, constantly under pressure, who just cannot cope with it, who turns to revenge against society in the haze of a bottle of spirits. Or maybe it was because I was just born an evil man?"

A second letter stated: "I am tragically a private person, not given to public tears. The enormity of the act has left me in permanent shock.

"The trouble was that, as my activities increased, so did the unbearable pressures which could only be escaped from by taking the best routes to oblivion via the bottle.

"I think I have sufficient principle and morality to know where the buck must come to rest. The evil was short-lived and cannot live for long inside. I have slain my own dragon as surely as the press will slay me."

In his third letter to Jay, Nilsen wrote: "I escaped from reality by taking increasing draughts of alcohol and plugging into stereo music which mentally removes me to a high plane of ecstasy, joy and tears. That is a totally emotional experience. I relive experiences from childhood to the present—taking out the bad bits.

"I played one record 10 times in succession until the Bacardi ran out. Music helps me into a trance."

The fourth letter talked about turning away a friend who had come from the city of Exeter, in the southwest, to visit him.

"I would obviously not admit him when I had

a headless, naked body lying on the floor of my front room," he wrote.

The trial of Dennis Andrew Nilsen began at the Old Bailey, London, on October 24, 1983.

Members of the public had been waiting all night to secure a place in the gallery of the famous Number One Court. This was the same court where Peter Sutcliffe, the Yorkshire ripper, had failed in his attempt to persuade the jury that voices from God led him to kill and mutilate 13 women.

Dr. Crippen and John Christie, legendary London murderers, had been sentenced to death in that court too.

Nilsen arrived neatly dressed and well groomed. Certainly he was one of the smartest men in the court.

Presiding over the case was Mr. Justice Croom-Johnson, a softly-spoken man, but renowned as a no-nonsense judge; a hard-liner.

The jury of eight men and four women were sworn in without a single objection from prosecution or defense.

The prosecuting team comprised Mr. Allan Green and Mr. Julian Bevan. Defending Nilsen were Mr. Ivan Lawrence, QC, a Member of Parliament, and Mr. Robert Flach, the junior of the formidable partnership.

During the trial, it was revealed by the prosecution that Nilsen had admitted to several psychiatrists that he had derived "enormous pleasure"

111

from the ritual killings and that he had performed "revolting sexual acts" on the bodies after they were dead.

The charge stated that he had committed the murders during a four-year period from December 1978. He'd also been charged with two attempted murders. In a clear, resonant voice, Nilsen pleaded "not guilty" to all counts.

He admitted the killings—and attempting to kill—but denied murder and attempted homicide, claiming "diminished responsibility," the British equivalent of insanity, at the time of the crimes.

Nilsen's long, meandering statement was read to the court. Of the first killing, he had said: "After having a damned good old drink together, the next morning I had a corpse on my hands. My tie was still around his neck. There was no argument. I was shocked, horrified.

"I got two plastic bags and put one over each end of his body, and I put it under the floorboards surrounded by bricks and dirt. I burnt him on August 11, 1979 (eight months later). I remember that date. It was the end of a sorry period. I did not dismember his body.

"When I took it up, it was remarkable. There was very little decomposition. He was fully clothed and the morning was bright and sunny. I put string around the body to lift it. I had built a bonfire the day before. I burnt him at the bottom of the garden about three feet from the fence.

"It was a relief to be rid of the body. Burnt

meat smells but I had made sure to burn rubber in the fire. It cancelled out the smell."

Of the second victim, Ockenden, the Canadian, Nilsen stated: "When he was lying dead at my feet, I put on earphones and listened to some great music. It wasn't until several months later that I dissected him."

Duffey was victim No. 3 and Nilsen's statement dealt with the disposal. "I wrapped and packed the pieces of Ockenden and Duffey in suitcases. Two suitcases were full of parts and there were excess parts of Duffey. The two heads were in carrier bags and the arms and hands of Duffey would not go in the suitcases at all. Outside the French windows, the arms and hands went into a hole by the bush.

"I put the suitcases on the floor of the shed and built a brick barrier around them and covered them with ordinary house bricks. I took magazines from under the stair cupboard and covered these. The heads were in carrier bags.

"The shed was not locked. They remained there all summer. People lived next door, but there were never any complaints. I sometimes sprayed disinfectant there once a day. On my last day at Melrose Avenue, I dug up these bones. The long bones I cut up with a spade and threw them as far as I could into the waste part of the garden."

Of victim No. 7, Nilsen had written: "I couldn't cut him up. He was so thin he reminded me of concentration camps. I didn't want to look at him."

Victim 9 . . . "I remember sitting on top of him and strangling him with a tie. I remember at the moment of strangulation, for some biological reason which I don't understand, he urinated and made my trousers wet. That was the first time I was aware of something like that happening at the actual time of killing somebody."

Victim 12 . . . "This was a young man who was taken ill in the street near my home. I helped him indoors, gave him a drink. He wanted me to call an ambulance because he suffered from a serious condition. I didn't want all the fuss of being confronted by ambulancemen, so I killed him instead. By that time, I was surrounded by dead bodies."

Victim 13 . . . "After a minute or more of strangling him, his heart was still beating quite strongly, although he was unconscious. I couldn't believe it. He was dressed only in underpants. I dragged him into the bathroom, where I pulled him over the rim of the bath. His head was hanging into the bath, I put in the plug while still holding him firmly and turned on the cold water full. His head was on the bottom of the bath and in a minute or so it reached his nose.

"Rasping breathing came on again. The water rose high and I held him under. He was struggling against it. There were bubbles coming from his mouth, nose, and he stopped struggling. The water had become bloody. I left him there.

"He had urinated in the bath as he died and feces was coming from his underpants. I decided to let him soak all night in the bath. I cut him up the next day," the statement concluded.

The jury retired to consider their verdict late on the afternoon of Thursday, November 3rd, nine days after the trial had started. It was not until the following afternoon that the jury announced 10-2 "guilty" verdicts on all the murder charges.

It was also a 10-2 "guilty" verdict on one of the attempted homicide charges and unanimous on the other.

The judge immediately sentenced Nilsen to life in prison, with the recommendation that he should not be considered for release for at least 25 years.

Nilsen, standing meekly in the dock to receive his sentence, showed no emotion.

And everyone at the trial will remember the words of Dr. Patrick Gallwey who told the court: "Nilsen really believes that he is the most important person of the century. He said he is the murderer of the century. He talks about himself as a creative psychopath who, under stress, lapses into a destructive psychopath . . ."

"THE PIECE OF MEAT WAS PAMELA'S THIGH!"

by Gary C. King

The case which follows contains such gruesome and coldblooded elements that it has been described by many people, including Lane County District Attorney Pat Horton, as "unparalleled" in the history of Lane County crime. And justly so, for during the course of the investigation, homicide detectives uncovered shocking, horrifying details of a sordid, sado-masochistic sex orgy that led, ultimately, to the stabbing and dismemberment of an unwilling participant.

This bizarre story opens in the college city of Eugene, Oregon at approximately 12:30 on the morning of February 24, 1978 when two human scavengers were rummaging through one of the dumpsters of a west side shopping center in a search for cardboard. They found plenty of what they were looking for, the intended use of which was known only to them and God. However, as the couple dug deeper in the trash bin, one of them came across a plastic bag that apparently warranted further investigation.

The bag must have weighed at least 25 to 30 pounds, but it was easy to pull free. They had it lifted out of the bin and onto the pavement in no time at all, anxiously tearing open the bag to examine their "find."

At first glance, the contents of the bag simply appeared to be a couple of chunks of discarded meat, one small piece and one large piece, probably spoiled and thrown out a couple of days before from the meat department of the adjacent grocery store. However, upon closer examination, the cold, rancid smelling meat suddenly looked frighteningly familiar, almost human!

While examining the large piece of meat, one of the rummagers noted there was very little blood, about as much as would be present in butchered, prepared beef. Although the smell of the meat was nearly intolerable, the men's curiosity compelled them to examine the smaller piece. Although the smaller piece was nearly unrecognizable, it faintly resembled a severed, mutilated female breast!

Sick and retching from revulsion, the man threw the meat to the pavement and vomited. Following a few moments of illness and nausea, the two regained some of their composure and rushed to the nearest telephone and called the Eugene Police Department, informing the cops of the wretched discovery.

Due to the lateness of the hour, not to mention the seriousness of the trash bin discovery, the police dispatcher who took the call knew he would have to wake up someone with higher authority. He chose to wake up Lt. Don Lonneker, detective division commander.

When Lt. Lonneker and the first police units arrived, officers immediately cordoned off the area to hold back the curious onlookers and the graveyard shift of press members in an attempt to preserve any bits of evidence that might be present.

After the area had been completely sealed off, police detectives took statements from the two midnight rummagers regarding the events that led to the discovery of the two pieces of meat.

The police personnel set up lights and began going through other trash bins and garbage cans in search of still more body parts, but when it was evident there was nothing more of any significance to be found, the two pieces of meat were wrapped up and sent off to the medical examiner's office.

In the meantime, the Eugene Police Department launched a massive search effort of other garbage dumpsters and cans in the vicinity of the west side supermarket where the alleged body parts were discovered. Unfortunately, their efforts were futile.

A few days later Dr. Ed Wilson, deputy Lane

County medical examiner, reported that tests had determined that the larger piece of meat was that of a female thigh, which had been severed just above the knee and from the groin to the waist, and that the smaller piece was a female breast, ravaged by so many human teeth marks that it was nearly indistinguishable as a human anatomical part! Dr. Wilson reported that further tests were being conducted in an attempt to identify the victim's blood type.

Meanwhile, police detectives began checking their female missing persons files, singling out two young women who were reported missing at approximately the time the body parts were discovered in the shopping center dumpster.

The cops considered Elizabeth Green as the most likely victim, although no hard evidence had been found linking the 24-year-old mother to the mysterious and gruesome thigh and breast. Mrs. Green was described by friends and relatives as a dependable and a devoted mother, and was reportedly to have picked up her infant daughter at the hospital on the day of her disappearance.

According to hospital officials, Mrs. Green arrived at the hospital on the day in question at approximately 11:00 a.m., and she nursed her baby that had been born five weeks prematurely. She was last seen by a parking lot attendant as she drove away from Eugene's Sacred Heart General Hospital shortly after 11:00 a.m., and her car and purse were found the next day in separate parking lots in the 1400 and 1500 blocks of Franklin Boulevard.

Pamela Lee Bruno, 24, was another woman the cops added to their list of possible victims. Mrs. Bruno, a childless housewife, was described as white, 5 feet 8 inches tall, and approximately 165 pounds. She had blonde shoulder length hair and hazel eyes. She lived with her husband in the 4600 block of Main Street in nearby Springfield in one of several run-down, almost uninhabitable, apartments.

According to Springfield Police Chief Brian Riley, Mrs. Bruno was last seen by her husband, Johnny, at their apartment on February 16th. According to Riley, she was wearing a short brown plaid coat, blue jeans, and brown shoes. She did not own a car, and relied on hitchhiking and taxicabs for her transportation. Considered by many to be a heavy drinker, Mrs. Bruno was known to frequent the local bars and taverns.

According to Mrs. Bruno's husband, Pamela was gone when he awoke on the morning of February 17th. However, he didn't report her as missing until February 22nd.

"This has happened several times in the past, according to Mr. Bruno," said Chief Riley. "It's not unusual for her to be gone this long." According to Chief Riley, Mrs. Bruno was reported missing eight or nine times in recent years. But, he said, her most recent disappearance was different and unusual because none of her friends or relatives heard from her for over two weeks, and she was never gone for more than two or three days at a time.

In the meantime, with only the thigh and the breast to work with, forensic scientists from the Oregon State Police Crime Labs in Eugene and experts from the University of Oregon were able to determine, by studying the bones, the victim was a young woman between 18 to 30 years of age, and that she was of medium weight, approximately 140 to 160 pounds. They also determined that the blood type found in the severed parts was not of the same type as Mrs. Green, thus eliminating her as the possible victim.

However, the scientists were continuing to work round the clock in an attempt to connect the severed body parts with Mrs. Bruno. But unless they could locate some kind of official record listing her blood type, little progress in linking the parts was likely. The scientists did say, however, that the description they arrived at fit more accurately with Mrs. Bruno than with Mrs. Green or any other woman who was reported missing at that time.

The technique the scientists used to confirm that the thigh came from a woman was relatively simple. They merely examined tissue samples under a microscope in search of "Barr bodies," which was simply tiny specks or dots appearing in the nucleus of a cell that are present in females but not in males.

The detectives turned to the help of an anthropologist specializing in bone structures to help narrow down the age gap of the victim. The techniques involved were far more complicated than those used in determining whether or not the victim was male or female. They had to make estimations and calculations based on measurements of the length and diameter of the thigh bone and compare their findings with statistical tables and graphs. But when their tests were completed, they determined that the victim was between 25 and 30 years of age.

"We're taking a further interest in Springfield's missing woman," said Lt. Don Lonneker, detective division commander, after conferring with other detectives from several local law-enforcement agencies.

In the meantime, Springfield police stepped up their efforts in their search for Mrs. Bruno, and checked further into the backgrounds of the missing woman and her husband.

The cops soon discovered that the Brunos had lived in the Springfield area for about three years, having moved there from Vancouver, Washington. They were married for seven years, but had no children.

Digging still further into their background, police detectives soon discovered that Johnny Bruno was convicted in Vancouver for driving while under the influence of intoxicants and for hit and run, and that both he and his wife were convicted of contributing to the delinquency of a minor.

According to the Bruno's former probation officer, the latter charge was a result of an incident in which Mrs. Bruno invited two 15-year-old girls into their apartment and gave them alcoholic beverages, then proceeded to have explicit sexual intercourse with her husband as the two girls excitedly looked on! Johnny Bruno then had intercourse with one, possibly both, of the young girls during the incident after arousing their prurient interests.

Meanwhile, police divers searched the area near the university and the parking lots where Mrs. Green's car and purse were found, but they found nothing to help them locate the missing woman. According to Lt. Lonneker, however, divers did find a rusty knife in the water, but denied that it had any significance to the severed thigh and breast case. "It unquestionably has no bearing on our investigation," he said.

Lonneker did say, however, that the severed thigh "appears to have been cut with a knife." He also said that he had temporarily suspended the search for additional anatomical parts and other physical evidence connected with the murder and missing persons cases after a week of exhaustive efforts. "We've simply run out of places and directions to go," he said.

In the meantime, on February 28th, detectives went to the Bruno's cottage in Springfield to obtain hair samples from Mrs. Bruno's hair brush, and they attempted to find out what her blood type was by conferring with her husband. But he simply repeated that he didn't know her blood type, and all detectives were left with were a few strands of long blonde hair and the frustration of knowing that it was likely to be some time yet before positive identification of the severed thigh and breast could be made.

According to Dr. Ed Wilson, deputy Lane County medical examiner, investigators knew that the female victim had not been dead for long, unless the thigh and breast were preserved by freezing, which they seriously doubted. He also said they could only retrieve a small blood sample from the body parts, but stressed that it would be enough for the Oregon State Police Crime Labs to establish the victim's blood type, the results of which would soon be known.

If the scientists could have obtained more blood, said Wilson, they would have attempted to measure the amount of prolactin (a hormone) in the blood and could possibly have determined whether or not the victim had been nursing a child, a clue that could have been of vital importance to an investigation of this nature. But considering the small amount of blood they had to work with, the blood type identification was the best they could hope for.

The first real breakthrough in the case came when detectives finally learned Mrs. Bruno's blood type through her medical records in Vancouver, Washington, which they wouldn't release to the press. And almost as soon as they had discovered the missing woman's blood type, the Oregon State Police Crime Labs reported to detectives that their samples were of the same blood type as Mrs. Bruno's type.

Considering that detectives now knew that the victim was a female Caucasian, 5 feet 4 inches to 5 feet 7 inches in height, and that she weighed approximately 140 to 160 pounds, they now felt Pamela Bruno might be the victim that had been so savagely butchered.

A short time later, Springfield police Detective Don Bond paid a visit to the Bruno apartment. He told Mrs. Bruno's husband that it was likely his wife was dead, and that it was now believed that the thigh and breast were parts severed from his wife's body, although they were not one hundred percent certain Mrs. Bruno was the victim. While Detective Bond was relating the details to Mr. Bruno, Bruno's dog came barking into the room, at which time Bruno became irritated and angry with the animal.

"I've got to get rid of that damn dog, too," Bruno remarked to Bond. It was at that precise moment that Bond began to suspect that Bruno killed his wife, although he didn't immediately acknowledge Bruno's apparent Freudian slip of the tongue. Instead, he acted as if he hadn't noticed and asked Bruno to visualize the severed thigh found in the trash bin. Astonishingly, Bruno described to Detective Bond precisely how the thigh had been severed!

The investigation continued, and finally, on March 10, the severed thigh and breast were positively identified through laboratory analysis as being parts of what was once Pamela Lee Bruno.

With this sudden new development, police went to the Bruno apartment with search and arrest warrants, but in spite of their efforts they could find no traces of blood or other physical evidence that would indicate the murder occurred inside the Bruno's residence.

Police arrested Johnny Charles Bruno just the same, and took him to Springfield Police Headquarters for further questioning. Bruno was cooperative for the most part, and seemed to want to help the police. On a "cop's hunch," Detective Bond told Bruno that they thought someone else was also involved in the grisly murder.

"Well, you know, don't you?" Bruno told the cops. He then broke down and cried, making a full confession of how his wife was repeatedly stabbed and dismembered, and implicated one of his friends and co-workers, Charles Haynes, 31, and Haynes' wife, Lionetti Anita, also 31. The two men worked together for nearly three years as tree planters for a local firm, and Mrs. Bruno and Mrs. Haynes were known to associate with each other when the Brunos would visit the Hayneses.

On Saturday, March 11th, police went to the Haynes' rented house in Eugene, located in the 800 block of West Fifth Avenue, a poor area of town, and arrested Charles Leroy Haynes. The next day, when Mrs. Haynes appeared at Springfield Police Headquarters, she too was arrested.

All three suspects were accused of "acting in concert" with each other when the stabbing of Mrs. Bruno occurred, which police alleged was on or about February 21st, and each allegedly participated in the subsequent ritualistic dismembering of the victim's arms, legs, breasts, and head.

District Attorney Pat Horton would only describe the murder weapon as a "stabbing instrument." "There is a certain uniqueness in this case which I think is unparalleled in Lane County," said Horton. Springfield Police Chief Brian Riley stated he couldn't remember a murder case as gruesome, and went on to praise the cooperative efforts of the Springfield and Eugene Police Departments.

"I've seen a lot of investigations of crimes involving more than one jurisdiction done in other places," said Eugene Police Chief Pierce Brooks, a former detective division commander at the Los Angeles Police Department. "But I've never seen it done as effectively as here."

In the meantime, Lane County District Court Judge Gregory Foote ordered the suspects held without bail at the Springfield city jail, where they would be appointed attorneys by the court.

Police now alleged that Pamela Bruno was killed and "slaughtered" at the Haynes' residence in Eugene, and Chief Brooks sent crime lab supervisor Mary Ann Vaughn to the house to investigate.

Wearing an oxygen mask and tank inside the house, Ms. Vaughn used special chemicals that emit toxic fumes to search for "trace evidence" in each of the rooms of the house. Brooks said they were looking for evidence "so minute that it might not be visible to the naked eye."

However, District Attorney Horton and police officials refused to comment further on the case, saying only that a Lane County grand jury would be asked to indict the three suspects. When asked whether additional body parts had been found, Horton replied, "To my knowledge, (additional) body parts have not been found."

On Thursday, March 16th, a Lane County grand jury returned murder indictments against Johnny Charles Bruno, Charles Leroy Haynes, and his wife, Lionetti Anita Haynes. The three suspects were transferred to the Lane County Jail in Eugene, where they were held without bail.

As the weeks passed and turned into months, detectives continued their investigation of the butcher-murder of Pamela Lee Bruno, but chose to remain tight-lipped about their results, preferring to save the details for the soon-to-begin trials.

It was Tuesday, May 23, 1978, and the Lane County Circuit Court of Judge Roland Rodman was filled to capacity, with hopeful spectators being turned away. Johnny Charles Bruno was the first to go on trial for the brutal slaying and butchering of his wife, a trial that the people of Eugene and Springfield would not soon forget. Inside the courtroom, opening arguments were being heard.

Deputy District Attorney Brian Barnes' opening statement was a recounting of the events of the February 24th discovery of the severed thigh and breast, a synopsis of the investigation leading to the arrests of the three suspects, and details of Bruno's confession.

"At the end of this case," said defense attorney Harry Carp, "no matter what evidence the state presents, you're not going to have a pretty picture. You're going to be looking at a charnel house."

"I suggest to you it was more than a charnel house," countered Prosecutor Barnes, "which, as I understand it, is a place where dead bodies and bones are deposited. It was more like a slaughter house, an unparalleled ritualistic killing involving blood, guts, and gore. It's something you will not easily forget."

It was noted that Carp had filed notice of intent to argue his client's defense of extreme emotional disturbance or mental defect which, under

Oregon status, is the same as an insanity plea. However, he reserved the right to change his defense theorem if necessary.

When Prosecutor Barnes described how Mrs. Bruno's body had allegedly been strung up over the bathtub in the Haynes' residence and "disentrailed and butchered like an animal," Mrs. Bruno's mother, grandmother, and aunt all left the courtroom hurriedly.

To visualize how a loved one had been drained of her blood, and had her entrails scraped out into a cold porcelain bathtub, then to hear details of the grisly dismemberment, was understandably more than a relative of the deceased could bear.

In his statements, Barnes said the state would prove that Mrs. Bruno's death was caused intentionally by her husband and Mr. and Mrs. Haynes during an evening of alcohol, marijuana, and group sex which included sado-masochistic acts.

Dr. David Myers, assistant Lane County medical examiner who examined the tissue of the thigh and breast, told the court that the breast was so mutilated by human teeth marks that he could not immediately recognize it. He also told the court that the body parts had almost no blood, leading him to believe that Mrs. Bruno's body had been drained of blood through a cut or a wound caused by the woman's killers.

The feeling in the courtroom was cold and dismal in a psychological sense rather than physical. It was generally felt that in order for Mrs. Bruno's body to have been so completely drained of blood, her killers would have had to have her strung up over the bathtub for quite some time, a clear indication that her killers were in no hurry to get rid of the body, and that they might well have even enjoyed the ritualistic killing and subsequent hacking up of the victim's body.

On the third day of Bruno's murder trial, a packed courtroom of curious spectators and a shocked jury listened intently as a taped statement Bruno made to police was played.

In the taped statement Bruno made while being interviewed by Springfield police detective Donald Bond, Bruno described how he and his wife Pamela hitchhiked into Eugene and arrived at the Haynes' home about 8:00 p.m. Bruno said that after some heavy drinking (he was known to down a six-pack of beer in less than 20 minutes) and pot smoking, Charles Haynes and the Brunos decided to have a session of group sex.

According to the tape, Pamela Bruno had agreed at first to participate in group sex with her husband and the Hayneses. "Pam agreed at first," said Bruno on tape, "then she didn't, so we took her in the other room and tied her up." He also stated on the tape that he bit one of his wife's breasts so hard that he took off part of the nipple.

He also stated on the tape that Mrs. Haynes

was the first one to stab the victim because she was enraged when she saw her husband having sex with Mrs. Bruno. He further stated that Charles Haynes stabbed the victim several times after Mrs. Haynes passed him the knife, and that he (Bruno) stabbed his wife only once.

Bruno said he stabbed his wife in the chest after Charles Haynes passed him the knife, but "not very far 'cause I was so weak and leaning against the wall and everything. I couldn't believe this was happening.

"Haynes stabbed her quite a few times," Bruno's taped voice said, repeating that he stabbed his wife only once. "I don't even think I got into her far enough because I was so weak at that point and so scared." The tape continued, and the defendant's voice told the details of what occurred after the stabbing.

"Chuck (Haynes) says," according to the tape, 'We gotta do something about this now. We're gonna have to cut her up,' he says." Bruno then described how he helped Haynes drag Pamela into the bathroom, occasionally breaking down and crying as he told the horrible details—the blood, the torn flesh.

According to the tape, once they had the victim's body over the bathtub, her blood was drained. Some time later, the Hayneses and Bruno allegedly cut up Mrs. Bruno's body with a butcher knife, placing the severed parts into several plastic garbage bags. They then drove away with the packaged parts, according to the taped testimony, and deposited the parts in trash containers around various areas of Eugene. However, the only body parts that were recovered were the breast and thigh found on February 24th.

When asked by Detective Bond in the taped interview if he knew what he was doing on the night of the murder, Bruno replied he did know right from wrong at the time. Bruno's attorney had been trying to show Bruno was too drunk on the night of the murder to form the specific intent to commit murder.

When asked "if this act of sex and violence" would have taken place had there been additional people present Bruno answered, "I would have gotten some help. I would not have been so scared to be alone with him (Haynes)." In yet another statement, Bruno made the implication that Haynes had ordered him to participate in the killing and savage butchery.

Warren Reid, a neighbor of Bruno, took the witness stand and testified that the Brunos fought regularly. He testified that Bruno had attempted to throw his wife in front of an oncoming car, and that he saw Bruno kick Pamela in the back of her head while he was wearing his work boots.

Reid also told the court that Mrs. Bruno would very often insult her husband in front of others, telling all about her sexual activities with other men.

"He would sit back and take it for a long time," said Reid. "But then he would become violent with her, and she would fight back." He further stated that the Brunos were drunk or becoming drunk every time he was with them, and that they fought in his presence almost every time he visited with them.

As Reid continued his testimony, he said that after Pamela's disappearance Bruno told him "he knew Pam wasn't going to return," and said that Bruno asked him at least two or three times "if I (Reid) was able to kill someone." According to Reid, Bruno often talked about killing and death in relation to Bruno's army experiences in Vietnam, where he received a Bronze Star for bravery before being reduced from the rank of specialist 4 to private for leaving his guard duty post to see his wife.

On the seventh day of Bruno's trial, the defense called Portland psychiatrist Dr. Barry Maletzky to testify that Bruno "blacked out" on the night of the murder. Maletzky, an expert on alcohol's effects on the brain, testified that Bruno appeared to remember very little about what occurred on the night of his wife's murder, and that his apparent lack of memory was caused by alcohol.

"In a blackout," said Maletzky, "a person is not processing and retaining information in a normal way." He also said Bruno didn't forget or repress what happened the night his wife was killed, but that memories were never formed in his brain in the first place due to alcoholic blackout.

It was clear that the purpose of the defense was to show that Bruno didn't intentionally commit murder, even though he admitted to the police that he was involved. It is necessary to point out at this stage of the trial that even if the jury accepts the arguments of no intent, Bruno could still be convicted of felony murder which, according to legal statutes, "is a murder committed in the course of another felony such as rape or sodomy."

"I think Pamela was a big part of Mr. Bruno's life," continued Maletzky, "and he would not have planned to murder her. John is not a leader. He's not a strong person. It's absolutely inconceivable to me that he could plan such a crime." He went on to say that Bruno was constantly struggling to be accepted by others, and he always wanted to be accepted in a group.

"I think if people suggested things for him to do," testified Dr. Maletzky, "he would go along. Under the influence of alcohol, he would have gone along with anything . . . just to be accepted."

Several other defense witnesses also took the stand and testified that Mrs. Bruno was a very promiscuous woman, and that she drank heavily. And according to Daniel Olsen, a volunteer for the Eastside Baptist Church in Springfield, Mrs.

136

Bruno jeered at her husband when he attempted to become a Christian in the spring of 1977.

Olsen testified that he went to the Bruno's apartment after Bruno called the church seeking to "accept the Lord," but when he arrived Bruno was drunk. Olsen said he told Bruno to wait until the next night because he should be sober for the religious experience.

But when Olsen returned to the Bruno residence the following night, he testified, Bruno wasn't home yet so he sat and talked with Mrs. Bruno, who "indicated to me she was too far gone to be saved," and further stated that Mrs. Bruno started bragging about her numerous affairs with other men.

Another defense witness, Philip Wright, who was an attendant at the service station near the Haynes' home in Eugene, testified that he observed Mrs. Bruno walking down the middle of Sixth Avenue about 3 a.m. on a morning in mid-February. Wright testified that he called her off the street because she appeared to be intoxicated. When she walked over to the station, she asked to use the women's room. But when he told her the station had no restrooms, she dropped her pants and squatted, and urinated on the ground in front of him.

In a rebuttal to the defense contention that Bruno blacked out on the night of the murder, the prosecution presented Medford psychiatrist Dr. Hugh Gardener, who testified that Bruno couldn't have possibly blacked out the night his wife was killed because he "indicated in several ways that he remembered his role in what happened that night.

"Bruno had sufficient understanding of what was going on around him to form an intent to kill his wife that night," said Gardener. "He's an amoral, selfish, sociopath who is quite capable of using anybody or anything to satisfy himself."

June Lerner of Newport, Mrs. Bruno's grandmother, was called to the stand as a witness for the prosecution. She testified that Bruno called her on February 24th.

"He wondered if Joan (Mrs. Bruno's mother, also of Newport) and I could take this and if we were ready for it," said Mrs. Lerner. "I asked him what he meant," she continued, "and he said there had been a stabbing. I asked what he meant, and he said 'forget it,' and hung up."

Nearing the end of the trial, John and Rose Martin both testified that they were living at the Haynes' home and were, in fact, sleeping in the next room on the night Mrs. Bruno was allegedly killed! They astonishingly reported that they heard nothing unusual. However, both the defense and the prosecution agreed during the trial that the Martins were deceptive in their answers when they were questioned during a lie detector test about whether or not they were involved in the killing, a clear indication that both defense and prosecution felt their testimony in court was questionable.

After closing arguments were orated by the prosecution and the defense, which took most of the last day of the three-week trial, all that could be agreed upon was the uncertainty of whether they would ever know the full story of what happened on the night of February 21st.

"We don't know yet whether we have the full story of what took place that night in the Haynes' house," Barnes told the jury only minutes before they were charged with their obligations and went into deliberations.

Although it seemed longer, the Lane County Circuit Court jury of five men and seven women found Johnny Charles Bruno guilty of felony murder after barely three hours of deliberations, because they decided that his wife's death occurred during the course of sexual assault.

In the meantime, while Bruno was awaiting sentencing for his conviction, Charles Haynes' trial date was fast approaching. It was June 13th, only one day before his trial was to begin that Haynes surprisingly waived his right to a jury trial and was swiftly convicted by Judge William Beckett in a "trial by stipulated facts." Judge Beckett immediately sentenced Haynes to life in prison.

It should be pointed out that in his agreement to a trial by stipulated facts, Haynes did not plead guilty to the crime of which he was charged, but simply admitted that the state had enough evidence to convict him. In such an agreement, the defendant retains the right to appeal the verdict. If he had pleaded guilty, he would not have had the right to appeal for there would not have been a verdict delivered.

Jack Billings, Haynes' attorney, stated that his client would appeal the verdict on the grounds that a portion of the state's evidence was "improperly admitted" in the case by a ruling of circuit Judge Douglas Spencer. According to Billings, Spencer ruled on May 18th that statements made by Haynes to the Springfield police about his role in the killing would be admissible in Haynes' trial.

However, Judge Spencer rejected Billings' argument that Haynes' statements were inadmissible as evidence. Billings had argued that Haynes' rights were violated because Springfield police allegedly refused to let the defendant talk to a lawyer hired by Haynes' family. But the court ruled the statements as admissible because Haynes had not hired the attorney in question himself, and furthermore had no knowledge that an attorney had, in fact, been retained. The attorney in question had been retained and dismissed within only a few hours, supposedly because Haynes' family decided they couldn't afford the cost.

In the meantime, Mrs. Haynes was still being held in Lane County Jail awaiting trial. Her trial was postponed four times, and she was denied bail three times. By November, 1980, it was beginning to look like she may not go to trial at all, due mainly to the fact that she had remained incarcerated since her arrest in March, 1978.

The Oregon Supreme Court heard oral arguments concerning that very issue from Mrs. Haynes' attorney, who pleaded with the court to set his client free because he contended that she had been denied a speedy trial.

But the Supreme Court denied the requests, ordering Mrs. Haynes to remain in jail. But the court said "that any further postponement of her trial will no longer be 'trial within a reasonable period of time.' " The court stated that charges against her would have to be dropped if she could not be tried or released on bail.

Meanwhile, the Oregon Supreme Court reversed Charles Haynes' conviction on the grounds that Springfield police kept him from seeing an attorney, a charge that Springfield police repeatedly denied. Nonetheless, a new trial with a change of venue was ordered, this time to be held in Salem.

Johnny Bruno and Lionetti Haynes were not so lucky. Bruno's conviction was upheld after his appeal, and he is currently serving a life sentence. Mrs. Haynes was finally brought to trial and convicted of first-degree manslaughter following a trial in which she vehemently maintained her innocence. She was sentenced to 20 years by Judge William Beckett, but the judge ruled that Mrs. Haynes be given credit for the time she spent in Lane County Jail awaiting trial.

In May, 1981, Charles Haynes received his new trial in Marion County, but was convicted after a two-week trial and sentenced to life in prison.

Haynes and his wife appealed, but on March 18, 1982, the Oregon Court of Appeals upheld their convictions. More than four years after the gruesome murder of Pamela Lee Bruno, her convicted killers' cases were now fully adjudicated, and all are serving their sentences at the Oregon State Penitentiary and the Oregon Correctional Institution for Women.

EDITOR'S NOTE:

The names Warren Reid, Daniel Olsen, Philip Wright, June Lerner, John and Rose Martin, and Elizabeth Green are fictitious and were used because there is no reason for public interest in these persons.

"A VAMPIRE DRANK HIS VICTIM'S BLOOD!"

by John Benson

Marshfield, a seaside town 35 miles south of Boston, is normally a pretty quiet little community. Its population of 21,000 is largely working class and its people go about their business just as people do in small towns everywhere. For the most part, it's work, the family, TV after supper, and on the weekends, church and perhaps a movie.

The pace of life does pick up in June, July and August as the day-trippers from inland southeastern Massachusetts flock to Marshfield's pleasant beaches and the summer folk move into their cottages. The off-season, though, comes quickly and by mid-September Marshfield is once again back to the usual routine.

The fall of 1981, however, proved to be a dramatic exception.

The last week of October, Marshfield was hit

by more crime, tragedy and violence than at any time since the town was founded in 1640.

All the news that week in Marshfield was bad news. For whatever reason, the town was plagued with tragedy during this time. There were reports of murders, lethal accidents—all the things few would ever attribute to a quiet village like Marshfield.

"Everything's whacky," a Marshfield restaurant owner commented in an interview with the Brockton Enterprise. "Everyone coming in here is wondering what type of town this community is getting to be."

"Most people are in a state of shock that such things can happen in this town," one town government official ruefully acknowledged.

These incidents, as tragic or scandalous as they were, however, took second place as far as the amount of bad publicity being earned for the town of Marshfield. At the fore of the news that strange week was a bizarre murder trial that held Marshfield firmly in the public eye. An elderly Marshfield woman had been slain in a gruesome manner and the trial of the suspect received a great deal of the kind of newspaper and television coverage that no town likes to get.

The events that culminated in the aforementioned trial occurred some 18 months before. They are the subject of our story here.

On the afternoon of April 10, 1980, Marshfield was getting belted hard by a springtime storm, and Bob Edwards was just as happy to be working inside. Edwards, a carpenter and handyman, was painting some ceilings in a house situated only a few hundred feet from the roiling Atlantic, and the rain and the wind weren't pulling any punches that day.

Mid-way through the job, Edwards realized that he hadn't brought in enough paint and that he'd have to go out to the truck for more.

He made the dash to his vehicle for the supplies and was met there by an electrician working on the house next door who excitedly pointed out the smoke pouring from the little bungalow at 19 East Street, just across the road.

Having grown up in the town, Edwards knew the occupant of the dwelling, an elderly woman confined to a wheelchair, and he knew he would have to move fast.

The telephones weren't hooked up in the two houses the men were fixing up, so Edwards ran the short distance to his brother's home, located by coincidence the next street over, and called the fire department while the other man headed in the opposite direction for help.

Edwards made it back to the burning building first and attempted to enter by the back door, but the door handle was too hot to touch and the billowing smoke forced him to retreat.

He checked for other ways to get in, but had no luck. He could do nothing but wait.

A few minutes later, the fire trucks roared

down the street and set up as a crowd gathered.

Fire Lt. Roy McNamee and two firefighters donned air masks, grabbed a line and fought their way into the home through the thick, choking smoke. They quickly located the source of the fire in a front room and knocked it down without any problem.

But it was too late: 74-year-old Carmen Riva Lopez was already dead. Her frail, lifeless body lay curled on the floor beside her bed. The body was badly burned and portions of the corpse had been charred by the flames.

The date was April 10, 1980. The time was 3:45 p.m.

Although the authorities could not know it then, Mrs. Lopez had been viciously murdered. They would not know that fact for certain until the following day. And it would be more than two months before they would know the bizarre and chilling story behind the brutal slaying.

Even so, Marshfield Police Det. Sgt. James Lopes was suspicious almost at once. Call it intuition or a sense developed after 14 years of police work, but Lopes had a strong feeling that the death was not an accident. Later that day, the veteran detective would begin what amounted to a murder investigation — even before there was any concrete evidence of a murder.

At the scene, however, there was nothing that pointed to murder.

Plymouth County Medical Examiner John C.

Angley took a cursory look at the body, but because of its burned condition, could not establish the cause of death. Angley tentatively listed asphyxiation as the cause of death and ordered the body removed to a local funeral home for an autopsy the following afternoon.

Meanwhile, fire officials attempted to determine the cause of the fire. They found no easy answer. It was clear the fire had started in a corner of the bedroom under a window and had spread to the bed and the body, but they could not figure out what had caused it.

Mrs. Lopez didn't smoke, so there had been no smouldering cigarette. There was no faulty wiring, no gas explosion, and the TV, radio and the light fixtures were all intact. Arson was also considered—a cruel joke on an old lady that got out of hand, for example, or after a robbery to hide clues of the crime—but there was no indication of either. Fire Chief Louis Cipullo noted the fire as undetermined and called in the state Fire Marshal's office.

Firefighters checked through the small dwelling for any hot spots that might ignite later on. They also checked for any valuables that should be removed for safekeeping, and in the process, Lt. McNamee found a small metal box in an upstairs bedroom which would prove to be of some interest later on. The lieutenant saw that the box contained personal papers and bills, and without looking further, turned it over to his superiors.

Marshfield Det. G. Patrick Davis examined the box at the police station a short time later and made a startling discovery: under the papers, there were six .38 caliber bullets, five of which had their tips painted gold. That was not exactly what the detective had expected to find.

Judging by the papers, the box was the property of James P. Riva II, the 24-year-old grandson of the victim. Riva, who had lived with his father, who was divorced, and grandmother until the elderly woman had tossed him out three weeks earlier because of his long hair and lack of a job, was well known to the police.

Over the years, Riva had had numerous brushes with the law for incidents ranging from theft to illegal possession of a gun. As a teenager, he had been involved in drugs, and he'd been expelled from at least one high school as a result.

Riva also had a reputation as being a very strange young man. He was often observed skulking around town at all hours at night, and there were various tales about his odd behavior. One story, which the police verified, told how Riva had strangled a cat with a shoe lace and had removed and dissected its brain to learn about his own brain.

Less well known was that Riva was actually mentally ill, rather than just a bona fide eccentric, and that he had been treated at half-a-dozen state and private hospitals in the past ten years.

The doctors had diagnosed him, in his early teens, as a paranoid schizophrenic and had prescribed long-term psychiatric care.

Riva, at this point however, wasn't a suspect in the fire—the police weren't even sure they had a crime—but he was an individual worth keeping an eye on.

That night the case got slightly more curious when the two chief investigators, Lopes, Massachusetts State Police Trooper Robert A. Fernandes and Trooper Lee Garrison, interviewed the carpenter who had reported the fire.

Edwards said he had seen a young man acting oddly in the neighborhood about 3 p.m. that day, half-an-hour before the fire was discovered. The man had driven down East Street in a rust-colored Ford Maverick, had parked the car at an access road to the nearby beach, and had walked back up the street and then around behind the Lopez house. The carpenter had worked in the neighborhood in the past and had seen the young man repairing cars outside the Lopez home, so he didn't think anything of his presence there. He described the individual, but didn't know his name. The sleuths were mindful that the young man in question might be James Riva.

The next day, a Friday, they interviewed Riva's father. The 55-year-old man cooperated fully with the investigators, giving them a candid view of his son and Mrs. Lopez, and as complete a rundown as possible of the family's activities.

On the day of the fire, the father, an engineer in a firm making blood processing equipment, said he left home about 8:30 a.m. and drove to his job in Braintree, a Boston suburb, 20 miles from Marshfield. Jimmy, he said, met him there early and borrowed his car, a rust-colored Ford Maverick, in order to shop for some brake parts for his broken-down Volkswagen. He also had to go to his grandmother's to get his fishing pole and a shirt, which he had not taken when he had moved in with relatives in the Jamaica Plain section of Boston a few weeks before. A far as the father knew, Jimmy had done his errands, visited his grandmother about two o'clock and had gone to a job interview before picking him up at the plant at 4:30.

The father admitted frankly that relations weren't good between grandmother and grandson, but the visit that day apparently had been one of the most cordial in recent weeks. In the past, the pair constantly clashed about Jimmy's appearance and attitude, the father said.

The son was waiting at the plant for his dad to finish work when the call came about the fire. Jimmy, the father said, "appeared to be stunned and very upset." They went directly to the home, he said, the son driving.

The father told the officers that Mrs. Lopez had gotten out of the hospital only two weeks earlier after a nerve block operation because of a tumor at the base of her spine. She was still in a lot of pain and depressed, but he doubted that his mother had set the fire in order to take her own life. Mrs. Lopez also had heart problems, the son said, and knew she probably did not have long to live. They had discussed her will and had made the funeral arrangements to be ready when the time came.

Mrs. Lopez owned the modest house and, he believed, had no money to speak of. What she had was to be divided equally among several family members. He said she was a spunky woman who worked hard at being self-sufficient and getting around the house in her wheelchair as much as possible.

After interviewing the father, the police returned to the neighborhood for another chat with the carpenter, but before they could get their first question out, the carpenter abruptly pointed to a young man across the street as the one who had been at the Lopez house just before the fire. The young man was James P. Riva II. He agreed to an interview that was tape recorded that afternoon at the Marshfield Police Station.

Jimmy Riva's story was similar in most respects to his Dad's, but nonetheless some questions began to emerge. Riva said he had visited his grandmother about 2 p.m., but he wasn't sure of the time because his watch was not working properly.

"I had my watch on," he told the police, "but I didn't look and sometimes it sticks for like ten minutes, a half-hour sometimes and then it starts ticking and even if I did look, it might not have been accurate and precise."

The visit apparently wasn't as friendly as the father had thought. Jimmy said casually that Mrs. Lopez had greeted him "with her usual sourness. She said, 'I'm sick and tired of you walking around like a woman. You cut your hair off or don't come in this house again.' "

Riva said he did some chores for her, took a load of laundry to the cellar, and Mrs. Lopez had then "sweetened up a bit. She's always sour at me and then when I do a few things she shuts up and acts a little nicer."

The grandson said he didn't argue with his grandmother. "I just agree. I just say yeah, yeah. You know you can't reason with an old woman. It, ah, it's really very aggravating, you know? She does it every time."

Riva said he left quickly, his grandmother still sitting on the couch where she was when he arrived.

"I just walked out before it hurt my ears, before she could get on my case about my hair too much."

The grandson said he continued his hunt for the brake parts (he offered a sales slip from a Marshfield auto parts store, which the detectives took to check out later) and then went to pick up his father, who was about ready to leave for the day.

"I was there about 15 minutes," he told the officers, "and I was sitting around talking with the guys that are in the place. They make blood processing equipment and there was this big thing of red liquid to simulate blood so they can test it out. So I started making jokes with them and we were talking about that, and then my father got a telephone call from his girlfriend. He was told that his mother was dead and the house was on fire. And then I drove to the house in Marshfield and we stayed around for about 30 minutes and that was it."

Asked if he knew how the fire might have started, Riva said, "I didn't see any potential fires in the making when I left." But he did offer a unique theory on what might have happened. His grandmother, he said, may have set the fire accidentally by dozing off while smoking one of his marijuana joints.

"Once, I could swear she pinched a joint off me because I smelled pot in the house about two years ago," he explained. "I came into the place and I smelled pot and nobody's been there except for her for the last five hours."

He said he didn't notice any of his marijuana missing, "so I didn't point any fingers. I just changed my stash around, you know, so she wouldn't be digging her fingers and cutting it with oregano.

"You know, you figure old ladies—what the hell they going to do all day? If they are in pain, smoke it all up on you?"

To say the least, Riva's attitude was hardly what the detectives had anticipated from a man whose grandmother had died in a fire only the day before. But that didn't prove anything other than that Jimmy Riva was Jimmy Riva.

Later on in the afternoon, Massachusetts State Police Lieut. John A. Mowles, from the state fire marshal's office, and senior state police chemist Francis Hankard, went to the Lopez home for the second time to try to determine what had caused the fire. This time, they brought a combustible gas detector, a machine used to sniff out any residual fumes from a substance such as gasoline that could be used to start or accelerate a fire. The ultra-sensitive machine, however, found nothing. The investigators took samples of the flooring and insulation for laboratory testing. They kept in mind the possibility that an accelerant had been used, but had been consumed without a trace. The cause of the fire would have to remain a mystery for the time being.

Also that afternoon, the police spoke with the victim's housekeeper, a woman who lived a few streets from Mrs. Lopez. The woman said she had gone to the Lopez house about 11:30 on the morning of the fire and had helped the elderly woman with her bath and had put a load of laundry in the washing machine. She had stayed at the house until about 1:55 p.m., but had gone out between 1:25 and 1:35 to pick up her daughter. She said she finished the laundry and then made some preparations for a meal that would be cooked as supper by Mrs. Lopez's son that night. Then she left for the day. She assured the detectives that no one had come to the house while she was there.

The police had their doubts that Jimmy Riva had visited his grandmother's in the housekeeper's 10-minute absence, but it was possible. The young man said his visit was brief, that he had come and gone quickly, but surely the housekeeper would have learned from Mrs. Lopez that the grandson had visited.

Next, the investigators went to the Marshfield auto parts store to check out Riva's sales slip alibi. The manager recalled seeing Riva, but couldn't narrow the time down to be of help one way or another. He suggested that the officers speak with two local high school teachers who were in the store at the same time as Riva and had talked with him about his purchase. The teachers were not around at the moment, but they wouldn't be hard to catch up with, and according to the manager, they would be able to pinpoint the time. The detectives agreed among themselves to follow that lead up at the high school.

Medical examiner Angley and state forensic pathologist Ambrose Kelley began the autopsy Friday at 4:30 p.m.

Before their autopsy would be completed, however, the case would take a dramatic turn.

That night, about 5:45 a.m., Jimmy Riva went to the Marshfield Police Station and asked for the metal box containing the papers and the gilded bullets that had been taken from his grandmother's home. Sgt. Lopes informed him that the box was in the custody of Det. Davis, who was not at work at the time, but who would call Riva when the box was available. Riva didn't like the answer and told the sergeant he was leaving town in five minutes and he wanted the box immediately. He then stormed out of the police station.

Sgt. John Ewart, however, noticed that Riva had headed around the back of the station, toward an area where the police park their personal cars. Ewart, Lopes and Patrolman John Cheesman, went out to see what Riva was up to. They found him trying to get in the restricted entrance at the rear of the building. Lopes ordered Riva to stop, but instead Riva turned and cursed the officer, fists clenched and began swinging at Lopes. The officer took a blow off his shoulder and told Riva he was under arrest. Riva spit in the officer's face and swung again. Now the officer moved in. Lopes, Cheesman and Patrolman Dennis Buetner then wrestled the young man to the ground and cuffed him. Riva lashed out with his feet as the officers brought him into the station, and after being placed in the cage, Riva spit in Lopes' face again.

Quickly as Riva's temper had flared, however, he became calm. He apologized to Lopes and explained that he was angry because Lopes had thrown away his marijuana on an earlier occasion. Riva was booked and searched, and in the course of the search, Lopes made a significant find—a small, silver, folding fish knife which he took from Riva's back pocket. Lopes was even more surprised to see what appeared to be blood and hair on the knife. Lopes wasted no time getting the knife to the funeral home, where the autopsy was still in progress.

In the meantime, the doctors had made some shocking discoveries: Mrs. Lopez had suffered three severe wounds—two punctures of the heart and a traumatic injury to the head. There was no question about it, she had been murdered.

The medical men noted the wounds: one a thin cut one and one half inches deep; the second, three fourths of an inch in diameter, through the lungs and heart, both apparently made by a knife; the third, a massive epidural hematoma of the brain.

Dr. Angley ruled that any of the three injuries could have killed the woman. Tests showed that there was only a small percentage of poisonous fumes in her lungs, which indicated that she was already dead when the fire enveloped the room.

With these findings, the doctors had solved the quandary about the fire. It had to be arson.

Sgt. Lopes arrived at the funeral home and

turned over the Riva knife. The detective's gut reactions were right. The doctors said the knife could not be ruled out as the weapon that had caused two of Mrs. Lopez's wounds.

Lopes returned to the station and Riva agreed to another interview. Nonchalantly, he consented to talk about the fire, but not about his temper tantrum.

Riva repeated his story about the visit, but when informed that other witnesses' accounts contradicted his, he ended the interview and asked for a lawyer.

He was then booked for murder and arson.

"Oh, I don't think you can prove it," he blithely told the officers from his jail cell.

The next day, the case against him grew stronger when several relatives of the dead woman made an unsettling discovery in the fire-damaged house where they had gone to straighten up. As they were putting a living room couch back in place, a son-in-law of the victim spotted a mark on the wall, and on the floor below, the man discovered what appeared to be a bullet slug—a gold bullet slug. A closer look at a pillow on the couch and an afghan showed what appeared to be bloodstains. The police were informed and removed those items, as well as a rubber mallet, which might have been used to strike the victim in the head, and pieces of red-stained carpeting, for testing.

Riva was formally arraigned Saturday, April

12th, in Plymouth District Court for murder and arson in connection with the Lopez death and for assault and battery on Sgt. Lopes. Judge Robert Anderson sent Riva to the state mental hospital at Bridgewater for 30 days' observation.

On Monday, the police continued to close the net on the suspect. The detectives spoke with the two high school teachers who were in the auto shop at the same time as Riva. The men said they had talked with Riva between 1:45 and 2 p.m. on the day of the killing. They knew the time because they had left the store in time to be back at the school for traffic duty at 2:05 p.m. Those times, the police knew, virtually ruled out the possibility that Riva had been at his grandmother's house in the brief interval of the housekeeper's absence.

At this point, Plymouth County District Attorney William C. O'Malley Jr. stepped into the case for a brief and important role.

With the evidence of gilded bullets and the gilded slug, plus Riva's earlier gun troubles with the police, the DA wondered if Mrs. Lopez had been shot. The autopsy had not indicated any bullet wounds, but O'Malley theorized that if there were any, the charred flesh might have concealed them.

O'Malley ordered x-rays of the victim, and his hunch was borne out. The pictures revealed two small objects lodged in the body. Two bullets were removed from the corpse's torso—and they, too, were gold.

The gold motif didn't end there. That day the investigators executed search warrants on Riva's VW, his room at his relative's house in Jamaica Plain and the father's Maverick. The warrants paid off: a driver's license, a cardboard cutout of a woman's face, a catalogue advertising women's clothing — all had gold paint on them. The officer also took from the Maverick a towel with blood-stains on it which later were found to be of the same blood group as the victim's.

Riva was brought back to court May 15th after his 30-day stay and evaluation in the state mental hospital, but Judge George A. White returned him to the institution for another visit.

About that time, the case against Riva took a turn for the worse. The tests on the knife showed that the stains which appeared to be blood were actually paint, and the strands of hair from the blade were not, in fact, human hair. Despite these findings, Fernandes and Lopes were still confident that circumstantial evidence against the grandson would stand up.

A probable cause hearing was scheduled for June 18th, but a few days earlier, the case took another turn, this one so incredible that investigators could only shake their heads in disbelief and wonder if they were dreaming some fantastic nightmare.

James Riva's mother came into the Marshfield Police Station on June 14th, and told Sgt. Lopes that her son had confessed to the murder while she was visiting him an hour earlier at the Plymouth House of Correction.

The mother, an articulate 44-year-old woman who taught mathematics in high school and at a prestigious college, had a horrific tale to tell.

She said her son had claimed he was a vampire directed by voices and that he had shot his grandmother to death with gold bullets. He said he had attempted to drink blood from her wounds and then had poured dry gas over her body and lit her on fire. The son said he had been a vampire for four years and the voices had told him he would have to kill Mrs. Lopez that day or she would kill him.

As he told his macabre tale, the young man alternately laughed and cried and shook uncontrollably, saying his brain was burning and that he needed help that he was being controlled by the devil, by vampires and by voices from outer space.

Riva said he had tried all day to fight the voices, but found it was no use. He had driven to his grandmother's home that afternoon. He said he had brought a load of wash to the cellar at his grandmother's request and had gotten his .38 caliber revolver there, which, like the bullets, he had painted gold to guarantee the killing would succeed.

Riva told his mother that he then took the gun and went upstairs where he found his grand-

161

mother lying on the sofa.

"I didn't want to do it," he said. "She was yelling at me and I shot her but she didn't die."

He said she threw a glass at him and pleaded, "Jimmy, please, Jimmy, don't do this."

He continued: "And then I had to drink her blood. I tried to, but there wasn't enough of it because she was old and it was all dried up. That's when I dragged her off the couch and into the bedroom and I put the dry gas on her. I set the room on fire because I wanted just the room to burn."

Riva said he left the house and drove to the North River Bridge in the adjacent town of Hanover where he thought of suicide. He considered drowning or shooting, but said the voice told him not to mutilate himself and that he would be all right. He then threw the gun in the water and drove to pick up his father.

He told his mother that he had become sick by drinking a bad vampire's blood and that he had been sick for "a long time." He said he had no control over the voices and what they might tell him to do. "Even if my lawyer could get me out of here," he confided to her, "you would have to lock me up because I never know when that voice would come and tell me to get another gun.

"I know that people are trying to kill me, and the voice told me that if I kill the people that hated me, I would be handsome and I'd have girls and I'd have cars and that I would have all the things I wanted."

That was the crime, but it was obvious that there would be much more to the case than the facts of the murder—because of Riva's mental illness—if the case ever made it to court.

That night, the mother gave detectives a detailed history of her son's mental problems. It was a history she would have to give several more times in the next 18 months as the case moved through the judicial system.

The mother said Jimmy had been diagnosed as a paranoid schizophrenic in his early teens and in later years he had experienced lengthy periods of psychosis in which his behavior was twisted and demented. Jimmy, she said, had punched her and roughed her up more than once and had threatened to kill her and his father and other members of the family. The mother, divorced two years before from Riva's father and remarried, said her son had been treated in many medical facilities and had been counselled by a score of psychiatrists.

The woman said the signs of her son's illness emerged early in his childhood. As a tot, Jimmy was very bright, she said, but had a bad temper. Once, believing his father had stolen coins from his piggy bank, he set up an elaborate trip-wire trap that would bring a hammer crashing down from atop a door on his father's head.

Jimmy began to show his preoccupation with violence while still a preschooler, she said, drawing vivid war scenes of violence and slaughter. After a hospital stay for pneumonia, the youngster developed a fixation with hypodermic needles and blood, themes which became subjects for his artwork for years to come.

In junior high school he began using drugs, and his grades, which had always been good, began to drop. Often, his teachers found him walking the halls in a dazed condition. It was at that time, she said, Jimmy started chumming with the wrong crowd—kids who stole cars for joy riding and who had numerous brushes with the police. At one point, she said, the youngster had a tremendous burst of creativity and built a guitar and crafted a flute from a lead pipe that played perfectly and amazed the experts at the Boston Conservatory of Music. But that artistic side was never to emerge again.

In his teens, Riva became interested in witchcraft, a subject his mother had researched in college, and he took to wearing a clove of garlic around his neck and practicing rituals with wax and candles. He became convinced of the positive powers of pyramids and built one in the woods and sat beneath it. His mother, who also taught astrology in college and was interested in the occult and bizarre parapsychological phenomena, related a thought-provoking experience which occurred when her son was 13. A guest speaker in the mother's course, a self-proclaimed witch, visited the family after a lecture and conducted an experiment in "mind running," a kind of self-hypnosis which supposedly brings a person back to a previous existence. Jimmy was directed into a trance and told the onlookers a strange story, which seemed to have taken place at the time of the Revolutionary War. He said his name was Isaac and claimed he was seeing himself in a burned-out building. He said he had been stabbed, and a man in a red coat was standing over him with a rifle.

His mother and the police noted the dreadful similarities to the grandmother's death ten years after the story.

At first, the family and the doctors felt that Jimmy might outgrow the difficult periods he was going through, that he would get over his troubled times. But their worst fears were realized eventually when the doctors found Jimmy seriously mentally ill and in need of long-term help.

Treatment was some benefit, but not for long, and during his psychotic periods, Jimmy would deteriorate before the family's eyes, his mother recalled. He would stop taking care of himself, stop bathing and combing his hair. He wouldn't change his clothes and he smelled vile. His room would become a mess, its condition reflecting his abnormal state of mind. His mother told how he would have a hot plate in the room which he used to cook up weird concoctions made of catsup, tomato paste, onions, garlic and pieces of raw fish and clams he had scavenged from the beach. He would eat this food and no other and keep it in all manner of jars and bottles in his room. His teeth became stained brown from these meals, his mother said.

His mother related how Jimmy had run away once and lived in the woods on Cape Cod, some 75 miles from his home, for several weeks avoiding all contact with his family, surviving by living off the land and breaking into homes and stealing food, until a brother found him and brought him home.

Jimmy had gone to court-arranged counselling, but the day he turned 18 years of age, he stopped and would not continue. On that same day he informed his mother that he wanted a gun, a desire that turned into an obsession. He needed a gun, he said, because there were people who were out to get him. He tried to get a gun legally, but the police refused to issue him a permit. He managed, however, to get more than one his own way. His mother said she found two of his firearms, a rifle attached to a beam in the house and wrapped with insulation, and another in his room under dirty clothes. She also discovered a cache of women's clothes in the room from some unknown source. Possibly, she said, they were from the many house breaks Jimmy was pulling off around Marshfield. The mother said she was constantly trying to correct Jimmy's misdeeds by bringing back the things he had stolen.

During these burglaries, she said, he used to

find his way to the bedroom, where he would stand watching as the unsuspecting people slept peacefully.

Just after a major snow storm hit Massachusetts in February 1978, devastating the coastline, Jimmy disappeared from the room he was renting in Marshfield. His family didn't hear a word from him until he telephoned from Florida a month later, saying he wanted to come home but the police had set up roadblocks and barricades in towns and he couldn't get through. The family sent him money and he returned.

He underwent more treatment and while at Boston University Hospital told the doctors remarkable tales about drinking blood from all types of animals, including a horse which he had stunned with a fence post. On one occasion, he said, the blood was too thick to drink and he mixed it with crackers in order to eat it. Riva said he was 2,000 years old and needed the blood to survive.

The hospital determined Riva was too dangerous as an outpatient, and they wouldn't keep him. He went to the State mental· hospital at Taunton as a voluntary commitment, but ran away twice, and the courts decided that holding him there would violate his civil liberties because he hadn't done anything bad enough.

Early in 1980, his mother related, Jimmy told another relative about his desire to kill his grandmother. He said he had taken a pillow and was going to smother her but had stopped himself.

The last the mother saw Jimmy before the killing was Easter Sunday at a family gathering, shortly before the day Mrs. Lopez died. The mother saw sadly that he had gone bad as in the past. That was just after the grandmother had kicked Jimmy out of the Marshfield house and he had gone to live with her brother in Boston.

The probable cause hearing was held June 18th in Plymouth District Court. Judge White bound Riva over to the grand jury on all charges, and Riva was indicted July 15th on the same charges.

Over the next year, Riva made some 20 court appearances as the defense and prosecution psychiatrists studied him and reported their findings about his competency to stand trial and his criminal responsibility at the time of the crime.

In August 1981, Riva was adjudged competent, and his attorney John T. Spinale of Halifax informed the court that the defense would be not guilty by reason of insanity.

Fifty prospective jurors were interviewed before 16 were chosen to hear the case which began October 22nd in Brockton Superior Court before Judge Peter F. Brady.

Assistant Plymouth County District Attorney Henry A. Cashman, the prosecutor, faced a doubly difficult task. Not only was this his first murder case, but he had to contend with the insanity defense. Not only did the government have to prove Riva did the killing, but it now had the burden of proving that Riva was sane, a seemingly impossible task if there ever was one.

Cashman, in his opening argument, purposely avoided even a single reference to Riva's mental history, stressing instead the defendant's planning and premeditation and his attempt to hide the crime. Cashman pointed out Riva's circuitous entry to the house, the parking of his car down the street, the dry gas used to conceal the murder, the auto shop alibi.

One problem the prosecution had to deal with was the testimony of the mother, who was called as a government witness. Her testimony would be a double-edged sword. As expected, the woman took the stand and clearly and honestly testified about her son's confession, but at the same time, much evidence of Riva's mental problems came out in graphic detail. The mother hoped to show that her son was insane and should go to a mental hospital rather than a prison. The chips would have to fall where they may. It would be for the jury to sort out.

The prosecutor did not call a single psychiatrist to the stand, a potentially dangerous move because of the insanity burden, but a move Cashman had carefully planned and discussed with Assistamt Plymouth County District Attorney John Corbett, head of the DA's appeals staff.

The government's strategy was challenged at once by the defense. As soon as Cashman rested his case, Spinale, seizing the moment, moved for a directed verdict of innocent, arguing that the government had not upheld its burden of proving Riva was sane.

Judge Brady, however, denied the motion and the case proceeded.

Spinale called several psychiatrists for the defense, all of whom said Riva was not legally responsible.

Dr. Mandel Cohen, from the world-famous Massachusetts General Hospital, told the court:

"In my opinion the defendant has been insane for a number of years. He was insane at the time of the killing of his grandmother. He is insane now and could be dangerous to himself and others and belongs in a maximum security mental hospital.

"He was obviously not responsible for the murder by reason of insanity. He did not appreciate the wrongfulness of his act. He did not have a logical and emotional understanding of the wrongdoing. He was unable to resist the urge to do something wrong."

He and other psychiatrists maintained their position despite withering cross-examination by Cashman, who skillfully scored valuable points when he got one forensic psychiatrist to admit that Riva had tested out to be a "normal person" on one widely used psychological test.

In addition to the doctors, the defense introduced some 200 pages of Riva's psychiatric history and records from numerous hospitals.

Cashman, on the other hand, presented a quick, tidy case on the sanity issue. The DA called only one rebuttal witness, Dr. Martin Kelly, a highly-regarded forensic psychiatrist and frequent prosecution witness in Massachusetts trials involving insanity pleas.

Kelly, a psychiatrist at Brigham and Women's Hospital in Boston, and a teacher at Harvard, contradicted all earlier psychiatric testimony. He said Riva was sick, but sane and responsible.

"Riva has a mental illness," Kelly told the jury, "but it is not one which demonstrates his capacity to recognize wrongdoing."

Kelly referred to the tape-recorded interview which Riva gave to police the day after the killing.

"The interview showed his state of mind, cogent responses to questions, well-organized thoughts, normal responses and the ability to handle the interrogation," Kelly said.

"He did not appear to be confused, was consistent and his behavior was not that of a person who was not criminally responsible. I could find no convincing evidence that he lacked the capacity to appreciate his act."

A jury of nine men and three women deliberated for just over three hours, and on Friday, October 30th, at 4:20 p.m., convicted Riva of second degree murder, arson and the assault charges on Lopes.

Judge Brady imposed the mandatory life term in Walpole on the murder finding and added 19-20 "on and after" for the charge of arson. The charge of assault and battery on the police officer was filed.

Riva must do a minimum of 27 years before being eligible for parole — 15 years on the murder and 12 years on the arson.

One month after the conviction, Riva was transferred from Walpole, the state's maximum security prison, to the state mental hospital at Bridgewater where he is now being held.

The defense has appealed the verdicts, alleging there was insufficient evidence. The defense has also claimed that Riva's mother was acting as an agent of the police when she visited her son at the house of correction and heard his confession, a violation of the young man's constitutional rights.

Riva's father, who was present every day at the trial except for the day when the jury brought back the verdicts, still visits his son every week at the state mental hospital at Bridgewater.

EDITOR'S NOTE:

The name Bob Edwards is fictitious and was used because there is no reason for public interest in his true identity.

"THE RELUCTANT HOOKER WAS COOKED ALIVE!"

by Andrew Lowen

It was a few minutes short of midnight. Business was brisk at Greenwich Hospital in London's dockland, with the usual night-trade beginning to heat up.

The drunks, the winos, the derelicts, the victims of road accidents, muggers and bar brawlers, battered wives, battered children, battered husbands.

They were all arriving, some on foot, the majority by ambulance, private car or taxi.

Through the doors of the casualty department staggered 27-year-old Philip Georgiou, carrying a young woman over his shoulder.

"Someone help . . . please!" he called out, almost dropping the unconscious woman.

A nurse and a porter came running.

"I think she's dying," said Georgiou. "I've carried her more than a mile. I never thought I'd make it."

The porter and the nurse laid the woman onto a trolley, covered her with a blanket, and headed swiftly for the first available emergency treatment room.

Georgiou was told to go to the official waiting area, where someone would be along to see him and take details "as soon as possible."

Within seconds, the nurse and porter who went to the treatment room were joined by an intern, Dr. Julian Parsons. When he pulled back the blanket, both he and the nurse grimaced at the horrific sight before their hardened eyes.

The patient, who had been transferred from the trolley to a medical couch, was so badly burned that she had been turned into a shrivelled up black mass of human cinders. Her face was unrecognizable. All her hair had been burned from her head, leaving her bald. The smell of smoke filled the air. The very sight of this pathetic woman in such a condition was enough to repel the most jaded among them.

And she was still alive. Her blackened lips moved. She gasped for breath. Dr. Parsons looked into her eyes—even the whites were black.

"Oxygen," he said tersely. Then he went to the wall telephone and made a call. This was something he could not handle alone. This was a case for a senior surgeon. Dr. Parsons spoke with Dr. Peter Montgomery, who had just finished an emergency operation.

"I'll be with you right away," said Dr. Montgomery.

While waiting for the senior surgeon, Dr. Parsons noted several points. He was struck by the fact that the patient was only partially clothed. Her skirt, reduced to ashes, had become embedded in her flesh.

But from the waist upwards she was completely naked. Nor was she wearing anything under her skirt, except for the remains of her stockings. She was wearing no shoes nor any rings on her fingers.

Dr. Montgomery was appalled by what he saw. He knew from just a cursory examination of the patient that there was no chance of saving her life, though he still would do everything within his power to try. He instructed a saline drip to be set up and he started making preparations for immediate emergency surgery. However, before they could get the patient into the operating room, she was dead.

Dr. Montgomery assumed that the woman must have been the victim of a house blaze, so he went out to speak with the man who had taken her to the hospital.

Mr. Georgiou was in the waiting area reading a magazine. He got up as he saw the doctor approaching.

"How is she?" Georgiou asked.

"Are you a relative?" the doctor inquired, before answering the question.

"No," said Georgiou. "I've never seen her before in my life. I just brought her in."

"Well, I'm afraid she's dead," the doctor confided. "Where did you find her?"

Dr. Montgomery expected to hear that she had been trapped in a blazing house or car.

"I found her in a dustbin (garbage can)," Georgiou replied. "I was just passing, and there she was. I couldn't believe my eyes. So I pulled her out and ran here with her on my back."

Dr. Montgomery told Georgiou to stay where he was. "I'll be back in a moment," said the doctor. "Don't you go away."

The senior surgeon then hurried to his office and called the police.

Within 15 minutes of Dr. Montgomery's call, uniformed Sergeant Harry Mabbett and Constable Peter Jones had arrived at the hospital. After a brief conversation with the nurse, porter, and Drs. Parsons and Montgomery, the officers questioned Georgiou.

After giving the police his full name and telling them that he was 27 years old, lived at No. 72 Pepys Estate, Deptford, in southeast London, and worked as a chef in a local restaurant, Sergeant Mabbet said to him, "Now, I want the whole story, chapter and verse, from beginning to end."

Appearing relaxed, Georgiou repeated what he had told Dr. Montgomery, except in more detail.

As Georgiou spoke, Jones made copious notes.

The man explained, "It was my night off from the restaurant. I took myself out for a meal. I had a few drinks and then I decided to walk home, instead of taking the bus.

"I was just passing a block of flats (apartments) in Camberwell, when I smelled something burning. I couldn't see any flames anywhere, but the air seemed full of smokey fumes. So I started looking around and then I came across this dustbin. It was all black and disintegrating."

"How could you see its color in the dark?" the sergeant asked.

"Because the area's well-lit," Georgiou replied.

"Okay, go on."

"For a second, I didn't think anything of it. I mean, people are always setting light to things in dustbins, aren't they?

"I was about to walk off, when I noticed something hanging over the side of the dustbin. It looked like a human arm, but I couldn't believe it. Then I stopped and looked again. This time I could hear something. It was a groaning, moaning sound.

"So, I took a closer look . . . and there was this woman's body inside the dustbin. You can imagine how I felt?"

"No, you tell me," the sergeant retorted tartly.

"Well, I was stunned. I thought of telephoning for the police and an ambulance . . ."

"Why didn't you?" Mabbett interrupted.

"Because I realized she needed medical treatment as fast as possible. I knew it wasn't far to this hospital. In fact, it turned out to be further than I thought. Anyhow, I pulled her from the dustbin, threw her over my shoulder, and started running. I just wanted to give her the best chance she had."

"And you've never seen her before?"

"Never sir. Not in my life. I swear to it."

"There were no possessions, like a handbag, in or around the dustbin?" the sergeant pressed.

"I don't know about inside the dustbin," the chef replied, "but certainly I didn't see anything on the ground."

Realizing that this was no accidental death but a case of murder, the sergeant returned to his car and radioed his report to headquarters. He was instructed to remain at the hospital with Georgiou until a team of Murder Squad detectives arrived.

The team was led by Detective Chief Inspector Wally Banks. He and his men took over from Mabbett and Jones, who were both thanked for their preliminary work and asked to present a written report by the following morning.

The chef was made yet again to recount the whole story, and after he'd finished he was then asked to take the detectives to the spot where he found the woman.

The drive to the apartment block in Camberwell took no more than a few minutes. The dustbin was still there on the ground floor, all burned out as Georgiou had described.

Forensic experts took charge of the dustbin and started combing the area under arc lights for clues. Crowds began to gather even though it was in the middle of the night, and ropes were set up to establish a "No-Go" area.

Georgiou was made to retrace his route that night, showing from which direction he'd approached the apartments, and having to explain yet again what had attracted him to the dustbin.

Everything he said was carefully noted down. Meanwhile, detectives were knocking up every resident in the apartment block in an attempt to identify the homicide victim. It was first thought that the victim must have lived in one of those apartments. But no one was missing. Everyone in the apartments was accounted for.

Georgiou was allowed to go home at 6:00 a.m. on November 16, 1981, with the cops still being none the wiser as to the victim's identity.

The autopsy was commenced at 9:00 a.m. in the Greenwich Hospital. Two pathologists conducted the examination. One was attached to the hospital. The other was an official police pathologist.

There was no doubt about the cause of death. The young woman had died from shock as a result of her extensive burns. But in her body the pathologists found evidence that she'd taken a large quantity of barbiturates shortly before her death. And the amount of semen in her vagina

suggested that she'd indulged in sexual intercourse several times recently in the last few
hours.

Banks was told by the police pathologist, "The
barbiturates would have very quickly sent her
into a coma. It was a very large overdose. If she
hadn't died from the burns, I doubt whether she
would have survived. I would say that the overdose would have proved fatal.

"The intercourse took place shortly before her
death, so it looks as if she was raped rather than
her having sex voluntarily. She was almost certainly unconscious when she was raped. There
was no damage to the vagina, other than that
caused by the fire.

"The grisly fact has to be faced that this poor
wretched girl was set alight while still alive and
burned to death."

The police pathologist said that from tissue
tests the victim was between ages 18 and 25.
"Certainly no older than 25," he assured Banks.
"Apart from that, there's nothing more I can tell
you."

The forensic scientists discovered that the dustbin had been sprayed with paraffin before a
match had been used to set it alight. The remains
of the one solitary match had been recovered
from the bottom of the burned out dustbin.

Amazingly, no neighbors had heard anything,
nor had anyone seen the blaze.

At a briefing with his men at Greenwich Police

Station that afternoon, Banks stressed that there were two priorities — to identify the victim and to find the rest of her clothing.

That evening, Banks and a detective sergeant called on Georgiou at his home, where he lived alone. He said his boss had given him another day off because of his "ordeal."

Banks asked if Georgiou minded if the detectives had a look around his apartment.

"I've nothing to hide," said the chef, shrugging, then following the cops from room to room.

In a wardrobe in the bedroom, the detectives found a woman's overcoat. Under the bed there was a pair of women's shoes. And in a drawer there were a bra, panties, stockings and a blouse. A search of a box in the living room produced several beating canes, two whips, handcuffs, masks, rope and a hangman's noose.

"Explain?" said Banks when he'd come to the end of his tour.

"Explain what?" replied Georgiou.

"The women's gear. Who does it belong to? I thought you said you lived alone?"

"I do live alone," answered Georgiou, "but I have girlfriends. I'm quite normal that way. Sometimes they stay with me and they may leave their things, their belongings, for a few days, even months. Sometimes they never come back for them."

Banks then asked Georgiou the name of the woman who owned the female articles in the bedroom.

"I don't know her name," Georgiou answered. "She was just a one-night stand. We met at a bar late at night, came back here, and when I woke in the morning, she'd gone. She'd also taken what money I had in my wallet."

Banks then speeded up the interrogation. "Did you report the money missing?"

"No."

"Why not?"

"Because . . ."

"Because what?" Banks pressed.

"Just because," Georgiou replied.

"Which bar did you meet her in?"

"I can't remember."

"Which night?"

"A few nights ago."

"Which one?"

"I'm not too sure."

"You're not sure of very much, are you?"

"We were bombed."

"What are all these canes, whips and handcuffs for?"

"What do you think?"

"I'm asking you."

"I like sex to be something extra special."

"Do all your girlfriends think the same way?"

"I tend to gravitate towards the more adventurous kind of women."

"How do you know that's the way they are until you've got them back here?"

"Just by talking. You can tell. *I* can, anyway."

"You're a connoisseur of this kind of thing, are you?"

"I've told you . . . it's what turns me on."

"What if a woman you bring back declines to take part in your kind of bedroom fun?"

"Then we have it straight."

"Wouldn't you try to bring her 'round to your way of persuasion?"

"Of course."

"And if you failed?"

"I've already told you. We'd have it straight."

"Might you not be tempted to use force to get your own way?"

"Do me a favor!" Georgiou snapped.

"How can you be certain you'd be able to control yourself when sexually wound up?"

"Because I'm not an animal, that's why."

"The woman these clothes belong to . . . did she share your taste for sado-masochism?"

"She did. But I can't recall what happened . . . whether she tied me up, or if it was the other way around."

"Did this woman you're talking about have a suitcase or overnight bag of some kind?"

"No."

"What was she wearing when she left, then?"

"I don't understand."

"Well, if she left these clothes behind and she didn't have any others with her, that means she must have walked away from here into the streets half-naked. Why would she do that?"

"I don't know. You'd better ask her, not me. I told you, I was asleep when she left."

"You can remember that you were asleep and that she took your money, but you can't remember her name, where you met her or what day it was? That sounds to me very much like a convenient memory."

"I think the time has come for me to consult a lawyer. I don't want to say anything else," Georgiou said.

Banks paused, then said, "I don't think I have anything more I want to ask you . . . at this stage, Mr. Georgiou. But don't leave town without letting me know, will you? I'll be back. That's the one promise I can make."

Banks and his men then set about testing Georgiou's alibi for the evening of the murder. They also took the erotic equipment and women's clothes from Georgiou's apartment for scientific examination.

The owner of the restaurant where Georgiou worked confirmed that his chef had been off duty the previous evening.

"Any idea where he might have gone?" Banks inquired.

"Why don't you ask Danny Links?" replied the restaurant owner. "He's a waiter here and he and Philip knock around together. They always have the same night off so they can go drinking together."

Links, age 18, was on duty, and the cops interviewed him on the premises, in the owner's office.

"Sure I was with Philip last night," Links said. "We met at seven, had a few drinks, then went for a meal, and went home our separate ways a little after eleven-thirty."

Banks and his men were thinking the same thoughts. Why hadn't Georgiou mentioned Links? He'd given the impression that he'd been drinking and eating alone the previous night.

"Which restaurant did you eat in?" Banks asked.

Links volunteered the name of the establishment without hesitation.

"What do you know about your pal's girlfriends?" Banks asked.

"Nothing," replied the young waiter. "When he's got a date, I don't see him."

"You've never seen any of his women friends?"

"Never."

"Did you know he went in for kinky sex?"

"I know nothing about that. What do you mean?"

The cops then said Links would have to go with them. He protested feebly, but then saw the sense of it after a few words with his boss.

"We just have a little checking to do with you," Banks reassured the waiter.

They drove to the restaurant where Links said he'd had a meal the night before with Georgiou.

"That's right," said the owner, "he was in here last night with his friend, the chef. Philip somebody or other."

"Can you remember what time it was they were here?" Banks pressed.

"No," answered the restaurant owner. "They didn't leave until late, nearly midnight, but what time they came. . . ? No, it's impossible for me to say. We were very busy. It could have been ten, ten-thirty . . . or even earlier. But they arrived together and left at the same time. No doubt about that."

Outside the restaurant, Banks said to Links: "Do you live alone?"

"Yes," the waiter replied, "I have a bedsit flat near where Philip lives."

"Mind if we take a look?"

"Why?"

"Just to help our investigation."

"I'd rather you didn't."

"What have you to hide, son?"

"Nothing. But my home's private. You've no right."

"We can get a search warrant."

"Get one then."

Links then attempted to run off, but was felled by a flying tackle by one of the detectives.

"Not so fast," said Banks. "We have not finished with the questions yet. And by the time we have finished, we'll have the search warrant, so there's no way you're going to be able to get home and tamper with anything. You can forget that idea . . . completely."

While another senior detective went off to write up a magistrate in order to obtain a search warrant, Banks and other officers drove the waiter to Georgiou's apartment. There they initiated a confrontation between the two men.

"Why didn't you say you were out with him last night?" Banks asked Georgiou, pointing at the young waiter.

"Because I didn't want to involve him," replied Georgiou. "There didn't seem any point. Look, I tried to do a favor. I desperately tried to save a woman's life, and here I am being treated like a criminal. You should be out hunting her killer, not pestering the life out of the person who rescued her."

"They're getting a search warrant for my place," said Links.

"The bastards!" Georgiou exploded.

Banks was beginning to get the feeling that the big breakthrough might well come at the waiter's one-room apartment. And his instincts were not to fail him.

It was in the early hours of the morning before Banks and his men were ready to search Links' place. In a set of drawers, they found a stack of black and white color prints of a girl being subjected to every conceivable kind of perversion.

In all the prints, which had been developed recently, the girl was naked. In some of them she was bound and gagged with rope. In others she was handcuffed. In one she had a noose around her neck, and in many she was being shamelessly abused.

In some shots, Georgiou was doing the beating. In the others, it was the waiter. Numerous shots showed sexual intercourse taking place while the girl appeared to be unconscious. Banks immediately recognized the background in the photographs. They had all been taken in Georgiou's bedroom.

"Who is this girl?" Banks demanded. "You'd better come clean or you're the one who's going to be doing all the sweating."

"Her name is Sheila Gohill," said Links.

"Where is she. . . ?" Banks asked.

"I don't know. She was tied up at Philip's place. If she isn't there now, I don't know where she is, but I haven't harmed her, I swear."

"You've got a lot of explaining to do," said Banks. "Let's go. I want a full statement from you at headquarters."

A check of the Scotland Yard Missing Persons File revealed that a Sheila Gohill had been reported missing by her parents from her home in the Midlands city of Birmingham on October 27th that year.

Although the body was unrecognizable, it was quickly identified through her teeth. A Birmingham dentist was able to confirm that the woman who had been burned alive in a dustbin was, in fact, the missing Sheila Gohill.

Georgiou's doctor also contacted the police to report that he had prescribed the chef with barbiturate sleeping tablets a few days before the girl's murder. The tablets were of the same kind that were found in Sheila's stomach and blood.

After being kept in custody for two days, Georgiou still maintained his innocence and refused to make a statement.

However, faced with the mounting evidence, Links agreed to turn Queen's Evidence and make a full confession, thus becoming a witness for the prosecution.

He told Banks that the plan was to blackmail Sheila into becoming a prostitute and force her to work for Georgiou and himself.

They met her at a bar, drugged her drink, took her back to Georgiou's place, where they photographed her in all kinds of degrading positions.

The next day, they showed her the prints and threatened to send them to her parents if she didn't do as they wanted.

However, Sheila refused to be intimidated and tried to escape. She was physically restrained and tied up. For several days she was kept a prisoner, with both men having sex with her whenever the urge surfaced.

On the day she died, Georgiou forced Sheila to swallow the overdose of barbiturates, which he had obtained from his doctor. As soon as she was in a coma, more perverted sex sessions followed.

As soon as it was dark, the two men carried the body down to Georgiou's car and hid it in the trunk.

"The idea was just to dump her body and forget all about forcing her to work for us as a prostitute," the waiter maintained.

When they reached the apartment block in Camberwell, they removed the body from the trunk of the car and squeezed it into the dustbin, Links explained.

"It was a miracle we weren't spotted," commented Links.

While the two men were in the restaurant, Georgiou told his friend that he wanted to return to the dustbin and check that Sheila was "all right."

He was only gone about 15 minutes and that's when Georgiou set the woman alight. When he got back to the restaurant, he told Links: "She'll be okay now. She hasn't any more problems."

The same day, Philip Georgiou was charged with the murder of Sheila Gohill and with administering a noxious substance.

When Georgiou appeared on trial at the Old Bailey, London, on November 9, 1982, he did not deny the charges.

Mr. Michael Worsley, prosecuting, said that the two men had befriended the girl and then had drugged her while she was in a stupor, taking photos of the debauchery that followed. The plan, he said, had been to blackmail her into prostitution so that the two men could share her earnings from the work.

When sentencing Georgiou to life on the murder charge and to three years imprisonment for administering the drug, Judge David Tudor Price, QC, told him: "Such callous and cruel destruction of human life means you have forfeited your right to live among decent people for a long time to come. You threw her in the bin like some rag doll and set fire to her," he said with disgust.

He recommended that Georgiou should serve at least 20 years in jail.

EDITOR'S NOTE:

The names Dr. Julian Parsons, Dr. Peter Montgomery and Danny Links are fictitious and were used because there is no reason for public interest in their true identities.

"FREAKY BATHING FETISH TRIGGERED A SEX SLAYING!"

by Joseph Koenig

The sound of the school bell released a torrent of chatter, about boys and movies and teachers and clothes, about sports and friends and homework, about anything at all that interests teenage girls. It poured across the schoolyard and filled the bus on the long ride through the country. There was an interlude of quiet when Sheli was dropped off and Cindy rode the rest of the way alone. It lasted until Cindy came home and put down her books, when the phone began to ring.

"Hi," began the familiar, girlish voice, "it's me."

The girls picked up exactly where they left off, as if they had stopped only to catch a very long breath. During a lull in the conversation, Cindy thought she heard a harsh rasping at the other end of the line. After a brief pause, Sheli said, "Hold on, someone's knocking at the door."

Then there was the sound of diminishing footsteps, a distant, "Hi, how are you," and a man's muttered reply. After that there was nothing.

When two or three minutes had gone by, someone hung up the phone without another word. Cindy held the receiver to her ear, as if not quite believing what she had heard, and then called her friend back. Two more times she dialed the number without an answer. Puzzled, and more than a bit worried, she gave up and went away from the phone. It was about 3:45 when she glanced out the window and saw the red car . . .

About 5:45 on that warm Thursday afternoon on April 22, 1982, a desk officer at the Ellenville barracks of the New York State Police scribbled a brief entry in the blotter.

"Received a call from hysterical woman calling from Wilkinson residence regarding possible death of daughter."

Fifteen minutes later, according to the entry, State Police Lieutenant Daniel Scribner arrived at the house, a secluded A-frame set back in the woods at the end of a long driveway fronting Highway 209 in the town of Wurtsboro.

Scribner was met at the house by two first aid squad members and the mother and brother of 15-year-old Michele "Sheli" Wilkinson, an honor student at Monticello High School. After a few words he was led into the bathroom, where he found the bloodsoaked body of the attractive blonde draped over the bathtub. Clad only in a shirt, sweatshirt jacket and knee socks, her hands were tightly bound with white masking tape. Protruding from her chest was a butcher knife with an eight-inch blade.

After alerting headquarters, Lieutenant Scribner searched the Wilkinson home for evidence. In a recreation room on another floor, he found a pair of bloodflecked white sneakers, blue jeans and underpants, which appeared to have been torn from the teenager's body during the assault that claimed her life.

When detectives reached the scene, they learned that Sheli Wilkinson was a lifelong resident of Wurtsboro, a Monticello High School student since September, when she transferred from John S. Burke High School in Goshen.

"She loved to ski," a friend said, "and to swim and to play video games at the arcade on Broadway in Monticello. She was so beautiful, so very intelligent . . ."

At Monticello High School the probers learned that, as was her habit, Sheli took the bus home when classes let out about 3:00. From school officials they obtained the names of some of the other students who rode the bus and then fanned out through the Wurtsboro-Monticello area to speak with them.

"Was there anything out of the ordinary that you noticed on the ride home this afternoon?" the sleuth asked after breaking the news of their classmate's death. "Anything at all you think we should know about?"

A number of students revealed to the investigators that, as the bus made its way through their neighborhood that afternoon, it was followed by a car driven by a sandy-haired man.

"What kind of car?" a detective asked.

"A red car," one of the students answered. "A Chevy, I think. A mid-sized model, maybe a Nova."

One youngster told the officers that, after she got off the bus, she noticed Sheli Wilkinson talking with a strange man at the bus stop. As the bus continued on its route, the stranger made an obscene gesture at the driver. The witness added that, as they rode in the bus that afternoon, a number of the students had noticed the red Chevrolet and had speculated about what its driver was doing.

The news of the brutal slaying of Sheli Wilkinson sent shock waves throughout the normally tranquil communities of the Catskill Mountain foothills. The following day, some 25 to 30 students from Wurtsboro stayed home from classes at Monticello High, still upset by the death of the pretty blonde.

"Everybody was down," reported a 16-year-old Monticello boy. "Most of her friends were crying."

"I was shocked," said a 17-year-old boy who had dated Sheli Wilkinson on a casual basis during the winter. "I was asleep and my mother woke me up. I was shocked. I am still. I'm shaking like a leaf . . . She was so pleasant."

Early on Friday morning, April 23, nine New York troopers began scouring woodland near the Wilkinson home for evidence. Lieutenant Scribner reported that as many as 30 troopers were taking part in the murder investigation.

That afternoon, investigators erected a roadblock where Wilsey Valley Avenue crossed Route 209, close to the Wilkinson home, asking motorists if they had been in the area at the same time on Thursday. On Saturday, as some 400 mourners gathered at St. Joseph's Roman Catholic Church for funeral services for Michele Wilkinson, the homicide probers continued to press the hunt for the elusive red Chevrolet.

There were no major developments the rest of the weekend. Late on Monday evening, April 26, however, detectives began interviewing residents along Katrina Falls Road in Rock Hill. Several hours later they took into custody on murder charges a 32-year-old prison parolee with a rap sheet showing three Nassau County, New York, sex convictions in 15 years. Arraigned Tuesday morning on a second-degree murder charge, Joel Ferkins of Rock Hill pleaded innocent and was ordered held in the Sullivan County Jail without bail pending a preliminary hearing.

At an afternoon press conference, District Attorney Stephen F. Lungen revealed that police had been led to Ferkins by witnesses who had seen him behind the wheel of a maroon Chevrolet and by information from Monticello police and the State Division of parole. He refused to comment on whether or nor Sheli Wilkinson had been sexually assaulted by her slayer.

That night, the county coroner, Dr. Sydney P. Schiff, informed the district attorney's office that the teenager had been stabbed 18 times in the chest, abdomen and neck. Three of the wounds had been fatal, those which pierced her heart, lungs and a major vein. The girl also had suffered numerous hand injuries as she attempted to ward off the deadly thrusts with her open palms.

Other marks on the body included the imprints of the masking tape on her wrists and three bruises on a breast which seemed to have been made by the intense pinching pressure of the slayer's fingernails.

Joel Ferkins, newsmen learned, had been released from the Auburn Correctional Facility in Cayuga County, New York, on March 5, 1981, after serving two thirds of a five to ten-year sentence on a first-degree attempted sodomy conviction from February, 1975. In 1971, Ferkins had been given a four-year term for first-degree sexual abuse which was vacated the following year by the Appellate Division. In 1967, when he was 18, the record showed, he had been convicted as a youthful offender of sexually abusing a female store clerk in Cedarhurst, Long Island.

In Rock Hill, where Ferkins lived with his

girlfriend and her eight-year-old daughter in a modest, two-bedroom home, acquaintances described the murder suspect as a quiet man with boundless energy for playing video games.

"He worked as a waiter at one of the resorts in the mountains," one acquaintance said, "but more often than not, you could find him at the video arcade in Monticello. He'd usually show up about 5 p.m., to play PacMan. He was an OK player, but nothing more."

"He's a blond, lanky guy," a neighbor said, "very tall, about six-foot-seven. Though we didn't see him very often, whenever we did he'd wave."

One Rock Hill teenager told reporters that, although it was an open secret that Ferkins drove a car like the one police were looking for, no one had thought of contacting the authorities.

"I kept telling people the guy had a maroon Nova, that we have to do something," he said, "but everyone said he was too nice a guy to do something like that. I was looking in every red car I could find for something. We all knew Sheli. We didn't know he knew her."

On Wednesday, April 28th, a Sullivan County grand jury returned a seven-count indictment charging Joel Ferkins with one count of second-degree intentional murder, two counts of second-degree felony murder committed in connection with the crimes of sexual abuse and burglary, one count of first-degree sexual abuse, two counts of first-degree burglary and one count of third-degree criminal possession of a weapon. The following day Ferkins pleaded innocent to the charges at his arraignment before Sullivan County Court Judge Louis B. Scheinman.

That same day, it was revealed that in recent months the Sullivan County Mental Health Clinic had notified state officials that it could not provide psychiatric treatment for Ferkins, despite an apparent need for counseling, and that he would be better handled by the legal system.

"We felt we could not handle the degree of treatment he needed," a county official told reporters. He went on to hint very strongly that clinic counselors had been apprehensive about treating the ex-con because of his record of criminal violence.

County mental health officials reportedly had notified the state in January that they could not treat Ferkins and that the "prognosis was poor." One source said that officials were concerned about female counselors having to treat Ferkins because of his record.

A spokesman for the State Division of Parole said that the Parole Board had turned down Ferkins' bids for parole in July of 1979 and December, 1980 because of his criminal record of sexually deviant behavior and violence.

"We perceive you as a continuing threat to the community," the parole board had told Ferkins.

However, under the state's "Good Time Law," his release from prison had been mandated after he completed two thirds of his term.

"We treated this as a serious case from the outset," said a senior parole officer on Friday, adding that the regional parole office in Poughkeepsie had "a number of contacts" with Ferkins since his conditional release.

One county source described the legal release from prison of someone with Ferkins' background as one of those cases which falls "through the cracks" of the system.

More than a month after the initial seven-count indictment was returned against him, Ferkins was indicted on additional counts of sodomy and felony murder.

At Joel Ferkins' murder trial, which got underway in Monticello in April, 1983, District Attorney Lungen told the jury that two of Sheli Wilkinson's friends would testify about seeing a red car following them when they got off the school bus a year earlier. The girls would testify that the driver of the car matched the defendant's description.

Armed with the description provided by the girls, as well as other evidence, state police began tailing Ferkins, Lungen said. During the two days after the killing, they took a number of photos of the ex-con, whom they linked to the slaying when they learned he drove a Chevrolet Nova. The car was registered to Ferkins' girlfriend, and undercover photos were taken of him driving the vehicle.

When police initially brought Ferkins in for questioning on April 26th, Lungen said, the suspect told them that he had expected to be questioned about the slaying of Sheli Wilkinson.

"The reason she is dead today," Lungen said, "is because if she weren't, she would have been able to take that witness stand and prove he sodomized her. It's the classic elimination of the witness."

Nevertheless, he promised, before the end of the trial, "Sheli Wilkinson is going to have something to say to you about the identification of the murderer."

"There's no question about what happened," responded defense counsel. "The only question is whether or not Mr. Ferkins did it."

On Thursday, April 21st, State Police Senior Investigator Wilfred Holik testified that, although Ferkins' fingerprint was in his girlfriend's red Nova, none of his prints were found on the death weapon or in the Wilkinson home. Holik was quick to note, however, that it was considered rare to find a print, rarer still to come up with one on a knife.

During a comprehensive search of the crime scene, Holik went on, he found no sign of a struggle. The only blood in the house was in the bathroom and on one of Sheli Wilkinson's sneakers. Holik added that he had found a hair on the floor of the recreation room. Coroner Schiff, during his stay on the witness stand, mentioned that he found two bloody hairs in one of the defensive wounds on the victim's hand.

On Monday, April 25th, Sheli Wilkinson's best friend, Cindy, told the court that at 3:45 on the afternoon of April 22, 1982, after speaking with Sheli on the phone, she had looked out a window of her house and seen the same red car which had followed the school bus out of the Wilsey Valley area. Earlier, she said, she had noticed the car when she got off the bus and began walking toward her home. The man in the car, she testified, waved and smiled at her, "evil-like."

The teenager also identified a pair of sunglasses which police had found in the red Nova as those worn by the man who followed the school bus.

A 13-year-old Wilsey Valley Road girl said that she, too, had noticed the red car following the bus. When she got off and began walking to her house, the driver had looked at her and then turned away.

Both girls, it was noted, had selected Joel Ferkins from a police line-up as the man they had seen that day. In addition, Cindy had identified him at a hotel where state police had brought her while maintaining surveillance of the ex-con.

On Tuesday, April 26th, State Police Investigator John Gallagher testified that after the girls had identified him as the man who had followed the school bus, probers had picked up Ferkins for questioning. Ferkins, who was not told why the police wanted to speak with him, readily agreed to accompany troopers to the Ellenville barracks. There, he told them that he had been paroled from a rape conviction and assumed they wanted to speak with him about the Wilkinson case.

Ferkins initially told police that he had not been in Wurtsboro in more than a month and had spent the day of the slaying working at a hotel, shopping, washing his car and trying to locate a friend. However, according to Gallagher, after being told that a witness could place him in the vicinity of the Wilkinson home, Ferkins broke down and said.

" 'I need help . . . I didn't mean to hurt that girl. I don't want to go back to jail.

" 'Oh God, help me,' " he repeatedly cried, rocking back and forth with his hands clasped in his lap.

When he was asked why he had slain the girl, Gallagher continued, Ferkins had replied, " 'She's dirt. She was dirty.' " Asked why he had slain her in the bathtub, he had answered that the victim " 'had to be cleansed.' "

After he had made his admission, Gallagher said, police decided to arrest Ferkins. But as he approached the suspect with handcuffs, Ferkins punched him under the left eye and jumped on another investigator, whom he attempted to choke.

Wednesday, Investigator Michael Cahill testified that, when state police drove Ferkins to the Wilkinson home and showed him a photo of the victim's body sprawled across the tub with a carving knife in her chest, the defendant's eyes filled with tears.

" 'I feel sick,' " he reportedly said. " 'I feel sick.' "

" 'Can you tell me you did not kill her?' " Cahill said he asked.

Ferkins, according to Cahill, shook his head no.

Cahill added that Ferkins nodded affirmatively when asked if he had stabbed the girl because he wanted her to perform oral sex.

On Thursday, April 28th, State Police Forensic Scientist Ralph Maruccio testified that two hairs found in the Wilkinson home were "microscopically similar" to Joel Ferkins' pubic hair. Such evidence, he noted, "is not absolutely conclusive" as an identification tool.

Of two bloody hairs found in a stab wound on Sheli Wilkinson's left hand, the witness said, one had characteristics similar to the victim's scalp hair while the other was similar to Ferkins' pubic hair. The other pubic hair identified as being similar to the defendant's was found on the floor of the recreation room.

On Monday, May 2nd, Robert Shaler, a serologist from the New York City medical examiner's office, testified that semen removed from Sheli Wilkinson's body during the autopsy fit at least three characteristics of Joel Ferkins' seminal fluid. Statistically, the witness explained, those characteristics would eliminate 92 per cent of the male population as suspects in the case.

The final prosecution witness, State Police Senior Investigator Ronald Keillor, told the court that detectives did not attempt to confirm the defendant's purported confession in writing, because he was upset and crying at the time he made it.

"This was one of the more difficult interviews I've ever been involved with," Keillor testified. "I had never been exposed to this type of reaction."

In his final argument on Tuesday, May 3rd, defense counsel asked the jury to consider the possibility that the police had fabricated his client's purported admissions. Never, he noted, had an attempt been made to get Ferkins to sign a statement.

District Attorney Lungen countered by telling the panelists that Ferkins had selected Sheli Wilkinson as the target of his lust because "she was a darn pretty, young, 15-year-old girl."

Ferkins, he said, gained entrance to the Wilkinson home by telling the teenager that he was distributing religious pamphlets. He killed her after the sexual assault because she would have been able to identify him.

As Lungen discussed Ferkins' account of his whereabouts at the time of the slaying, the defendant, who had remained silent throughout the proceedings, rocked back and forth in his straight-backed wooden chair.

"I wasn't looking for an alibi," he blurted, tears glistening in his eyes.

Admonished by Judge Scheinman for speaking out, he added, "I'm sorry, your honor, but my life is at stake here."

Around 5 p.m., the jury retired to the deliberation room to debate Joel Ferkins' fate. They returned to the courtroom four hours later to report that they had found the defendant guilty of one count of second-degree intentional murder, two counts of second-degree felony murder in connection with the crimes of sodomy and burglary, first-degree burglary, first-degree sodomy and third-degree criminal possession of a weapon. Charges of felony murder in connection with sexual abuse, first-degree sexual abuse and first-degree burglary had been dropped by the prosecution.

District Attorney Lungen told newsmen that he would seek an extremely stiff prison term for Ferkins. Although, under New York law, the defendant faced a maximum 25 years to life term, the prosecutor said that he would research the law to determine if a longer term could be meted out.

On Tuesday, May 31st, saying that his crimes called for the death penalty, Judge Scheinman sentenced Ferkins to three 25-year to life prison terms for murder, two 12 1/2 to 25-year terms for burglary and sodomy and 3 1/2 to 7 years for weapons possession. Although the murder, burglary and sodomy sentences must be served concurrently, the jurist ordered that Ferkins serve the sentences for each group of convictions consecutively. Under New York law, Joel Ferkins will not become eligible for parole for a minimum of 30 years.

EDITOR'S NOTE:

Cindy is not the real name of the person so named in the foregoing story. A fictitious name has been used because there is no reason for public interest in the identity of this person.

"LINDA'S KILLER FED HER TO THE PIGS!"

by Andrew Lowen

Main Road is the mile-long spine of Biggin Hill, a rather colorless town but famous during World War II as a base for fighter aircraft and currently for its racing circuit for the highest-powered cars.

No address could sound more mundane than 80 Main Road. Yet great mysteries are often set at the most prosaic addresses. And no address typifies this tradition more starkly than 80 Main Road, Biggin Hill, a little white bungalow with a drab tiled roof. It doesn't deserve a second glance . . . yet it receives long, speculative stares.

For here, in July 1981, a 29-year-old mother, wife and mistress called Linda Sturley vanished as suddenly and inexplicably as if she had stepped off the edge of the world.

As soon as Linda was reported missing—an oddly-belated alarm, raised a year later by her

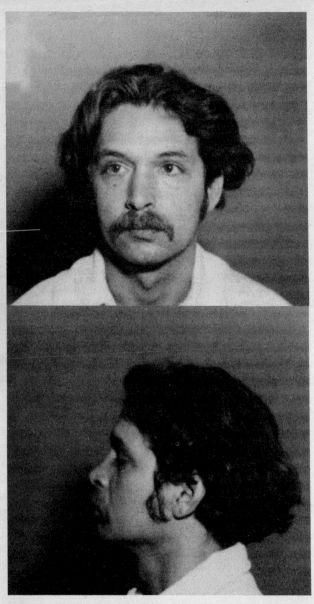

MICHAEL YARBOROUGH

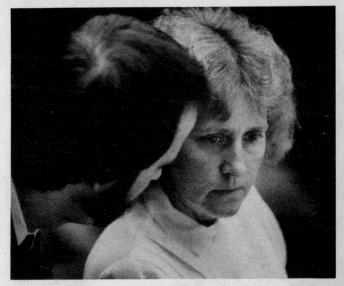

PAULINE ROGERS (Photo Credit: *Courier-Journal*)

MICHAEL WOODMANSEE
(Photo Credit: AP/World Wide Photos, Inc.)

CHARLES HAYNES

JOHN BRUNO

JAMES RIVA (Photo Credit: AP/World Wide Photos, Inc.)

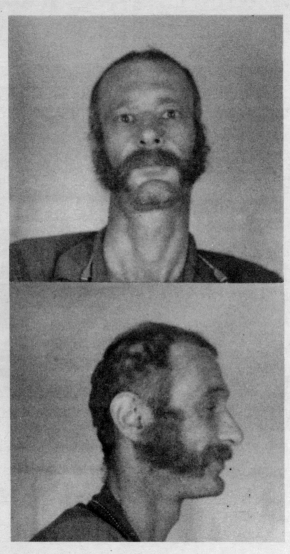

TIMOTHY BURGESS

WILLIAM DOUGLAS
(Photo Credit: AP/World Wide Photos, Inc.)

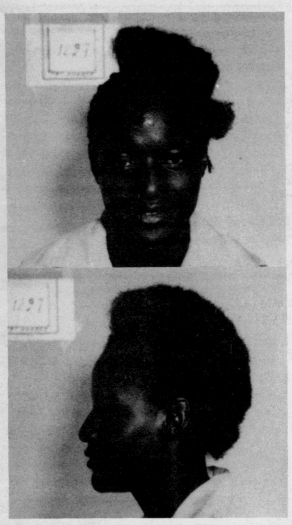

NORRISSA MILTON

RUTH NESLUND (Photo Credit: AP/World Wide Photos, Inc.)

MARIE WITTE (Photo Credit: Steven Peterka/*News-Dispatch*)

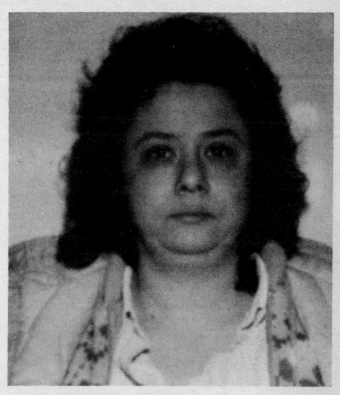

DIANE DOWNEY

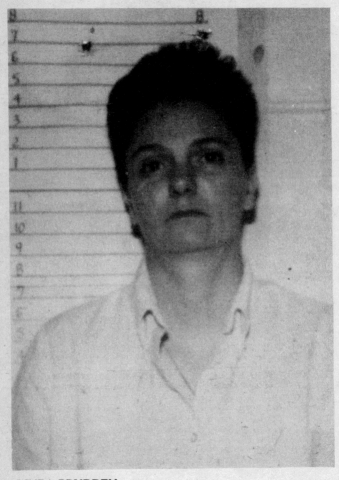

LINDA PRUDDEN

CHARLES PALMER

parents—there was no doubting the principal suspect. Murder, cynical cops say, for good reason tends to be kept in the family.

On one side was Graham "Rick" Sturley—solid, prematurely silver-haired. On the other, a Scotland Yard veteran, Detective Chief Inspector George Cressy.

At 50, Cressy had been a detective for 28 years and had led 50 homicide investigations, resulting in 50 prosecutions. Some record! A record that Cressy had no intention of allowing to be spoiled.

Sitting in Sturley's bungalow, the two of them might have been a pair of businessmen feeling their way towards the climax of a transaction.

There was a faint smell of furniture polish. A 34-year old married woman, who had worked for Rick Sturley and moved in with him immediately after his wife "went missing," kept the place immaculate.

Eighty Main Road was crowded, with two children from each partner, but there was nothing untidy or slipshod about this very ordinary home.

Sturley—pallid, portly and genial—leaned forward with a tiny grunt of effort and poured tea into two cups, passing one to his visitor. Eerily, he seemed flattered to be of major interest to one of Britain's top cops.

The cup did not tremble as Sturley passed it questioning: "Do you still think I murdered my wife?"

Cressy answered without hesitation. "I am more certain than ever!"

There was a pause. When Sturley eventually replied, he said, "Then we're at war."

When Cressy shook hands and climbed into his car to head for P Division—covering Lewisham and Deptford, southeastern suburbs of London—he was already framing the report which he felt certain would result in a charge of murder for Graham "Rick" Sturley.

Cressy's blunt accusation of Sturley's guilt had shaken the man, who had felt the situation was, at worst, a stalemate.

Because no trace of Linda Sturley had been found, living or dead, her husband had felt free to treat the matter as a kind of chess game, with a rather avuncular cop for an opponent.

But Cressy had signalled that he was going ahead, seeking an arrest and a trial in court, despite the drawback of not having a body.

Sturley projected himself to the world as a property speculator. Yet, as so often was the case with this complex man, reality was more humble.

Rick had gotten his hands on a house on the coast in the county of Kent, hoping for a swift conversion and profit, only to find that it was a bigger and costlier job than he'd expected. The property was still unsold when he declared war on Cressy. As for 80 Main Road, Biggin Hill, also in the county of Kent, not far from

London—that one his elderly mother had helped him buy.

While most people reading about the homicide investigation in the newspaper assumed Sturley was a property tycoon, Cressy saw him as a Walter Mitty character—someone who was always going to make a fortune—tomorrow. When things went wrong though, it was always someone else's fault, never his own.

"He liked to think of himself as a ladies' man," said Cressy. "No woman ever helped him merely out of kindness, she had to be desperately in love with him."

Cressy is a bespectacled man and very fit for a 50-year-old. He has a hatchet of a nose and a moustache and hair that is swept back. He goes in suits and waistcoats. He glories in being an old-fashioned cop. But he set out to understand Rick Sturley, to get into his skin, and he succeeded.

In Cressy's eyes, Sturley had always been a loser. He'd opened a grocery store in Deptford some years ago and found a way to cut overheads by handling stolen goods. He was jailed for 12 months.

When he was freed, he drove taxis for a while. That was how he first met Linda, who was to become his wife.

Cressy didn't know Linda as well, but he reckoned the key to her promiscuity was her good nature and her weakness for lame ducks.

Linda was something of a lame duck herself. After an insecure childhood—her mother was married four times—Linda ran away from home at 17 to live with a guy whom she married but ditched before she was 20.

One night she flagged down a taxi with Rick as the driver. Instead of going where she had intended, they ended up together at a hotel that night. They were together from then on until the time she disappeared.

They married and had two children—ages seven and four. Both were born by Caesarian section.

In the summer of 1981, Linda was six months pregnant and due to enter the hospital in October for another Caesarian birth. The essential operation was to be a significant point in the inquiries following her disappearance.

It was common gossip that Linda had boyfriends—one regular lover often calling at the bungalow in the afternoon.

Rick claimed that another of his business disasters, a diner in southeast London, was caused by Linda shutting the place to dally with customers in the bedroom when she'd been left in charge.

After being a taxi driver, Sturley drifted into being what he called a private detective; in Britain you don't need a license or an official badge. Despite his boasts that he'd once been a private detective, Cressy knew that this was yet another exaggeration. All Sturley had ever done in that line of business was serve the occasional writ and once give evidence in court for a client.

All the time his wife, Linda, had an insatiable appetite for men. She even dated one of her lovers while in a maternity hospital waiting to give birth.

Sturley was becoming suspicious, so he bugged his home telephone. And this way he learned of one of his wife's love affairs. He confronted both his wife and her lover, demanding that they end the affair. It did stop for a short time, but was resumed shortly after the birth of her four-year-old son.

Tension in the little white bungalow must have been building all the time. The Sturleys were struggling, not in the traditional triangle, but in a sort of crazy extramarital polygon, involving two couples and a few supporting characters.

His live-in girlfriend had worked for Rick for about three years. She was married with two children, and Rick and her were at least cemented friends. In addition to everything else, she was a qualified nurse.

Not that the woman was a femme fatale. A plump, homely, eminently stable person looking more mature than 34, she gave Rick affection and loyal support for his hungry, fragile ego.

Then her husband found out. He gave her an ultimatum—end the liaison or leave within a month.

Parallel with all this, Linda and Rick told relatives that she had stopped taking the pill and that they were trying for a third child to save their marriage.

A minor, though arguably potent, aspect of the case was Sturley's aspirations. Biggin Hill, forever woven into the "Battle of Britain" tapestry, isn't exactly the "Garden of England," although it lies in the "garden county" of Kent.

Describing the community in which the Sturleys lived, Cressy said: "It's full of people who hope they've arrived, but aren't quite sure . . . Cocktails before Sunday lunch, but sometimes no lunch!"

Rick, with his silver hair, neat suits and property developer image, found it easier to survive in this artificial environment than he might have in the genuine article.

Cressy was to observe, "It became clear that Rick and Linda thought they belonged to the jet-set, but with their financial circumstances, it was champagne tastes on beer money.

"Actually, they rarely went out anymore socially. Linda wasn't a drinker, and if she did go to a bar, then all she'd have was lemonade.

"But Rick made a few jet-set gestures, like hiring a plane for 200 and taking the whole family up for a spin."

Cressy was sure that their emotional time-bomb exploded on a hot summer night in July, 1981 — some time after Friday, July 17th.

Rick admitted to Cressy that he and Linda had an argument. She taunted him that the baby she was expecting would be "born black," Rick claimed.

Sturley also made no secret of having assaulted her. The scale of the violence differed according to whom he was talking. It ranged from a smack in the mouth and a punch in the stomach to a "good tuning up."

After the violence, according to Rick's version to the cops, he went to bed, leaving Linda sitting in the front room. When she was not there the next morning, he started to rearrange his life.

"I was glad she was gone," he admitted to Cressy.

Linda dropped from a cheek-by-jowl community, on the fringe of one of the world's biggest cities, without leaving a ripple.

Her mother lived not far away. So, too, did her sister.

Linda never missed birthdays or other anniversaries. She always sent cards and presents. She phoned her mother daily and met her once a week without fail.

Yet it was a year after her disappearance before her parents went to the police and officially reported her missing.

"That was the biggest mystery to me of the whole case," said Cressy. "It was beyond my comprehension."

Her sister, in fact, had lunch with Linda on

Friday, July 17, 1981. Linda promised to phone back later, confirming some clothes sizes before her sister posted an order to a mail-order firm. But the call was never made. The young woman phoned Linda the following day, only to learn from Rick that Linda had "gone away."

No one ever saw her or heard from her again.

When the investigation got under way, Linda's mother and sister claimed they had no reason to disbelieve Rick.

"He always seemed straight and honest with us," Linda's mother told Cressy.

The first cop to visit Sturley after Linda's mother had finally gone to the police was a uniformed sergeant. Sturley said that Linda was safe and well and was in regular phone contact with him. She had cashed checks in September, 1981.

The sergeant went through the motions and filled in a missing persons' report, recommending "no action."

But Detective Chief Inspector Rodger Williams was dissatisfied and sent a detective constable to make further inquiries.

As a result of that young detective's suspicions, the case was handed over to Cressy, arguably Britain's top cop.

"When I'm on a case, I go home only when there isn't anything else to be done," said Cressy. "And I play havoc if everyone else on the team isn't in the office with me at nine sharp the following morning.

"I decided on a low profile inquiry and obtained the assistance of only one other officer, PC John Asmus. I particularly wanted him, not only because he lived in Biggin Hill, but he also carried out there his hobbies of jousting, archery, falconry, hunting and fishing. In other words, he was a local character—probably more of a celebrity than Sturley. I knew that witnesses in the area would respond to John. I also knew that he was meticulous, totally reliable and worth his weight in gold."

It was several days before Cressy and Asmus knocked on the door of the bungalow and came face-to-face with Sturley.

Rick Sturley was sleepy. It was 7:00 a.m. Sturley's girlfriend opened the door, then fetched her lover.

The woman made tea while the two detectives and Sturley sat down in the living-room, all of them smoking.

After the tea had arrived and the woman had joined the party, Sturley said to Cressy, "Can I ask you a question off the record?"

Cressy agreed, and Rick said, "What do you think happened to Linda?"

Bluntly, Cressy replied. "You killed her. Didn't you?"

Sturley was visibly shaken. He put his head in his hands, and according to Cressy, showed all the normal signs of a man about to unburden himself with a full confession.

But after remaining silent for about a minute, he took his hands away from his face and said defiantly to Cressy, "You'll have to prove it."

And that moment of confrontation marked a complete change in Sturley's mood. The tea party was over.

Cressy said he wanted to make a complete search of the bungalow. Sturley's girlfriend was escorted to the nearby St. Mary Cray police station with a woman cop. Cressy insisted that the four children be moved into the house of a neighbor. The chief inspector agreed that the children should be moved.

Sturley followed Cressy and Asmus around the premises, including the garden, giving the impression that he was enjoying every minute of it. More cops were called in to dig up the garden.

Cressy was later to say, "In all honesty, I never expected to find Linda's body in or near the bungalow. It just was a facet that had to be covered. We had to go through the motions."

The clues were indoors—Linda's jewelry-box, complete with her watches, and her personal checkbook.

Sturley had assured Linda's parents that she had been using that checkbook months after "going away." But now he volunteered that he had forged her signature, transferring her money into his account. His justification was that Linda had stolen money from him when they ran a diner and he was merely recovering what was rightfully his.

He also admitted forging a claim for Linda's maternity benefit. He had now admitted a criminal offense, so Cressy immediately cautioned him, making sure Sturley had been read his rights.

Cressy already had information of Sturley showing semi-nude photographs of Linda while she was in an advanced state of pregnancy.

Rick produced them for Cressy from a drawer, saying he found the film after Linda had left and had had it developed. He claimed that he was so disgusted with the photographs that he had thrown them in the drawer.

Sturley accused one of his wife's boyfriends of being the photographer, but agreed that they "were probably" taken with his own camera.

Long before that first confrontation, Cressy and Asmus had spoken to Linda's family and friends, gathering what they considered to be "good ammunition."

They had learned that Linda was an attentive daughter and a doting mother. They'd also discovered that Sturley had told his wife's sister how Linda had given birth to a black baby in October 1981 and that she had phoned while drunk from the city of Birmingham, despite the fact that she was known by everybody to be a non-drinker.

Sturley also said that Linda wanted to return home and that she'd been living with two men in Brixton, a notorious district of inner London.

Cressy was well aware that impulse was a part of Linda's style. It would not have been out of character for her to be living with two men and then deciding in a flash to return home. But Sturley's story had a massive flaw.

Linda was utterly devoted to her son, who was a toddler at the time his mother vanished. She took him everywhere, including the times when she indulged in extramarital sex in cars.

She had discussed leaving Rick with many friends, but one theme had remained constant. She was prepared to leave her daughter with her husband, but never her son. He would have to go wherever she went.

A neighbor remembered seeing Linda at 9:00 p.m. of Friday, July 17th, 1981. Linda had appeared very happy. She'd met one of her boyfriends that day and had arranged to phone him on that Saturday. She also arranged to attend a fete with her neighbor and her children the next day. She did not make the phone call and neither did she keep the appointment.

For more than a year, Linda had not been seen or heard from. And, unless Rick could be believed, she had not contacted anyone. Her clothing, jewelry and other possessions were still at the bungalow.

Rick admitted forging Linda's check, emptying her bank account and trying to obtain her maternity benefits. If Linda was alive, then she would have given birth to another child, and it could only have been done by Caesarian section. Yet no hospital or clinic in the country had any record of having admitted Linda.

On the Saturday following her mother's disappearance, Linda's daughter had gone into her parents' bedroom to be told by her father that Linda had "gone away." Not "gone shopping," not "visiting friends," just a bland "gone away."

Linda had not made any phone calls to friends or relatives. Cressy could trace only one phone call from Sturley's bungalow that weekend. It was made by Sturley at 10:00 a.m. on Saturday—to his girlfriend, asking her to move in with him.

Sturley's allegation of the expected baby not being his contradicted a discussion during Christmas, 1980, when Linda and Rick had told relatives they would try for another baby to save their marriage.

Sturley's girlfriend had been faced with the ultimatum from her husband—stop seeing Rick or leave within a month.

Cressy's questioning of Sturley was intense. After seven hours on the opening day, he sent Sturley to a hospital for a check-up, aware that Rick had a heart condition.

Cressy's main problem was that Sturley had already admitted a criminal offense and this meant, under British law, that all interviews had to be conducted under caution. Each question had to be written down, a reply invited and then recorded.

Cressy asked the questions, his partner recorded the answers. Sturley, on average, took about 30 seconds to gather his thoughts before replying to each question.

It was evident that Sturley was genuinely proud of his home and his children. His girlfriend had no problem coping with four children and keeping a tidy home.

The county of Kent alone covers a million acres or so. Cressy believed that Sturley had all of that fateful Friday night—possibly 12 hours—in which to dispose of the body.

"Draw a radius of six hours driving, one-way from Biggin Hill after dark with traffic relatively light, and she could be literally anywhere," Cressy told his partner.

The investigation took a dramatic turn on October 28, 1982, just 12 hours after Cressy had told Sturley that he was "more certain than ever" that Rick had killed his wife.

Sturley woke his mistress in the early hours of the morning, complaining of "a crushing pain in the chest." The woman took one look at her lover's blue-colored face and called an ambulance.

When Cressy arrived in his office at 9:00 that morning, there was a message waiting for him on his desk. It said simply: "Graham Sturley is dead. He died in the hospital of a heart-attack at 7:30 a.m. today."

Cressy had had an appointment with the Director of Public Prosecutions at 10:00 a.m. that

223

same day to officially draw up the charge of homicide against Graham "Rick" Sturley. The appointment was cancelled.

Cressy and his partner attended Sturley's funeral five days later. They were intrigued by the bizarre message on the wreath from his lover which said simply: "Well, you got that out of the way, Sturley." It was signed: "All my love," followed by three kisses.

When asked to explain the message, Sturley's mistress told the cops to "get lost," adding, "You have caused enough trouble already. If it wasn't for you, Rick would be alive today. You killed him with all your filthy questions and dirty accusations."

After the funeral, Cressy told reporters, "Everything we discovered, and all my experience, convinces me of two factors — Linda is dead and her husband killed her."

The police officially closed their file on the case and that might have been the end of the matter if it had not been for Cressy's nagging curiosity. He just couldn't get the case out of his mind. He was not sleeping at night, even after a few beers and a tablet which was supposed to relax him.

"I'll never be satisfied until I've found that body," he told his wife. "Even though the case is closed, I've got to go on. Even if only in my spare time, as a sort of hobby."

His wife knew better than to protest. He was

as much in love with his work as he was with her. Work and marriage had to learn to co-exist.

On November 13, 1982, Cressy returned to Sturley's bungalow. No one was at home, but the garage door was unlocked and the car Sturley had driven was still there. Cressy tried the driver's door and found it was unlocked.

The detective started looking around inside the car. Under the seat he found a map of Britain. Although it was old and rather tatty, it had definitely not been in the car or on the premises during the time of any of the police searches. One thing was certain, however, the map was more than a year old.

Intrigued, Cressy started browsing through the pages of the detailed map. Suddenly, he spotted a faint X, marked with a pencil, at the location of a farm just five miles away.

Cressy drove the five miles to New Haven Farm in Farmborough, Kent. As soon as he arrived, her realized that this was no ordinary farm. It was a pig farm. The whole place was alive with snorting, grunting pigs.

After a frantic phone call, the case was immediately reopened. Asmus joined Cressy on the farm. A hundred uniformed officers and soldiers from a nearby regiment were recruited to dig up the land.

"I'm not very happy about this," said the farmer, "but I realize it's something that has to be done. I can't very well refuse to help the police, can I?"

Two days later, a woman's shoe was dug up, plus three small bones. Laboratory tests showed that the bones were human and had formed the toes of a woman.

Suddenly, the appalling, harrowing truth dawned on Cressy and the searchers.

Nothing else was found on the farm, but the cops now knew where Linda Sturley had been taken on that fateful Friday night and how she had disappeared.

In his definitive report to his superiors, Cressy wrote: "As horrific and grisly as it may be, I'm afraid there can be no other conclusion than that Mrs. Linda Sturley, already dead, was driven to New Haven Farm on the night of July 17, 1981, and fed to the pigs.

"There was no evidence of the body being dismembered at the Sturley home. If the body had been cut up there we would have found traces of tissue and bloodstains, even if they were invisible to the naked eye.

"The owner of the farm knows from his diary that he was out late that night with his wife and did not return until at least 3:00 a.m. on Saturday.

"We also know that Sturley was familiar with that particular farm. We have discovered that Sturley tried to rent a cottage on the land a few months before his wife disappeared.

"Sturley must have killed his wife at home and

then drove her to the farm where he cut her up on the land, a remote spot, knowing that there was little or no chance of his being disturbed.

"Then, bit by bit, he fed his wife's flesh to the pigs until she had been devoured.

"It is an horrendous proposition, but it is impossible to come to any other conclusion."

The farmer pointed out to Cressy that 600 tons of bones were removed every month from the farm. There was little chance of any of Linda's remains being found there.

But the shoe and the three human toes were enough.

"I knew right from the beginning that Rick was our man," said Cressy. "It was a game of chess that I always believed I was going to win. The important thing was not to fall into the trap of rushing and over-reaching. It was vital that I should not charge him until I was as near certain as it's ever possible to be that I would get a conviction.

"Then he went and died on me ... And to think I had him checkmated for sure!

"WEIRDO CUT UP A CORPSE WITH A CHAINSAW!"

by Terrell Ecker

The 50 acres of woods known as the Foster Farm wasn't really a farm at all in the conventional sense. To the untrained eye it was just 50 acres of woods, briars and palmettos surrounding one small cleared area in which a previous owner had erected an open air "pole barn." The only other structure on the property was a vacant house trailer.

More knowledgeable eyes could see a scattered crop growing on the Foster tract in 1981, although how large it was and whether it was intended for sale or personal consumption remain matters of speculation to this day. Its existence came to the attention of authorities by chance while they were looking for the property's missing owner, Allen T. Foster III.

Foster, a 34-year-old yacht salesman, left his Gainesville, Florida home Saturday afternoon,

March 28th, saying he was going to make some repairs on the house trailer, for which he had found a tenant, and add some pine straw to a mulch he was making at the farm. He loaded several green plastic bags of pine straw into the bed of his blue pickup truck, climbed into the cab with his German shepherd and headed for the farm in Fairbanks, a small community about five miles northeast of Gainesville in Alachua County.

When Foster didn't return home Saturday night his worried wife called the sheriff's office and reported him missing. It wasn't like him to come home late, let alone not come home at all, she told the police.

Sunday afternoon Mrs. Foster and a deputy sheriff made a cursory search of the farm but saw no sign of Foster or his blue truck. There was no sign of the farm's only current occupant, either, but no one thought anything of that. Mrs. Foster explained that the tent under the pole barn was the temporary home of an old friend of Foster's from Miami. She said she didn't know much about him except that he'd been down on his luck lately and Foster was letting him camp on the property, rent free, until things improved. The house trailer was vacant, but apparently a new tenant was supposed to be moving into it soon.

By Monday afternoon Mrs. Foster was thoroughly alarmed, and Foster's friends and co-workers had become worried as well. Missing work was no more like Allen Foster than was his unexplained absence from home.

Sheriff Lu Hinderey agreed that a thorough search of the Foster farm seemed in order, but using the manpower on duty would stretch the county's regular patrol coverage too thin. For that reason the sheriff authorized a search by his highly trained Special Emergency Response Team (SERT), Alachua County's version of the well-known SWAT, under the command of Lieutenant Jerry Hansen. Fifteen of Foster's friends and co-workers joined the seven SERT officers, making a total of 22 men who began a systematic search of the Foster property at 3:00 p.m. Monday, March 30th.

The plan was literally to comb the entire 50 acres in a series of sweeps. The searchers spread out at arms' length in the southeastern corner of the tract and walked northward side by side, examining every briar patch and palmetto thicket in their path. By the time they reached the northern boundary it was raining heavily. They shifted westward and started southward on the second sweep.

The search party had advanced several yards on the second sweep when it came upon an odd pile of brush. It was too big, for one thing, a little larger than a vehicle, and too neatly rectangular. In fact the brush pile, which included a few small trees, was shaped roughly like a pickup truck. Peering into the brush at close range, searchers could see the blue sheet metal. They had found Allen Foster's truck.

Because the poorly hidden truck could be a crime scene, it was left covered as found, with only enough brush removed to allow a closer look. The bed appeared to be empty except for a length of nylon rope, and the only thing visible in the cab was a chainsaw.

About ten yards south of the truck, searchers found the body of a black German shepherd. Leaving one SERT officer to watch the truck and the dog's body, the other 21 men reformed their line and continued south through thickening underbrush and driving rain.

About 50 yards farther south, Deputy Pascucci's attention was captured by a bare plant stalk lying in a heavy palmetto thicket. To the evidence technician's trained eyes, it looked suspiciously like the stripped stalk of a harvested marijuana plant. Walking toward it through the thick palmettos, Pascucci tripped on something but kept his balance and thought nothing of it since whatever it was didn't bite him. Picking up the suspicious looking stalk for a close look, he saw that it was indeed a fully grown and carefully stripped marijuana stalk with its dirt-laden roots intact. It had not been touched.

Deputy Pascucci looked around for a hole from which the plant might have been pulled. Not seeing one, he started walking around among the palmettos and promptly tripped again. Still no bite, and this time it occurred to the deputy that he could have tripped on the stump of another marijuana plant. He reached down and got hold of something, then bent down for a close look.

He had a bone in his hand.

Pascucci brushed some pine straw from around the bone and saw that it seemed to be protruding from a buried green plastic garbage bag. He tugged on the plastic enough to open it slightly and saw what looked like human flesh adorned by fine, scattered dark hairs. Peering closer with the aid of his flashlight, the deputy saw what appeared to be blue denim. Foster had left home Saturday wearing blue jeans, a cowboy shirt and moccasins.

Pascucci's discovery brought a halt to the search and precipitated a host of new and considerably more grim activities. For starters, the civilians were removed from the property and the entire tract secured as a crime scene. Sheriff Hinderey himself was soon on the scene along with his chief of detectives, Captain B.E. "Bubba" Roundtree, and a growing army of investigators, evidence experts and medical people.

The buried plastic garbage bag obviously contained a human corpse, apparently dismembered and buried in a more or less upright position. The poorly hidden pickup truck and the dead German shepherd were strong indications that the human corpse was that of Allen Foster, but positive identification could be a problem under the circumstances. The detectives were not yet sure whether they even had a complete body. The only thing they knew for sure was that they had an uncommonly grisly murder on their hands and they didn't want to risk losing evidence through improper procedures. The thing to do was shut the scene down for the night and come back Tuesday morning with a search warrant and the best technical help available.

The state crime lab in Jacksonville agreed to send a team of experts with a portable lab, housed in a van, first thing Tuesday morning. The sheriff also requested and got help from a resource closer to home: the University of Florida's archeology department. Dr. William Ross Maples, who has dug up and studied dismembered bodies around the world, said he too would have a team on the scene Tuesday morning. And with that the crime scene was shut down, undisturbed and heavily guarded, for the night. But the investigation wasn't.

While the search had been going on, Captain Roundtree's investigators had been questioning such neighbors of the Foster property as could be found at home. Virtually all of them knew Allen Foster in a very casual way, but none knew him well or had any idea where he might be. After all, Foster didn't live among them, just owned some property that he visited occasionally. Most of the neighbors were much more familiar with the guy who lived on the property, although no one had seen him that day. A tall, skinny "weirdo" named Tim Burgess who lived in a tent, the man had no visible means of support and walked around the property wearing guns much of the time.

As the afternoon struggled on through the rain toward darkness, and more neighbors began arriving home from work with bits and pieces of information about Tim Burgess, the detectives' interest in his background and current whereabouts increased sharply. In the first place, the body could be his; it wouldn't be identified until Tuesday morning, if then. In the second place, if the body was that of Allen Foster, as suspected, Burgess would have to be an automatic suspect until cleared, if only because he lived in a tent less than 100 yards from the buried corpse.

It was late evening when Sergeant Kenny Mack obtained, thus far, the most startling bit of information about the mysterious Mr. Burgess. A 14-year-old neighbor told Mack that he had had a curious conversation with Burgess on Friday, March 27th, but hadn't really thought much about it because, he said, all conversations with Burgess were curious.

The boy said that Burgess, high on marijuana as usual, had bragged in gory detail about how he was going to murder Allen Foster, with whom he was terribly upset for some reason. Burgess had said he was going to ambush Foster with a shotgun, dismember his body, bury the pieces and cover them with lime. Burgess had seemed to relish the prospect, but the boy hadn't taken it seriously because Burgess was always carrying on about the horrible things he intended to do to whomever he happened to be angry with at the time.

Sergeant Mack took it seriously, however, especially when conversations with officers who had discovered the body confirmed that the remains and immediate surrounding area appeared to have been sprinkled with a lime-like substance of an extremely corrosive nature.

Tuesday morning brought welcome sunshine and a three-pronged attack on the bizarre case. One group of detectives and uniformed deputies cooperated with the state crime lab technicians and the University of Florida archeologists charged with digging up and identifying the mutilated corpse. As Dan Pascucci recalled later, "It took quite a while. They did it with teaspoons and brushes, and what have you. It was a very, very slow process. They documented it all the way down."

What they ended up documenting was the body of Allen Foster, killed by three shotgun blasts, its legs severed and its head scalped after death, the entire mess buried head downward in a plastic garbage bag, sprinkled with lime and covered with pine straw.

A second group of deputies, armed with a search warrant, began a painstaking three-day search of the entire Foster tract with special attention to Burgess's apparently abandoned home. It looked more like a garbage dump than a campsite, and nothing of particular interest was obvious. One thing the searchers did find of interest was a substantial marijuana crop growing here and there about the property.

A third group of detectives concentrated on the missing Mr. Burgess. They had no luck at all in finding him, but each new bit of information they obtained strengthened their determination to do so.

It turned out that Burgess was on probation from Washington, D.C., and a bit of routine checking into that interesting fact revealed a fascinating story.

On October 6, 1979, the White House was under even more scrutinization than usual by both the public and the police as President Jimmy Carter awaited the imminent arrival of Pope John Paul II. Across the street in Lafayette Park, police eyes were attracted to a tall, skinny redhead leading a Great Dane around on a leash. The huge dog was enough to attract attention but no cause for alarm. But having noticed the guy, the police couldn't help noticing the heavy vest he wore—much too heavy for the warm weather.

As officers moved closer and watched the man with professional curiosity, the dog started getting frisky and jumping playfully at its master. One jump knocked the guy off balance and opened his vest — revealing three .45-caliber semiautomatic pistols and two big knives. Their curiosity now thoroughly aroused, the officers wrestled the man to the ground for a closer examination and found 200 rounds of ammunition for the three fully loaded pistols.

In the interest of presidential and papal safety, the officers took the precaution of hauling Timothy Robert Burgess off to jail.

Charged with carrying the concealed weapons, ammunition and three marijuana cigarettes, Burgess, then 35, pled not guilty and explained that he was just trying to draw a little attention to himself in order to publicize a problem he was having with the Veterans Administration. Something about having been injured in a motorcycle accident while in the Navy and being unable to get any financial help from the VA.

Naturally, before the case could proceed any further, Burgess's competency to stand trial had to be established, so he was turned over to the mental health unit of the D.C. Department of Human Resources. Eventually one of the unit's 18 part-time psychiatrists reported to Superior Court Judge Robert M. Scott that the suspect's competency couldn't be determined because Burgess wouldn't talk. But the doctor said he had the "impression" that Burgess was suffering from a mental illness of psychotic proportions.

Judge Scott allowed Burgess to plead guilty to one count of carrying a pistol without a license, gave him a one-year suspended sentence and three years' probation.

Now, with Burgess possibly in trouble again, a spokesman for the D.C. mental health unit said they couldn't ethically discuss the case, and anyway they were too busy trying to determine John Hinckley's competency to stand trial for the attempted murder of President Reagan.

While that information was being digested, Deputy Gregory Weeks was following a lead to Burgess's possible current whereabouts. The lead came from the proprietor of a mom and pop type grocery store near the Foster property.

The grocer told Deputy Weeks that he last had seen Burgess about 9 o'clock the previous morning, Monday, and knew where he might be now. He said Burgess had come into the store carrying a large canvas duffle bag and said he needed a place to stay. He'd said his landlord was missing and the police probably would blame him because of some trouble he'd had in the past. Actually, he'd said, his landlord was probably just off with a woman somewhere having a good time.

The grocer said he knew that old Harvey Hanks, who lives down the road a ways, sometimes takes in roomers, so he had taken Burgess down there and left him. That had been about 10:00 a.m. or so. He hadn't seen or heard from Burgess since then.

It was 11:45 a.m. Tuesday when Deputy Weeks found and questioned Harvey Hanks at his house. Hanks confirmed that Burgess had spent Monday night there, but said he didn't know where he was now. Hanks said Burgess had behaved very strangely and had given Hanks the impression that he was running from the police. Then, this morning, Hanks had heard on the radio that a body had been discovered in the Fairbanks area. After thinking that over for a few seconds he had told Burgess he'd have to leave. So Burgess had left, and Hanks said he hadn't seen him since about 9:00 a.m. and didn't know where he might have gone.

Others heard the news on the radio, too, and the expected flood of phone calls started. As is usual in such cases, most of the calls were useless, but all were listened to carefully and a few proved to be of genuine value. One in particular proved to be of great value. One caller named Ginny Burnside said she had Tim Burgess's sawed-off shotgun if an officer would like to drop by her office and pick it up.

Detective Martin Snook promptly dropped by Miss Burnside's office and was given, from the trunk of her car, a sawed-off Stephens 16-gauge pump action repeating shotgun in a green plastic garbage bag. She said Burgess had left it with her Sunday morning—the last time she'd seen him. She and her boyfriend had let him out at that little grocery store in Fairbanks after he'd accom-

240

panied them on a grocery shopping trip into Gainesville. Miss Burnside's boyfriend, Greg Thompson, verified her story and added some very interesting details, including a possible motive for murder.

Thompson said there had been a dispute between Allen Foster and Tim Burgess over the use of the house trailer on the property. It was not exactly a landlord-tenant dispute because Burgess wasn't a paying tenant, just an old friend down on his luck whom Foster allowed to camp on the property. Burgess didn't see any reason why he shouldn't live in the trailer and simply moved in—without Foster's permission. Foster explained that he had rented the trailer to a paying tenant who would be moving in in a few days, and ordered Burgess to move out. Not off of the property, just out of the trailer. That was on Tuesday, March 24th. Foster told Burgess to be out of the trailer by the following morning, then had carefully cleaned up Burgess's mess while Burgess watched, silent and pouting.

Later Foster had told Thompson about the incident, Thompson said. Foster was concerned about Burgess's welfare, of course, and had done the best he could for the guy. Burgess had electricity in his tent, after all, through a long extension cord from the trailer. He cooked with electricity and had television. He had no bathroom, of course, but no one ever brought that subject up.

But Foster was also worried about Burgess's effect on the new tenant. Burgess was a weird looking dude, six feet four and 150 pounds, unkempt red hair and ragged clothes, walking around armed to the teeth. He usually wore a pair of .357-magnum revolvers and carried a sawed-off shotgun. Moreover, Burgess said if his probation officer ever showed up he'd blow her away. No one else really took him seriously, though. Burgess just liked to talk that way.

Thompson said he had seen Burgess three times since that incident. Friday night, March 27th, Burgess came to Thompson's trailer, located very near the Foster property, for a cookout. Saturday night Thompson heard that Foster was missing and went over to Burgess's camp to see if Foster was there. He wasn't, but Burgess said he apparently had been there during the afternoon while Burgess was away and had left some fertilizer.

Then, about 8:30 Sunday morning, Burgess had accompanied Thompson and Ginny Burnside into Gainesville to do some food shopping. Burgess had worn his guns into town, which was unusual, and wouldn't get out of the car. He just waited in the car while they shopped. When they let him out later in Fairbanks, he left the shotgun with Ginny.

Thompson said he hadn't seen Burgess since then.

In the meantime, the press had gathered in

force about the perimeter of the Foster property, but wasn't allowed onto the property itself and was given virtually no information beyond the fact that Allen Foster's body had been found. One enterprising reporter managed to gather a few odds and ends of information and misinformation, including the non fact that the victim's head as well as the legs had been severed from the body, and something about a chainsaw being found, and wrote an interesting if not accurate story for the Wednesday morning paper. From that point on the case was known, to the eventual embarrassment of the press, as the "Chainsaw Murder."

Actually, by then the University of Florida's Dr. William Maples had determined that the legs had been chopped off with considerable effort, while the lifeless body lay face down on the ground. There had been no chainsaw involved, although one had been found in the cab of Foster's pickup truck.

Also by then, a new witness had come forth with some intriguing information. Bill Herring, another Fairbanks trailer dweller, arrived at the sheriff's office in Gainesville accompanied by his lawyer after the lawyer had arranged a meeting with detectives. Herring had taken that precaution because, he said, he knew so much that he was worried about his own vulnerability to possible criminal charges.

Herring said he met Tim Burgess in October

243

1979. At the time, Foster was living in his trailer on the "farm" and he and Herring were neighbors and friends. Burgess lived in a tiny trailer on property adjacent to Foster's with a big dog, a Great Dane. About a week after Herring had met him, Burgess got himself arrested in Washington, D.C., and wasn't seen locally for several months.

Foster bought a home in Gainesville and moved into it, Herring continued, but made frequent trips to his farm property and usually stopped by to visit Herring. In the spring of 1980 Foster asked Herring if he'd like to go partners on a marijuana crop. Herring told Foster he would consider it, he said, and was considering seriously when, in the early summer, Tim Burgess showed up again, broke and homeless—and on probation for a weapons conviction.

Herring said that when he asked Foster about Burgess, Foster said that Burgess would be camping on the farm rent free and would be helpful in the marijuana project, but that it was understood there were to be no guns on the property. Well, okay, Herring said he told Foster, but the proposed pot crop deal was off, period. Herring wasn't about to get mixed up in any kind of operation that included Tim Burgess.

Herring said he did get pretty well acquainted with Burgess, however, and as the year wore on it became obvious that Foster and Burgess were cultivating a marijuana crop. They didn't try to hide that fact from Herring, and occasionally discussed the crop's progress in his presence.

Then the trouble started. One day late in the summer Burgess came to Herring's trailer and said 30 marijuana plants had been stolen. Later the same day, Foster told Herring that he suspected Burgess of having stolen the plants himself. A few days later Burgess showed Herring a .22-caliber rifle he had bought. Burgess said he also had a sawed-off shotgun, but Herring didn't see it. Still later, Burgess showed Herring a pair of .357-magnum revolvers.

Herring said that at that point he started getting paranoid about Burgess and talked to Foster about the guns. Foster said not to worry, that he could handle Tim Burgess.

Not reassured at all, Herring considered trying to contact Burgess's parole officer but decided that would just invite revenge from Burgess. He said, "I was extremely skeptical of the state's system of supervising such a dangerous person because I had witnessed the complete lack of supervision of what I thought was a demonstrably dangerous person."

In a December, 1980, conversation, Herring said, Burgess stated he was at the end of his rope. He had decided to go to town and blow up the parole office—take a can of gas, spread the gas around and light it, then shoot the secretary, janitor, anyone who got in the way.

Then, Herring said, "He started describing the glory of death, of watching people die, the sensuality of that death look as they knew they were dying, experiencing physical agony and emotional stress at the moment of death.

"I talked to him about twenty minutes on that occasion, turning the conversation to suggesting that he commit suicide rather than kill all those people if he was that distraught over his life and the uselessness and pain of it all.

"He said he wanted to go out in a blaze of glory. He told me at that point he had killed six or seven policemen and had never been caught, that he particularly liked to kill policemen and that he wanted to kill as many as he could before he died.

"At that point I was afraid for my own life and maneuvered myself out of the situation. I got in my truck and drove to a phone, called Allen Foster and talked to him at length. Allen said he would go out and talk to Tim and find out what the situation was."

Herring said Foster told him in a later conversation that he had tried repeatedly to contact Burgess's parole officer but couldn't get any response.

Herring said he then removed himself from the frightening situation by simply moving and avoiding any further contact with Burgess. When he heard what had happened to Allen Foster he felt obligated to tell the police what he knew. But he was worried enough about his own legal position that he contacted them through his lawyer.

Wednesday, April Fool's Day, brought an intensified search for Timothy Burgess. But the 37-year-old suspect, normally so conspicuous, seemed to have evaporated. Press coverage was intensified as well as the "Chainsaw Murder" label spread through the journalism community.

The break came late Wednesday afternoon with a phone call from Harvey Hanks, who evicted Burgess from his home after one night. Hanks said Burgess had simply moved into the woods behind the house, pitched a tent and apparently had been there the whole time. Anyway, Burgess was again in Hanks's house, and Hanks was out of it for the duration.

At 6 o'clock Lieutenant Hansen and his SER Team, armed with an arrest warrant among other things, secured the Hanks house. Hansen yelled for Burgess to come out and surrender. Burgess yelled that he wanted Deputy Gary Buchanan. He said he knew and trusted Buchanan, who lived in the Fairbanks area. Hansen yelled that he had a warrant for Burgess's arrest and demanded that he give up. Burgess yelled that he wasn't going to surrender to anyone but Gary Buchanan.

Hansen then left the scene to fetch Buchanan, leaving Sergeant Curtis O'Quinn in charge at the scene. During Hansen's absence, O'Quinn and Burgess exchanged shouts, mostly concerning treatment of prisoners. At one point Burgess shouted that the killing had been in self-defense. O'Quinn quickly changed the subject and they shouted about other things. "Just whatever I could think of," O'Quinn recalled later.

Gary Buchanan, it turned out, didn't even know Burgess and could not remember ever having seen him. But he must have seen him sometime, somewhere, or at least *been seen by* Burgess. In any event, he was glad to be of service. He called Burgess on Hank's telephone.

"Tim," Buchanan said, "this is Gary Buchanan. I understand that you wanted to talk with me and give up to me."

"Yes, I feel like I can trust you," Burgess replied.

Buchanan said, "Well, you know, I'll do my best to uphold that confidence in me."

"But you think you can get me something to eat?" Burgess asked. "My ulcers are really bad."

"Well, I'm sure we can find you something to eat," Buchanan assured him.

"Cigarettes?"

"Yes."

"Okay."

"Now, Tim," Buchanan said, "when I approach the house I'm going to tell you who I am and at that time I want you to come out the front door with your hands straight in the air and with no shirt on."

The arrest was accomplished without incident and Buchanan drove Burgess to the sheriff's office in Gainesville where he was given a hamburger, a coke and a pack of cigarettes.

"It was pretty gory, wasn't it?" Burgess said as he consumed his goodies. "This is the first food I've been able to hold down since I got rid of him."

After finishing his hamburger, Burgess asked for a lawyer. "I want to get my story straight before I talk to you about what happened," he explained.

In the meantime, however, he was perfectly willing to talk about his unsuccessful trip to Washington. He told Sergeant William "Bear" Bryan that he had gone to Washington intending to shoot President Carter, and would have pulled it off if his dog hadn't screwed up. Then maybe the VA would have listened to his complaints.

After talking to a lawyer Burgess decided that he wasn't guilty of the Foster murder or possession of a short-barreled shotgun and so pled on April 2nd.

Burgess's arrest brought a new round of publicity about his 1979 Washington adventure, and it occurred to some reporters that perhaps a would-be presidential assassin ought to have been under Secret Service surveillance. All a Secret Service spokesman would say on the subject was, "Let's just say we have been very much aware of Mr. Burgess."

On January 27, 1982, Timothy Robert Burgess, then 38, went to trial before a capital jury of seven men and five women. The trial didn't last long. The jury heard detailed testimony about the death of Allen Foster, then was shown photographs of his dismembered body. Watching the jurors' reactions to the grisly photographs, Burgess decided to call it off and plead guilty.

Circuit Judge John J. Crews immediately sentenced Burgess to life in prison with a mandatory minimum of 25 years before parole eligibility.

EDITOR'S NOTE:

Harvey Hanks, Ginny Burnside, Greg Thompson, and Bill Herring are not the real names of the persons so named in the foregoing story. Fictitious names have been used because there is no reason for public interest in the identities of these persons.

"KILLER KEPT ROBIN'S BRAIN TISSUE AS A SOUVENIR!"

by Bob Carlsen

Robin Nadine Benedict was an extremely talented graphic artist and could have made a fine living on her artistic ability alone. But that wasn't enough for her. Her stunning looks also provided the opportunity for her to make vast sums of money at another profession, according to investigators in Norfolk and Suffolk counties in Massachusetts.

But her sex games apparently were too much for at least one lover to handle, because police learned that the beautiful 21-year-old woman met a grisly death.

Massachusetts authorities didn't know that something terrible had happened in their state until a trash picker accidentally found some horrible evidence along State Route 95 near the Mansfield highway exit south of Boston.

It just looked like an innocuous plastic trash

bag, and the scavenger who had pulled off the highway into the rest stop was just idly curious as to what might be in it.

He spied the plastic bag and opened it up. In one respect, he wished he'd never done so, but on the other hand, his find would prove to be a valuable link in a bizarre chain of events which eventually would solve a horrible murder.

When the trash picker first saw the contents of the bag he didn't realize what he'd found. It just looked like some slimy garment, a corduroy blazer. But the bag was too heavy for just that, and as the trash picker moved the blazer he got some of the slime on his fingers. Then he realized what he was into—a bloody bag of clothes.

A bloody bag of clothes at a highway rest stop is not the type of thing a person finds every day. The motorist knew something terrible must have happened, and he notified the Massachusetts State Police.

A trooper responded to the scene and agreed with the motorist. The bag of clothes obviously was evidence in an assault, and perhaps even a murder. Careful examination of the bag revealed that it contained a bloody jacket, a bloody shirt and a 2 1/2-pound hammer. Trooper and crime scene technicians determined that the evidence had merely been disposed of in that spot, and the rest area was not a crime scene.

Robin Nadine Benedict lived in Malden, Massachusetts, which is approximately 12 miles north of Boston as the crow flies. On March 5, 1983 she did not return to her home, and the following day she didn't show up for work. Friends became very worried about the girl and reported the incident to local authorities.

Police could easily see from a photograph which was provided that Robin Benedict was a knockout. She had alluring eyes, soft lips, and pretty, shoulder length hair. Any man would have been proud to be seen with her.

She had attended the Rhode Island School of Design and worked in the daytime as a graphic artist, her friends told detectives. They also revealed that Robin owned a car, a silver Toyota. A statewide alert was later broadcast regarding this auto.

Meanwhile, in talking to the woman's friends, detectives had the feeling that they were holding something back. They knew something about Robin that they didn't want to reveal. Detectives made it clear that by withholding information, they could actually be doing Robin a disservice. The truth was learned, however, when a friend of Robin's told police that Robin was good with her hands as an artist, but she earned a lot more money at her other jobs, dancing naked and giving men a good time.

At first her friend didn't want to sully Robin's reputation, but she realized that Robin's life might be in danger. It wasn't like Robin just to leave without telling somebody, so the friend told everything she knew to the police.

Robin, the friend said, worked the notorious Boston Combat Zone, and she apparently had done so for a couple of years. The Combat Zone is a section of the city which houses seamy clubs, porno parlors, peep shows and second floor apartments in old buildings, out of which hookers ply their trade.

When it became apparent that several jurisdictions were involved in the investigation into the disappearance of Robin Benedict, the case was given to Massachusetts State Police, which worked in cooperation with local police departments.

Investigators started checking into the background of the pretty woman and learned that she had been working the Combat Zone as far back as 1981. She was a bottomless dancer in one of the seamier nightclubs on the strip, according to what police could learn. Because of her looks, the detectives knew that if she was hooking too, she would not come cheaply. And they were right. Their investigation revealed that she could fetch as much as $100 for a single session.

But investigators realized something else as well. The average John frequenting the Combat Zone didn't have $100 to drop for a single thrill. Most of the men would only be able to afford one of the cheaper hookers who worked out of the old apartments, which meant that whoever was responsible for her disappearance was no derelict. He had to be a man who could afford such talent, detectives reasoned. He was probably upper middle class with a good job. Robin was careful and wouldn't associate with anybody who looked dangerous or suspicious.

Working on that theory, investigators questioned Robin's friends and asked if she had any particular John whom she may have been fleecing. They learned that indeed there was a man who had played a prominent role in her life during the past year.

"Who was that?" an investigator asked Robin's friend.

"His name is Bill Douglas," the friend told investigators. "He's a professor, or something like that at a university."

It was not a difficult task for Massachusetts State Police Sgt. Richard Zebrasky and other investigators working the case to learn the identity of the university professor. Dr. William H. Douglas, 41, was a professor of anatomy at Tufts University in Cambridge.

Investigators continued their probe into the girl's disappearance and learned that on March 5th, she had an appointment with the university professor at his home in the exclusive suburb of Sharon, south of Boston.

Investigators paid William Douglas a visit and asked him pointed questions about his actions on March 5, 1983. To their surprise, he was cooperative and readily admitted that Robin Benedict had made an appearance at his home that evening. Another person living in the house could even verify that, the professor told the detectives. But Robin left his house about 11 o'clock or 11:30 p.m., according to his recollection.

The time was closer to midnight, the person who also lived in the house told detectives. The witness could be sure of the time because, at 11:30, she was returning to the home and saw Benedict's car in the driveway. But Robin was gone by midnight, the witness assured, and William Douglas was in bed at that time.

It appeared to investigators that they'd come to a dead end. William Douglas apparently was not involved in the disappearance of Robin Benedict. He merely had the misfortune to be the last one to see the lovely young woman before she vanished. Investigators realized that after Robin delivered some graphic art design to Douglas, she may have left his home for another appointment at somebody's else's residence in the early morning hours of March 6th.

"Did she mention anything about where she was going after she left here?" a detective asked.

William Douglas and his witness both said they had no idea what was on Robin's agenda for the rest of the evening and the next morning.

"What did you do the next morning?" Douglas was asked.

Douglas said he hopped on a bus at Foxborough and went to South Station and then took a commuter train from there to Washington D.C. The witness again verified his statements.

The case was a real puzzle. With the witness backing up everything the anatomy professor said, it appeared that the sleuths were on a wild goose chase. Perhaps nothing had happened to Robin after all, and she had just taken off on a lark, theorized sleuths.

After all, she did lead the type of life in which opportunities pop up at the most unexpected time. Maybe she had the chance to take a trip with somebody else and had just decided to leave without telling anybody. After all, if she had taken off with another rich man, there certainly wouldn't have been any reason for her to pack a bag. She could just buy a new wardrobe and leave her old clothes at her Malden apartment until her return, whenever that might be. If things were good enough in her new circumstances, maybe she would never return, detectives speculated.

All of the scenarios were possibilities that weren't without merit, and they had to be seriously considered. But still, detectives wanted to find out what happened to Robin Nadine Benedict, regardless of what the answer might be. They desperately wanted to account for her whereabouts as did her friends and relatives.

Investigators checked into the relationship which Robin and William Douglas allegedly had. Witnesses told them that the relationship was hot and heavy, and at times could have been construed as frightening.

Robin met William Douglas in 1982 while she was working as a bottomless dancer and prostitute, witnesses told the detectives. There was nothing unusual about that. And it wasn't even very alarming that Douglas allegedly became one of the girl's regular customers. But then the relationship got much more serious, according to what the state police inspectors learned. In April of 1982, William Douglas was beyond the point of being infatuated with Robin—he was possessed, according to witnesses who knew Robin, and knew details of her freelancing in the evenings.

Douglas was willing to do anything to win the woman's affection. State inspectors decided to delve further into that allegation, and they soon discovered that it had considerable merit. A check on the doctor's financial affairs revealed that he, indeed, was willing to do almost anything for the pretty girl, including misappropriating university funds to the tune of approximately $67,400.

He apparently used this money to live in his fashionable home in Sharon but also to provide comfortably for Miss Benedict.

As detectives dug deeper, however, they learned that the problems began to set in on their relationship when his money well began to run low. You can only draw from it for so long, and then the supply is exhausted. That was the case with Professor Douglas and his money, as nearly as detectives could figure. Perhaps the doctor had visions at one time that Robin would fall in love with him and he would no longer have to buy her favors. Nobody knows what thoughts were going through his mind toward the close of 1982, when the couple started arguing on what witnesses said seemed to be a regular basis.

With the new year, Robin had resolved to have the anatomy professor out of her life, state investigators learned. The sleuths got hold of romantic letters which allegedly were written by Dr. Douglas to her. In those letters it was obvious that Robin was trying to end the affair, and the doctor was pleading for her to continue it even though his money supply was exhausted.

It was clear in the letters that Dr. Douglas feared the relationship was nearly over. Upon questioning friends of Robin, inspectors learned that three days before she disappeared, she had made it clear that the affair was over. That explained why she had taken some graphic art work up to his home on March 5th, detectives realized. Under the pretense of wanting her professional talents, Dr. Douglas could lure her to his home one more time. She wouldn't have come to provide sexual favors because she'd terminated the relationship.

State Police investigators reasoned that if the affair was on the rocks by January of 1983, then perhaps some incidents had occurred between the two which were reported to other police departments.

Their hunch was correct. After contacting other departments in different jurisdictions, the state inspectors got still more evidence which seemed to indicate that Dr. Douglas was their man.

The Lynn Police Department contacted the State Police in connection with the case. Lynn is a coastal town near East Point on Boston Bay.

According to Lynn Police, in February of 1983, Dr. William Douglas of Tufts University had filed a complaint against Robin Nadine Benedict. In the complaint, Douglas alleged that Robin had stolen from him some very important slides, papers and a key to a joint safety deposit box which they had at a national bank in Lynn.

Then later in 1983, state detectives learned, Douglas filed a similar complaint with the Sharon Police Department. A Sharon policeman told the State Police that he had observed an argument between Dr. Douglas and Robin Benedict. Both of them accused the other of stealing, the policeman told detectives. As near as he could determine, Robin admitted she did go to the safety deposit box and removed something. But they never revealed what it was.

If Dr. Douglas did murder Robin, detectives speculated, he at least had two motives. He didn't want their relationship to end. Perhaps the thought of her loving another man would drive him to murder. And his second motive, of course, was to protect his own hide. He probably finally realized that the affair was indeed over, and that if she wanted to, Robin could easily blackmail him because she knew he'd filched funds from the university research fund.

She could continue to bleed him for more money, and he'd have to resort to filing even more false reports and vouchers and the vicious circle would go on forever. If she didn't care for him anymore, it was doubtful she would have reservations about fleecing him for even more bucks, the professor could have figured. If he thought along those lines, then he may have concluded his only escape from the dangerous situation was to go directly to the source of the trouble and snuff the threat, detectives surmised. Thus, jealousy and self-preservation were his two sound motives.

Even though Dr. Douglas seemed to have the motives, and there was the circumstantial evidence involving his relationship with the woman, the fact that he had a sound alibi and a witness puzzled detectives. And things became more complicated when they learned that Robin had left a message with her answering service sometime around midnight after she supposedly left the Douglas residence in Sharon.

While checking into the young woman's background, detectives had tried to learn as much about her as possible. One of the details they discovered is that she had an answering service she periodically checked in with.

"She said she was going to visit Fred in Charlestown," the operator at her answering service told detectives when she checked the company's records.

Perhaps, detectives speculated, they had been on the wrong track all along. Maybe Fred was their man. After all, Dr. Douglas said Robin left his home and he was in bed by midnight, and his witness verified that. The answering service seemed to verify it too, and it would have been a reasonable assumption to say that Robin was alive at midnight.

And so a new suspect had entered into the picture. Since police believed Robin was an expensive call girl, it was reasonable to assume that lurking somewhere in the shadows was a man she might be supporting. Perhaps that is why she was so firm in breaking off her relationship with Dr. Douglas. Maybe there was a jealous boyfriend who had decided that things had gotten too cozy, and she was thinking of really hitching her wagon to the professor. It was a possibility that had to be checked out. To ignore such a thing would not be sound police procedure.

Charlestown, New Hampshire is located approximately 509 miles north of Massachusetts on the New Hampshire/Vermont border. It's nearly a couple hours' drive from Robin's home, which was Malden, Mass. It seemed odd that she would make the drive so late at night. And if she left the doctor's house around 11:30 or 11:45 p.m. and telephoned her answering service around midnight, she must have been south of her hometown, which would have made the drive even longer.

Detectives questioned Fred who lived in Charlestown. Although he had to be considered a suspect, the sleuths couldn't get anything on him. He wasn't too thrilled about talking to police, but relished even less the idea of turning himself into a prime suspect through belligerence. He denied ever hearing from or seeing Robin during the early morning hours of March 6, 1983.

So sleuths were at another dead end.

Meanwhile, the body bag of clothing and hammer that were found by the motorist at the rest stop near Mansfield had been taken to the state crime laboratory for examination, and the report came in.

"A strand of dark hair was found on the hammer," a technician told detectives working the case. "There was blood on the hammer and the clothing," he continued. The clothing consisted of a woman's corduroy jacket and a man's shirt, and the blood on the clothing and hammer was type "A," the same type of Robin Benedict's.

Friends identified the corduroy jacket as belonging to Robin. Detectives could reasonably assume that Robin had been attacked and possibly murdered somewhere in Massachusetts. Part of the evidence had been disposed of at the rest stop. If that was the case, how was she able to telephone her answering service and say she was heading in just the opposite direction, north toward Charlestown, New Hampshire.

"What if she didn't make the call?" a detective speculated. "What if it was somebody else, disguising her voice?"

It was a cinch that the answering service, which has a huge list of clients, couldn't positively identify the person as Robin. It could have been just about any woman, or even a man adept at disguising his voice to sound like a woman, who called and said it was Robin Benedict and left the message. But how could the detectives prove that? Perhaps, the sleuths reasoned, the person had made the mistake of calling long distance. Not more than a half hour prior to the incoming message, Robin had been in Sharon, Massachusetts. It was a logical assumption that whoever snatched her and maybe killed her was in the same territory, and that was long distance.

State Police detectives checked the telephone records and learned that the call that Robin Benedict allegedly placed had been long distance. And the call had come from the home of Dr. William Douglas. The message that she was going to see Fred in Charlestown was a smokescreen to throw detectives off the track. Now the cops were sure that Douglas was their man. He'd gone to elaborate lengths to cast suspicion elsewhere, and the plan had failed.

That being the situation, Dr. Douglas definitely was trying to hide something, the investigators concluded. And since the witness had supported his alibi, it was reasonable to think that the witness might be lying to protect the professor. Thus, detectives decided to find out if Dr. Douglas had been in bed at midnight and had gone to Washington D.C. the following morning, as he'd claimed. Only this time they would have to find some evidence, since it was obvious they couldn't depend on the witness for any accurate information.

The evidence broke unexpectedly. Robin's silver Toyota was found in New York City. Forensic experts descended upon the vehicle, and traces of blood and tissue were discovered in the rear portion of the car. Robin Benedict's body had been transported in her own car. But where was her body?

Detectives realized that it is possible to prove a murder case even without a body. But they also knew they'd have to link Douglas with the victim. All they had was a fake phone call to her answering service. It wasn't enough, and they knew it.

But the fact that Douglas had made a major mistake with the telephone led probers to believe that he perhaps made other errors. If he was the person who drove Robin's car into New York, then maybe he placed a phone call from there to his home.

Following that line of reasoning, investigators learned that Dr. Douglas had a Tufts University credit card which he could charge long distance telephone calls on when he was not at the university.

Detectives checked the telephone company records of the Tufts account and discovered that their theory had been sound—Douglas had made a second mistake, and it was a big one. He had charged several telephone calls on the credit card at 11:42 p.m. on March 5, 1983. And the telephone that he used was directly across from the rest stop where the bloody hammer and clothing had been found by the motorist.

In October of 1983, charges were filed in Suffolk County Superior Court against Dr. Douglas in connection with the alleged stealing from the Tufts University research fund. He pleaded innocent to ten indictments charging him with 30 counts of larceny and 31 counts of filing false reports. Prosecutors said he stole $50,000 in research funds, although university officials claim about $67,400 can't be accounted for.

State detectives were still piecing together their case. They managed to crack the professor's alibi of going to Washington D.C. on March 6th. By checking bus and train records they determined that he did no such thing.

They finally had enough evidence for a search warrant, and it was promptly issued.

A search of the suspect's home was conducted and more damning evidence was found. Robin Benedict's purse, her credit cards, newspaper clippings about prostitutes, birth control devices and pornographic magazines and a pair of pink panties were found in a closet in the doctor's home.

A bloodstained jacket was also found in his ranch-style home on Sandy Ridge Circle in Sharon. All the evidence was turned over to forensic technicians, who went over it with a fine toothcomb. In so doing, they made another grisly find, one which is probably the most damaging link in the entire chain of events. It was found in a pocket of the doctor's bloodstained jacket.

It was turned over to Suffolk County Medical Examiner George Katsas who confirmed that the item was a piece of brain tissue. There is no way that the person from whom that tissue came could still be alive, the medical examiner told investigators. It was a piece of tissue from the interior of the head. The person is definitely dead, he determined.

Detectives continued their probe and found a witness who said the bloody shirt that was found at the rest stop along with Robin's jacket belonged to Dr. Douglas. Furthermore, another witness said, the hammer, believed to be the murder weapon, had been lent to Dr. Douglas

"There is probable cause that Mr. Douglas may be responsible for the murder of Robin Nadine Benedict and that the murder occurred in his home," State Trooper Paul Landry, one of many who investigated the killing, said. Other investigators, the prosecutor and a judge agreed, and a warrant was promptly issued for the doctor's arrest on a charge of murder.

Dr. Douglas was arrested in Cambridge, and according to Norfolk County Assistant District Attorney John Kivlan, the anatomy professor seemed somewhat surprised. The doctor didn't believe he could be indicted without a body, according to DA Kivlan.

In November of 1983, a grand jury was seated to determine whether Dr. Douglas should be indicted for murder. DA Kivlan laid out the evidence in much the same manner the detectives had uncovered it. He went into the background of the professor and Robin Benedict and their alleged affair.

The physical evidence was presented. The circumstantial evidence supported it. Kivlan didn't believe the lack of a body would hurt the case that much. The fact that a portion of the victim's brain was found in the professor's coat pocket seemed to be ample proof that Nadine Benedict was bludgeoned to death with a hammer lent to the doctor.

Kivlan said Douglas was unable to explain why Benedict's purse, personal papers and other items were found at his home during a police search. Kivlan said Douglas had claimed that they were planted by Benedict's boyfriend or else by the

State Police.

The grand jury returned the indictment, and Kivlan asked Judge Thomas Dwyer to hold Dr. Douglas without bail, which was done.

"There is no basis for the judge to hold him without bail," the defense attorney said, adding that he'd appeal the ruling. "He has shown up on many, many occasions throughout the course of this investigation," the attorney said. "He went about his business and was working at his job."

That made little difference in the final analysis. Dr. William Douglas was ordered held without bail.

Police, in the meantime, continued their search for Robin Nadine Benedict. State Police Sgt. Richard Zebrasky, one of the investigators on the case, speculated: "With an expert knowledge of anatomy, a person could easily dissect a body and hide the pieces."

The search for Robin Benedict dragged on with no results. The continuing investigation revealed that Douglas was so obsessed with Robin that he was always telephoning her, writing her notes, following her around, and was extremely jealous of her seeing other men.

He even paid her $100 per hour just for her company, detectives learned.

In December of 1982 he was so jealous of her that he broke into one of her apartments and stole her two Panasonic answering machines and used them to intercept her messages, the investigators learned.

That incident was one of several which caused conflict between them in early 1983, probers learned.

The case dragged on with still no sign of the corpse. The doctor did a good job of disposing of it. Assistant DA Kivlan decided to go ahead with the murder trial without the body. He was confident he could prove his case.

Jury selection began and it was a tedious process. Judge Roger Donahue presided at jury selection in Superior Court in Dedham. Prospective jurors were kept in a church across the street from the courthouse and, when called, they heard tape-recorded questions designed to weed out those who wouldn't be impartial in the case.

But then on April 27th, 1984 the case took on a new twist. In a packed courtroom on the morning his trial was to begin, William Douglas now 42, pleaded guilty to a charge of manslaughter.

Assistant DA John P. Kivlan explained he was willing to settle for the plea bargain in exchange for Douglas revealing where he hid the body of the victim. Relatives of the victim wanted to provide her with a Christian burial, an attorney representing the family explained.

"Did you murder Robin Benedict?" Judge Donahue asked Douglas.

"Yes sir," Douglas replied in a high voice.

Then Assistant DA Kivlan spent 45 minutes revealing the facts of the case, the investigation and evidence. Judge Donahue asked Douglas if the prosecution's description of the murder was as accurate as possible.

"Respectfully, I don't agree with every detail of what Assistant District Attorney Kivlan stated, but I do in fact agree with it substantially," Douglas replied.

"Did Robin Benedict come to your house on the night of March 5, 1983?" the judge asked.

"Yes, sir."

"While she was at your home, did an altercation between you and Robin Benedict occur?"

"Yes, sir."

"And during that altercation did you take up a hammer, or was a hammer in your possession with which you struck Robin Benedict?"

"Yes, sir."

"And as a result of striking Robin Benedict, did you cause her death?"

"Yes, sir."

"Did you dispose of her body thereafter?"

"Yes, sir."

"And you will cooperate with law enforcement authorities and take them to where you placed Robin Benedict's body?"

"Yes, sir."

The defendant's attorney said that Douglas finally had peace of mind after telling the truth about the matter. The attorney conceded that the evidence was insurmountable.

After pleading guilty, lawmen interviewed

Douglas for four hours. District Attorney William D. Delahunt told newsmen that when Robin's body finally was found, details wouldn't be given to the press because the victim's family had been through enough torment.

"We don't want to turn the search into a matter of public display," the prosecutor explained.

During his conversation with authorities, Douglas did reveal that he had hit his victim several times in the skull with the sledgehammer. The blows dislodged the brain tissue, he told them. He then said he disposed of the body by leaving it in a dumpster at a Providence, Rhode Island shopping mall.

The prosecutors had consulted with Robin's family prior to accepting the plea-bargain arrangement. The family had agreed to it on the condition that Douglas reveal where he hid the body and account for all of his actions on the night of her murder.

On May 7th, William Douglas was sentenced by Judge Donahue to the maximum (which the prosecution had recommended) 18 to 20 years in prison for the manslaughter.

"Manslaughter it may be, but it's about as close to murder as you can get," Asst. DA Kivlan said Monday in arguing for the maximum sentence.

It must be stressed that at the time this story was written, the theft charges against Douglas in connection with the Tufts University research accounts had not been resolved, and he must be presumed innocent of those charges unless proven otherwise in a court of law.

EDITOR'S NOTE:

Fred is not the real name of the person so named in the foregoing story. A fictitious name has been used because there is no reason for public interest in the identity of this person.

"SHROUDED THE NAKED BODY IN CAT FOOD!"

by Gary Ebbels

The morning of Dec. 30, 1983 was a windy one in downtown Las Vegas. It was a Friday and another work week was about to come to an end. An apartment manager was in his office reviewing the weekly rent receipts.

But his work was interrupted by a knock on the door. The manager answered the knock. It was one of the tenants and he was looking for Az "Jack" Peterson.

He told the manager he hadn't seen Jack or his latest lady for several days. It was the 70-year-old Jack's pattern to bring a prostitute to his apartment for a few days each month when he received his military pension, and he had not broken the pattern this month. He had been seen with a prostitute earlier in the week, as a matter of fact.

The apartment manager shrugged off the tenant's worry over the prospect of something bad having happened to Jack. But the tenant insisted the manager use a pass key to check out Jack's apartment.

The manager agreed, and the two went to Jack's apartment. The manager put the pass key in the lock and slowly turned it. He started to open the door wide but a putrid odor backed him up. He closed the door and turned to the tenant, who had also caught the horrible smell in his nostrils.

The two men exchanged worried glances.

Then the manager again tried to open the door, only this time he held his breath to lock out the foul odor. The eyes of both men widened at the sight that greeted them in the living room. Sprawled on the floor was the half naked body of Jack Peterson.

The old man's head was bashed in. What appeared to be a piece of bone was lying beside his left hand.

And the body was covered with cat food.

The manager and the tenant backed out of the apartment. Horror was etched on their faces.

Leaving the apartment door open, the two men ran back to the manager's office and immediately placed a call to the Las Vegas Metropolitan Police Department. Fighting the urge to vomit, the manager spoke in short bursts. He told the operator who took his call that there was a battered corpse in one of his apartments.

The operator transferred the call to the homicide division where Det. Joe McGuckin took it.

The detective tried his best to calm down the manager so he could get the story straight before going to the scene with uniformed officers and a lab crew. The manager, who was growing a bit calmer at this point, explained to the detective that he and another tenant checked out the Peterson apartment with a pass key and were greeted with the grisly find.

McGuckin told the manager to wait in the office for him. He said he and other officers would be at the scene in a matter of minutes. Although the wait seemed an eternity to the manager and the tenant, it was only four or five minutes before the wail of a police siren pierced the air.

McGuckin followed the cruiser in an unmarked car. The two vehicles sped into the apartment complex parking lot. Det. McGuckin went into the office while the two uniformed officers waited in the cruiser. The apartment manager pointed across the complex to the Peterson apartment.

He told the detective the corpse was inside and that he did not want to go back over there.

McGuckin nodded in agreement and went outside. He and the uniformed officers went to the Peterson apartment and went inside.

Meanwhile, the lab crew was pulling into the parking lot in a van. McGuckin stepped to the door of the apartment and motioned the crew to come to him. Then he went back inside to check over the corpse.

He remarked to one of the lab crew members that it appeared the body had been there for a few days because of the smell. An autopsy would be done later in the day to confirm the assumption.

The detective was informed by a member of the lab crew that an ambulance had been called to get the body for the ride to the morgue where the autopsy would be performed.

When the ambulance arrived, the body was placed on a stretcher. McGuckin picked up the piece of bone that lay by the left hand of the dead Jack Peterson and placed it on the stretcher with him. While this was going on, the lab crew began combing the crime scene for physical evidence.

In another part of the room was a hammer and a vacuum tube. Both were caked with blood.

A member of the lab crew examined them both. A fingerprint could be seen in the caked blood on the vacuum tube. Slowly and skillfully the lab member lifted the print.

Although the two bloody items would be taken to the lab for testing and an analysis of the blood, the lab member did not want to take a chance in having the fingerprint damaged during its transport. That was why he decided to lift it at the crime scene, even though it would have been easier to do it in the lab.

McGuckin, meanwhile, had been quietly looking over the apartment. Blood seemed to be everywhere—the walls, the floors and even the ceiling. It was apparent the hammer and the tube had been used in the beating death.

The detective returned to the office where the manager and the tenant waited. One asked if the body of Jack's latest lady friend had been found, too.

McGuckin said only one body—that of Jack Peterson—had been found. He asked what lady friend the two men were talking about, and they told him of Jack's monthly pattern.

The detective asked if they could give him a description of the prostitute who had been Jack's lady friend this month. After all, she could be a suspect. And if she were a known prostitute, the chances were good that she had been arrested at least once and that her fingerprints would be on file. And if her prints matched the blood-caked fingerprints, the case against her would be strong.

But the two were unable to offer much of a description. Neither man had paid much attention to her. They'd seen her outside the apartment with Jack one or two times. But since he lined up a prostitute every month, there was no need for either man to single this one out.

The detective elected to check with other tenants.

Maybe one of them had taken particular notice

of the prostitute.

But it appeared none had. The ones who had seen her could offer only very sketchy descriptions. Those descriptions were all about the same but they were too general to narrow down. The police mug books were full of photos of women who fit the general description.

A discouraged McGuckin was ready to leave the complex when a man came out of one of the apartments. He said he had heard the detective was looking for someone who could describe the mystery prostitute.

He said he might be able to do it because he had gotten a good look at her three days earlier when he was outside working on his car. The man said the prostitute, with her two small children, ran across the parking lot that particular morning. He remembered she was clad only in a red nightgown.

The witness said he got a pretty good look at her face when she ran by him and then thought little more about it.

Later that day, he continued, he saw the prostitute return to Jack's apartment in the company of a man and another woman. He recalled the trio went inside and came out a few minutes later.

The description of the prostitute which he offered was much more detailed than the ones the others had given. McGuckin hastily wrote down the description and returned to headquarters.

Here he checked the mug books for known prostitutes. He found a photo of a face that fit the detailed description and returned to the apartment complex with it.

Again he knocked on doors. The first woman to answer his knock identified the photo as that of the prostitute with whom Jack had been living.

But she was the only one who did.

Other tenants said that that was not the prostitute. The man who gave the detective the detailed description said it was definitely not the prostitute but that it did look somewhat like her.

McGuckin returned to headquarters and began a preliminary file on the Peterson murder. The day was drawing to a close and the autopsy report would not be available until the following morning.

The report was on the detective's desk when he arrived at headquarters the morning of Dec. 31st. The details were far from pretty.

Jack Peterson had been slammed on the head at least 15 times, according to the report. And that piece of bone that had been lying beside his left hand was a part of his skull.

All five fingers of the victim's left hand had been broken. There were numerous cuts and bruises on both hands and both arms, according to the report. The cause of death was put at a skull fracture.

When he was through reading the report,

McGuckin telephoned fellow Det. Al Leavitt on the inter-office hook-up and asked if he would like to help him on the case. He briefly outlined the situation for Leavitt, who agreed to assist in the investigation.

Leavitt entered McGuckin's office and the two then went over the statements and descriptions offered by residents of the apartment complex. But with no further leads, that was about all they could do at this point in the probe. This day passed and so did another two with no break in the case.

On the morning of Jan. 3rd, though, a woman telephoned police headquarters. She asked to speak with the detective who was investigating the Jack Peterson slaying.

McGuckin took the call.

The woman said she had a girlfriend and that her girlfriend's mother might know something about the killing. She gave the sleuth the name of the woman and then hung up without identifying herself.

McGuckin rang Leavitt's office, told him of the possible break in the case and asked if he wanted to go to the woman's home with him. Leavitt agreed to go.

The woman was home when the two detectives rang her bell. And when they confronted her with the fact she had been referred to them by the anonymous caller, she agreed to cooperate.

The woman said she had reason to believe the

murder was committed by her daughter's boyfriend's sister. She said she had learned that the boyfriend's sister had been living with Jack Peterson for a few days and had ended up killing him. She said the boyfriend's sister had two small children and that they, too, had been living with Peterson.

But she said she did not know the woman's name.

She said she knew only that this woman had admitted the killing to her brother and his girlfriend and had taken them to the crime scene a few hours after the killing.

This confirmed what the one neighbor had told McGuckin. That neighbor had recalled seeing the prostitute, with a man and another woman, return to the apartment the same day he had seen her running from it with her two children.

The woman promised the detectives she would contact her daughter and find out the name of the suspect. She said she would telephone them at headquarters as soon as she found out.

The detectives returned to headquarters and added the woman's statement to the Peterson file.

McGuckin called Hank Truszkowski in the identification lab. He asked if the fingerprint in the blood was good enough to make a match.

The expert said he believed he would be able to match it. McGuckin said he hoped to have a print very shortly.

It was later afternoon Jan. 3rd when the

woman who had promised to get a name for the suspect called headquarters. Leavitt took her call.

She said the first name of the prostitute was Norrissa. She said that was the only name she knew because her last name was different from that of her brother.

Leavitt and McGuckin obtained the files on all the known prostitutes in Las Vegas. Using these files, the two worked backwards, using a first name rather than a last name as a point of reference.

The name Norrissa is not a common one so chances were the first time they came across anyone with that name it would also be the last. They came to the name Norrissa Louise Milton, a 26-year-old known prostitute.

McGuckin pulled the woman's fingerprint card and took it to Truszkowski in the lab. He waited while the identification expert began making the comparison. Carefully, the expert worked up the comparison.

When he was finished he turned to McGuckin and told him the prints matched. He said there was no doubt the print furnished by McGuckin was that of the killer.

Now all the sleuths had to do was find Norrissa Milton.

They put the word out on the street that they were looking for her. They let the snitches know they wanted her for murder.

Two days passed, though, and nothing came

back from the street. The stool pigeons were unable to find out where she might be hiding.

But, just as the detectives had had to work in reverse to find out the suspect's last name, the idea of putting the word out on the street was also about to work in reverse. While the street people with whom the detectives were working were unable to find the suspect, somehow word had gotten to her that the police were closing in. That word had reached her indirectly from the stool pigeons and other street people through whom the detectives had spread the word.

It was late afternoon Jan. 6th when a young woman walked into police headquarters. She calmly told the receptionist at the homicide division she understood she was wanted for murder.

She said her name was Norrissa Milton.

The receptionist buzzed McGuckin's office and told him he had a visitor and that her name was Norrissa Milton. The detective hurried to the reception area.

When the woman identified herself he hastily gave her the Miranda warning.

Then he took her back to his office. Before he left the reception area, he told the receptionist to contact Det. Leavitt and send him to his office. The receptionist buzzed Leavitt's office and told him the suspect had surrendered and was with McGuckin. Leavitt went to his partners office as soon as he heard the news.

McGuckin had elected to hold all questioning

until Leavitt could join him.

At this point he wasn't sure the woman was going to make a statement. When Leavitt entered the office McGuckin again gave the suspect her Miranda warning. Upon being told she had the right to remain silent, she said she would talk. She said she wanted to tell her side of the story.

Milton said Peterson was just another trick to her. She said he had some money and offered to take her and her two children off the streets for a few days.

She said she agreed to move in for a price. The price was met and she moved in.

She said Peterson was drunk the morning of Dec. 27th and was being mean to one of her children. She said she hit him over the head when he wouldn't back off and then ran out of the apartment with her two children.

McGuckin asked her how many times she hit the old man over the head and she said only once or twice.

The detective told her the autopsy report showed at least 15 blows to the head. The woman said she didn't know anything about 15 blows and exercised her right to silence at this time.

The woman was booked into the Clark County Jail on a charge of open murder. The detectives, while figuring she lied about the number of times she had slammed Peterson over the head, knew she was telling the truth about one thing.

The autopsy had shown the victim had a

blood-alcohol count of .21 at the time he was murdered. In Nevada and in most states, a blood-alcohol count of .10 is enough for a legal presumption of intoxication. In this case, Peterson's blood had more than twice the amount of alcohol necessary for a legal presumption of intoxication.

Milton, meanwhile, had nothing more to say about the case.

In mid-February, a Justice Court preliminary hearing was held for her. Such hearings are open to the public, unlike grand jury hearings, and witnesses are subject to cross-examination. It is the duty of the prosecution at these hearings to show the presiding justice of the peace, in this case Kelly O. Slade, that there is enough evidence against the defendant to warrant a trial in District Court.

Deputy District Attorney Chris Owens handled the case for the state. Using the bloody fingerprint and the confession, self-serving as it was, Owens easily won on the Justice Court level. Slade bound the case over for trial in District Court.

The defense offered nothing at the hearing, which is normally the case. The defense never likes to tip its hand on the Justice Court level. It merely sits back and listens to what the state has up its sleeve.

While Owens had no problem with the case on the Justice Court level, he knew things might be different in front of a District Court jury. He knew the defendant was going to say Peterson was drunk and molesting her children and that whatever she did to him she did to protect the little ones.

On April 2nd, trial was scheduled in the courtroom of District Judge Donald Mosley.

With the charge being open murder, it would be up to the jury to choose a degree in finding Milton guilty. The panel could find her guilty of first-degree murder, second-degree murder, voluntary manslaughter or involuntary manslaughter. The jury could also find her innocent, but that did not seem a possibility in light of the state's evidence, which included her confession.

But D.A. Owens was worried about a possible manslaughter verdict. After all, the autopsy showed the man was intoxicated, and this backed up Milton's story.

If the jury were to find Milton guilty of first-degree murder, it would be up to its members to sentence her to life in prison, with or without the possibility of parole, or to death by lethal injection.

Any lesser finding of guilt would result in the judge's handing down a punishment.

While Owens worried about jury-sympathy coming into play for the defendant, Milton's public defender attorney was worried that an unsympathetic jury might send his client to her death. Both attorneys agreed the case was ripe for plea-bargaining if Milton would go along with it.

D.A. Owens was offering a deal that would spare Milton's life but that would also keep her locked up for many, many years, if not forever.

The prosecutor said he would reduce the charge to second-degree murder in exchange for the guilty plea. But he also alleged the use of a deadly weapon in the commission of a crime. This allegation automatically brings about a double punishment.

Whatever sentence Mosley might hand down for the second-degree murder plea would be mirrored with the allegation of the use of a deadly weapon.

The public defender lawyer approached Milton with the state's offer. At first she was reluctant to go along with it. But when the attorney noted her life would be hanging in the balance if she were to go to trial and be convicted of first-degree murder, she took the deal.

On March 30th, the Friday before the scheduled Monday start of the trial, Milton pleaded guilty to second-degree murder. She was then returned to her county jail cell to await an April 30th sentencing.

Second-degree murder in Nevada is not probationable. It is punishable by a term of five years to life behind bars with parole a possibility as soon as five years have been served. In the month between the taking of the guilty plea and the sentencing, a pre-sentencing investigation and report was carried out.

Judge Mosley reviewed the report before meting out the punishment.

When Milton stood before him for sentencing April 30th, the judge told her she had turned Peterson's face "into hamburger" with the beating she had administered.

Then he handed down twin life prison sentences. Milton would be eligible for parole after serving five years of the first sentence. If she were lucky enough to be granted parole upon first becoming eligible, she would then have to serve at least five years of the next term before once again becoming eligible for freedom.

In commenting on the case after the sentencing, D.A. Owens said he was happy with the outcome of the plea-bargaining.

He said he wanted to get the woman off the streets for a good long time and that the guilty plea had served the purpose without the risk of a sympathetic jury finding her guilty of nothing more than manslaughter.

Even with the allegation of the use of a deadly weapon, the maximum prison sentence the woman would have faced would have been 20 years on a finding of voluntary manslaughter and 12 years on a finding of involuntary manslaughter.

"DRAG QUEEN SMEARED MAKEUP ON HIS NUDE VICTIM!"

by Eric Wakin

New York City, August 6, 1983. Years of cleaning hotel rooms might have prepared Jane Daly for many surprising and shocking incidents, but no amount of experience could have readied her for the horrible sight that awaited discovery in suite 1603 of the elegant Gorham hotel in New York City.

The eight million inhabitants in New York City have produced more than their fair share of degenerates, psychopaths and common criminals. It was a strange combination of these three types that descended upon the Gorham hotel on that humid night in the form of a solitary man. That man was a murderer.

The city of New York is a sprawling metropolis with the 23 square-mile island of Manhattan at its center. Its residences range from decayed tenements to opulent block-long apartments in luxury buildings. The broiling dog-days of summer in the city, when you can really fry an egg on the pavement, as the proverbial expression goes, usher in a restless, uneasy time for residents. Violent crimes, particularly murders, increase as people, hemmed in by the blazing concrete and steel, struggle to escape.

Murder isn't anything new in the Big Apple. In fact, there are thousands every year, hundreds of which remain unsolved forever. Only the most diligent police work and the most dedicated investigators prevented this particular slaying from falling into the open but unsolved file.

By the time Jane Daly reached the top-floor suite, it was late in the afternoon. She knew that the only residence above the sixteenth story was a single penthouse, roofside apartment, and its maintenance was not her responsibility. Daly was hoping to be finished with her round of duties ahead of schedule so she could enjoy the early evening hours resting in a cool place. At precisely 4:10 p.m. she entered suite 1603 to perform her routine cleaning. However, any thought of finishing up early for the day was cut short by the ghastly scene that greeted her in the bedroom.

Daly's roving eyes first noticed a few articles of clothing strewn about the floor. They seemed to be out of place in the usually neat rooms. But, as she moved further into the suite, knowing it was her job to straighten the disarray, it became clear beyond any doubt that this was no ordinary

292

mess. The entire bedroom was strewn about with clothing, cosmetics and personal articles. Daly's eyes were now riveted to the room's double bed. Stunned and unbelieving, she tried to comprehend what she was seeing. There, face-down, with her nightgown pulled up over her waist, lay the cosmetic-smeared body of a middle-aged woman.

Although stunned, the housekeeper had the intelligence and good sense not to disturb the crime scene. Her voice choked with horror, she did what every good citizen would do in a similar situation if he or she could keep from going into shock—she immediately sought help. The hotel management was equally stunned, but quickly summoned the police. Murder may be common in the flea-bag tenements that pass for single-room occupancy hotels and homes for prostitutes, pushers and pimps in New York City, but it is a rare happening, indeed, in the elegant midtown hotels of the wealthy.

Police officers arrived almost instantly at the hotel's 55th street entrance. They were ushered through the beautifully-mirrored foyer and up to the sixteenth floor. It only took the uniformed officers a few moments, after surveying the extent of the damage and murder, to realize that the investigation would need to be broadened to include detectives skilled in the specialized examination of homicides. Fingerprint experts, crime lab photographers and a medical examiner were also summoned.

While the three-room suite was dusted for fingerprints and pictures of the victim and crime scene were being taken, Detective John Johnston of the Midtown North Detective Unit arrived to take over the investigation.

Johnston began by ascertaining who the murder victim was and how long she had been a guest at the hotel. Preliminary information of this kind was obtained from the hotel management. Johnston was told the woman was socialite and journalist Lenore Gilbey who had checked in on Saturday, July 30th.

She was in a predicament that many New Yorkers find themselves in, police were told. Having moved out of one apartment, Gilbey was waiting to move into another. The midtown hotel had seemed a safe place to wait out the move.

The Gorham is a small but elegant hotel opposite the famous City Center, where various cultural events, such as ballet, are performed. It is within easy walking distance of the Museum of Modern Art, the Fifth Avenue shopping district and many other places the well-to-do guest might want to visit. It was in this hotel that Mrs. Lenore Gilbey rented a $105 per night suite, complete with living room and bedroom. It certainly had seemed pleasant until the early morning hours of the following Saturday, when the socialite was killed in what a judge would later call, "one of the most vicious crimes in the city."

Detective Johnston learned that Gilbey was currently a professional fundraiser for charitable and non-profit organizations, and she mostly divided her time between New York City and London, England. Lenore Gilbey had once been married to Anthony Gilbey, heir to the multi-million dollar English Gilbey gin fortune. During the hectic decades of the 1950's and 1960's the Gilbeys were part of the group of wealthy international travellers known as the London and Paris "jet set." They both had worked as journalists: he, for various racing publications, and she, as a freelance writer for women's magazines. The most saddening fact to come to light was that the pair had three children who would never see their mother alive again.

The medical examiner pronounced Mrs. Gilbey dead and listed suffocation as the possible cause of death, pending an autopsy. The fingerprint experts informed Detective Johnston that they had found no complete prints, only smudges, in addition to those of Mrs. Gilbey. The preliminaries were over with and Johnston pounced on the suite. He searched every ransacked inch looking for clues.

The complete rifling of Gilbey's clothes and personal effects led the detective to surmise that the killer was looking for something. However, the complete disarray made it impossible to deduce what, if anything, had been taken. Detective Johnston examined the bed, floor, bureaus, closets and bathroom of the suite but found nothing. After a complete sweep of the interior, he walked over to the small balcony overlooking the street below. There was a set of drapes hanging down from the penthouse above. There was a possibility that the killer entered by way of the balcony, but he would have had to be a particularly daring and determined person to attempt the steep, 15-foot-climb, even if he used the drapes.

Despite his exacting study, the detective was left with only the most basic facts: a middle-aged woman was murdered, possibly by suffocation, in her hotel suite; parts of her body were smeared with cosmetics in what appeared to be a sexual assault; her room was thoroughly ransacked by a killer who may have entered through the balcony. With only these facts at hand, the detective's analysis could lead him to consider burglary, rape or murder, or a combination of these, for the motive of this horrendous crime.

Johnston was troubled by the lack of any stranger's fingerprints in the suite. It indicated the killer was either very careful or very lucky.

Gilbey's past associations with numerous people might've given someone reason to kill her, but Johnston doubted it. Perhaps she had something in the room that someone wanted. Perhaps a random cat-burglar had climbed into her room expecting to find jewels or other valuables. Whatever the motive, Johnston was determined to crack the case and find out.

He broadened the scope of the investigation. The next phase called for intensive manpower, so Detective Johnston requested assistance from two fellow detectives with whom he had worked before.

Detective Juan Crosass-Medina and Detective Jerry Georgio of the Detective Borough Manhattan Task Force had helped him crack the Waldorf-Astoria stabbing in 1982, but that was another story. Now they were working together in an effort to piece together the events that led to this murder and to apprehend the killer.

The three detectives questioned every hotel guest and employee. They needed to find out if anybody knew anything about the crime or had any knowledge of weird occurrences or had heard noises during the night of the murder. This was no small task, considering the hotel has 16 U-shaped floors with eight rooms on each. The investigators walked the halls knowing that their painstaking work would turn up something. Indeed, it was during these hours of diligent and careful questioning that the three investigators learned of several strange occurrences on the night of the murder and on the morning after. These leads grew into concrete results.

Detectives learned that on the night before Gilbey's body was discovered, two women reported to the desk clerk the sighting of a nude black man in the hallway outside their room. But the management was unable to locate the stranger in the hallway. Hotel life can lead to some wild pranks, but the detectives thought this particular incident was very much out of the ordinary. Although the women had already checked out, sleuths got their home address and telephone number in the event further information would be needed, which seemed likely.

The investigators then turned to Jane Daly, discoverer of the body. They asked the distraught woman if she had noticed anything unusual on Friday or Saturday. The housekeeper could only recount one incident that she thought odd. While still early in her shift, at a time she said was about 10:00 a.m., she noticed a young black Muslim in the hallway. She identified him as such by the traditional Islamic skullcap he wore.

Muslims in flowing robes and skullcaps are a common sight in New York City, but Daly hadn't seen any in the hotel lately. She only glanced at his face briefly but described him as best she could to the detectives as a young black man in his early twenties. Other than this, there was nothing she had noticed until finding Gilbey's body.

The spells of monotonous, room-by-room questioning were punctuated by the occasional person, like Daly, who had something of possible interest to tell the detectives. Another break came when they questioned a hotel porter.

He mentioned that a woman had casually remarked to him about a man in drag leaving the hotel at the same time she had left. She described him to the porter as wearing a woman's pair of blue shorts, a red top, some sort of slippers and a bath cap for a hat. The strangeness of his outfit, even in New York City, struck her. By questioning the porter further, the detectives learned that this woman was one of the two women who had reported a nude man in the hall the night before. Even more importantly, the woman noted a similarity between the nude man and the transvestite. She thought them to be one and the same!

The detectives now had something tangible to work with. A Muslim, a nudist, and a transvestite had all been sighted in the hotel around the time of the murder. The similarity in the witness' descriptions of them led probers to surmise that several different people had seen the same man.

As they worked their way through the hotel in an attempt to gather more information about the mysterious nude, the detectives reached the ninth floor room of Richard Davis, a visiting businessman staying at the hotel. Davis cooperated fully with the detectives and provided the payoff clue that made all of their painstaking work worthwhile.

He admitted to having had a male black visitor whose description fit that of the hallway nude, as a guest in his room on Friday night. The detectives knew they were on to something and told

Davis to tell them the whole story from the beginning—everything he remembered.

Davis said he had met a young man, who called himself Lawrence Smith, on the street on Friday afternoon. He suggested they go out in the evening. Smith accepted. They went to the Times Square area for a few drinks. Later the two returned to the hotel with a non-working antique radio that still was sitting in Davis' room. After spending some time together, Davis said the two had an argument, and he chased Smith into the hallway where the young man disappeared in the hotel.

However, in his haste to flee the room, the mysterious Mr. Smith left behind some things. These included his clothes, two tickets to a New York Jets football game, a religious book written in Arabic, and several photographs of himself. He left no identification, perhaps because he wasn't carrying any in the sweat suit he wore that evening.

When the detectives showed the picture to the housekeeper, Daly identified the man in it as the Muslim she spotted in the hallway on Saturday morning. The two women who had spotted the transvestite leaving the hotel also described him in a way that fit Smith's picture.

The detectives had ferreted out at least one suspect through their intensive police work. They had the "Lucky break," (as Detective Johnston called it) of his clumsiness to thank for leaving behind a picture. If Smith was the same man who murdered Lenore Gilbey, his good luck at not leaving any fingerprints in suite 1603 was eliminated by his bad luck at leaving Davis' room too quickly to pick up his things. Of course, as skeptical sleuths, the detectives were not about to believe the nude man's name really was Smith. But, whatever his name might be, they began to focus on him as the prime suspect.

In an unlikely, but vaguely possible scenario, the detectives first considered the chance that Smith might've simply left the hotel after Davis last saw him. They checked out the lobby and noted the location of the elevator. It is far from the front desk and near the main entrance. But, even in the so-called "Naked City" of New York, a nude man exiting a prominent midtown hotel would be noticed. He would've had to obtain some covering for himself and some money to take a taxi. These were readily available in Gilbey's room. No, the detectives thought, Smith didn't leave the hotel immediately after exiting Davis' room.

The detectives picked each other's brains attempting to follow the trail that may have led Smith to Gilbey's suite. By reenacting the steps the murderer took, they sought to discover his method and motives.

Detectives agreed that it was unlikely Lenore Gilbey, an intelligent city dweller for some time, allowed a nude stranger into her suite through the front door. They examined the layout of the three-room suite and discovered the only other possible way of entrance was through the balcony, actually more of an ornamental balustrade, facing the street. The hanging drapes that Johnston noticed from the penthouse above further indicated this.

The detectives traced the path of the nude Mr. Smith from the ninth floor, up a clean gray staircase bordering the elevator shafts to the seventeenth floor. Here, he bypassed the penthouse apartment and went out through an open metal door to the roof. Once there, he wandered around the outer brick walls of the penthouse on the tiled roof. He looked for an escape route but found none. He then passed through an open wrought iron gate in an archway and approached the front of the hotel. Only a yard-high iron fence held him back from the street 200 feet below. Closer than the street, only about 15 feet beneath him, was the balcony of Lenore Gilbey.

Probers reasoned that the killer didn't know who lived there but figured he could get in by climbing down the drapes and side of the building. The detectives surmised he went in search of clothing, money and an escape route. He entered the suite, and she surprised him. He attacked her in an effort to keep her quiet. Somehow, his fear, anger and determination was twisted into something else. He mercilessly sexually assaulted and killed the innocent woman and then proceeded to ransack her possessions. He dressed in what clothing he found, either before or after sleeping with Gilbey, and then left in the morning.

The repugnance of the crime would cause Justice Sybil Hart Kooper to remark: "You would think that a woman in a 16th floor hotel room would be assured of privacy and safety. What terror she must have felt when she saw a naked man enter through her window!"

The detectives now had a clearer picture of how the killer entered the suite and what he did. They figured the three strange men sighted in the hotel corresponded with Smith soon after leaving Davis' room, Smith in Gilbey's bathing cap (mistaken as a Muslim skullcap by Daly) soon after leaving the room, and Smith leaving the hotel dressed in Gilbey's clothing. Probers intended to apprehend the suspect and confront him with this information to judge his reaction.

The detectives returned to Richard Davis' room and asked him to rack his brain for any other facts that he might have forgotten to tell them about Mr. Smith. After much thought, Davis remembered something his visitor had casually mentioned. Smith said he worked at a midtown printing shop located a short distance from the hotel.

The detectives decided to pay him a visit on the next business day to find out just what he had been up to on the night of August 5th.

On Monday, they went to the shop and showed

the manager the picture of Lawrence Smith. He told the detectives that the man in the picture was employed in the shop as a messenger, but that his name was Lawrence Foye not Lawrence Smith. The detectives knew Foye thought he was a lucky man who had fooled everyone through his use of a pseudonym. Unfortunately, his luck had run out. As the carefree Mr. Foye returned from his lunch break, they arrested him for suspicion of murder. Detective Johnston was the arresting officer. He hoped a confession from Foye would confirm their hypothesis of his entry into suite 1603 and the subsequent assault and murder.

Back at headquarters, though, Foye played the sly fox, claiming he knew nothing about the murder of the socialite. The detectives told him to recount what he was doing in the Gorham hotel last Friday night. Foye was evasive at first, but decided to talk when the detectives confronted him with the fact that Davis told them a lot about him. Once detectives have amassed all the evidence about the suspect, it is often only the confrontation of him with the evidence, even if it's circumstantial, that results in a confession.

Foye knew they were on to him, but tried an alibi anyway. He told them that he met a man named Davis on the street and agreed to go out with him later in the evening. He used a business card of the out-of-towner to gain entrance to the hotel as his guest. Foye said he returned with the businessman after a night on the town. He said he was drunk from the many brandies and beers he had consumed. He claimed to have passed out and awakened to find himself the victim of a homosexual assault. He said he panicked, grabbed a brown pair of pants from Davis and fled the hotel immediately.

The detectives listened with interest to their suspect's clever story. They allowed him to finish and, as he sat hoping to have outwitted them, they confronted Foye with the discrepancies in his story. They said they knew he left Davis' room nude and somehow made his way to suite 1603, where he strangled an unsuspecting woman. They asked him if he was confident enough to take a lie detector test. He said he was.

Foye soon found himself strapped to a polygraph machine that was measuring the tiny physiological variations in his body as he spoke. Foye's simple lies were detected. He decided to tell the detectives the truth.

He said he left Davis' room in a panic without any clothes. He wandered around the hotel and made his way to the roof. He said he was looking for an escape route when he spotted a man in a blue shirt on the roof also. He said he heard sirens below and feared the police were after him. To escape, he climbed over the short fence and down Gilbey's balcony.

Since there had been no call to the police from the Gorham on Friday, the detectives determined the man Foye saw was a hotel employee whose blue shirt was mistaken for the standard uniform of New York City police officers. Sleuths looked Foye over and noticed the bruises on his arms caused by the perilous climb down the side of the hotel. He was clearly a dangerous and determined man who would have stopped at nothing, and didn't, to escape from the hotel.

Foye went on to tell how he killed Mrs. Gilbey and left wearing her clothes and using two cosmetic cases for shoes. Detective Crosass-Medina said, "He just very nonchalantly walked out wearing a bathing cap and ladies shorts and a red blouse, a sort of see-through blouse."

The detectives knew they would need concrete evidence, beyond Foye's confession and the bruises on his arms, to use as exhibits for the courtroom drama that was soon to follow. They pressed Foye to tell them where he'd hidden or disposed of the items. Whatever his testimony at the trial might be, they wanted it to be clear that the crime was heinous and the escape executed by a cold and very calculating individual. Foye told them he disposed of the items in the trash outside of his apartment. The detectives were finally satisfied he had told them everything. They brought the suspect to the offices of the Manhattan district attorney where he made a full confession that was recorded with sophisticated video equipment.

Now the investigators began a race to track down as much evidence as they could to aid in convicting the killer. They dispatched technicians to the hotel again. This time they were instructed to fingerprint and photograph the path Foye took to the roof. This included the stairwell, doors and iron fixtures that he might have touched. The detectives also proceeded to the killer's neighborhood, the South Bronx.

Foye lived on the 700 block of East 168th street in the South Bronx section of New York, where the local police precinct is known as "Fort Apache." Detective Johnston described the inner city neighborhood like this: "There is, maybe, one occupied building on the block." The remainder of the plots are burned-out shells or rubble-strewn lots.

Although the detectives didn't have a search warrant, they were aware of a method that made its use obsolete. They called the Department of Sanitation to check if the dumpster at Foye's building had been emptied. Sanitation said it hadn't. The detectives knew they could sift through the uncollected refuse outside the building and discover valuable evidence without being accused of illegal search and seizure. They rushed to the dumpster only to find that a bureaucratic snafu had occurred. The trash had already been picked up.

The detectives returned to the station-house disheartened, but their spirits lifted when Foye, under further interrogation, admitted having discarded one of the cosmetic cases in the street near his building. Again, they returned to the South Bronx hoping for success. They pried into every hole and corner in the alleys and lots around the building in an effort to unearth the cosmetic case. In an alley, between two abandoned buildings, they found it.

In the early morning hours of Tuesday, August 9th, after he confessed to the murder of Lenore Gilbey, Lawrence Foye was charged with felony murder, burglary and robbery. He denied having "done anything" with regard to sexual assault.

The cosmetic case was one of several pieces of evidence linking Foye to Gilbey's murder. A family member later identified it as a gift he had given to Lenore Gilbey.

Before the trial, Foye was made to undergo a blood test to determine if Gilbey was sexually assaulted by him. The absorption inhibition test indicated a particular blood type other than Mrs. Gilbey's was present on the body. It was determined that Foye was a "secreter," one who had blood substances present in non-blood body fluids, such as saliva. This was a positive step. However, further testing that was required, could not prove beyond the shadow of a doubt that it was Foye who sexually assaulted Gilbey, possibly due to the extensive purple cosmetic smears on the victim. As a result, all that could be determined was that Foye had been in Gilbey's room and Gilbey had been sexually assaulted. Once again, the difficulty of proving sexual assault on a dead victim was demonstrated. Even with all of the scientific technology available to modern-day police departments, a victim's personal identification of his or her attacker is still of primary importance. In any event, the evidence was enough for Assistant District Attorney Martha Bashford to remark about the bizarre nature of the cosmetic spreading.

Foye's trial was not set to begin until March 1984. Despite all of the bizarre twists to the story and all of the evidence the detectives had gathered, there was still a surprise for them to face — Foye's incredible assertion that he was not legally responsible for the murder of Lenore Gilbey!

On an unusually warm Monday in March, Foye, who had spent his 22nd birthday in prison, appeared in Manhattan at the State Supreme Court of Justice Sybil Hart Kooper. He was met by his court-appointed defense attorney. Section 18-B of the criminal procedures law of New York dictates that a person who cannot afford an attorney must have one appointed for him. Assistant District Attorney Martha Bashford was prepared to prosecute Foye to the full extent of the law. A jury of six men and six women sat ready to listen to the proceedings and render their verdict of guilty or innocent.

Foye's lawyer must have been upset at the candid revelations of his videotape confession, but he was prepared to refute the admission of guilt the three detectives had gotten from his client.

309

The evidence, including the cosmetic case and bruises from climbing, were arrayed against him. Remarkably no prints were located on the stairwell or anywhere on the roof when the technicians returned to dust these areas. Foye's strategy was to plead not guilty to the charges because he had been in a state of extreme emotional disturbance on the night of the incident.

Foye recounted his meeting with Richard Davis. He said the homosexual assault that he had been subjected to caused him to flee the room. A defense psychiatrist testified that this incident, combined with the alcohol and marijuana ingestion that Foye now claimed, had rendered him temporarily emotionally disturbed. In this state, the psychiatrist claimed, Foye was not legally responsible for his actions.

It was an interesting defense and one that had been used before with both favorable and unfavorable results. It might have worked for others but Foye's chances were bleak. Any compassion the jury might have had for him eroded as he told of the murder.

"She woke up," he testified. "I told her I'm not going to hurt you. I put my arm around her neck. I drew her close and then her head went limp. I put her on the bed and passed out on top of her."

The twelve men and women weren't taken in by Foye's defense. After a brief six-day trial, they deliberated for five hours before finding the defendant guilty of felony murder, robbery and burglary.

Less than one month later, Justice Kooper offered no sympathy to Foye at his sentencing. She described Mrs. Gilbey as pleading, "Take whatever you want but don't hurt me." Foye could have shown her mercy. Instead, Kooper said, "Without benefit of a lawyer, judge or jury, he sentenced her to die. Her life ended at fifty-four. She was executed. He then slept with the body and in the morning dressed in the clothes he stole from her and left." Kooper said the Gilbey murder was one of the "most vicious cases" ever before her. She sentenced Foye to 25 years to life in prison, recommending that he never be paroled.

EDITOR'S NOTE:

Jane Daly and Richard Davis are not the real names of the persons so named in the foregoing story. Fictitious names have been used because there is no reason for public interest in the identities of these persons.

"PARANOID PSYCHO SAID DOG BLOOD MADE HER KILL!"

by Gary Miller

Anna Armstrong's children were awakened by the shouting in the living room. They lay in their beds for a few minutes, trying to go back to sleep, but the arguing got louder, so they decided to go out and investigate.

The harsh light in the living room made their eyes blink, and they tried to wipe away the sleep. They could see their mother standing in the middle of the living room arguing with a man. Off to the side was a woman, apparently just observing.

When Anna noticed her children, she told them to go back to bed. They obediently returned to their room, but couldn't go back to sleep. The voices in the room grew louder, harsher, more strident, until suddenly, there was an explosion.

The children trembled with fear. They stayed in

their beds, too frightened to move.

Then, again, another bang! And moments later, the man appeared in the children's doorway, peered at them, then wheeled around and left. The children dared not make a move. They remained in their rooms for approximately 45 minutes when a family friend arrived at 8:00 a.m. that Friday morning of December 10, 1982 to pick up the youngsters for school.

As he approached the Armstrong home, he noticed the door ajar. Realizing instantly something was wrong, the man opened the door further and walked inside. That was enough.

Anna Armstrong lay on the floor near the living room couch in a pool of blood.

In desperation, the friend called out to the children, but received no answer. Fearing the worst, but still hoping, he ran into their bedroom, and found the children alive and unharmed but in a state of shock.

He immediately took hold of the children and went to a neighbor's house and called the Montgomery County police.

Detective J.W. Barnes responded to the scene with his partner, Sgt. Ricky Moore. Barnes has been with the Montgomery, Alabama, Police Department approximately seven years, three of them working homicide. Barnes arrived at the scene at about the same time the ambulance personnel were removing the body.

After securing the scene, he questioned the two

children and the friend. There was little the man could tell Barnes, and the children gave only vague descriptions of the people arguing with their mother.

As for physical evidence at the scene, Barnes had already noticed when entering the Armstrong home that it was bitter cold inside. Upon checking, he discovered that the window pane in the living room had been removed. Reasoning that the killers probably had entered the house through that opening, Detective Barnes knew there was a good chance fingerprints might be recovered from that area.

Checking further, Barnes also discovered that there were window putty filings found lying on the windowsill. Apparently the killers had scraped away the putty from the window and then removed the pane, he surmised.

There was another curious fact Detective Barnes noted: The weather at this time of year was cold and blustery. And yet the filings were not swept off the windowsill. The only possible reason for this was that Anna Armstrong must have been shot not long before. If the killers had entered much earlier, the winds would certainly have blown away filings that were on the windowsill.

Forensic experts from the Montgomery Police Department informed Barnes and Moore that the tool used to file away the window putty could not be found anywhere outside or inside the house.

As for the fingerprints on the windowpane, they had already dusted the glass, but it appeared that the killers had wiped it clean. This information wasn't too promising.

One approach that could be taken was question the victim, Anna Armstrong. But when Detective Barnes phoned the doctors, he was told the victim was in serious condition and unconscious. For now, at least she would not be able to provide any information that would help shed light on what happened.

The next order of business was canvassing the neighborhood. Investigators and officers went from house to house asking neighbors if they heard a shot or if they saw any suspicious persons near the Armstrong residence during the night or early morning, but, for whatever reason, all the residents either refused to speak with the lawmen or explained that they didn't see or hear anything at all.

After several hours of this frustrating effort, detectives returned to headquarters and did some checking on Anna Armstrong. Perhaps there was something in her past that might help investigators focus on a suspect.

But this approach also proved futile. Anna Armstrong had no criminal record whatsoever. Other files holding her name provided no clue as to why anyone would want to shoot her.

Then J.W. Barnes hit on something. Anna

Armstrong had been involved in a serious auto accident only months before and wasn't covered by insurance. Perhaps the victim in this accident was angered enough to shoot Mrs. Armstrong.

An investigator was dispatched to check on this suspect, but the person had an airtight alibi for Dec. 10th, the night of the shooting.

Barnes also checked back with the Montgomery hospital and spoke with Anna's doctors. The physician informed him that Anna's condition was getting worse, and it was unlikely she would ever regain consciousness.

The doctor also explained that the victim had been shot in her chest area and head. He had decided not to remove the bullets since they were both in vital areas, and any attempt to remove them would probably cause lethal hemorrhaging. The doctor added that there were gunpowder burns on the victim's temple, apparently indicating that whoever had shot her had made sure they were doing a good job of it since the burns indicated she had been shot from extremely close range.

After this conversation, Barnes contacted the forensic lab and received further depressing news. The technicians had already conducted tests on most of the evidence recovered at the scene. The only fingerprints recovered were of Anna Armstrong and the children.

The probe had now entered the evening of the murder and investigators from the Montgomery

Police were going nowhere fast. Barnes and his partner decided to get a little shut eye before continuing the probe full force the following morning.

The next day had hardly begun when a phone call came into the Montgomery police headquarters. Sergeant R.T. Ward who had arrived early that morning, took the call.

The woman caller said there was a dead body at an address on Cloe Street. Ward, together with Investigator E.T. Davis, responded to the scene. Ward knocked several times on the door of the house but received no answer. Upon trying the knob, however, the door gave way and opened.

When the investigators entered the house, they were overcome by a musky, foul odor. As they got closer to the kitchen, the smell grew stronger. It appeared to emanate from the closet in the kitchen. When they opened the door, the investigators made a grisly find.

Inside was the body of a man, apparently dead for some time, since his body had already begun to decompose.

Inside his pants pocket was a wallet with identification in the name of Jack Woods.

The corpse was transported to the morgue, where the medical examiner had the onerous task of performing an autopsy.

Detectives Ward and Davis had already returned to headquarters when they received word from the medical examiner. The corpse was not a "natural." Somebody had killed him with a small caliber handgun. The bullet had entered the victim's throat. It was a clear case of murder!

As for the approximate time of death, the best determination the pathologist could make was either three or four days earlier.

Only shortly after this conversation, another phone call came into the Montgomery Police Department. The woman asked to speak with a detective investigating the Woods-Armstrong cases. J.W. Barnes took the call. The woman caller said that the same person who'd shot Armstrong killed Woods.

Asked for the name of the killer, the caller said it was Juanita Poole. Then the woman told Barnes that Poole was the person who'd called earlier that day about the dead body of Jack Woods. The caller explained that she was a neighbor of Poole's and that, after Poole had called the police, she had brought a gun to her house and had told her to stash it for her. But she didn't want to get involved in any murder.

The caller gave Barnes her address, and soon detectives were at the woman's home. The witness gave detectives the gun and answered all their questions. According to the witness, Juanita Poole had been living with Jack Woods. She didn't know too much about the murders. All she could tell them was what Juanita Poole had told her—she had killed Jack Woods and had shot Anna Armstrong with the gun.

With this account, it appeared that the Armstrong shooting and Woods murder cases were ready to be resolved.

Of course, the woman might have been lying, and the only way to make certain that she was telling the truth was to check out this Juanita Poole.

First, the sleuths had to discover where the suspect was living. Questioning neighbors and acquaintances of both Poole and Woods, Barnes and other investigators learned that Poole was close friends with a woman by the name of Millicent Burns. From various sources, they learned Burns' address, and responded to her residence.

Sure enough, Juanita Poole was staying there. The detectives began questioning the suspect, but apparently she had just consumed a great deal of alcohol and was not in any rational frame of mind. She was brought back to headquarters and placed in a holding cell until she sobered up.

In the meantime, the revolver recovered at the witness's house was test fired at the ballistics lab and compared with the bullets removed from the throat of Jack Woods. The test bullet was a perfect match with the slug.

The facts were beginning to fit into place. But the investigators still had a lot of work cut out for them. First of all, according to the children, their mother had been arguing with a man and a woman before she was shot down. If Poole was the woman, then who was the man? It couldn't have been Woods since he was dead at least a day before Armstrong was shot.

There were other details that had to be worked out as well. Up until now, there was no evidence linking Juanita Poole to the Armstrong shooting. The matching bullets were only able to link Poole to the Woods shooting.

Barnes checked on the gun to determine its ownership, but there was no record of the gun being licensed to anyone.

Jack Woods, lawmen learned in the meantime, had an extensive criminal record, mostly involving small time theft and assault charges, but this fact would mean that Woods would not have been able to obtain a gun permit. Perhaps the gun had been purchased in one of the many pawnshops throughout the country.

As the following days progressed, Barnes and other investigators began checking out these shops.

As it turned out, there was a record in one of the stores that Jack Woods had purchased the revolver. So, here, they had one link. If Jack Woods owned the gun, and Juanita Poole was living with him at the time, she had the opportunity of obtaining the murder weapon and perhaps using it.

Still, one of the major obstacles facing the probers was the apparent lack of a motive for the shootings. What was it that triggered Juanita Poole to shoot Anna Armstrong or Jack Woods, if in fact she did?

Until Poole sobered up, the only avenue sleuths could follow was to canvass the neighborhood again, but this time their questioning of residents focused on the relationship of Poole with Woods and Armstrong.

Was it a love triangle? Was Juanita Poole jealous of Woods and Armstrong?

This theory, however, was discarded almost from the beginning. During the canvass detectives learned that Woods and Armstrong hardly even knew each other.

It was while interviewing Armstrong's family that investigators began to get a handle on the different relationships involved in the baffling case. Barnes learned that a relative of Armstrong had at one time been the boyfriend of Juanita Poole.

The relative was brought down to headquarters for questioning and admitted that, yes, he had been going out with Juanita Poole for a while. He explained that she would get violent at times—usually when she drank, which was often—and that he decided to break it off with her because of her bouts of aggression.

Asked why Juanita Poole would want to hurt Anna, he told investigators he didn't know of any reason at all. He had thought they were friendly with one another. In fact, he had met Juanita just because she was friends with Anna. He had visited Anna, and Juanita happened to be there on several occasions. That was how they started going out with each other, he explained.

So Poole and Armstrong knew each other; more than that, they were at one time close friends. But the investigators still knew of no real motive for the shooting.

The next day, Juanita Poole was taken from her holding cell, read her Miranda warning and questioned again about the Armstrong shooting and Woods murder. She would only say that she didn't know anything about it.

At this point, she was returned to her holding pen, and Detective Barnes contacted ADA Frank Hawthorne and related the details of the murder investigation. Hawthorne advised the investigators to charge Poole with murder.

The investigators felt that if they were going to obtain any evidence about the murder, it would not come from the suspect, so they continued canvassing the neighborhood and questioned friends, acquaintances and relatives of the victims and suspect.

As the canvass proceeded, one name kept popping up during the questioning, and that was the woman at whose residence Poole had been staying, Millicent Burns.

According to witnesses, wherever Poole went, Burns was right by her side. They would go to the store together, go shopping together, even go to bars together.

And, Detective Barnes wondered, perhaps even

killed together.

Millicent was brought down to headquarters, read her rights, and then interrogated. When she was asked her whereabouts on the night and early morning hours of December 10th, she explained that she was in bed asleep, but detectives noted the nervous desperation in her voice. Their gut instinct told them the woman wasn't telling the truth.

The next few hours saw the detectives in an intensive grilling session with the suspect. Finally, she cracked. Yes, she was with Juanita Poole at the Armstrong house when Anna Armstrong was shot and when Jack Woods was killed, but she had nothing to do with it. She only accompanied Juanita to the Armstrong house. She didn't realize Juanita would shoot the woman.

She told the investigators that Juanita was a believer in Voodoo and thought that Anna Armstrong had been secretly practicing it on her.

According to Millicent, Juanita felt that it was because of Anna's witchcraft that she (Juanita) broke up with Anna's relative and that now Anna was destroying her life further by casting these spells on her.

The final straw occurred when Juanita felt that Anna had somehow injected her with dog blood, and that she was now pregnant with a litter of puppies. Juanita decided to go to Anna's house and warn her to stop putting curses on her.

Before going to the address, she rode in a cab

through the area. Then, having determined that Anna was home, she asked Millicent to accompany her. They both went to Anna's house on Thursday night around 10:00, December 9th.

There was another person inside the house with Anna at the time, so they waited until the very early hours of the morning when the person left.

Then Juanita filed away the putty from the living room window, and, covering their hands with their blouses in order not to leave any fingerprints, they both removed the pane of glass.

Juanita then climbed through the opening, went to the front door and opened it for Millicent.

Once inside, Juanita went to Anna's bedroom and called her into the living room. She warned Anna not to practice Voodoo on her anymore.

According to Millicent, Anna denied even knowing anything about Voodoo, but Juanita would hear none of it. Anna had been practicing it on her, she believed, and had destroyed the beautiful relationship she had with Anna's relative.

Anna, though, didn't seem to know what she was talking about. The argument grew heated, explained Millicent, and during this time, Anna's children had awoken and entered the room. Anna told them to go back to bed. Shortly afterwards, Juanita pulled out her .22 caliber RG revolver and shot Anna in the chest.

Anna went down, and then Juanita walked

calmly over to the prostrate body, bent down, pressed the gun against the victim's temple and fired a second shot. She then walked over to the children's bedroom, peered into the doorway and left with Millicent in tow.

There were questions that still plagued Barnes. Why did the children say they had seen a man and a woman talking to their mother? It was true that Juanita had close-cropped hair, which might have led the children to make an error.

"What was Juanita wearing when you were at the Armstrong residence?" Barnes asked the witness.

Millicent hesitated for a moment, and then replied: "It was dungarees and one of those red and black plaid shirts."

In other words, thought Barnes, clothing normally associated with what a man usually wears. This, together with the fact that Juanita's hair was cropped close to her head, would explain why the children had mistaken her for a man.

The investigators now asked Millicent about the Woods' murder. Here, as in the Anna Armstrong case, the motive contradicted all reason. According to Millicent, she had gone to the Woods home with Juanita to help her pack her things. Juanita was moving out. The events leading to the murder were the following: When Juanita finished packing her clothes, she began collecting small items in the house, including an electric stove. Woods was quiet during most of the packing, but when Juanita took the stove, he said, "No, that's mine. You can't have it." After this incident, more arguing ensued over a chair and table.

Then, without warning, Juanita pulled out Woods' gun, aimed it at his face and fired. The bullet entered his throat.

Later, the two women dragged the victim into the kitchen closet and left him there.

With this confession, detectives had a case against Poole and Millicent. The only problem was that it was difficult to confirm most of Millicent's testimony. Since, in the both murders, the only witnesses were the victims and Poole and Burns, investigators had to rely on Burns' testimony.

There was, however, one detail which could be confirmed if, in fact the witness was telling the truth. During the interrogation, she had stated that before the Anna Armstrong murder, Juanita had taken a cab to the address to make sure Anna would be home that evening.

Barnes sent an investigator to check with the cab company. Within a few hours, the detective returned with the cabbie's manifest. Written in plain black and white, the log contained one round trip call on December 9th, Thursday night at 9:00 p.m. The taxi had passed by the Anna Armstrong residence and then returned to Cloe Street, Juanita Poole's home.

Another detail Barnes hoped would provide

some more evidence was the clothing worn by Juanita Poole. Juanita had been picked up by police with apparently the same blue jeans and plaid shirt that she had worn when she'd shot Anna Armstrong. These garments had already been tested by the forensic lab, but no bloodstains were recovered. Barnes contacted the lab again and asked them to give it another go over. There was always the chance that a speck of blood had been missed. The lab complied with the request, but several hours later, they contacted Barnes and told him, "No go." There just wasn't any blood on the clothing.

At about this time, Barnes learned the depressing news that Anna Armstrong died at 10:00 in the morning on December 16th.

It was also at approximately this date that Barnes was notified from the Montgomery County prison that Juanita Poole asked to speak with him. She was taken to headquarters and, there, confessed to the murder of Anna Armstrong. Her statement coincided in every respect with the testimony of Millicent Burns, but Juanita adamantly denied murdering Jack Woods. She didn't know anything about that murder, she maintained. After grilling her for several hours, Barnes realized he was getting nowhere with Juanita regarding the Woods murder. She was returned to prison, and proceedings were gotten underway for her murder trial.

ADA Frank Hawthorne would handle the

state's case against the two suspects, Juanita Poole and Millicent Burns. They were both charged with murder. The actual trial took place in August of 1983, approximately a year after the murders. There were many delays caused by legal technicalities, the major one being an attempt on Millicent Burns' part to suppress her damning statement to the investigators.

Finally, in August, the trial of Millicent Burns was held in Montgomery County Circuit Court, Judge Randall Thomas presiding.

During the trial Juanita Poole shocked the jury when she testified that she had shot both Anna Armstrong and Jack Woods. She also testified that Millicent Burns had nothing at all to do with either of the murders.

Once hearing this testimony, the jury acquitted Millicent Burns of the murders.

In October of 1983, Juanita Poole went to trial. She pleaded guilty to the murders of Anna Armstrong and Jack Woods and was sentenced by Judge Randall Thomas to 20 years in prison on each count, the terms to run concurrently, so, in effect, she was sentenced to a total of 20 years in prison.

EDITOR'S NOTE:

Millicent Burns is not the real name of the person so named in the foregoing story. A fictitious name has been used because there is no reason for public interest in this person's true identity.

"ROLF'S REMAINS WERE USED FOR FERTILIZER!"

by Jack Heise

Lopez Island is one of the San Juan group, a popular tourist attraction that has been described as an emerald necklace lying between the Washington State coast and Vancouver Island.

Among its better known residents was Captain Rolf Neslund. Neslund gained the dubious honor of having been charged with causing the most expensive ship accident on Puget Sound.

Locally, however, the 80-year-old retired sea captain and his wife Ruth, 20 years his junior and married for 18 years, were better known as the battling Neslunds.

Their fights, both verbal and physical, at home and in local bars and restaurants, were the talk of the sparsely populated island residents.

But it wasn't until after Captain Neslund mysteriously disappeared that one of the Neslunds' carefully guarded secrets became public.

The Norwegian sea captain, who had sailed the seven seas, became a member of the Puget Sound Pilots Association, a select group of navigators who guided Pacific Ocean-going vessels through the narrow Strait of Juan de Fuca into the Puget Sound waters.

On June 1, 1978, Rolf Neslund boarded the big freighter Chavez at Port Angeles and threaded its way into Elliot Bay. He was about a mile away from where the ship was to be berthed in the Duwamish Waterway when it happened.

The big freighter slammed into the West Seattle bridge. It took out the draw span and foundations, leaving the bridge a total wreck beyond repair and it also severed the main artery between the West Seattle residents and downtown. It took five years and $180 million to install a new bridge.

A Coast Guard inquiry board found Neslund negligent in causing the accident. After 68 years as a seaman, Rolf Neslund announced his retirement. Neslund said he was ready to take it easy in what he called his Shangri-la on Lopez Island.

The house he had built, complete with swimming pool, on considerable island acreage, cost $500,000. It wasn't a financial strain for the Neslunds, though, since Rolf had saved considerably during his years as a ship captain and there was a large retirement fund and monthly pension checks from the pilots association.

It wasn't quite the Shangri-la Rolf had envisioned. He and Ruth had gotten along fairly well when he spent most of his time on ships, but around the house day-in and day-out, they appeared to agree on very few things, except their appetite for liquor.

Ruth, neighbors said, could match him drink-for-drink, not to mention punch-for-punch when their arguments became violent.

Shortly after August 8, 1980, Ruth Neslund told friends that Rolf had gone on a vacation to Norway to visit relatives. She didn't know when he would return, hoped it wouldn't be soon, and said she would be delighted if he stayed there.

A few weeks later, Rolf's car was located in a parking area at the mainland ferry terminal in Anacortes. It wasn't unusual because many of the island's residents left their cars at the terminal to save ferry fare. It was thought most likely that Rolf had taken a bus into the Seattle-Tacoma International airport.

Ruth placed an ad in the San Juan Island newspaper to sell the car.

When friends of Rolf inquired of Ruth if she had heard from him, she said she hadn't, which didn't surprise her one bit. She said she wouldn't be at all surprised if he wasn't shacking up with some of his old girlfriends. She quoted Rolf as having bragged that he didn't have a girl in every port, but had a girl on every davenport.

A couple of months later, the Coast Guard held a second hearing into the wreck of the West

Seattle bridge. A subpoena was issued for Rolf Neslund to appear.

Ruth informed the board that Rolf was in Norway visiting relatives. She didn't know their address and hadn't heard from him. She said it was entirely possible that he did not intend to return because he was fearful that he might be found responsible for wrecking the bridge and would be sued.

The explanation, however, did not satisfy relatives of Neslund who were living in Washington State. They had called the relatives in Norway and learned that they had not seen or heard from him. They had also checked at the airport for overseas flights for around the time he was supposed to have left and were unable to find anyone by the name of Rolf Neslund who had booked a flight to Europe.

Ruth was unconcerned when the relatives imparted the information to her. She said it was possible he had used another name, or, on the other hand, possibly he had not gone to Norway. She suggested the possibility that he had committed suicide.

Ruth said that after his retirement, Rolf had hallucinations about wrecking the bridge, drank a lot, sat staring out the window and he might have decided to end it with a deep-six off the ferry.

The relatives didn't buy the theory that the crusty, old sea captain would take his own life.

They paid a visit to Lopez Island to talk to some of the residents who had known him.

They learned that Neslund hadn't appeared to be depressed over the bridge wreck. In fact, he had joked about it and said a new bridge had been needed for a long time and that the West Seattle residents should be grateful that he had provided one for them and should name it after him.

As far as the relatives could learn, Rolf hadn't mentioned to anyone that he was planning a trip to Norway. His prime interest in life after his retirement was his large swimming pool that he kept heated year-around and in which he went swimming daily.

The relatives went to the sheriff's office in Friday Harbor on San Juan Island to inquire if there had been any investigation into the mysterious disappearance of Rolf Neslund.

The relatives learned some of the facts of life and law as they pertained to living on the island.

A deputy informed them they barely had enough staff to control the tourists. No one had issued a complaint. And if Neslund had committed suicide, as Ruth suggested, and the body hadn't surfaced, he would most likely have become crab food and the remains would never be found in the deep, cold water of Puget Sound.

The family next visited San Juan County Prosecutor Gene Knapp. They suggested the possibility that Neslund had never left home for Norway, nor had he committed suicide, but might be dead and buried on some of the large tracts of land around his new home.

Knapp conceded that it was an interesting theory, but pointed out a flaw in it. Neslund was up in years. If he could not be found, it would take seven years to have him declared legally dead. If Ruth was out to gain the considerable estate, it would appear that she would be better off to wait until he died naturally.

The relatives then imparted a carefully guarded secret concerning Rolf Neslund.

They said Rolf had been married and divorced in Norway. After the divorce, he had married his former wife's sister in 1958. She had borne him two sons. They moved to Vancouver, British Columbia, because Rolf was navigating on the Pacific Ocean.

Ruth had been brought into the home as a housekeeper. Then, it was learned that Neslund's second marriage was not valid because his divorce from his first wife had not been finalized.

A relationship began between Rolf and Ruth and they were married, although Rolf kept in close contact with his sons and their mother. The sons took their mother's maiden name.

Knapp said it was an interesting story, but it didn't appear to be relevant to the fact that they thought something had happened to Neslund.

The family members said there was more. They related that about two weeks before Rolf was supposed to have gone to Norway, he stopped by to visit them. He said he was changing his will to leave his entire estate to his sons and their mother.

At the meeting, he told them that in the event of his death they should insist upon an autopsy. He said he feared Ruth might poison him.

Knapp pointed out that it was fairly obvious Rolf hadn't been poisoned or there would be a body. Additionally, he suggested that it appeared more to be a civil matter and explained that if they wanted to inquire into the will and Neslund's estate, it would be best to hire an attorney and possibly a private investigator. However, Knapp said he would check at the island and see what additional information might be had as to Rolf's whereabouts.

The relatives took Knapps' advice and hired an attorney and private investigator. They were back with the attorney a couple of weeks later.

The attorney said he felt that if Neslund was still alive he would have to have money to live on. He had checked at the bank where Neslund had his account and turned up some very interesting information.

Neslund had not made a withdrawal prior to a week before he was said to have left for Norway. There hadn't been a sum large enough to have purchased air fare or for his sustenance.

The attorney had obtained a court order to examine the bank account of the missing man and learned that a week before his disappearance Rolf had come in to cash a $75 check. At the time, the teller had informed Rolf there weren't funds in his account to cover the check.

Neslund was furious. According to his calculations, there should have been in excess of $100,000 in certificates of deposit, savings and a checking account.

A bank official brought out the records and found that the money had been in a joint account with his wife. Apparently, Ruth had withdrawn all of the money and deposited it in her personal account so that it could not be touched without her signature.

It was all perfectly legal, the bank official had assured Rolf . . . Any adjustment of the arrangement would have to be made with his wife.

When confronted with the information, Ruth had readily admitted to having withdrawn the funds. She offered two explanations for her actions.

She said she was concerned that there might be a civil action as the result of the bridge accident and the bank account would be attached.

Another reason was that when Rolf started talking about going to Norway, she suspected that he might not return and would withdraw the money and take it with him.

The private investigator had also learned that Ruth had been talking about selling the home and property on Lopez Island.

"At the rate she's going, there will be nothing in Neslund's estate," the attorney said. "She won't have to wait the seven years to have him legally declared dead. She'll have it all."

Meanwhile, Ruth Neslund had been angry with Rolf's relatives and the private investigator because when they had gone to the pilots association to inquire if they had any information concerning Neslund, who was missing and might be presumed to have committed suicide, they stopped his monthly retirement checks. The checks had been deposited directly into his account at the bank and withdrawn by Ruth.

Ruth informed the association that until such time as Rolf might be located dead or alive, or legally declared dead, they had best continue to send his retirement checks or she would sue them.

Pros. Knapp and sheriff's deputies had been doing some checking on Lopez Island. The residents were aware that Rolf appeared to be missing and there was some question as to what might have happened to him. The subject became a prime bit of conversation and rumor.

There were a number of stories about the battling Neslunds who had made no attempt to keep their quarrels a secret. Vocally and physically, they were pretty evenly matched. Rolf was in good condition for a man of his age. Ruth was shorter but outweighed him by at least 50 pounds and had 20 years on him in age.

It wasn't unusual to see either or both of them sporting black eyes and other marks of physical encounters.

One neighbor reported she had visited Ruth following a night of one of their more physical encounters. Ruth had a black eye and a bruised cheek.

The neighbor quoted Ruth as saying, "If that bastard lays another hand on me, I'll fill him so full of lead they can use him for an anchor."

Of course, the neighbor said, it was most likely just wild talk like people do when they get angry.

With Neslund missing for almost a year and no one having seen or heard from him, Pros. Knapp decided it was time to launch a full-scale investigation into the case.

Faced with limited funds, manpower and facilities in San Juan County, Knapp took advantage of a recently enacted resolution by the state legislature, authorizing the attorney general to actively participate in local criminal investigations when requested by local authorities.

Knapp contacted Attorney General Ken Eikenberry at the state capital in Olympia. He gave him the information that was known up to that point.

"I'm not sure just what has gone on," Knapp said. "I don't think Neslund went to Norway and his relatives are positive that he wouldn't commit suicide. It's become a pretty hot issue up here and we could use some help."

340

Eikenberry assigned his senior assistant, Gregory P. Canova, and two of the state's top investigators to go to the island to see what they could dig up.

The news media became aware that the investigation was going on, and the colorful pilot who had been charged with wrecking the West Seattle bridge made good copy. The published and broadcast stories stirred up more interest for the island residents. What had happened to Captain Rolf Neslund became one of the favorite topics of conversations.

Had he taken off and assumed a new identity to avoid any further involvement in the bridge accident? Had he committed suicide? Or was there something more sinister in his mysterious disappearance?

Checking out the rumors, the investigators located two contractors who had installed the swimming pool at the Neslund residence. They related that they had gone to the house to repair a leak in the pool and inquired of Ruth about Rolf. She told them that he had left for Norway to visit relatives and did not know when he planned to return.

While they were in the house, the men recalled, they noted that there were several spent cartridges in a shag rug in the living room. When they asked Ruth about the shells, she was quoted as saying, "I gave the old boy a royal send-off."

The information became more significant with

a statement from a neighbor of the Neslunds. She remembered that around the time Rolf was supposed to have left for Norway, she observed Ruth and the elderly relative living with her in the backyard. They were burning what appeared to be a perfectly good sofa and rug.

The woman said that she had wondered at the time why Ruth wouldn't have given the articles to charity rather than burn them, but hadn't questioned her about it.

Meanwhile, a grisly rumor was making the rounds that the investigators checked out.

They learned from a hardware store operator that around the time Rolf was reported to have gone to Norway, Ruth had come in to purchase a large commercial meat grinder.

He said he questioned her at the time about why she wanted such a big unit. She explained that she planned to slaughter some cattle she had and wanted the grinder to make hamburger. He suggested that it woud be less expensive for her to have the meat ground at the slaughter-house where the animals were to be killed and dressed.

The man said that Ruth had asked him sharply if he was in business to give advice or sell things. She bought the grinder.

Strangely, the investigators learned, a short time after the purchase of the expensive commercial meat grinder, Ruth sold it to a neighbor at a fraction of the price she had paid for it and, as far as they could determine, she hadn't slaughtered any cattle.

Discussing the incident, one of the investigators said, "Do you suppose she could have made hamburger out of the old boy?"

"If she did, she'd have to do something with the bones," another investigator responded. "Even those big commercial grinders can't take anything as big as shin bones."

The investigators took the information they were gathering to Pros. Knapp and Canova.

Laying it out, they pointed out that it was almost a certainty that Rolf Neslund was dead. He hadn't been seen or heard from in more than a year. He had no money to exist on if he were alive.

Ruth had been heard to threaten that she would kill her husband if he laid a hand on her again. It might have been just talk at the time, but there were the spent cartridges that were found in the living room.

They added to that the statement from the neighbor who had seen Ruth burning a sofa and rug, and the purchase of the commercial meat grinder.

"I don't think we're going to get much more until we can go out to the house and look around," one of the investigators said. "If she did knock him off and made up that story about him going to Norway, even if she used the meat grinder, the big bones must be somewhere."

"I think we have enough to get a search warrant," Canova said.

Canova and Knapp went to San Juan County Superior Court Judge Richard Pitt with the request.

Judge Pitt issued the warrant but warned, "I hope you find what you're looking for because what you have to date is purely speculation and I don't think there's any doubt but that she'll make trouble if you come up empty-handed."

With the warrants in hand to search the Neslund home and property, the prosecutors, sheriff, deputies and a couple of men from the county road crew showed up at the Neslund house with a small bulldozer and a power post hole digger.

Ruth screamed with anger when presented with the warrants. She described the men and their relatives in colorful terms and threatened to sue everyone in sight if they touched anything on her property or in her home.

The court order, however, was sufficient for the men to begin their search. The backhoe operator began to remove dirt from a septic tank. It was placed on a large screen where deputies raked through it looking for bones.

The post hole digger started a systematic probe of the ground around the house searching for any indication that the soil might have been turned over.

The investigators inside the house located what appeared to be bloodstains on the concrete floor in the bathroom and brownish flecks on the wall and ceiling in the living room. They sent out for an electric jackhammer and power saws.

Ruth continued to scream and hurl invectives as the crew with the jackhammer tore up sections of the concrete bathroom floor and loaded them into a pickup truck. Sections of the floor, wall and ceiling were also removed from the living room.

The post hole digger continued his operation in a widening area around the house.

The search went on for 13 days with 700 pieces of evidence weighing several tons hauled to the basement of the courthouse for evaluation.

The lengthy search, however, failed to turn up any human bones.

"I'll be damned," one of the investigators said. "I wonder what she could have done with them."

There was speculation that a night trip on the ferry would have been an ideal place to deep-six sacks of bones.

Canova and Knapp were well aware that if they were going to prosecute a case, it would be up to them to prove that a murder had taken place. Cases have been prosecuted without a corpse, but there were witnesses or other evidence to show that the crime had taken place.

Chunks of the concrete and sections from the living room were sent to a crime laboratory in Seattle. The report came back that tests revealed the stains were human blood of "A" type.

The investigators determined that Rolf Neslund had "A" type blood, but so did Ruth and a lot of other persons.

The prosecutors were reluctant to file a charge and go to court with the evidence they had. If they failed to get a conviction, under the law of double jeopardy, it could not be tried again even though additional evidence was discovered.

Ruth went through with her threat to sue. She filed a civil suit in federal court charging the prosecutors, investigators and other officials with violating her civil rights, destroying her personal property and causing her mental anguish and humiliation.

She asked for $840,000 in damages, listing $340,000 for mental anguish, humiliation, medical treatment, attorneys' fees and extensive damage to her home and property. The additional $500,000 was for punitive damages.

When Eikenberry was informed of the suit, he called Canova. "What are you guys doing up there?" he asked.

Canova responded that he felt certain Ruth had killed her husband. She possibly had used the meat grinder to get rid of some of the flesh, but they had failed to find any bones or any witnesses who could testify that a crime had taken place.

"If we file, we'll have to go to court," Canova said. "If we lose it, then it's over. We're just hoping to come up with something more positive."

"Well, let's hope you find it before we have to defend that civil suit in federal court," Eikenberry said.

Then, the break came that Canova and Knapp had been waiting for.

An investigator, acting on a hunch, checked the telephone calls that had been made from the Neslund home around the time Rolf disappeared. He learned that several calls had been made to a midwest city, one of them on the night of August 8, 1980. The call was to a Neslund relative.

Inquiring as to the nature of the calls, the woman who received them told him that Ruth had called her and emotionally, either from being disturbed or drinking, informed her that she and Rolf had quarreled over money. He had threatened her and she shot him.

The informant said Ruth had called her several days later and told her she and her elderly relative were in Bellingham. She made no mention of the previous call in which she allegedly said she had shot her husband. Instead, she said that Rolf had left for a trip to Norway to visit relatives.

Investigators were sent to interview the woman and obtain a formal statement. She repeated the statement she had given about receiving the call from Ruth, but could not recall that Ruth had told her what had been done with the body.

She said she had not gone to the police with the information because she thought Ruth must have informed the police about the shooting.

Later, when Ruth told her Rolf had gone to Norway, she questioned whether Ruth, who sounded partially incoherent in the first call, had said she shot her husband or if she said she planned to shoot him.

The information was a big break, but the prosecutors realized it might not be all they would need to prosecute the case.

They had only the witness's statement that Ruth had shot her husband, and Ruth undoubtedly would deny making such a statement. And if Ruth and the elderly relative had gone to Bellingham, it was possible they had taken the corpse with them. The remains could have been dumped off the ferry or left almost anywhere.

"The key to it all is the elderly relative who was with her," Canova said. "If there's a chance we can get him to talk, we might get to the bottom of this."

The elderly relative was no longer living at the Neslund home. A short time after Rolf disappeared, he had been sent to a nursing home in Illinois. Investigators were sent to question him.

Confronted with the statement that Ruth had told another relative that she had shot Rolf, the elderly man agreed to make a statement.

He explained that Rolf had learned that Ruth had withdrawn all of their money held in a joint account and deposited it into her personal account. They argued violently, Rolf had threatened Ruth that he would divorce her, and the court would force her to return the money.

Ruth left the room, went into her bedroom, and returned with an automatic pistol. Rolf was sitting on the sofa. Ruth told him that she was going to kill him. Rolf laughed at her. She fired two shots into Rolf's head.

The elderly man said that he had helped Ruth roll the body off the sofa onto a sheet and they dragged it into the bathroom and put it in the tub.

They discussed what they were going to do with the body and Ruth suggested that they cut it into pieces and burn it in a barrel in the backyard where they burned trash.

The elderly man related that he had used a broad ax and a hacksaw to cut up the corpse. He was unsure whether Ruth had put some of the flesh through the meat grinder, but they had taken the body out to the barrel. It took several days to reduce it to ashes.

He said they pulverized the burned bones and then mixed the ashes in a manure pile and Ruth used it to fertilize her flower garden. He quoted Ruth as saying that it would be the first time in Rolf's life that he ever smelled sweet.

The man's statement explained why the investigators had been unable to find any remains of the missing man and there was no way the remains could ever be identified.

However, with the sworn statements from the two witnesses, plus the bloodstains found in the house, the prosecutors felt that they now had sufficient evidence to proceed against Ruth for the murder of her husband.

The charges were filed just a little over 2-1/2 years following the mysterious disappearance of Rolf Neslund.

At a preliminary hearing, Ruth entered a not-guilty plea. She stated she had no recollection of the call she was alleged to have made to the relative in which she said she had killed her husband, and that if such a call had been made, she possibly had been drunk at the time.

She claimed that the relative, who said he was present at the time Rolf was killed and had chopped up the body and burned it, held a grudge against her because she had put him into a nursing home and would likely say anything the investigators had asked him to say.

The court ordered that there was sufficient evidence to warrant Ruth to stand trial on the charge, but allowed her to remain free on a $50,000 property bond pending the hearing.

It was the start of a legal hassle that took almost as long as the investigation had up until that time.

A trial date was held up when the defense attorney filed for a hearing on a complaint that the physical evidence obtained at the Neslund home and property had been taken illegally.

The charge was denied and a trial was set for May 6, 1985. Prior to trial, there was a hearing to determine if there should be a change of venue because it appeared that almost every resident of the sparsely populated San Juan Islands must have heard about the case and possibly formed an opinion.

Surprisingly, the defense insisted that there should not be a change of venue and asked that the case be heard in Friday Harbor with a panel picked from the island residents.

Judge Robert Bibb, who was to preside over the trial, ordered that a list of 400 potential jurors living on the island be selected at random by a computer. Those selected were sent a lengthy questionnaire in which they were asked if they would be able to disregard anything they might have heard or read about the case and consider only the evidence presented to them at the trial.

The original list was cut to 134 names by court administrators, with the others excused for various reasons revealed by the questionnaire.

Part way through the selection of a panel, the trial was again delayed when Ruth Neslund suffered a severe nose bleed resulting from high blood pressure. She was taken to a hospital in Bellingham.

The trial was heavily attended by the news media who were aware that the prosecution, unable to produce a corpse, would be relying upon the bloodstains found in the house to show that a murder had taken place.

One of the reporters commented, "Well there

goes the evidence for all of those bloodstains. The defense would claim that they came from Ruth's nose bleeds."

Pros. Canova, however, did not appear to be disturbed by the event. There was speculation as to what he could present to offset the defense claim concerning the bloodstains.

The trial was called into session a week later. A panel of nine men and three women, with three alternates, were selected to hear the evidence.

Before the opening arguments were heard, a vital point in the case had to be decided. Canova had introduced as an exhibit the statement given by the elderly relative who claimed he was present at the time Ruth shot her husband. Physicians at the nursing home stated that the elderly man was senile and not physically or mentally capable to appear as a witness.

Defense Attorney Fred Weedon argued that the statement was not admissible as evidence because the defense could not cross-examine the person, and further, it was likely the man had been senile at the time the statement was taken.

Judge Bibb ruled in favor of the prosecution. Canova had won the opening round, but there was much more yet to come.

Canova opened the state's case slowly and carefully, setting the background in which Rolf Neslund had first been reported to have gone to Norway and was later assumed to have committed suicide.

Witnesses were called to testify that Rolf had not appeared to be despondent before his disappearance. A relative, flown in from Norway, testified that Rolf had written him asking him to come to visit and that he had made no mention of any plans to vacation in Norway.

Bank employees related how Ruth had systematically drained the Neslund joint account and put the funds into her personal account while Rolf was still alive.

Technicians testified while the exhibits of the bloodstained articles taken from the house were shown to the jurors.

Then, the trial was delayed again when Ruth had another one of her severe nose bleeds.

After she had been taken from the courtroom, Pros. Canova petitioned Judge Bibb to have her placed in a nursing home and under supervision during the remainder of the trial. He informed the court that Ruth was admittedly a heavy drinker and it aggravated her high blood pressure.

Judge Bibb ruled that the bond that allowed her freedom while the trial was in progress would remain on the condition that Ruth agreed to spend her time out of the courtroom in a nursing home and under supervision.

With the court in session again, Canova called to the witness stand a forensic expert on bloodstains. He testified that the blood found on the ceiling of the Neslund home was a "high-velocity mist" of the type that could only be created as the result of a gunshot wound. This testimony eliminated any possible claim that Ruth's nose bleeds had caused the bloodstains.

"A person with a nose bleed couldn't have gotten that blood on the ceiling under any conditions?" Canova asked.

"Positively not, under any condition," the witness responded.

After two weeks of testimony, Canova introduced the state's star witnesses. The relative who had received the telephone call in which Ruth allegedly stated she had shot Rolf testified to the conversation. She was positive about the date being on the evening of August 8, 1980.

She was followed to the stand by a witness who identified himself as being a relative of the defendant, presently residing in California.

He testified to a conversation in which Ruth had told him that she had shot and killed Rolf and that she and another relative had burned the remains in a barrel.

Canova followed that testimony with the statement obtained from the relative who was present at the time of the shooting and who told of having cut up the corpse and helping Ruth burn the remains.

Except for being unable to produce a corpse, Canova had put on a strong case for the prosecution.

Weedon called Ruth to the witness chair to testify in her own defense. Ruth appeared to be as calm and collected as she had been throughout the state's case.

"Did you kill Rolf Neslund?" Weedon asked his witness.

"I did not kill Rolf," Ruth responded, looking squarely at the jurors as she answered the question.

Ruth admitted that she had withdrawn the funds from the joint account and deposited them in her personal account with the explanation that she was fearful they would be attached if Rolf was sued in a civil action as the result of the bridge accident.

She insisted that Rolf had been alive on August 14, 1980, six days after the state claimed he had been killed. She said he had told her he was going to Norway and she was under the impression that he was taking the mother of his two sons with him and did not plan to return.

She said if he had not gone to Norway, then the only explanation for his disappearance was the one she had given earlier, that he had become despondent and had committed suicide by leaping off the ferry into Puget Sound.

On cross-examination, Canova asked her to explain why, if Rolf had been alive as late as August 14th, she had called a relative on August 8th to say she had shot and killed him.

Ruth said she had no recollection of making the call, but had called the relative to say that

Rolf had left on a trip to Norway.

"And the statement and testimony you have heard from other relatives?" Canova asked. "How do you explain that?"

With a half-smile, Ruth quipped, "I have relatives who would say anything for $40."

With the defense case completed and prior to the summations, Pros. Canova informed the court that he had one more rebuttal witness to be heard from.

When the witness was called, it was obviously a surprise for the defense. The witness had earlier been listed as a defense witness to testify as a friend of the defendant and as to her character, but she had not been called.

The witness identified herself as a friend of Ruth for seven years who lived in the same area as the Neslunds on Lopez Island.

Canova questioned the witness with "at an earlier hearing you testified that you had no knowledge concerning the disappearance of Rolf Neslund?"

The witness stated that she had made such a statement.

"Why have you changed your mind and are willing to testify at this time?" Canova asked.

The witness said she considered herself to be a friend of the defendant. She had remained silent, but what she knew preyed upon her mind and it wasn't until the trial was in progress that she decided she could no longer keep the secret she knew.

The witness testified that on the night of August 8, 1980, Ruth had called her on the telephone and asked her to come over to the Neslund home. She said when she arrived, Ruth appeared to be agitated and had been drinking.

They sat talking in the music room, off the living room, and she had asked Ruth what was troubling her. Ruth blurted out that she had shot and killed Rolf. When asked where Rolf was at the time, Ruth had said that the body was in the tub in the bathroom and the elderly relative living with her was in there cutting it up.

"You didn't see the body?" Canova asked.

The witness explained that she had been shocked that Ruth had said the body was being cut up, but she was not completely surprised that Ruth had killed him because she was aware of the physical arguments between the couple.

"Did you see the relative she told you was cutting up the body?" Canova asked.

The witness responded that she had seen the man several times while at the house that evening. He came out of the bathroom, looked in to where they were sitting in the music room, and had smiled. She said he had made several trips between the bathroom and the kitchen, smiling but not saying anything.

The testimony, which could not be shaken on cross-examination, was a telling blow to the defense.

In his summation, Pros. Canova told the panel that the testimony they had heard and the exhibits they had seen was compelling evidence that Ruth Neslund had shot and killed her husband and then, with the help of a relative, had burned the body.

"Taken together, all the physical evidence is overwhelming beyond a reasonable doubt," Canova said.

Weedon addressed the jurors by telling them, "We put no halo on Ruth. It doesn't fit. Obviously she drank a tremendous lot, but that is no reason to think that she killed her husband."

Stressing the fact that the prosecution had not produced a body, Weedon told them, "We don't know where Rolf Neslund is, but that's not enough for a conviction. Just because he hasn't been seen since 1980 is no reason to believe he's dead, or if he is dead that he did not commit suicide."

In an impassioned plea, he urged the panel, "Send Ruth back to her home on Lopez Island a free woman."

After more than a month of hearing testimony, the jurors received instructions from Judge Bibb as to how they should consider the testimony they had heard and the verdict to be rendered. He stated they could find the defendant innocent, or if guilty, they could decide whether it was manslaughter, second-degree or first-degree murder.

It was late Wednesday night, December 11, 1985, when the instructions were completed. Judge Bibb ordered that the panel be sequestered in a hotel and begin their deliberations in the morning.

Reporters asked Canova and Weedon how long they thought it would take the jurors to reach a verdict. Both attorneys agreed that it probably wouldn't take very long. They would either come to a decision early that Ruth was innocent, or if they found the state's case sufficient for a guilty verdict, it would be only a matter of deciding the degree.

But, both attorneys were wrong in their assumptions.

The panel deliberated all day Thursday. Windows in the courtroom had been covered so that they could examine the numerous pieces of evidence that had been introduced as exhibits. They retired Thursday night without coming to an agreement.

The attorneys were asked for their reactions to the length of time it was taking to reach a verdict. Weedon thought it bode well for the defense. "The longer they take, the better it looks for us," he said. Canova was of the opinion that the panel was deliberating the degree in which the defendant was found to be guilty. He said he felt certain he had produced a case to show that a killing had taken place, but the jury might be taking into consideration the hectic life of the battling Neslunds and deciding whether the penalty should be manslaughter or second-degree murder.

The panel continued their deliberations on Friday. Reporters stayed on at the courthouse waiting for a decision, but the bell from the room where they were deliberating did not ring. They retired for the night.

Both the defense and prosecuting attorneys became concerned about the length of time it was taking the panel to reach a verdict. Weedon felt that they would have agreed soon if they found his client innocent. Canova was concerned that there might be a holdout, which would mean that they could not reach a unanimous agreement and a new trial would be required.

The lengthy investigation and the many delays, with the expense of bringing witnesses from out-of-state and lodging them in Friday Harbor had cost the state thousands of dollars.

The panel continued their deliberations on Saturday. There was no indication from the jurors as to what problem they were having in reaching a verdict. They had not asked the court for further instructions.

Judge Bibb also became concerned over the length of time it was taking the panel. He contacted Canova and Weedon and said that if a verdict was not arrived at soon, he wanted to confer with them and contact the panel to see if they were deadlocked.

Weedon, while not pleased that the panel hadn't returned with a verdict finding his client innocent, was not opposed to having the panel declared deadlocked and a new trial scheduled. It would mean that Ruth could remain free on bond until a new court date could be set.

Canova said he was definitely opposed to having the jury declared deadlocked until it could be positively determined that they could not reach an agreement. It had already been more than five years since Rolf Neslund was reported to have disappeared. More delays would mean locating the witnesses and preserving the evidence. He also pointed out that a number of the witnesses had been elderly and might not be available at a new trial.

The panel retired Saturday night without a verdict. The foreman announced that they would continue their deliberations on Sunday.

Speculation was rife among the courtroom observers and reporters as to what the outcome might be. One of them commented that it would be on Sunday and near Christmas as they went into session again. It might be that the holiday season would temper their decision.

The panel broke for lunch on Sunday. It was evident from the faces of the jurors as they were led from the courthouse to lunch and then returned to the room where they were deliberating that the length of time consumed in reaching a decision was taking its toll on them.

Shortly before six o'clock, the bell sounded. The foreman informed a bailiff that the panel had reached a unanimous agreement.

Judge Bibb and the attorneys were notified. The courtroom quickly filled with observers and reporters. With the court in session, the panel was called in to report their findings at eight o'clock.

It was noted that two of the women on the panel appeared to have been crying. The male members were grim-faced as the foreman handed a bailiff the slip with their findings on it.

Judge Bibb accepted the slip. The courtroom was silent with nervous tension as he read it and then announced:

"We the jury find the defendant, Ruth Neslund, guilty of murder in the first-degree, as charged."

There were audible gasps from the spectators, but no show of emotion from Ruth as the verdict was read.

The verdict carried with it a mandatory life sentence. Judge Bibb ordered that the bond for the defendant be rescinded and that she should be taken into custody and detained in the sheriff's jail until such time as a formal sentence was passed on January 13, 1986.

Reporters were eager to talk to the jurors who had taken so long to reach the verdict. The jury foreman, with tears in her eyes, told them, "It was not the decision we would have liked to reach, but the evidence was too much." She said each member of the panel had gone over the evidence numerous times until they found that there was no alternative but to impose the guilty verdict.

Media reporters followed Ruth out of the courtroom and to the walk up the stairs to the jail in the courthouse. She was assisted by deputies and used a cane and refused any comment except to say, "I can make it. I'm all right."

Pros. Canova said he was pleased with the verdict, but admitted the best he had expected was a finding for second-degree murder.

He had high praise for the investigators who had worked so hard and long to gather the evidence.

"There aren't many cases nationwide where there's been a conviction with no body," he said. "The jury did an incredibly thorough, conscientious job and did what the evidence indicated they should have done."

Defense Attorney Weedon told the reporters that he was disappointed and shaken by the verdict, particularly because they had found his client guilty of first-degree murder when they could have found for voluntary manslaughter or second-degree.

Asked how Ruth was taking the verdict, Weedon replied, "A lot better than the rest of us. She's one gutsy old lady."

Weedon said because of the age of Ruth and

the problem with her health, he would have to consider at a later time if he planned to appeal the decision.

Members of the communities on the island were contacted by reporters as to their reaction of the verdict. Many expressed surprise that it had been first-degree.

One of the residents summed it up with, "We're a small group on these islands. It isn't often that anything very interesting happens. It's been our entertainment for almost five years, almost like watching a soap opera."

In January 1986, Ruth Neslund was sentenced to life in prison. Judge Robert Bibb recommended that she serve at least 20 years in prison.

"GRANDMA WAS CHOPPED UP, THEN COOKED!"

by Jack Heise

Friends of Grandma Elaine Witte in Trail Creek, a small rural community a few miles east of Michigan City, Indiana, were pleased when they heard that she was going on a vacation. The 74-year-old widow had been through a few rough years, late in life.

First, her only son had been killed in a tragic accident on September 1, 1981. His oldest son had been playing with his father's gun when it discharged and the slug hit his father in the back of his head.

Then, a few months later, the house in which his widow and two sons were living in Beverly Shores mysteriously burned to the ground.

Granda Witte invited her daughter-in-law and two grandsons to come live with her in Trail Creek.

It didn't work out very well, however. The

boys, who were 14 and 17 at the time, were brats. Some said they were a pain to Grandma Witte.

John, who was called Butch, was the worse of the two. He managed to get himself expelled from school and then spent days smoking pot and drinking.

It wasn't to Grandma's liking and wasn't the way she raised her children, but her daughter-in-law, Marie, who doted on the boys, refused to hear her criticism and practically let them run wild.

Grandma knew more about her daughter-in-law than she had confided to even her close friends.

Her son Paul, a steel worker, had met Marie in a nudist camp while he was on a vacation in Florida. She was 16 years old at the time.

When Paul returned from his vacation, he called Marie's family and asked to marry Marie. The child bride took off on a bus to Trail Creek, and Paul brought her home. Elaine Witte thought Marie was awfully young to become a wife for her Paul, who was ten years her senior, but accepted that he wanted to marry her.

It wasn't Marie's first marriage, however.

At age 14, she had been married to a coast-guardsman in a ceremony at the nudist camp. Photographs from nudist publications covered the wedding, in which Marie was clad only in a wedding veil. Guests were charged admission and the photos appeared in a number of publications. But the marriage lasted a short while, when

Marie had a miscarriage and her husband of a couple of months divorced her.

A short time after Marie and Paul married, he bought a home and some acreage at Beverly Shores where he could maintain his hobby of breeding sled dogs.

Marie and Paul evidently hit it off all right, despite her young age, but Elaine Witte wasn't overly fond of her daughter-in-law and particularly the way she kept house. Dogs with their pups were kept inside the house, creating a smell and mess.

After the fire, Marie sold off all of the animals when she and her boys came to live with Grandma Witte.

In the late fall of 1983, Eric, the older of the two boys, joined the Navy and was sent to boot camp at Great Lakes, Illinois. Butch, as obnoxious as ever, stayed on with his mother and grandmother.

In January of 1984, Marie told neighbors that Grandma Witte had left on a well-deserved vacation. She was vague about where she had gone, except to say she was visiting relatives and didn't know exactly when she might return.

Neighbors noted in the spring that Marie had bought a new motor home. She and Butch left in it for a vacation to California, where Eric was stationed with the Navy. No one had actually seen Grandma Witte, and it wasn't known whether or not she had been with them.

In September, one of Grandma's relatives living in the east became concerned. She had been unable to reach Grandma or Marie by telephone, and then learned that the telephone had been disconnected.

She came to Trail Creek to find out what was going on, and was shocked when she went to Grandma Witte's house and noted it was practically devoid of furniture. Even the bed she had slept in was not there.

The relative went to the Trail Creek police to see if they could find any answers. She talked to Sergeant Eugene Pierce.

He suggested that possibly the best way to locate Grandma was to go to where she banked. She received Social Security checks and would need money to live on.

A shock awaited them when the bank manager checked on Grandma Witte's account. In January, she had transferred her considerable savings account into her checking account and the funds had been systematically withdrawn from a cash machine. It appeared to be more than a coincidence that the account of her daughter-in-law had been enriched by about the same amount Grandma Witte's account had been depleted.

Marie's account had been closed out at the time she purchased the motor home and went on a vacation to California.

The bank manager explained that all the transactions were perfectly legal. He had no address for Marie and hadn't seen or heard from Grandma Witte.

Pierce suggested another means of locating Grandma Witte. He contacted the Social Security office to learn where her checks were being sent. It took awhile, but they came up with the information that they were being mailed to general delivery in San Diego, California.

The checks were located. They had been endorsed by Marie Witte and cashed.

Sgt. Pierce requested that the checks be examined by a handwriting expert to determine if Grandma Witte's signature had been forged.

Meanwhile, Pierce contacted Detective Sergeant Arland Boyd of the Indiana State Police. "I don't know quite what has been going on," he said. "But it doesn't look good. The daughter-in-law is out in California and no one has seen or heard from the old lady since January."

"Let's wait and see what they come up with on those Social Security checks," Boyd suggested. "Maybe we'll have some leverage to pry loose some information."

In the early part of November, a report came in from Larry Ziegler, a handwriting expert with the Secret Service. He stated that, in his opinion, the signatures of Elaine Witte were tracings from an original signature.

The evidence was enough to support charges of federal forgery and conspiracy against Marie Witte and her son Eric, who had cashed the checks. They were taken into custody in San Diego.

Marie was questioned as to the whereabouts of Grandma Witte. She said she didn't know, didn't care, and if they wanted to locate the old lady, they'd just have to find her themselves.

Pierce and Boyd, looking for someone in Indiana who might have answers, learned that Marie's family had been living in Trail Creek.

They questioned one relative of Marie's, who told them that she didn't know where Grandma Witte might be and hadn't heard from Marie since she left for the vacation to California.

The detectives told her quite frankly that they didn't believe her, and if she was concealing information, she could be charged as an accessory.

Quite unexpectedly, the woman said she was willing to make a statement.

After being advised of her legal rights, Marie's relative said she knew that Grandma Witte was dead and that her grandson had shot her with a crossbow.

What's more, she added, Marie's husband Paul had not been killed accidentally. He had been deliberately shot by his son Eric on instructions from his mother.

In the statement, she related that Paul Witte had been seriously injured in a motorcycle accident. He had given up his work at the steel mill and went into breeding sled dogs full-time. The relative said that, at one time, Paul had as many as 70 dogs outside the house and 30 female dogs with their pups inside the house.

His injury had made him irritable, and he was abusive to his wife and sons. Marie had threatened to divorce him, but he had warned her that he would not pay her alimony or child support.

The relative claimed Marie had attempted to poison her husband by putting rat poison in his food, but somehow it wasn't effective. So then Marie came up with the plot to have Eric shoot his father, and she and Butch would swear that they had witnessed it and it was accidental.

The relative said Eric had shot his father in the back of his head as he lay sleeping on a davenport in the house on the mid-morning of September 1, 1981.

Relating the murder of Grandma Witte, Marie's relative said Grandma learned that someone had been using her bank card to withdraw money from her account and had accused Butch of it. Actually, Marie had withdrawn the money, and she became fearful of what would happen when Grandma Witte said she was going to the bank to find out what was going on.

The relative recalled that she had received a telephone call from Marie in early January of 1984 asking her to come to the house because she needed help.

When she arrived, Marie told her that Butch had killed his grandmother by shooting her in the chest with a bolt from a crossbow. After the old woman was dead, Marie had called Eric at boot camp and asked him what she should do with the body. He told her to put the corpse into the freezer they had in the basement, and he would figure out what could be done as soon as he could get a pass.

Marie told her, the relative claimed, that she and Butch had spent three days hacking up the old woman's body with butcher knives, a chisel, a hammer and finally with an electric chainsaw she had bought. Then the body parts were put in the freezer.

Eric came home from boot camp on an overnight pass. He advised his mother to have a garbage disposal unit and a trash compactor installed. They could get rid of the flesh down the disposal and crush the bones in the trash compactor.

Marie purchased the appliances. But it didn't work out. Parts of the flesh became enmeshed in the disposal and burned out the motor. They put Grandma Witte's head in the trash compactor and that machine, too, broke.

The relative said Marie called her for help because she was fearful that people might come checking on the old woman and, if they found the body parts in the freezer, it would be curtains for them.

The woman allegedly admitted that it had been her idea to cook up the flesh to make it look like a stew. They could freeze the bags of stew until

Eric could come home and figure out some way to dispose of them and the bones. She claimed that she and Marie had spent nearly a week cooking Grandma Witte into sacks of stew.

With the statement obtained from Marie's relative, Boyd and Pierce questioned Eric and Butch, advising them of the statement they had obtained.

Butch was the first to voluntarily give a statement, after being advised of his legal rights.

He said he had never gotten along with Grandma Witte, and she was always picking on him and accusing him of stealing money from her purse. His mother told him that the old woman was going to the bank to check on some withdrawals from her account using her bank machine card. She said, he claimed, that if the old woman found out what was going on she would toss them out of the house, so the only solution was to get rid of her.

He stated that his mother had awakened him at six o'clock on the morning of January 10th and told him that it had to be done right away.

He went to the basement, where his brother had a crossbow in a trunk. He brought it upstairs and went into his grandmother's room. She was still in bed sleeping. He shot her in the chest with the bolt and then called to his mother and told her the old woman was dead.

His mother told him that she had an appointment with the Social Security office in Chicago, and told him to clean up the mess as best he could and she would be back to help him.

He said he got a garbage can, shoved his grandmother head first into it and waited until his mother returned.

The statement detailed the trouble they'd had cutting up the body so that it would fit in the freezer before his mother bought an electric chainsaw to solve that problem.

Confronted with the statement given by his brother, Eric voluntarily gave the detectives an account of his involvement.

He said that his mother had discussed killing his grandmother even before he had left for boot camp, but he hadn't wanted any part of it because of the trouble he'd had after shooting his father. He said he was sure that the police wouldn't buy the story of two accidental killings.

Eric admitted that after his mother called him and he came home, it had been his idea to get the garbage disposal and the trash compactor. Several weeks later, he obtained a leave and came home again, bringing with him a buddy from boot camp. He said that he hadn't told his buddy about his grandmother's body being in the freezer until after this buddy had spent a couple of nights sleeping with his mother.

Eric said they had told his buddy that the killing had been accidental, that Butch had shot the old woman when he stumbled on the stairs while carrying the crossbow upstairs.

He said he had brought home some acid with him and planned to dissolve the bones with it, but it didn't do the job. So they mashed up the grandmother's head as best they could and pulled out all her teeth and cracked them with a pair of pliers so they couldn't be identified.

In his statement, Eric said that his buddy offered what appeared to be the perfect solution to getting rid of the body parts that were in the freezer. They were scheduled to leave boot camp shortly and assume duty in San Diego. They would drive to California and toss out the bags along the route. No one would recognize them as body parts.

Eric said his mother bought a used pickup truck with a camper. When he and the buddy were transferred to San Diego, they loaded up all the sacks with the grandmother's body parts in them. Then they tossed them out, at various places along the road in three states, as they made the trip.

Eric's buddy gave the detectives a statement, in which he confirmed what Eric had said. He entered a guilty plea to a charge of illegally disposing of a human body, and received a seven-months sentence in exchange for a promise to testify.

Eric was offered immunity from prosecution in exchange for his testimony in the murder of Grandma Witte, but not for the murder of his father. Eric faces a sentence of 20 years for that murder. He is currently in jail.

In a plea-bargaining session, Butch agreed to testify against his mother in exchange for a plea of guilty to the charge of involuntary manslaughter and a 20-year sentence.

Marie Witte was charged with first-degree murder and conspiracy to commit murder, but was not brought back to Indiana until after she and Eric had gone on trial for the federal charges of forgery and conspiracy in California. Both were convicted, but sentencing was delayed until after trials could be heard for the murders of Elaine and Paul Witte in Indiana.

The trial of Marie Witte for the murder of Elaine opened in the court of Judge Donald De-Martin in Michigan City on November 4, 1985. Prosecutor William Herrbach presented the state's case, and Attorney Scott King represented the defendant. A panel of ten men and two women were selected to hear the evidence.

Before the trial started, with the jurors out of the room, the attorneys presented Judge Martin with a difficult decision.

Herrbach requested the court's permission to introduce testimony concerning the slaying of Paul Witte. King objected. He said he represented the defendant against the charge of having murdered her husband. It would amount to having to defend her against both charges, and the testimony would be irrelevant and illegal.

Herrbach argued that the testimony would

show the mental attitude the defendant had toward murder, and the influence she had over her sons in committing the killings for her.

One of Marie's relatives was among the first witnesses to be called. Her testimony was a repetition of the statement she had given to police earlier, detailing her knowledge that Marie had attempted to kill her husband with rat poison and, failing in that, had cajoled her teenage son into shooting his father to death.

In a chilling recital, she told how she and Marie had spent nearly a week cooking up the flesh of Grandma Witte to make it appear to be a stew.

In cross-examination, King had the witness admit that her memory was not always good, but he couldn't shake her from the testimony she had given against Marie.

Butch was next to testify. He calmly related that his father had abused him, his brother and his mother. He said he was present when he saw Eric shoot his father, but felt no remorse for the slaying.

Discussing the death of his grandmother, Butch said he had never liked her because she picked on his and accused him of stealing money from her. He said when his mother told him that she had to be killed, he simply carried out her wishes.

While the panel and spectators appeared to cringe at Butch's gruesome testimony of how he and his mother had cut up the victim's body with an electric chainsaw, Butch appeared perfectly calm.

It wasn't until he was questioned in cross-examination that he lost his composure. When King suggested to him that his mother had not instructed him to kill his grandmother, but he had killed her because she had accused him of stealing from her, and his mother had only tried to protect him, Butch flared, used profanity, and called the attorney a liar.

At one point, the witness appeared as if he was going to leave the witness stand to strike the attorney and was restrained by bailiffs. Judge Martin called a recess until the witness could get control of himself.

Eric was then called to testify. He began by stating that he had not received immunity from prosecution or any promises for the charge he faced of having killed his father. He said he felt the time had come when everyone should tell the truth about what had happened.

Referring to the death of his father, he said his mother had come to him and told him that she could no longer stand the abuse, and that if he did not kill his father, she would kill him herself. He said that, faced with the choice of losing his mother or his father, he had agreed to kill his father.

He related that, prior to leaving for boot camp, his mother had discussed with him plans to kill Grandma Witte and to make it appear to be an accident. He said he had advised her against it because he thought the police hadn't been completely satisfied that he had killed his father accidentally and it would just open up the whole thing again.

Eric said he wasn't completely surprised when his mother called him to say that Butch had killed Grandma Witte.

He related coming home and advising her to get a garbage disposal unit and a trash compactor to dispose of the body. He said his involvement was simply to protect his mother and brother.

Cross-examination was similar to that heard when Butch had been on the witness stand. King asked him if it wasn't true that he had shot his father because he had been chastised, and that his mother hadn't been aware of it until after his father had been killed, at which point she had concocted the story about it being an accident in order to protect him. Eric said that it was not true. What had happened was the way he had related it.

Eric's buddy from boot camp was called as a witness. He testified to having sex with Marie, stating that Eric and Butch knew about it but hadn't objected because they felt that their mother needed a man.

He said he had been told that Butch had accidentally shot his grandmother with the crossbow, and he had helped dispose of the body parts in the freezer out of friendship for Eric and his relationship with Marie.

Prosecutor Herrbach concluded the state's case with testimony from the investigators, laboratory experts and witnesses who were aware of certain things that had taken place.

Employees from the bank testified how Grandma Witte's savings had been transferred into her checking account and then withdrawn by means of her bank machine card.

Testimony was heard from employees where Marie had purchased the garbage disposal and trash compactor. They said she had been insistent that the appliances be delivered and installed immediately.

With the state's case completed, courtroom observers wondered what kind of a defense King could offer to offset the testimony and evidence introduced by Herrbach.

King called Marie to testify in her own defense. Guided by her attorney, she related her life as a child in the nudist camp, with little or no supervision as she cavorted around the camp naked, and she told of older male members who had more on their minds than playing volley ball in the buff.

She told of becoming pregnant at 14, and of the marriage ceremony in which everyone was nude and she wore only a bridal veil. There was a brief stay with her husband until she had a miscarriage and he divorced her.

She related being sent up to Indiana to marry a man she had only known for a short time while he was at the nudist camp.

Her life with her new husband had been good, she said, up until the time of the birth of Butch. He was a sickly child. As he grew older, he was a bedwetter and often threw temper tantrums that annoyed his father.

The big break in her relationship with her husband came, Marie testified, after he had been injured in a motorcycle accident and spent all of his time at home breeding sled dogs. She said he became mean, beating his sons, and when she refused to have sex with him, he would tear off her clothes and rape her.

On the mid-morning that her husband was shot, Marie said she had been in the yard. Eric came out of the house screaming that he had killed his father. She said she was almost certain that it hadn't been an accident, because Eric and his father had been arguing. To protect her son, she said she had coached both Eric and Butch on what they were to say when the police came.

Testifying about the death of Elaine Witte, she related how her mother-in-law was critical of Butch, scolding him for being a worthless bum and accusing him of stealing money from her. She flatly denied ever entertaining any notion of killing the elderly woman.

She recalled that, on the morning Grandma Witte had been killed, Butch came to her crying that he had shot his grandmother with the cross-bow and sobbed, "I didn't mean to. It just happened."

Marie did not deny that she had helped dispose of the old woman's body, by cutting it into pieces with the electric chainsaw so that it could be placed in the freezer, or later enlisting the aid of her relative to disguise the body pieces as stew meat.

She maintained she had done all of those things only to protect Butch, because she knew the police would think it strange that Eric had accidentally killed his father and Butch had accidentally killed his grandmother.

She did not deny taking the money from Grandma Witte's bank account. She explained that she reasoned her dead mother-in-law would have no use for the money, and she feared it might go to other relatives.

Under cross-examination, Herrbach asked Marie how she could explain the difference in her account of what had happened and that which her two sons had testified to.

Tearfully, Marie responded that she had no answer. "I've been good to all of them," she said. "Now, they have turned against me."

In his closing argument, Herrbach pointed out to the jurors that the defendant had admitted her part in disposing of the body. The point they had to consider was whether she had influenced and conspired with her son to kill her mother-in-law.

He said that the only thing they had to deliberate was whether the defendant's two sons and relative had told the truth, or if they could accept her story.

"I think you will find that this is not a complicated case," Herrbach said. "The motive is as old as crime itself — greed."

Pointing to Marie, he added, "She is a scheming, greedy woman who used her own sons to kill her husband and her mother-in-law."

In his closing argument, King pleaded with the panel to consider that the state had made deals with the witnesses for their testimony, and they had been coached to lie to save their own skins.

"It is those lies that make no sense of the state's claim that they have produced evidence that is beyond a reasonable doubt."

Judge Martin instructed the jurors as to what they should consider in their deliberations and the various degrees of guilt that they might consider if they did not find the defendant innocent. The panel took the case to deliberate at two o'clock Friday afternoon, November 8, 1985.

They broke for dinner and then returned to continue their deliberations. At seven o'clock, they sent out word that they had reached a unanimous decision.

Judge Martin called the court into session. The jury foreman handed a bailiff the decision of the panel. Judge Martin took it and read:

"We the jury find the defendant guilty of murder, and we the jury find the defendant guilty of conspiracy to commit murder."

Marie gave no outward sign of emotion as the verdict was read.

Judge Martin announced that he would pronounce the sentences at a later date.

In a statement to news reporters following the trial, prosecutor Herrbach said that he had not asked for the death penalty, but would recommend to Judge Martin that she be given the maximum sentence of 60 years for the murder conviction and 50 years for the conviction of conspiracy, to be served consecutively for a total of 110 years.

King told the reporters that he had taken the defense for a fee much smaller than normal because it had been an intriguing case, but he had little hope of obtaining an acquittal after the testimony from his client's two sons. He said he would continue to defend his client in the trial, in which she was charged with having murdered her husband.

Asked if he planned to request an appeal, King said that he would consider it later, but added, "I have never been treated as well by the court and staff as I have been here, and I have enormous respect for Judge Martin."

Marie later went on trial for the murder of her husband in Valpariso, Porter County, before Judge Bruce Douglass. It was almost a replica of the first trial in which her sons testified for the state.

It took three days to present the evidence, and the jurors took eight hours to render a verdict. Marie was found guilty of murder and attempted murder.

Pending appeals, Marie will spend the rest of her life in prison.

"THE LESBIAN LOVERS SPUN A LETHAL WEB!"

by Pat Turner

To the arriving patrolmen, it appeared to be one of those modern tragedies — a routine burglary that went wrong, the killing of a home-owner who interrupted the break-in artist and paid for it with his life.

The killer-thief broke his way into the split-level in the Central New Jersey suburb of Piscataway and butchered Robert Downey when the 33-year-old father of three children apparently woke up early that morning two days before Christmas, Dec. 23, 1981 and found a burglar in his house.

Robert Richard Downey was not a guy who succumbed easily. He was tall, almost 5 feet 10 inches, about 200 pounds, with reddish brown hair and a reddish brown-trimmed beard.

He could probably take care of himself in a

barroom fight but Bob Downey didn't get into barroom brawls.

More likely his stature stood him in good stead as a volunteer fireman.

But Piscataway Police Patrolman Jack McDonald didn't know any of these things when he pulled his police car into the headquarters parking lot that morning, Dec. 23rd, about 11:30 a.m. McDonald is an ordinary cop. He's done his job for years and well knows his way around the sprawling township he has sworn to protect. Jack McDonald doesn't go looking for a fuss, but he knew what to do when a man he had never seen before ran towards him outside headquarters screaming that a woman had just come up to him saying she found her husband dead in the house.

Radioing for assistance, the cop sped to the address he was given on Stratton Street near the Middlesex borough.

It's routine for McDonald, and for every good cop, to make immediate observations and later to relate them in the impassionate language that keeps cops sane.

There were two vehicles parked in the driveway of the split-level house in question, McDonald would later recall, and two white females talking to each other in one of them, a white Chevy station wagon.

McDonald approached the car on the passenger side and quietly inquired if one of the women had summoned help. The woman, later identified as Diane April Downey said she did.

By now, McDonald's back-up for this incident, Patrolman Dennis Duvall, had arrived, and both lawmen were directed by the woman to a house across the street.

Upon entering, the officers were faced with a grisly scene. As McDonald recalled, "There was blood spattered on the walls, on the floor . . . buckets of blood. The furniture was overturned, the floor was covered with blood. We could see a body in an upright, sitting position, the pajama top open in front, his intestines sticking out."

Despite the horror, McDonald functioned as a cop. He walked around through the dining room and reached towards the blood-drenched form, careful not to step into the kitchen from the dining room entryway. McDonald checked for vital signs, a macabre task set against a grisly scene.

There was no pulse. The man was still and cold to the touch.

McDonald was very clear about this, and about another fact every cop will recognize: he never stepped into the kitchen. Nor did Duvall. Instead, he radioed headquarters and then followed the trail of blood.

McDonald and Duvall knew the body was cold, but they did not know whether the burglar-turned-savage-killer might be trapped inside the house with them.

Nonetheless, they knew their jobs. McDonald and Duvall saw, as McDonald told it later, blood splattered up the walls in the hallway, five or six feet. There was blood on the floors and carpet; a lot of blood in the bathroom, a pool of 12 to 14 inches across, coagulated and dry.

Carefully, their senses at a high pitch, the men checked the bathroom and then, at the end of the hallway, the master bedroom.

Here, in the matching bureau, McDonald and Duvall saw classic signs of a burglary: all of the drawers pulled out five or six inches.

But the cops' training paid off. They were quick to notice a major discrepancy from the usual household burglary: the drawers were undisturbed even though they stood yanked open.

"There were two big blood spots on the bed," McDonald said, "and the covers were pulled back."

McDonald notified his superiors of the magnitude of the problem and began his criminal investigation report."

"I had to get the vital information on the victim," McDonald recalled.

Although there were signs of a break-in, police would have to know whether the victim, however unpleasant it is to speak ill of the dead, had enemies; whether, on the other hand, he had a lover.

Then McDonald went outside again, in the cold gray air that precedes Christmas in New Jersey.

Aware now that the woman who sent him into the house was the victim's wife, now his widow,

McDonald began with all the obvious and important questions: Diane Downey, a stocky, 33-year-old woman, had last seen her husband alive at 10:00 p.m. the night before. She was talking to him at the place where he worked.

As McDonald took notes, Diane Downey told of the horrifying discovery. She and her friend, Linda Prudden the other woman with her, had decided to deliver some Christmas packages to Diane Downey's home at 11:15 a.m. that day.

They had pulled up to the house, and, finding Bob's car in the driveway, went into the house. Linda headed down the stairs to open the garage door so they could carry the boxes in. Diane took the right-hand stairs up.

For some reason neither woman could explain, they had instructed Diane's three-year-old daughter to remain in the car.

Unlike both McDonald and Duvall, whose first recollection was of the awkward and lifeless legs protruding into their consciousness, Diane Downey recalled first noticing that the kitchen telephone was off the hook. She reached over and replaced the phone on its hook. She didn't notice the blood, the furniture overturned or the body, Diane Downey told McDonald. Instead, she saw that typical suburban telephone, and it was out of place, so she returned it to its rightful spot.

McDonald's instincts were alerted. He noticed band-aids on Mrs. Downey's hands when he spoke to her again, she sitting in the stationwagon, he standing in the driveway.

Diane Downey had an explanation for the band-aids and the dried blood on her hands. Confronted, finally, with her husband's brutalized body, she reached towards him and cut herself on glass near his brown curly hair on the floor, she said.

"Where are the little papers band-aids come in?" McDonald asked. She knew she had found the band-aids in the car, but she didn't know where the papers had gone.

While this transpired, Duvall continued his routine investigation. He went into the cellar, found what looked like blood spots on the floor and back door open six inches. The striker plate was on the floor and there was a chip from the door. Was this the site of the break-in?

Duval merely looked; he touched nothing, disturbed nothing. By now, others had arrived, detectives more polished in the skills necessary at a crime scene.

Det. Sgt. Joseph Triano now spoke to Mrs. Downey. She told him of a marriage that had run nine years, of three children, 3, 5 and 7 years old. She said it was a normal marriage up until the time of an auto accident she suffered in March, 1980.

All of this Diane Downey recalled calmly outside her home, while her husband lay lifeless on the kitchen floor of the home they shared, slashed and stabbed almost 50 times.

After leaving the hospital, Diane Downey said, she found it impossible to care for that home and her three children unless she had more help than Bob could provide.

He was working two jobs, after all, and wasn't often around when she needed him. She went to live with the Pruddens. It was Linda Prudden who sat the driver's position in her station wagon, listening to all this.

For a while, the Pruddens had moved in with the Downeys, she said, but most of the time, she and her children lived with Linda Prudden, her husband and two pre-teen boys.

Diane Downey told Det. Triano that she and her husband had argued several times about this arrangement.

But he insisted that she return home with his children on Christmas. That's why she and Linda Prudden were there that day and why she saw the body.

Knowing his task, Triano probed. Diane Downey told him that because of her auto accident, she was unable to have sex with her husband. He remained celibate, Triano recalled her saying. He, Downey was handling everything okay, as she was.

But what kind of man was Bob Downey, Triano wanted to know. What was his nature? He was a very passive, introverted individual, his widow reported. Sometimes he became depressed and would cry. She had to make all the important

393

decisions.

No, he had not engaged in extramarital affairs. Yes, he was a wonderful family man, true blue, in her words. He wanted her to come home with the children.

Could he be the victim of a botched break-in? Triano asked. He was paranoid, his wife answered. He made sure all the doors and windows were locked before retiring for the evening. He was paranoid from being alone.

Maybe Bob Downey had reason for his concern, Triano said. Certainly he had died a horrible death, cut down, no, butchered, two days short of the Christmas he sought with his little family.

There would be no last minute Christmas shopping for Bob Downey, nor, this year, for the officers who sought to answer the questions of his savage murder.

The man across the street probably provided the first clues. He was a tractor trailer driver who fixed cars in a small garage across the street from the Downey home. He knew Bob Downey from high school and even sometimes parked cars he had finished in the Downey driveway which Bob had agreed to.

The woman he recognized as Diane Downey approached him that morning and told him someone had done a number on her husband.

Because he had no telephone in his garage, this man drove to Piscataway police headquarters.

That's where he met Patrolman McDonald.

There was an officer who found a neighbor who remembered seeing Linda Prudden in a white Chevy station wagon near the Downey house sometime around 11:30 the previous night, a time when both Diane Downey and Linda Prudden told probers they were nowhere near the Downey home.

There were the officers who executed the search warrant at the Prudden home in Bound Brook, the home to which Diane Downey had taken Bob's three beloved kids all those months before and from where he insisted they return home for a family Christmas.

Those officers found an incredibly sharp fishing or hunting knife hidden among falling ceiling tiles in the laundry room, the first place a woman with blood on her clothes would go, they reasoned.

Diane Downey and Linda Prudden, in fact, said they had done wash that fateful morning.

That knife was matched by New Jersey State Police Laboratory forensic experts to a rip in the blood-purpled pajama shirt stripped from Bob Downey's mutilated body.

And it was matched by the medical examiner to a wound which he traced five and one-half inches from the skin into the liver, one of 48 wounds to Bob Downey's scalp, head, throat, chest, back, arms, hands, abdomen and legs.

Smerecki and Nemeth took into account, too,

Diane Downey's wounds, the ones she said resulted from glass on the floor next to her husband's body. They photographed them and made sure they were ready to testify about them, should the matter come to trial.

And come to trial, it did; murder charges were lodged against the widow and against Diane Downey's companion, Linda Prudden.

But it's a long way from a murder charge to a conviction. Everyone involved, experts from the New Jersey State Police and the FBI, handwriting specialists, and blood specialists, fingerprint specialists and hair analysts—all had to work very hard for these convictions.

These investigators may have even pioneered New Jersey law in their use of a forensic anthropologist from Kent State University in Ohio, who testified that there were footprints which matched Linda Prudden's, and which proved that she had been sneaking around the bathroom and bedroom in her stocking feet during the night of the murder.

A certified locksmith and break-in expert further testified that jimmy marks found on the back basement door knob were faked because the marks were on the inside of the door.

To further enhance its case, the prosecution provided numerous photographs, charts and diagrams.

No one wants to speak ill of the dead, certainly not the victim's bereaved relatives. But someone, some sensitive and careful police officer had to solicit the information about what was clearly a marriage gone wrong through homosexuality and hatred.

It was crucial to investigators that Bob Downey's closest family discuss the problems they knew he encountered in his last year or 18 months.

It was even important to try to enlist the aid of Diane Downey's co-defendant, Linda Prudden.

For it was Linda Prudden's white Chevy station wagon that a neighbor saw that night outside the Downey home when both women said it couldn't be there, and Linda Prudden's home where the crucial knife was found hidden in the ceiling tiles.

Eventually, Linda Prudden would tell a sordid tale of lesbian love, claiming she had lied to help her friend.

Eventually, too, Diane Downey's lawyer would try to blame Linda Prudden for the foul deed.

Two separate juries made their own determinations: Diane April Downey and Linda Marie Prudden were found guilty of murder.

In his opening remarks to the jury, Prosecutor Thomas Kapsak termed theirs a bizarre relationship and described Diane Downey's hatred and contempt for her husband.

Diane Downey, Kapsak said, moved into the bed of Linda Prudden. Robert Downey accepted this, although he didn't like it.

Kapsak described Robert Downey as a simple, hard-working man, a man who held two jobs, adored his children and tried desperately to save his marriage.

But, Kapsak contended there were sinister forces at work in his life, forces that would lead to his death.

On November 24, 1982, Diane Downey was found guilty of murdering her husband. She was sentenced on January 17, 1983 to life in prison.

Linda Prudden was also convicted of murder on February 17, 1983 and was sentenced to life in prison on April 11, 1983.

Since Judge Nicola set no minimum term, both women will be eligible for parole in 12 to 14 years.

"MONSTER WHO SQUEEZED HIS VICTIMS TO DEATH!"

by Bruce Stockdale

Grand Island, Nebraska is a typical small Nebraska city of 33,276 souls which seemingly springs from out of nowhere in the windswept central Nebraska plains. It is the kind of small town which is so often heralded by Nebraska native Johnny Carson as the sort of All-American place which offers its inhabitants that which is best in life: law, order, security, stability and the opportunity to get ahead.

At least, 55-year-old Eugene William Zimmerman had found it so. Since coming to Grand Island 20 years before, he had prospered and his combination business-residence on West Second Street stood as testimony to what the American spirit of free enterprise could do for a man. Although "Zimmy" (as he was called by his many friends) dealt mainly in coins, his interests also embraced antiques, jewelry, indeed, anything of value. This universality of entrepreneurial spirit had provoked one friend to remark laughingly that, "Zimmy would buy your hat off your head and resell it for a profit."

It was cold that afternoon of March 6, 1979, with a stiff northerly wind pushing the wind chill factor down to a frigid zero degrees Fahrenheit. The coin dealer's wife had just returned home from work at 5:00 p.m., and upon entering the front door of the coin shop, she could readily see that something was radically wrong. The place had obviously been ransacked and repeated calls to her husband drew no response. Empty coin trays were strewn about with the coins missing. She continued to call out to her husband to no avail. Finally, with the realization that something was definitely amiss, she put in a call to the Grand Island Police Department (GIPD).

Uniformed officers responding within minutes secured the crime scene, and began a room by room search of the entire premises. In an upstairs bedroom, they were confronted with Grand Island's first homicide for the year 1979.

Lying on its back with the head facing east was the body of William Eugene Zimmerman, an electrical cord wrapped tightly around his neck, obviously beyond all mortal help.

Their discovery prompted an immediate call for detective division assistance. At 5:00 p.m., GIPD plainclothes detectives, under the command of Captain Howard Bacon, arrived on the scene. Shortly thereafter, they were joined by investigators from the Hall County Sheriff's Department (HCSD) and a mobile crime laboratory manned by the Nebraska State Patrol (NSP). (Typical of many small police agencies, the GIPD does not see many homicides; therefore, every homicide investigation of any complexity becomes a team effort of all the criminal law enforcement agencies in the area.)

Bending over the body, Captain Bacon noted that the electrical cord wrapped around the victim's neck led to a lamp and a clock. The plug of the cord had been disconnected from the wall socket. The clock showed a time of 4:30 p.m.

When the crime technicians from the state police laboratory had arrived, they began their duties by recording every detail in the room on film and sketchpad so that they could be referred to later. Meanwhile, a detective squad for the investigation was organized under the command of Lt. Carroll Ward, aged 40, an 18-year veteran of the department. Their orders were to fan out into the neighborhood in an effort to come up with anyone who might have seen anything suspicious that afternoon.

At a gas station located just across the street from the Zimmerman place, Jim Morris, the manager, told detectives that just that afternoon the victim had been in his gas station with a man and a woman with a baby. Since the manager had not paid much attention, he was unable to provide a detailed description of the couple; just that they were Caucasian, the man tall and the woman short.

A man, a woman and a baby. At least, they had a starting point for the investigation, thought Captain Bacon. He issued an appeal through the news media asking that anyone who had seen a couple on the area fitting this general description to come forward.

When their work was completed, Captain Bacon authorized the body's removal to the medical examiner's office for autopsy, and sealed the crime scene. No detective, as yet, had been able to interview the victim's wife, as she was too distraught. That would have to wait until morning.

The next day, March 7, 1979, dawned clear and cold over Grand Island, as Captain Bacon (now Chief of Police Bacon) reported for duty at 8:00 a.m. The news of the Zimmerman homicide had swept the small community like wildfire, and already a citizen had responded to the media appeal.

Donna Kingston told investigators that late the previous afternoon, she had been driving past the Zimmerman place and had observed a couple fitting the general description reported in the newspaper, walking south in front of the shop. The man appeared to be carrying a bundle in the manner one would carry a baby. The witness went on to say that after passing the couple, she had driven west to a grocery store about seven blocks away. It had been 4:45 p.m. Again, not much notice had been taken of the couple, and she was, therefore, unable to provide a detailed description of the man and woman.

Thanking the woman for her help, Captain Bacon and Lieutenant Ward returned to the Zimmerman's home, in hopes that an in-depth interview with the victim's wife might provide some more extensive information.

Mrs. Zimmerman had worked as a bookkeeper for her husband's business, and her meticulous record provided the detectives with an itemized list of missing property: a tie clasp made of a two-dollar gold piece; a silver-dollar bracelet; a silver-dollar belt buckle; a Waltham railroad watch set in an Illinois gold case; gold bullion bars; gold buttons; a diamond ring set in gold; and U.S. currency in excess of $2,000.

Captain Bacon noted that one item, the tie clasp, was readily identifiable, mounted as it was with an Indian head quarter eagle. Other easily identifiable items included a well-worn Masonic ring, with a half-carat diamond in the center of the Masonic emblem; a diamond-mounted gold wedding band; and an 1861 quarter eagle, which according to Mrs. Zimmerman once "had been chewed by hogs."

Captain Bacon copied the information and placed it in the case dossier, then began questioning Mrs. Zimmerman about the "mystery" couple. She recalled that as recently as the day before yesterday, her husband had been doing business with a couple with a small child. She described a white male abut 30 years old, six feet tall or more, with a stocky build, medium-brown hair, and ruddy complexion. The female was described as being in her mid-twenties, slightly over five feet in height, with long, medium-brown hair that was pulled back. The victim's wife was sure that she would recognize the couple if she ever saw them again.

With this, the lawmen drove the victim's wife to police headquarters so that she might work with the GIPD police artist, Det. Bruce Antonson, in an effort to produce composite drawings of the couple.

Upon his return to the Detective Division, Captain Bacon was pleased to find the autopsy report awaiting him. A quick reading confirmed his initial impression of the crime. The cause of death had been determined to have been due to strangulation with a cervical ligature (the electric cord, in this case), with the manner of death officially ruled homicide by Dr. Paul Sloss, Hall County Medical Examiner. The time of death was estimated at or very close to 4:30 p.m. on March 6, 1979.

It was agreed that the Zimmerman homicide was more than a garden variety robbery that had gone awry. This particular robber had not killed his victim in panic. Instead, the murderer had been especially cool, calculating and deliberate.

And the murder, especially brutal. One detective remarked that whoever had done it must have had a heart of stone, "the way he had wrapped that electrical cord around a man's neck and squeezed the life out of him." The detective also agreed that the killer must have had (what was to him) a very good reason for doing so—like eliminating a witness.

Obviously, the focus of the investigation at that point needed to be the identification of the mystery couple, but this was proving to be a problem.

It was at this point that Lieutenant Ward had an idea which would eventually lead to solving the riddle, but he didn't know it then. Later, as he explained in an interview with Inside Detective Magazine: "It seemed to me that in the Zimmerman homicide case, we were dealing with a typical case of murder committed in the course of a crime motivated strictly by greed. But, except for the cash taken by the perpetrator, his loot consisted of property with a very narrow market—antique coins and jewelry. In order to turn this type of property into quick cash, the killer would have little choice but to expose his merchandise to this relatively special marketplace. Therefore, it seemed to me that if we could alert the dealers in this marketplace to watch out for the stolen property, we might come up with our man. Furthermore, we knew that the legitimate coin and jewelry dealers throughout the country would cooperate with us, as they are well aware of the fact that they are always prime targets for the criminal element."

Captain Bacon quickly recognized the merit of Lieutenant Ward's idea and authorized the expenditure of agency funds for the placement of advertisements in all the coin trade journals describing the crime and the property taken. In addition, copies of the composite drawings produced with the assistance of the victim's wife were furnished to run with the advertisements.

In the meantime, sleuths continued their field investigation, attempting to turn up other witnesses who might be able to identify the couple.

Finally, on March 27, 1979, the frustrated GIPD got the break they needed to get the Zimmerman homicide investigation moving forward again.

At 6:30 p.m., Lieutenant Ward was just getting ready to head home when the telephone rang. It was Sergeant John Farrar of the Austin, Texas Police Department, advising him that they had taken into custody a person identified as one Charles Jess Palmer. Sergeant Farrar told Ward how on March 23, 1979, a man representing himself to be "J.B. Kirkpatrick" had sold one Joseph Garcia, an Austin coin dealer, the following items: a tie clasp incorporating a two-dollar gold piece; a silver-dollar bracelet; a silver-dollar belt-buckle; a Waltham railroad watch set in an Illinois gold case; gold buttons, and two necklaces.

Joseph Garcia, a reader of *Coin World Magazine,* had seen the department's advertisement concerning the stolen Zimmerman articles. After making the purchase from "J.B. Kirkpatrick," who, he noted, looked like the composite drawing run in *Coin World Magazine,* he had contacted the Austin Police Department, advising them of the transaction. The alert Austin lawmen had picked up immediately on the significance of what had happened and arranged for Garcia to set up "J.B. Kirkpatrick" should he attempt to do any more business with him. When Garcia was again contacted on the morning of May 27, 1979, Garcia agreed to purchase 23 gold presidential bars. The transaction was to be consummated at the Austin Airport.

When "Kirkpatrick" had met with Garcia at the Austin airport, he had been mightily surprised when he was suddenly surrounded by a detail of plainclothesmen, advised that he was under arrest, and given his rights under Miranda.

The Grand Island Police Department lost no time in chartering an airplane to take the joint investigative team from Grand Island to Austin. Mrs. Zimmerman went along, since she had observed the couple longer than any of the other witnesses and could give the best identification.

When the Nebraska party arrived in Texas, they were met by Sergeant Farrar who escorted them to Austin police headquarters, where the victim's wife viewed five mug shots. She identified

Charles Jess Palmer, alias J.B. Kirkpatrick, as the man who was present at the Zimmerman residence on the evening of March 5, 1979 in the company of a woman and child. She also recalled that this individual had been at her residence with the same woman and child on March 2, 1979. In addition, Mrs. Zimmerman personally identified a gold diamond ring being worn by the suspect at the time of his arrest as one which had belonged to her husband. Also identified as stolen were the items sold to Garcia during the initial transaction on March 23, 1979.

Fingerprints identified J.B. Kirkpatrick as Charles Jess Palmer, a.k.a. Charles Tinsley.

The now arrested suspect obligingly waived extradition, and space was made on the chartered aircraft for him by having one of the detectives fly back to Nebraska on a commercial airliner.

Once back in Hall County, charges of murder in the first degree were preferred against the suspect and he was placed in the Hall County Jail, without bail, pending trial. The suspect continued to deny any complicity whatsoever in the death of William Eugene Zimmerman and was appointed counsel to represent him in his upcoming trial.

Hall County prosecutors continued to buttress their case against Palmer with additional pre-trial investigation, learning from the NSP that one "C. Palmer" had been issued an equipment violation ticket in the early afternoon of March 6,

1979, at a highway intersection nine miles south of Hastings, Nebraska, a town located about 70 miles west of Grand Island. Further background investigation disclosed that the suspect and his wife had been living since August, 1977 in Guide Rock, Nebraska, a village about 60 miles away. Their child was born July 4, 1978. The suspect had been employed at a farm engaged in the business of producing greyhounds for the dog race industry. The owners of the farm had been absent, vacationing in Florida during the months of February and March of 1979.

One aspect of the case continued to disturb prosecutors. The identifications of the suspect and his wife by the three witnesses (i.e., the victim's wife, Jim Morris, and Donna Kingston) were understandably tenuous and would be subject to attack. Accordingly, in order to possibly refresh their recollections as to what they had seen, prosecutors arranged for these witnesses to undergo pre-trial hypnotic interviews. (Psychologists know that people sometimes observe things that they bury in their subconscious minds which a trained hypnotist can bring to the surface.)

Trial commenced in the case of the State of Nebraska vs. Charles Jess Palmer in Hall County Circuit Court on September 21, 1979. After a week long trial, at which the defendant elected not to take the stand in his own behalf, a jury of six men and six women found the defendant guilty as charged. A three-judge panel imposed the death sentence.

However, the Nebraska Supreme Court reversed the conviction and remanded the case to the lower court for a new trial. The grounds: the admission of the testimony of the hypnotized witnesses by the lower court was found to have been in error. The Supreme Court held that the hypnotism process had been too suggestive to the witnesses and, therefore, was unworthy of belief, especially in a murder case where the life of the defendant was at stake.

Prosecutors proceeded to try the case again, this time without the evidence offered by the hypnotized witnesses and, again, a Hall County jury found reason to believe beyond a reasonable doubt that the defendant was guilty of the murder of William Eugene Zimmerman. Again, the defendant was sentenced to death in the electric chair.

At the time of this writing, Charles Palmer was still pursuing his appeal through the judicial system. An inveterate jailhouse lawyer, he is also suing the Grand Island Police Department, the Hall County Sheriff's Department, and the Nebraska State Patrol for violation of his civil rights.

EDITOR'S NOTE:

The names Jim Morris, Donna Kingston, and Joseph Garcia are fictitious and were used because there is no need for public interest in their true identities.

APPENDIX
ADDITIONAL COPYRIGHT INFORMATION:

"The Cannibal & the Floating Body Parts!"
Inside Detective, April, 1986
"Who Laced the Ice Cream with Arsenic?"
Inside Detective, February, 1985
"Who Beheaded the Bisexual Nympho?"
Front Page Detective, February, 1985
"Chef Choked on a Bottle of Tabasco Sauce!"
Front Page Detective, August, 1985
"The Little Boy was Boiled in Lye!"
Inside Detective, November, 1982
"A Pile of Human Bones Filled the Chamber of Horrors!"
Front Page Detective, May, 1984
"The Piece of Meat was Pamela's Thigh!"
Inside Detective, August, 1982
"A Vampire Drank His Victim's Blood!"
Front Page Detective, December, 1982
"The Reluctant Hooker Was Cooked Alive!"
Front Page Detective, June, 1983
"Freaky Bathing Fetish Triggered A Sex Slaying!"

411

Front Page Detective, November, 1983
"Linda's Killer Fed Her to the Pigs!"
Front Page Detective, May, 1983
"Weirdo Cut Up a Corpse with a Chainsaw!"
Inside Detective, October, 1983
"Killer Kept Robin's Brain Tissue as a Souvenir!"
Inside Detective, October, 1984
"Shrouded the Naked Body in Cat Food!"
Front Page Detective, November, 1984
"Drag Queen Smeared Makeup on His
Nude Victim!"
Inside Detective, December, 1984
"Paranoid Psycho Said Dog Blood Made
Her Kill!"
Front Page Detective, August, 1984
"Rolf's Remains Were Used for Fertilizer!"
Inside Detective, May, 1986
"Grandma Was Chopped Up, Then Cooked!"
Inside Detective, May, 1986
"Lesbian Lovers Spin a Lethal Web!"
Inside Detective, March, 1984
"Monster Who Squeezed His Victims to Death!"
Inside Detective, July, 1983

PINNACLE'S FINEST IN SUSPENSE
AND ESPIONAGE

OPIUM   (17-077, $4.50)
by Tony Cohan
Opium! The most alluring and dangerous substance
known to man. The ultimate addiction, ensnaring all in its
lethal web. A nerve-shattering odyssey into the perilous
heart of the international narcotics trade, racing from the
beaches of Miami to the treacherous twisting alleyways of
the Casbah, from the slums of Paris to the teeming Hong
Kong streets to the war-torn jungles of Vietnam.

LAST JUDGMENT   (17-114, $4.50)
by Richard Hugo
Seeking vengeance for the senseless murders of his brother,
sister-in-law, and their three children, former S.A.S. agent
James Ross plunges into the perilous world of fanatical ter-
rorism to prevent a centuries-old vision of the Apocalypse
from becoming reality, as the approaching New Year
threatens to usher in mankind's dreaded Last Judgment.

THE JASMINE SLOOP   (17-113, $3.95)
by Frank J. Kenmore
A man of rare and lethal talents, Colin Smallpiece has
crammed ten lifetimes into his twenty-seven years. Now,
drawn from his peaceful academic life into a perilous web
of intrigue and assassination, the ex-intelligence operative
has set off to locate a U.S. senator who has vanished mysteriously from the face of the Earth.

PINNACLE'S HORROW SHOW

BLOOD BEAST (17-096, $3.95)
by Don D'Ammassa

No one knew where the gargoyle had come from. It was just an ugly stone creature high up on the walls of the old Sheffield Library. Little Jimmy Nicholson liked to go and stare at the gargoyle. It seemed to look straight at him, as if it knew his most secret desires. And he knew that it would give him everything he'd ever wanted. But first he had to do its bidding, no matter how evil.

LIFE BLOOD (17-110, $3.95)
by Lee Duigon

Millboro, New Jersey was just the kind of place Dr. Winslow Emerson had in mind. A small township of Yuppie couples who spent little time at home. Children shuttled between an overburdened school system and every kind of after-school activity. A town ripe for the kind of evil Dr. Emerson specialized in. For Emerson was no ordinary doctor, and no ordinary mortal. He was a creature of ancient legend of mankind's darkest nightmare. And for the citizens of Millboro, he had arrived where they least expected it: in their own backyards.

DARK ADVENT (17-088, $3.95)
by Brian Hodge

A plague of unknown origin swept through modern civilization almost overnight, destroying good and evil alike. Leaving only a handful of survivors to make their way through an empty landscape, and face the unknown horrors that lay hidden in a savage new world. In a deserted midwestern department store, a few people banded together for survival. Beyond their temporary haven, an evil was stirring. Soon all that would stand between the world and a reign of insanity was this unlikely fortress of humanity, armed with what could be found on a department store shelf and what courage they could muster to battle a monstrous, merciless scourge.

Available wherever paperbacks are sold, or order direct from the Publisher. Send cover price plus 50¢ per copy for mailing and handling to Pinnacle Books, Dept. 17-486, 475 Park Avenue South, New York, N.Y. 10016. Residents of New York, New Jersey and Pennsylvania must include sales tax. DO NOT SEND CASH.